STATION ETERNITY

MUR LAFFERTY

ACE
NEW YORK

T0036730

ACE
Published by Berkley
An imprint of Penguin Random House LLC
penguinrandomhouse.com

Copyright © 2022 by Mary Lafferty

Library of Congress Cataloging-in-Publication Data

Names: Lafferty, Mur, author.
Title: Station eternity / Mur Lafferty.
Description: First edition. | New York: Ace, 2022. | Series: The midsolar murders; 1
Identifiers: LCCN 2022004869 (print) | LCCN 2022004870 (ebook) |
ISBN 9780593098110 (trade paperback) | ISBN 9780593098127 (ebook)
Subjects: LCGFT: Science fiction. | Detective and mystery fiction. | Novels.
Classification: LCC PS3612.A3743 S73 2022 (print) | LCC PS3612.A3743 (ebook) |
DDC 813/.6—dc23/eng/20220203
LC record available at https://lccn.loc.gov/2022004869
LC ebook record available at https://lccn.loc.gov/2022004870

First Edition: October 2022

Printed in the United States of America
4th Printing

Book design by Alison Cnockaert

PRAISE FOR *STATION ETERNITY*

"What a glorious romp. Murder, sentient space stations, and banter. It had everything I wanted."

—Mary Robinette Kowal, Hugo and Nebula Award–winning author of *The Calculating Stars*

"Lafferty's characters stomp off the page, kicking ass and taking names as they do. If Jessica Fletcher ended up on Babylon 5, you still wouldn't get anywhere close to this deft, complicated, fast-moving book. *Station Eternity* kept me up way too late turning pages."

—T. Kingfisher, Hugo and Nebula Award–winning author of *Paladin's Grace* and *Nettle & Bone*

"A science fiction mystery has to nail both the science fiction and the mystery, and this book passes both tests with flying colors. As bingeable and satisfying as your favorite murder show. I couldn't put it down."

—Sarah Pinsker, Nebula Award–winning author of *A Song for a New Day* and *We Are Satellites*

"Mur Lafferty is turning into science fiction's Agatha Christie, with her mastery of ensemble casts and deft characterizations. *Station Eternity* builds a whole new universe of alien civilizations and wraps it all in an engaging mystery. This fun, fast-paced novel is sure to please fans of both *Six Wakes* and *Solo*."

—S. B. Divya, Hugo and Nebula Award–nominated author of *Machinehood*

"Mur Lafferty proves once again that she has the rare talent to blend and bend the sister genres of mystery and science fiction. She gathers her cast of characters, both humans and exuberantly imagined aliens, onto a sentient space station whose identity problems may cause the deaths of all aboard. Meet resourceful and mordant sleuth Mallory, already cursed with being a serial witness to murder, who's in a race to solve the mystery of *Station Eternity* and avert an interstellar fiasco. Smart and sassy, here's the book that will blast you into orbit."

—James Patrick Kelly, winner of the Hugo, Nebula, and Locus Awards

PRAISE FOR *SIX WAKES*

"A taut, nerve-tingling, interstellar murder mystery with a deeply human heart."

—NPR

"An exquisitely crafted puzzle box that challenges our thoughts on what it means to be human—*Six Wakes* is a sci-fi murder mystery of light speed intensity."

—*New York Times* bestselling author Scott Sigler

"This is a great book with so much going for it: clever structure, wonderful characters, and a fiendishly clever puzzle that you'll roll over in your mind for months after you close the covers."

—BoingBoing

"Mysterious and tense. . . . I wish I wrote this book."

—*New York Times* bestselling author Chuck Wendig

"Lafferty delivers a tense nail-biter of a story fueled by memorable characters and thoughtful worldbuilding. This space-based locked-room murder mystery explores complex technological and moral issues in a way that's certain to earn it a spot on award ballots."

—*Publishers Weekly* (starred review)

"Lafferty delivers the ultimate locked-room mystery combined with top-notch sf worldbuilding. The puzzle of who is responsible for the devastation on the ship keeps the pages turning."

—*Library Journal* (starred review)

*To Douglas Adams, who will never know the impression
he made on so many writers,*

and Alasdair Stuart, who is the world's best electric monk.

PART ONE

ALL IN YOUR HEAD

It's an art you partake in and just know
You all paid to watch, let's start the show
Come out, sit your ass down
Don't blink, don't make a sound
Just look, it's okay to cry
You live your best life when you watch them die.

—"The Show" by clipping.

1

WAS SHERLOCK LONELY, TOO?

NOBODY EVER BELIEVED murders "just happened" around Mallory Viridian.

Not at first, anyway.

Before 2032, she figured she was an unlucky kid in that she'd been adjacent to two deaths, at separate times. In college, she witnessed four murders (unrelated) and, this time, helped solve them.

She began to worry after she solved her third and fourth cases: two unrelated murders while on a college trip. She wasn't trained in crime scene investigation and she wasn't even a big fan of mystery novels. Still, she was the only one to spot that the key clue to the murder of a room service waiter was not the shotgun, but a tacky, wet popsicle stick.

Despite this solve, the detectives were not impressed.

"I would have found it eventually," Detective Kelly Brady had barked, his cheeks still pink from being teased by a beat cop about the popsicle stick.

Even the investigators who accepted her help in solving cases didn't believe Mallory had done this before. She was twenty-two, a college dropout, and a civilian. What did she know about a murder investigation?

After she'd solved five cases, the North Carolina State Bureau of Investigation started getting interested in her.

MALLORY KNEW WHAT to expect when she pounded on Adrian Casserly-Berry's door at five in the morning local station time. He would crack the door, eyes slitted in suspicion; he would see her and relax, and the air of suspicion would ease and annoyance would take over.

And if he didn't come to the door, or told her what she didn't want to hear, she would have to figure things out on her own.

I could always run. The thought was always at the back of her mind.

But he would see her, she knew. Adrian tolerated her because she was the only other human he knew of aboard the Space Station Eternity, and even ambassadors got lonely. Even if he was missing only the superior feeling he got when he pulled ambassador rank on a civilian. He was important and had a job aboard the station, while Mallory was pretty much a leech on society, or a hobo at best. He had political power; she had nothing more than sanctuary.

Mallory had found that she could easily placate people like that by not threatening their power directly and reminding them constantly of their titles. "Ambassador Casserly-Berry!" she called. Then she pounded again.

She normally didn't ambush him early in the morning, but she'd been up to use the restroom and casually glanced at the news. After she'd translated the symbols, she ran down the station hallways in her pajamas to pound on his door. But the ambushing might work in her favor, she reasoned, since she usually could startle an honest answer out of him when he let his Important Ambassador mask slip.

He was taking a while. She wondered if he was coming out of

a drunken sleep or wanted to get dressed before he answered the door. She guessed the former; few people stopped to get presentable when woken up early by insistent pounding.

It turned out it was both. The door finally slid open about four inches, and a bloodshot eye peered out. Mallory could smell vodka on his breath and took a cautious step backward. Adrian's eyes were thin with suspicion and barely concealed hostility. He saw her, relaxed, and then looked merely annoyed. But when he opened the door to her, not only was his hair combed, but he was wearing a dress shirt and blue trousers. A loose tie hung around his neck. Even hungover, he looked almost presentable, while she was still in the T-shirt and pajama bottoms she had slept in.

"Why are you dressed this early like you have a trust fund meeting?" she asked, baffled.

"Hedge fund," he corrected automatically. He sniffed. "I have an early meeting with station officials. What do you want, Mallory?"

She looked past him, trying to focus. She hated that he had been the one to throw her off, using nothing more than a tie and a comb. Still, judging by his looks, his hangover was a big one, and she could use that to her advantage.

"I figured you'd be in meetings all day, so I wanted to catch you beforehand," she said. She took a deep breath and relaxed her shoulders. "I have some human-related business. Can I come in, please?"

He didn't step aside. "What human-related business do you have that I don't already know about?"

"Let me in and I'll tell you," she said.

He sighed and stepped aside. The door opened all the way, and she stepped inside his quarters. The door slid closed behind her.

"God, it smells like my grandmother's freezer in here," she said, looking around his quarters. "Were you having a party of one?"

While stinking of vodka, his rooms still appeared neat and efficient (and larger than hers). The bed was made, the closet closed, the desk free of books or papers, the laptop turned off. Even the vodka bottles were arranged neatly, three full bottles on the right side of the small kitchenette sink, three empties on the left.

"Ms. Viridian, what do you want?" he asked stiffly. "I need to keep getting ready for my meeting. I like to look presentable before I leave my quarters. It shows people I respect them." He straightened his tie and cast a pointed look at her clothes.

She rolled her eyes. "Whatever. We need to talk. Can I sit?"

"No, say what you need to and then go." He gestured toward the door and manually slid it open.

She flopped onto his one easy chair, trying to force a casual position. "When were you going to tell me about the humans?"

He paused for a moment and then closed the door again. "What other humans beyond you and me are you talking about?"

"Adrian, I found out about the shuttle," she snapped. "The shuttle full of vacationing humans on its way to the station, who's apparently now just letting anyone on. Don't act like you don't know."

His face, already pale, grew white, emphasizing the small mole on his cheek. "Tell me everything you know."

"What, that Eternity is changing its position on allowing humans as a species to come aboard? That we won't be the only people here very shortly? Tourists, diplomats, businesspeople, even the military!" She took a deep breath and forced herself to lower her voice. "How could you not tell me?"

He rubbed his face with both hands. "I don't know anything about this. How did you find out?"

"Are you kidding me? You're supposed to be negotiating for Earth tourism, and it's happening without you doing anything? What the hell have you been doing, if not that?"

"How did you know?" he yelled. "Why did they tell you and not me?"

She sat up straighter and held her hands out. "Whoa, hold on, it's okay. Sheesh. Are they really keeping you in the dark?" He nodded. "Okay, I've been trying to learn the station layout, iconography, and basic universal symbols, on top of the laws so I don't accidentally get arrested. Again. Anyway, the early news this morning said a human shuttle would be here shortly. I thought you would get a daily news briefing as part of your ambassadorial breakfast or whatever your routine is."

He stiffened. "I do. An ambassador's report is read to me every morning."

"It's read to you? You don't read it yourself?"

His pale face flushed, two red spots appearing on his cheeks. "The station host reads it to me," he said.

"So you meet with Ren and he tells you what he wants you to hear," she said. "You know he doesn't like us, right? That's exactly why I have been trying to get the news that everyone else on this damn station has, not just what he wants me to know. Why would you trust him?"

"That's not the point," Adrian said, looking down at the carpet as if it offended him.

"Yeah, the point is we have to stop them," Mallory said. "Especially if you don't know what they're doing here."

"But why would they change their mind about allowing more humans to come?" he mused, ignoring her. "None of my arguments have worked."

"Well, someone did something, because the station is ready to allow humans aboard. You promised me you would tell me if that ever happened. Now I don't know who to be mad at. If you're telling the truth, of course. Usually not diplomats' and politicians' strong point."

He walked to the kitchenette and put the kettle on. "Have you been saying anything? Going above my head?"

"Are you kidding? Adrian, I came here to get away from humanity. I definitely don't want them following me," she said. "When I got here, the station seemed pretty adamant about allowing only a few humans on board, so it seemed perfect for me."

The kettle screamed its achievement of boiling water and Adrian jerked it off the element, wincing. *He must have a hell of a headache*, she thought. He retrieved a mug from his shelves above the sink and then a tea bag from a small basket on his counter. He went on with his tea-making ritual with his back to her.

Mallory grew tired of the silence. "Do you think Earth knows that someone else did the diplomatic negotiating? Think they're sending someone to take your place?"

"Don't bait me, Mallory," he said quietly, picking up the mug in both hands and facing her. He inhaled the steam, eyes closed.

Mallory nearly said she hoped a new ambassador would offer their guests tea, but Adrian was pretty tightly wound right now. There was something alarming about the way he was keeping himself perfectly still, like a waiting snake. She mentally prepared herself to dodge a mug of boiling water if he let loose.

She cleared her throat. "May I also have some tea, please?" She asked it just the way her mother insisted she do when she was young.

He looked at her for a long moment as if he didn't understand her words and then turned around, face still stony. Behind him, hanging below the shelves against the wall, was a wooden dowel. Slung over the dowel and secured with a thumbtack were about twenty used tea bags. He removed one and prepared her tea.

"An old tea bag? Really, Adrian?" she protested.

"I have to ration when I don't know when I'll get back home again," he said woodenly. "If I'd known they were coming, I could have asked someone to bring me some more tea. I was denied that option." He cleared his throat, and then his voice took on his smoother diplomatic tone. "About the incoming humans—it's a good thing, Mallory. Trade will increase. Doctors will visit. Diplomats will come to make the situation better on Earth. We might get closer to negotiating for FTL technology. People will bring us news. Media. More books and games. I know you don't like people, but it's undeniable—"

She stopped him before he got into full diplomat monologue mode, holding up her hand. "Wait, wait, wait, you still think I don't like people?" she echoed in disbelief. "Jesus, when are you going to believe me? I like people just fine. They just tend to not like me."

He had the full diplomatic face on, and he smiled benignly and spread his hands in the classic way to defuse arguments without actually conceding. "What can I do to make things better? Can we find a compromise?"

"You can listen to me when I tell you that letting that shuttle dock will very likely result in someone getting killed," she said, glaring at him from behind bangs that hadn't been cut in three months. "You can go to your meeting and tell them to send the humans back home."

"You knew this was what we were working toward, and it's much bigger than you and your personal problems. This is a big step for humanity and long overdue," he said patiently. "What if one of us humans gets appendicitis and there's no one who understands human anatomy? Having humans on board who can handle our medical needs is good for both of us!"

She got to her feet. "If you won't listen to me, I'll ask for a meeting with the station folks. I can still get this changed."

He shook his head slowly. "That's not going to work. They're not going to deny a new race access to the station based on one person's paranoia. And if you succeed you will be responsible for single-handedly holding back humanity from scientific evolution. Do you want that on your tombstone?"

"If humans come aboard, we will be writing the epigraph for someone's tombstone, but it won't be mine," she said, defeat weighing on her shoulders.

Nobody—really, *nobody*—believed murders "just happened" around Mallory.

AFTER TWO YEARS of college and four murders in six months, she had tried therapy.

Dr. Miller first said she'd seen too many murder mystery shows and didn't believe her when she said she wasn't a fan of them. Then he suggested possible paranoid schizophrenia. Or maybe just paranoia. She left the appointment with a prescription for brexpiprazole that she didn't fill.

During her second appointment, Miller's receptionist was murdered while Mallory and the doctor were arguing in the next room. When they discovered the body, Dr. Miller accused her instead of validating her, and then, when she obviously had a perfect alibi, refused to treat her further.

He didn't appreciate her solving the crime either. Probably because the killer had been his own wife, who had been convinced he was sleeping with the victim.

She'd turned to religion next. She didn't care which; she just made a list of places one could worship in Raleigh and rolled a die. Each holy leader she spoke with told her to trust in a variety of higher powers, give herself over to Christ, follow the Tao, meditate, pray, volunteer, whatever. They each thought she was presenting a troubled mind that their faith could focus, not a real problem. But she couldn't just magically believe in something; she had trouble believing in what was actually happening in front of her.

"Miracles happen daily if we just open ourselves to it," one priest had said while she was in confession. He hadn't wanted to call it a miracle when, while hearing Mallory's confession, a parishioner had been murdered in the church's parking lot. The church had not admitted she was right; they instead accused her of orchestrating the crime. This was her eighth murder and she should have known better.

She opened her private life to law enforcement, from local cops to the North Carolina State Bureau of Investigation, to prove she had nothing to do with the murders. The only result was that her computer got broken and they wouldn't replace it. They never found any evidence linking her to any crime, but they never stopped being suspicious.

She often found the bodies by accident. She almost always helped solve the crime.

"If what you say is true," the insufferable Miller had told her before his receptionist had died, "then why not enter law enforcement or become a private investigator?"

As if she'd never thought of that. Even though she'd had little interest in official police work, she had looked into it. Unfortunately, her proximity to the murders she'd already solved killed any chances she had of entering law enforcement herself. Suspicion was too high. She also had trouble getting her own PI license. Turns out a grumpy SBI agent had made it his career focus to investigate her, and even without evidence he said she was too dangerous to be allowed to go into any kind of professional investigation work. He'd hindered her every way he could to keep her from following the one career path she was good at.

It hadn't helped that she didn't graduate from college, thanks to a murder. She dropped out after sophomore year, having solved four murders.

Everyone left in her family feared her, except for her aunt, who thought she was insane and needed help by way of a mental institution. Her friendships dried up. Romance was out of the question; if someone dated Mallory, then someone close to them would die. Without fail.

After she left school, she'd foolishly attempted to date a few times. She met John in 2037. He'd taken her home one Easter to meet his family, but then his sister died at a Christmas party. When Mallory figured out that their childhood friend next door was the murderer, John didn't appreciate it. She got the line, "I have to be here for my family and mourn my sister," and then six months later his wedding announcement appeared on social media—the bride was the cop who'd investigated the murder.

Another disaster came in the form of dating Sarah, Mallory's first girlfriend. That relationship had ended after Sarah's English teacher died. Mallory had accompanied her to his office hours to recite the opening to *The Canterbury Tales* and found him dead in his office, strangled by his broke brother-in-law, who'd just been released from prison.

She still remembered the opening lines to *The Canterbury Tales*, at least. Her small knowledge of Middle English had come in handy during a murder investigation a few years later, so that was something.

Then there was the bright, hot regret that was Bob in 2038: she'd found a job, met him, and had been happy for a full year with no murders. Mallory had been naïve enough to relax and think life could become normal. But then they went to a Charlotte Hornets game and Bob got down on one knee during halftime. The jumbotron focused on them, and Mallory gasped in delight. Before Bob said anything, his eyes focused past her just as people started screaming. Two rows behind them, shown on the screen for all to see, was a still-bleeding dead body. A woman slumped to her right over an empty seat, a precisely severed artery in her neck ruining the upholstery.

Bob had gone home; Mallory stayed to help solve the case. The woman had been killed by the former foster child she had abused. Not a lot of people mourned her, but unmourned murder was still murder.

The video of the "worst proposal ever" had been a hot meme for a while, with Bob in the foreground on his knee and the woman bleeding out two rows above them. Talk shows had asked to interview them, but she refused. She hadn't seen Bob again. By now she couldn't blame him.

In 2044, with more than ten murders behind her, she moved east of Raleigh. She had kept her distance from her neighbors and made friends only with the night volunteers at the local animal shelter. She shopped online or late at night in twenty-four-hour grocery stores. She tried to avoid groups of people at all costs.

And she was so, *so* goddamn lonely.

"WHEN I ASKED to live aboard, the station promised me sanctuary," she told Adrian, crossing her arms. "What am I supposed to do now?"

"I suppose you will have to run away again," he said. "Let me show you the door to get you started."

Mallory bristled. "Run away? Is that what you think I do?"

He nodded matter-of-factly and held up his hand to count off his fingers. "That *is* what you do. You left home after a murder, you left college after a murder, you moved after a murder, you changed jobs after a murder. You told me you were never in an apartment longer than a year—"

Her cheeks flamed as he laid out her past in stark, embarrassing detail. "I'm never having a drink with you again if you're just storing up shit to use against me!" She put aside all plans to throw him off balance to get information. Now she just wanted out.

Now I just want to run away.

Adrian continued, "—and then you got a chance to run away from the entire planet and you couldn't escape fast enough. You are always running. So, you've found out that humans are coming to the station—something you knew would happen because I told you that was my goal—and the next logical step is for you to decide where to run to next." He took a meaningful step toward the door, extending his arm as if it were a favor to guide her the hell out of his space.

"We didn't think you would actually succeed," she muttered, looking at the carpet.

"What was that?" he asked, voice tight and alert.

She cleared her throat and raised her head. "I didn't think you would succeed. The station made it clear they didn't want a lot of humans here at once, and let's face it, Adrian: you're not great at this diplomacy thing. I knew more about the humans coming than you did, and that was your one job!"

"Get out," he said. He had taken on that perfectly still pose again, reminding her of a snake.

She relented and walked to the door. "And I am not trying to run. I am trying to keep the humans away from me to keep them from dying. That's hard to do if they're going to follow me."

"Sounds like running to me," he said.

"I can't believe you're my Earth representative when clearly you don't give a shit about my situation here."

"I'm not here for you, Mallory!" he shouted.

She flinched.

"I don't care about your paranoia; I don't care about your fears. I'm not here to represent you right now; there's supposed to be only one human on the station to negotiate for Earth. Not one ambassador and one societal leech. And even if you're right, even if you do have some weird murder virus that causes people to fall on each other like wild animals, that's a small price to pay for galactic-level diplomacy. The space program has killed a lot more people than you have, and that didn't stop NASA. The universe is bigger than you."

Mallory balled her fists. She wasn't self-centered. People refused to acknowledge that she tried legitimately to help. She tried to stomp out the door, but Adrian's plush carpeting softened her steps, denying her even that. She paused at the open door and turned to face him. "That's the problem. Everyone talks about acceptable losses until they are the ones doing the losing. You're cool with people dying so you can do your job, but you never even considered that you might be the one who dies. Are you cool with it then?"

He gave her a little shove, getting her fully into the hall. "You know, the more I get to know you, the more I wonder if people around you killed themselves just to get free of your drama."

The door slid closed before she could hit him.

The loneliness threatened to cover her with its shroud again, but she took a deep breath and straightened her back. Adrian was not the only person she knew on the station. She could find help elsewhere.

She trudged back to her rooms, well down the hall from the diplomatic wing. She had to get cleaned up and dressed for an appointment, but after that she had to break the news of the humans' arrival to the other person on the station this would directly affect.

2

. . .

THE SCENT OF FEAR

MALLORY LEARNED EARLY in her time on Station Eternity that if you missed an appointment with your doctor, the appointment came to you. The result of that happy accident was that she'd been examined in her own room instead of the doctor's "office," which was much more public.

She didn't care that aliens didn't know what a nipple was; the average Joe Phantasmagore didn't need to learn it from her.

Her first appointment had included undressing with nothing but drooping purple branches making a wall to shield her from view in a public area. She could still remember the movement of various people enjoying the parklike common area of the station, but the doctor had assured her that they couldn't see her. She tried to enjoy the natural surroundings to keep calm while naked, in public, while a swarm of wasplike aliens buzzed around her and asked her questions in a voice that consisted of thousands of humming wings.

That had been a bad day.

For this exam, she sat on her bed, clothed and keeping very still as a blue wasp about as long as her thumb crawled over her wrist. Countless other wasps buzzed around her, some landing on her head and shoulders, then taking off again, leaving nothing but a whisper-brush of an antenna against her skin. Human physiology changed from day to day with hormones, which they found fascinating in sentient beings. They'd explained that most beings had evolved to hide the scent of strong pheromones from other species, which Mallory found nearly as strange as the fact that humans were the only species discovered that didn't regularly bond with another sentient race symbiotically. According to the Sundry, humans were wandering around advertising their every hormonal shift to anyone paying attention.

She also discovered that her doctors were obsessed with how *wet* humans were. Some other races had blood, or something like it, but humans were the only race that had blood, and bile, and waste, and saliva, and tears . . . all liquid. Their organs needed these liquids to function, which also made them squishy inside. With no exoskeleton, and hormones acting like a siren to alert predators, how in the world had humans evolved instead of being devoured or falling apart in a big wet puddle of goo and bones?

And how could their skin keep all that inside? Mallory had pricked her own skin with a needle from her sewing kit (after politely refusing their offer to sting her), and the wasps had seemed almost disappointed that she didn't pop like a water balloon.

Still, it was terrifying to be examined by a swarm of wasps. Mallory used deep breathing to calm her nerves, which usually worked. Today, however, she choked on a breath when they asked if she was on her period.

"Your hormones are different today. Taut. Spicy. Sour. Musky. Are you bleeding? Frightening. Messy. Safe."

Mallory coughed and took a moment to compose herself. They were not using the question to passive-aggressively call her a bitch: they really wanted to know. And it was her job to answer direct questions (or what her grandmother would have called "rude-as-all-get-out" questions). Many aliens had wanted to learn more about humans, and Mallory had no other skills that were usable in a completely alien setting—they wouldn't even accept her offer to do janitorial work. So she had offered herself to the alien scientists as their human guinea pig to study, or their Barbie to dress and undress.

The doctors were dissatisfied with studying only a female-presenting body; Adrian had flat-out refused to allow them to study him. He protested that he didn't have time and that he was afraid of wasps; one time, he used a cold he had caught on a supply trip back to Earth as an excuse. Mallory just thought he couldn't stand the idea of explaining human testicles to aliens in the morning and then negotiating with the same aliens in the afternoon.

Mallory couldn't afford pride. After she'd mentioned her availability to the doctors in the medbay, two of the five dominant species on Station Eternity had approached her and offered to pay so they could study her. Thinking of every conspiracy theory on earth, she set some ground rules (no impregnation, no harming; the aliens must fully explain every test they run, etc.), and then she allowed them twice-weekly study.

Her best clients by far were the blue wasp hivemind that called themselves the Sundry. The station housed two separate factions, blue Sundry and silver Sundry, and the silver ones had shown no interest in her. She'd tried to ask about the differences between them, but the blue Sundry reminded her she was there to inform, not to ask.

The blue Sundry wanted to know everything about human physiology and had been totally flummoxed by menstruation. Humans were so messy! Trying to explain her period to a xenobiologist of another species made her revisit high school and all the shame her period had brought to her life. No, it didn't hurt, not like bleeding usually did. Yes, it was a little scary the first time, but now it was just a part of life. And it was useful, as it gave her clues as to her own reproductive health; namely, if she ever didn't bleed during a month, it was indicative of pregnancy or illness or menopause.

Why did she expel the lining as waste and not absorb it for energy, or let another species absorb it?

She explained she didn't have any control over involuntary functions. That was the day she learned that other species sometimes "consume biomass." She'd changed the subject after that.

The shame and embarrassment of talking about her period to a bunch of strangers was magnified by the fact that she was terrified of stinging insects. She'd had a bad experience with a bee sting as a girl, and had been armed with Benadryl and epinephrine ever since. During her exams, she kept telling herself that she had an EpiPen across the room.

She just hoped it was strong enough to handle the venom from an insect that made an Asian giant hornet look like a ladybug.

Mallory sighed and ran her free hand through her hair, pushing her bangs out of her eyes. "No, I'm not bleeding right now. I told you how often that happens, right?"

"Yes, but your moon cycle is meaningless here. Obsolete. Ineffective. Missing," the swarm replied. Most of them buzzed about her small quarters, some landing and crawling over her furniture and belongings, but three or four dark blue wasps perched on her arm, antennae probing her skin. "Your concept of 'days' is meaningless as well. Solar. Lunar. Sidereal. From the information you gave us, we calculate it may come every seventeenth day, but we aren't sure yet. Intense. Studious. Time."

Oh, great, so I'm a teenager again, getting it any time my body decides I need some extra anxiety and embarrassment. She cleared her throat and added, "Well, I'm still not bleeding. Maybe it's stress hormones?"

"Please do go on producing stress hormones. Fascinating. Enthralling. Delicious. Is this another aspect of your body that evolved to make you overreact to things? Pointless. Tiny. Safe."

"I guess so, yeah," she said, rolling her eyes. "And again, I can't just reassure myself that I'm not really under attack. I can't argue with my own hormones."

"We understand. Learning, clarity, study," the swarm said. A few more wasps dove down and lit on her arm, probing gently. "Is this fear we taste? Terrifying. Scary. Tharn."

"*Tharn*? Where did you get that one?" she asked, distracted.

"Human literature translations. Available. Entertaining. Simple." They paused, hovering. "Rabbits."

"So you've read *Watership Down*. This is a weird day," she said, shaking her head. "But, yeah, you're probably getting fear, panic, dread, any and all of those." Her skin twitched at the sensation of insect legs crawling on her.

"What is the hormone driving you to do?" the swarm asked. "Fight, fly, freeze?"

She was painfully reminded of Adrian's dismissal of her fears, of him accusing her of always running away.

"Flight, I guess. I want to get out of here," she said, shifting uncomfortably. "Run to the shuttle bay and hop on the first ship that would take me away."

"Where? Escape. Flee. Avoid."

She glared at the wasps, not sure which one to focus on. "Et tu, Brute?"

The wasps answered right away, "Yes, we said that. Who else had? And who is Brute? Confusion. Inattentive. Brain damage."

Why did they understand Latin but still not know some of the living Earth languages? Whatever, not her problem. She needed to remember they were likely to take obscure sayings literally. "No, I'm fine. It's a saying on Earth, but never mind. Where would I go—I would go somewhere . . . else. I don't know where yet. I can't go home, and I don't know anywhere else that would accept me, so I'm here right now."

"So the hormone isn't driving you to deal with the actual

source of the fear," the swarm said. "Ignore. Circumvent. Obviate. You want to escape and leave the danger here for someone else to fight. Shirk. Eschew. Duck."

"Hey, that's rude!" she exclaimed, and the wasps on her arm took flight. They buzzed around the room, agitated. "Sorry," she muttered. They landed again. "And that's not it. No one else has to fight it. It's not something you can just kill with a weapon. There's no monster coming to the station; it's just my problem alone."

"I don't know how you evolved. Baffling. Weak. Perplexing."

"I'm pretty baffled too," she said. She waited for the Sundry to ask her what was bothering her, but it didn't.

The wasps flying around her head all dove at her at once. She winced, closing her eyes tightly as each one found a place to sit on her body. By this time she could avoid reacting outwardly, but they had not agreed to her request not to crawl over her face, which always made her shudder. Still, this frightening action signaled the end of her exam, which was always a good thing.

"Thank you. Payment will be delivered to your account in the station bank as usual. Appreciations. Admirations. Trust."

Huh. They've never indicated trust before.

They continued. "We would like to offer you double your current payment to chronicle the changes if you ever decide to produce young. Nurturing. Life. Cycles."

Mallory choked out a laugh. "Not planning on it anytime soon," she said, trying to imagine getting pregnant aboard the station and trying to find another species' version of an epidural that wouldn't kill her. "It's not as simple as laying an egg for us."

"Is birth messy? Fluids. Floods. Mopping." The voice had a distasteful tinge to it. They took off from her skin and formed a swirling mass in the center of the room.

"Yeah, it's pretty messy, or so I hear," she admitted. "Messy and painful."

"We request again for you to ask the male humans aboard the

station to allow us to inspect them as well. Convince. Coerce. Seduce."

"No, I'm not seducing anyone so you can examine him!" she said, shuddering. "Especially not Adrian."

"Second male, then. Secret. Perplexing. Sexual."

"Sexual? That doesn't—" Mallory broke off, her cheeks flaming. She couldn't deny her reaction when they could smell and taste her hormones. She rubbed her arms to rid herself of the residual crawling feeling. "I have asked. Really. No one is interested. And remember, there is only one male officially aboard the station. Adrian can't know anyone else is here."

"And you have our discretion. Secrets. Subterfuge. Misdirection," the voice said, sounding slightly puzzled.

Mallory took a deep breath of relief. The Sundry knew just about everything happening on the station; they had thousands in their swarm, and they could get anywhere. They had known that Xan was secretly aboard the station before she had.

She opened the door for the swarm to exit. "You may be able to find another male soon, though. I heard that more humans are coming to the station."

There was a pause, and then the wasps closed in on her, several landing on her bare arms and neck. She flinched. "That's what you're afraid of, even more so than us. Terror. Guilt. Dread. Why are you afraid of your own people? Family. Comfort. Home."

She shook her head. She wasn't in the mood to explain, nor to explain that "family" and "home" held little comfort for her.

"Never mind. We can talk about it next time."

MALLORY TOOK A very hot shower to shake off the feeling she always had at the end of her appointments with the Sundry. She knew she needed to get to the shuttle bay, but if she didn't shower right now, she would feel crawly all day.

After she'd toweled off vigorously to scrub that last tactile memory of tiny legs on her skin, Mallory dressed and took a lift to the main deck of the station to go through a heavily traveled common area that led to the shuttle bay.

She slowed to enjoy the public area, with a park, various alien restaurants, and shops that sold or traded incomprehensible alien items. It reminded Mallory of any park on Earth in a major city—Central Park or Hyde Park came to mind—but she was the only human, and all of the shops and restaurants were made to accommodate the Gneiss, which were the largest alien race on the station. Those places dwarfed Mallory, but some of them had seating areas that fit people around her size, at least.

It also held a Grand Central Station of sorts, encompassing a tram system that went around the station and was more versatile than the lifts—but you could count on the lifts. The trams were only guaranteed to be in their bay; you couldn't be sure you would catch one elsewhere in Station Eternity.

The tram system was also unique in that it had been built by outside aliens. The statuesque Gneiss had offered one of their newest modes of transport, and the station had accepted. With the station's help, they built a marble track upon which translucent pods hung while they zipped around. The cars looked as if they were made of mica, but they couldn't have been because they were made to carry multiple Gneiss aliens, which stood around seven to eight feet tall and were made of solid stone.

It was still relatively early in the morning, and Mallory was alone in the Gneiss car. She preferred traveling alone so she wouldn't have to remember what the proper morning greeting was for each alien. Just because they could all understand one another's words didn't mean she wouldn't say the wrong thing. She spoke aloud that she wanted to go to the shuttle bay, and the car hummed back at her and began its trek through the station.

She liked the Gneiss, though. Though taciturn and slower to

respond than most humans, they definitely weren't stupid, and she'd even managed to bond with a few of them that she assumed were of a similar generational mindset—adults that were still a comfortable distance from middle age. On Earth her contemporaries would include young parents, but that wasn't a possibility for her.

The tram car ran right through the shuttle bay, entering at one end, skirting around the edge, and exiting at the other. She signaled the tram to stop at the entrance, near a Gneiss that was tending to a shuttle.

The ship's footprint was about ten by ten, but it was nearly twice as tall. It looked as if someone had sheared off a hunk of a shatter cone in New Mexico and claimed it was space-worthy. No landing gear, no doors, no portals, no apparent engines or exhaust. Just a big rock. But it sat here among the other shuttles, so she had to assume it was a vehicle of some sort.

The Gneiss standing beside the rock was purple with white veins of marble running through her hard skin. She stood about eight feet tall and was terrifying to an average-size human—until you got to know her. She had introduced herself as Stephanie the first day Mallory was on the station, and they'd become friends of a sort.

Mallory raised her hand to wave. "Hey, Stephanie!"

The huge rock woman didn't respond. She just kicked the corner of the cube, and then a rumbling, vibrating noise came from her chest. She opened her mouth, and the words were broadcast more than spoken with tongue and lips.

Stephanie said, "I don't care about his problems; he never cared about mine. Now be quiet so I can work on you. You don't want me to put you down below, do you?" She closed her mouth and the vibrations cycled down to nothing.

"Down below? Where's that?" Mallory asked.

Stephanie ignored her again. She started to work on the shuttle, which apparently meant . . . sanding? She slid massive gloves over her hands and rubbed at the ship now, little puffs of dust rising around her.

The vibrations and rumbling started again. "Yeah, I'm shouting because the human is watching us," Stephanie said without turning around to acknowledge Mallory. "If you didn't act childish, then she wouldn't be able to see you acting childish, now, would she?"

Mallory remembered that the Gneiss usually preferred to talk to one another via vibrations that humans couldn't hear, and if they were verbal it was only for the benefit of species who needed language. Had Stephanie been wanting to shame the shuttle in front of Mallory?

"Steph, is your shuttle *alive*?" she asked, edging closer to get a better look.

"Go away, Mallory," Stephanie said in a low rumble.

She'd been hurt the first few times Stephanie had told her she didn't have time for her, but she soon learned that Gneiss bluntness was just conservation of energy; it took them more effort to vibrate on a level for other species to hear. For them, speaking was the human equivalent of trying to hold a conversation during a sporting event.

"Okay, but let me know when you're free. I could use some help," Mallory said, and left Stephanie to her sanding and her argument, which had softened to gentle vibrations too quiet to translate.

Mallory moved on down the line of shuttles. The ship she was looking for was more geometric and attractive to human eyes than the cubist Gneiss ship. She finally found it, dwarfed by a large, chalky Gneiss shuttle.

The shuttle *Infinity* had a coppery sheen and looked as if it should be a ten-million-dollar sculpture in front of a Very Important Building in New York or Dubai. Icosahedral in shape, it balanced impossibly on one of its corners, always humming slightly. Mallory figured it was probably creating some kind of field to allow itself to balance on its tip. She approached the ship and raised her hand and hesitated—knocking always felt wrong, but she didn't know how else to tell its resident that she was here. She probably should have called via station communication, but in her haste she'd not thought of that option. Working the communicator took understanding the iconography, and her logical brain had shut off when she had gotten news of the human shuttle.

Before she could knock on the thick, reddish metal, one of the triangular sides hinged open and unfolded to present a walkway. From inside the shuttle came the words "Mallory? Are you okay?"

She smiled slightly. "It's complicated. Can I come aboard?"

"Yeah, sure, come on in," he said after a moment. "So long as you're alone."

She boarded, feeling an unfamiliar reluctance to do so. Anxiety gnawed at her, and she squeezed her hands into tight fists to fight it back.

The interior of the ship was as gorgeous as the exterior, with coppery fixtures and a cushy captain's chair that faced several screens, currently showing the shuttle bay and the exterior of the station. The chair bothered Mallory, but she couldn't put her finger on why. On the far wall was a ladder that led to other floors both above and below the main deck.

"Mallory?" His voice, coming from the room below, was concerned. "Are you alone or not?"

"Oh. Yeah, I'm alone. Thought that was rhetorical," she said, laughing nervously.

Like a powerful headache remedy finally offering relief, the veil of anxiety and distrust lifted. Behind her, the walkway refolded itself and closed the hatch as Xan Morgan climbed the ladder to the main deck.

"Thanks for seeing me so early," Mallory said, then cleared her throat and looked at the captain's chair again.

Xan had a towel slung over his bare shoulder and a T-shirt in his hand. After he stepped off the ladder, he rubbed the towel over his naked torso. He wore sweatpants and little else, causing Mallory to hate the blush that warmed her face.

"Going shirtless because the aliens don't know what a nipple is?" she asked lightly.

When she was able to glance at his face, he was giving her a strange look with a wry smile. "I thought you were supposed to teach the aliens about nipples."

"Sorry, I mean, I can come back when you're dressed," she stammered. She looked behind her, but the exit remained closed. Escape from total embarrassment was denied.

"Why? You never come to see me here, and now you're running away? What's the trouble?" He pulled the gray T-shirt over his head.

Running away. She pursed her lips. *No, I'm not.* She squared her shoulders and looked him in the eye, much easier to do now that he was wearing his gray ARMY shirt.

On Earth, Xan had been a soldier in the US Army. He was a little taller than Mallory, with a shaved head, light brown skin, and cheekbones that could cut glass. He had a wide smile when he chose to show it. He wore small, round glasses that magnified his dark brown eyes. A few shiny scars marked his lean torso and arms, including a freshly healed one on his arm close to the shoulder. Little round scars dotted his forearms like polka dots.

In short, it was damn hard to look at him and think of anything else.

He tossed the towel through the hole in the floor and then smoothed the stained gray shirt over his chest with a grimace.

"What's wrong with the shirt?" she asked.

"This is the only shirt I have, so I have to wash it every night. I went to bed late, so it's still damp." He walked over to the cushy captain's chair and sat down.

Something weird about that chair, her mind insisted. But she wasn't solving a crime, so she told her mind to focus on the matter at hand.

"I haven't seen you in days. Is everything okay?" he asked.

She shook her head. She opened her mouth to calmly tell him what was going on, but ended up blurting out, "We have to get out of here. Can you take this shuttle, can it take two people?"

He held his hands out, palms first. "Whoa, hang on. This isn't my shuttle to take, so let's keep our feet on the station for now. What's got you so spooked?"

She cleared her throat. "This morning I found out Eternity is going to allow more humans onto the station. This means tourists. Ambassadors. Walmart. People."

He froze, then sat up, back ramrod straight. "'People' probably means military." His face had gone ashy with shock. His eyes slowly focused on her like those of a calm predator. "Is this that ambassador's fault?"

"Not that I can tell. He seemed as surprised as us. Apparently, someone else convinced Eternity to agree to let humans aboard."

"Who would try to get humans here if not for us?"

"I don't know," she said, shrugging and then trying to shake out the tension in her shoulders. She spied a stool in the corner and sat down. "You think there might be someone else on board?"

"I have no idea." He swiveled in the chair and fixed his stare to the shuttle bay in front of him. "Why not ask those bugs that you see? Don't they witness everything that goes on?" He glanced around the shuttle as if looking for a solo Sundry scout.

"They see most everything, yes, but as for giving out any information, your guess is as good as mine," she said. "They collect data like nectar, but I've yet to see them do much with it."

He shook his head slowly. "When is this happening? Can we appeal to the station?"

"I was going to after I talked to you. Adrian is pretty pissed at me for wanting to stop them. He doesn't want people messing with his authority; he says whatever problems I have shouldn't stop humanity from expansion. I think he's just mad I found out first." She stood up suddenly, the nervous energy getting to her. She paced a few steps, but pacing a ten-foot-square area wasn't very satisfying. "We could still run. You know the army will be sending someone to look for you, and I can't have a bunch of humans around me. Having them here might even endanger you." She cut herself off, embarrassed. "Surely we know enough aliens to get help to get out of here. The station might take pity on us."

"Take pity on us *again*," he reminded her. "And go where? It was hard enough to get aliens to welcome me here. I don't want to be another planet's equivalent of E.T."

"I don't know, I think we're pretty close to E.T.–levels of pitiful!" she said, her voice rising. "Come on, Xan, neither of us can stay here if they allow humans on board."

"Mallory, we don't have the same problems," he said, frowning. "You could just stay in your room and avoid humans and you'd be fine. I have extradition to worry about. Whether the murder charge sticks or not, I've still been AWOL for months—"

He stopped all of a sudden, his eyes going glassy. Then he focused on her again. "My bad. That wasn't fair. Our problems are kind of similar. But it's easy for you, since you can just avoid humans, right?"

Mallory was sick of this idea, given by every well-meaning person who actually believed the things that happened to her. "The US may not even know you're here; they don't know where you went when you left Earth. The shuttle may not even be from the US. But no matter who is coming, my threat remains the same. You think staying in my room will fix everything? You think I haven't tried that in the past? It sucks, and it's lonely, and it still doesn't always work out." She stopped herself and took a deep breath. "I didn't realize we were competing over who had the worst situation. Whoever wins, it's bad news for both of us."

"You're right," he said, leaning forward and putting his elbows on his knees. "You're not the one I'm angry with. We should talk to—someone."

Mallory wondered what name he had been starting to say, but didn't ask. "I'll see if Stephanie is done yelling at her shuttle. She was in a pretty big fight with someone earlier. Are their ships sentient or something?"

Xan shrugged. "It's certainly possible."

"Okay, I'll talk to her, and then I'll see if I can talk to Ren."

He shook his head, clearly caught up in his own thoughts. "The Gneiss won't care about human problems. We should go directly to the station. Eternity let us on board; I can't believe she'd throw us to the wolves."

"She may not think that's what she's doing. We can't anthropomorphize her."

None of the main races had developed a positive view of humans since First Contact two years earlier, but they had agreed to allow Ambassador Adrian Casserly-Berry aboard Station Eternity, the nearest hub in the galaxy, to let him make a case for their inclusion. After Adrian had been established, both Mallory and Xan had, for different reasons, appealed to the station to be allowed sanctuary. Both stories had piqued Eternity's interest enough to grant them a short stay, and longer if they showed themselves worthy of being included in galactic life.

Mallory had offered to work for her room and board and got a job being examined by other species. She didn't like to think about what she'd do for income once the aliens were done examining her.

Xan hadn't made the same deal, but he never explained what

the station required of him. All Mallory knew was she was given small quarters, while he lived inside *Infinity*. She'd kept her distance from Xan for the most part, so she didn't know any more details.

Each of the three humans had managed to make a life aboard the station in the past few months, for better or for worse, and each keeping to themselves.

Best of all for Mallory, there had been no murders.

"Eternity never said we would be the only humans forever," Xan said, looking at his hands. "I just didn't think others would come this soon. When are they coming, anyway?"

"I don't know, but the shuttle has left Earth."

Xan cursed under his breath, shaking his head.

"Didn't Eternity guarantee you sanctuary?" Mallory asked. "Can't the station keep you safe?"

"She can only do so much. She may be able to stop them from extraditing me, but I don't know if she can stop an assassin from shanking me in the hallway." He closed his hands into fists and stood up with resolve.

Yes, here we go, a plan is forming! she thought. *He'll figure out how to convince Eternity to send them home!*

"I'm hungry. Do you want to get some food?" he asked.

She blinked at him. "Food? That's your plan?"

He raised an eyebrow. "I didn't hear you coming up with anything."

"But I did!" she said. "Let's get the hell out of here; if not aboard this shuttle, then ask one of the aliens you know."

"I can't do anything without food," he said. "And Ferdinand's is always a good place to talk to people, so we can still look for passage while we eat."

Mallory looked around, frustrated, hoping a solution would fall out of the ceiling or something. She finally shrugged and said, "Fine, let's get some food. But then can we talk to other people?"

He frowned at her. "Mallory, I'm not stopping you from getting help from someone else. Go talk to the station; talk to your friends; do whatever you need to do. Make your own plan. I need to eat."

"Me? I can't plan. I am the problem people plan around," she said, confused.

"I think you need to figure out who told you that, and go punch them," he said. The exit unfolded then, making Mallory jump. "Or tell me and I'll punch them," he added, walking past her to the exit.

Mallory followed.

"If we could get a human restaurant here, I might be okay with humans coming aboard," Xan said as the walkway folded in on itself and withdrew into the shuttle. Xan hadn't said anything or pushed any buttons; it had just happened.

On their way out of the shuttle bay, they passed Stephanie, who was still sanding her ship in silence. Mallory stopped and looked at the unmoving slab of rock and then back at *Infinity*. She started to suspect why Xan wouldn't talk much about the ship.

Maybe that's why he's changed so much. I wonder what happened to him.

3

. . .

A FIRST EDITION OF
SLAUGHTERHOUSE-FIVE

XAN AND MALLORY first met in 2033 at the University of North Carolina at Chapel Hill in a twentieth-century American literature class, bonding first over Octavia Butler and then over their mutual dislike for Vonnegut Guy.

Mallory thought Vonnegut was fine, but this guy made fandom for the author look tacky. Vonnegut Guy was a thin white dude walking around with a beret and glasses that Mallory was sure were plain glass. When they started their Vonnegut section of the syllabus, he proudly came in with a first edition of *Slaughterhouse-Five*, ready to discuss.

The professor had calmly told him they were covering *Cat's Cradle* first, and they might not even get to *Slaughterhouse-Five* because they had more books and authors to cover.

Mallory and Xan had spoken at the same time.

Mallory said, "What about *Parable of the Sower?*"

Xan said, "Like Octavia Butler?"

They had looked at each other. Xan had pointed at her and grinned widely. "She gets it."

"Oh, come on, she's not nearly as important as Kurt," Vonnegut Guy said dismissively. "I've never heard of her."

"That says more about you than it does about her," Mallory said.

"You may want to search under 'MacArthur genius grant,'" Xan added, pointing to the phone in Vonnegut Guy's hand.

"Butler was brilliant, but we didn't have room for her," said the professor, taking control of the class again.

"You had room; you just gave it to someone else that everyone here has read a hundred times," Xan countered. "I'm reading *Heart of Darkness* in two other English classes! You think I have anything more to learn about that book?"

"You haven't been taught *Heart of Darkness* in my class yet," Professor Rudnick said coldly.

Mallory raised her hand and started talking. "Hey, I've been meaning to ask: *Heart of Darkness* was written in 1899, so it's not even twentieth-century lit. Can we cover something relevant?"

Professor Rudnick's face was growing pink. He focused past Mallory and Xan and on the rest of the class. "Today we will talk about *Cat's Cradle*'s historical significance, and close discussion on the first half of the book will start on Wednesday. Vonnegut was prolific, but his books aren't long; I'm sure y'all can handle it."

"So you're not going to address just leaving Butler out?" Xan asked as the professor started to write on his tablet, displayed on the wall behind him.

"I'm not debating my syllabus with students," he said without looking up.

Without another word, Xan grabbed his laptop and backpack and walked out. The rest of the class stared at him, but the professor still didn't look up.

After class, Mallory had found him sitting on a bench outside the library. She sat beside him.

"It's the Butler girl," he said by way of greeting. "Why didn't you come with? I thought we were united." He didn't look up from the e-book he was reading.

"I agreed with you, but I didn't get your memo about the walk-out," she said. "I'm Mallory, by the way."

"Good to meet you, Mallory," he said, grinning at her and shaking her left hand awkwardly with his right. "I'm Xan."

"And I stayed because I actually liked *Cat's Cradle*," she said, shrugging.

"That's a fair play," he said, nodding.

"Although class is going to suck this year if that Vonnegut Guy keeps talking like that," she added grimly, and Xan laughed. The friendship was formed.

After a few months, Mallory was determined to ask him out, but always lost her nerve. There had been an awkward moment on the Poe-focused spring break trip to Baltimore where something might have happened, but the moment was shattered when Vonnegut Guy and a room service waiter were murdered. Even better: the murders were unrelated.

Mallory had left college soon after. She didn't plan on seeing Xan again.

Over a decade later, Xan had shown utter surprise when he ran into Mallory at a birthday party for one of his friends.

Three weeks after that, he was absolutely baffled beyond words to find her on Eternity.

Mallory wasn't surprised. By then, she had stopped being surprised by anything—especially coincidences.

MALLORY HAD KEPT her distance during her first few days on the station. She wanted to keep him safe, which meant keeping him away from her. What finally drove her to seek him out was hunger. Asking aliens what she could eat was pointless; they knew as little about her biology as she did about their food.

Adrian hadn't been too sympathetic to Mallory's situation, saying she should have thought about that before she left Earth forever. His stature and income allowed him to visit the finest restaurants where he could test his stomach's limits, but Mallory was strapped for cash in the early days and couldn't afford to pay for food she might not be able to digest. When she complained, Adrian told her that thousands of life-forms found something to eat every day, and his fellow diplomats had promised there would be food for human consumption, so she should just look harder.

So she went to Xan for help.

"You haven't eaten in how long?" he'd asked, his eyes growing wide.

"Two days, I think?" she asked, running her hands through her hair, distracted.

"Did you tell the station? I don't think she'd allow someone to starve."

"I'm not going to be an adult woman going to someone asking for a peanut butter sandwich like a seven-year-old," she'd snapped.

He smiled at her. "So instead you came to me asking for a sandwich?"

"We're on the same level, both here under strange circumstances, both not having much more than what we brought with us, and both human," she said. "Don't give me a fish; teach me to fish! Or whatever you do for food around here!"

They started testing the cheaper places to eat. Xan admitted that his testing had been rough at the beginning, with burns, vomiting, and intense stomach cramping as he sampled alien food. But he'd found a few dishes that would sustain him, and once they began working together, they had eventually found food that was first digestible, then nourishing. Once they had found a few items that were somewhat tasty, eating almost became a thing to enjoy again rather than dread. They most frequently ended up at Ferdinand's Crush, which Mallory considered a Gneiss dive bar. It was open all day and night to suit the needs of a never-closing shuttle bay. Ferdinand had, once he had met the humans, also been open to stocking more food that their systems could handle.

Ferdinand was on duty as usual (Gneiss didn't sleep). He was short for a Gneiss, about seven feet tall and stocky, looking like he was made of dark gray rock veined with silver. Mallory and Xan waved at him when they entered and headed for the only seating area with a table and chairs low enough for them to sit comfortably. Most places seemed amenable to altering their interior to suit all the differently sized aliens on the station, but they'd learned that if your species had only a few aboard, most didn't want to change things for that small a number. This had lifted Ferdinand even higher in Mallory's eyes.

Every other table around them was about five feet off the ground, and the chairs were massive, reinforced stone that could handle a thousand pounds of sentient rock sitting to enjoy a beer— or the equivalent intoxicant.

Ferdinand lumbered over to their table and began vibrating in the way that signaled he was about to speak at a level that non-Gneiss could hear.

"How are things, Ferdinand?" Mallory asked, filling the silence with a greeting.

"Things are standard, the clients are about the usual numbers," Ferdinand finally said. "It's early for you to be in here, isn't it?"

"Mallory had something to talk about and I was hungry," Xan said.

"'Something to talk about' is a dire thing for humans, as I understand it," Ferdinand said, turning to Mallory. "Are you ending your sexual relationship with the male? I will need to collect payment in advance, then, in case there are arguments that end with a storming out."

"Has everyone been reading novels and watching soap operas from Earth?" Mallory demanded, hoping the low light would hide her warming complexion. "And no, I'm not, I mean—we're not—I don't even know how to answer that." She took a deep breath and started again. "Look, you're way off base."

"No, we're not talking about anything that personal," Xan said, cutting in smoothly. "It has to do with other humans."

Ferdinand waited for a moment, and Mallory wondered if he was trying to parse "way off base." She had forgotten it was safer not to speak in vernacular phrases. "'Way off base' means you're wrong, essentially," she said.

"Oh," Ferdinand said, and shrugged with a sound like a tomb being opened. "I'm pleased to see you regardless. I had heard about the humans arriving, yes. They will arrive today. Are you pleased?"

"No," they said in unison.

"Unfortunate. Do you need time to find things you can eat?"

"No, I think I'll have my usual," Xan said.

"Just a coffee," Mallory said, and Ferdinand turned, grinding, and shuffled back.

"I thought communication would be easier, but it's like the more they learn about humanity, the more awkward things get," Xan said with a grin.

Mallory thought about her exam that morning and hunched her shoulders. "You have no idea." She looked around toward the door. "I had hoped Stephanie would come by once she was done sanding that shuttle or whatever she was doing."

"Speak of the giant rock devil," Xan said, pointing across the bar.

A purple head appeared in the doorway. Mallory waved at her, yelling, "Stephanie! Over here!"

The Gneiss heard her name, or the approximation of her name, and began shuffling over.

Everyone aboard the station who had auditory receptors had been fitted with a tiny translation device that painfully (for humans, at first) attached to their eardrums. Once you got used to it, it could translate any language in the universe, provided the language had been added to the massive central databases. Since humans had made First Contact with the rest of the universe,

Earth languages were being added to the database. When last Mallory checked, the central database already had several English, Chinese, and Indian dialects, in addition to some of the dead languages like Latin. As for the names, the translating device created names that were generally understandable to the mother tongue of the listener. It was strange to look at a thin humanoid that resembled a walking stick and call her Bertha, but if that's what the translator said, then that was what they used.

Nicknames, however, sometimes stymied the translator. It could only do so much when languages evolved on the fly. Which, Mallory realized, nicknames sometimes did.

When it came to ordering in restaurants, Mallory had been delighted to find that nearly every race so far had their version of "hot pleasant morning drink" that translated to "coffee or tea" and so far she could drink all but one of them.

The odd thing about such a powerful little translation device was that the species who had created it had such poor eyesight compared to other races that they didn't see the point in creating a similar tool to allow you to read any alien writing. And there was a lot of alien writing around Eternity.

She still did enjoy ordering "coffee"—or the equivalent—and she could close her eyes and imagine that for a moment she was fifteen and in a diner back home, drinking coffee with too much sugar and whining about life. Back when life was simple and her biggest problems were an upcoming math test or whether her aunt was going to yell at her for being late or whether the point guard on the basketball team had noticed her. (He never did.)

"Do you know who's coming?" Xan asked as Stephanie lumbered their way.

"No, from what I got in the news feed this morning, it was essentially 'humans, welcome, shuttle, soon.'" Those are all the words I recognized. I messaged Stephanie for a translation and she confirmed it. Humans are being welcomed to the station now; a shuttle is on its way. And Adrian says he doesn't know anything about it."

Xan said nothing, appearing lost in thought. Stephanie reached them and sat at the tall table next to theirs. She began warming up to speak.

"Do you think the army will send someone right away?" Mallory asked.

He shrugged. "I don't know how hard they're looking for me. I don't know if they're going to piece together that I'm here. How much does that ambassador know at this point?"

She shook her head. "He's super-paranoid and is bad at hiding it, so I think it's safe to say he doesn't know you're here. But if he found out about you, I wouldn't put it past him to turn you in to get the Earth military to like him more."

"Why did Earth send him?"

Mallory shook her head, having no answer for him.

Stephanie started making a sound that was more like a voice. "Good morning," she rumbled. "My grandfather is a backend waste hole. Is your day going any better?"

The translator had problems with vulgarities, too.

"It's bad all around," Xan said. "Humans are coming, but we don't know who. We also don't know why. The army could be sending someone to find me, or the shuttle could be full of tourists. And I don't even know if they're still trying to pin the murder back home on me."

Mallory winced. "A lot of unknowns. And anyone who comes here is in danger from me, so I'm not looking forward to it."

"If humans are in danger around you, why is Xan here?" Stephanie asked.

"You don't see us together that often," Mallory said. "But every once in a while we need to talk."

"Is that why? You're afraid of me dying?" Xan asked, looking at her thoughtfully.

Their food and drinks arrived, and Mallory busied herself with her mug instead of looking at him. Her "coffee" looked like watered-down lava and was almost as hot. It was made "mild" for humans and still pushed the limits of what she could handle, but she soldiered on, blowing on her mug until she could sip without burning her mouth. It had a smoky, spicy, almost fruity sweetness. It was surprisingly good once you got past the texture and the temperature.

Xan was eyeing a flat piece of something that looked like orange bread but came with a hammer and chisel. He started knocking off little pieces and sucking on them. Mallory didn't see how he could digest rock, but it was his innards, his choice.

"It could happen," Mallory said. "You were with me the last time it happened; you know there's a risk."

IN A FIT of loneliness and against her better judgment, Mallory had agreed to attend a birthday party with her pushy neighbor, Anira. She was from the upstairs apartment and was part friendly person, part textbook nosy neighbor. She'd decided that Mallory needed social time and insisted she attend a party with her.

Mallory went to the party, someone died, and that's when she realized she was done with humanity.

Early in the evening, Mallory was actually enjoying the party, especially when she found her old college friend reading a book in the corner.

The party was in a residence inside the new North Carolina base, Fort Bowser. A very bubbly woman Mallory didn't know had hosted a birthday party for someone else she didn't know. After Anira introduced her to everyone ("everyone that matters, anyway!" the hostess had said), Mallory tried to do what she historically did at parties, which was gravitate toward a bookshelf and try to figure out her host's personality by their book collection. After that, she planned on eavesdropping on conversations.

Unfortunately, the hostess didn't have any books. Mallory stared at the pictures of drunken parties and messy kisses between the hostess and a man, unsure of where to go from there.

There was one book in the house: an old copy of *Slaughterhouse-Five* was currently in the hands of a bored-looking bald man in a light gray ARMY T-shirt and jeans who sat alone on the couch with a bottle of beer in front of him. He yawned as he flipped through the orange book. The beer had a peeling label, and he fiddled idly with it whenever he put the bottle down.

"Are you the guy I have to fight to look at the only book in this place?" she asked in greeting. "Or did you bring that yourself?"

He looked up at her and blinked. "Holy shit. Mallory? Is that you?"

He shut the book, but not before Mallory saw several notes scrawled in the margins.

The wave of emotions was surprising. Delight bloomed when she spotted an old friend, then her palms started to sweat because he was even better looking than she remembered, and then her stomach dropped into her boots when she realized it was a massive coincidence that she would run into him.

Coincidences were usually followed by murder.

She gestured to the book. "And what are you doing reading that?"

"Does this look like an Octavia Butler–loving house to you?" he asked in a low voice. "I brought the book as a gift for Billy, but"—he gestured to the bookcase that was full of pictures of the hostess and bowls of wooden eggs—"I unwrapped it to read because this is what the hostess has instead of books, and I got bored." He stifled another yawn. "What are you doing here? Did you enlist?"

"Oh, no, never been on the base before. I'm here with a friend who made me get out of the apartment. I don't know anyone here. I figured I would be the one who wandered around asking people uncomfortable questions about themselves and their relationship to one another." She glanced at his ARMY T-shirt and his defined muscles, something she hadn't remembered from college. "I assume you did enlist."

"Yeah, I had to leave school and enlist. It's a long story." He frowned, then continued. "Been in the service over a decade. Started in Fort Lee, then Afghanistan, then Sam Houston, and was transferred here about a year ago."

"But if you know these people, why did you get bored?" Mallory asked.

He shrugged and pulled some torn wrapping paper out of his jeans pocket. He smoothed it out on the coffee table. "I'm not feeling very social tonight. But Billy's a friend, so I promised I'd come." He put the book in the center of the paper and carefully wrapped it up. It was a bit messy, considering the tape had torn the paper in a few places, but it showed real effort. There was a word written on the inside of the wrapping paper, but she could only see half of it—"KEMM."

"I don't mean to assume, but how many people do you know who would appreciate a used Vonnegut?" she asked, grinning.

"No one still alive," he said, and the joke fell flat as they both remembered the last time they had seen each other, eyes meeting over the broken body of their classmate. They hadn't liked him, but he hadn't deserved to be thrown off a balcony.

"Maybe he'll be into a book about a soldier named Billy given to a soldier named Billy? Like those children's books you could order with your kid's name in it."

"I doubt he'll get it, anyway." He looked around the room. "Who did you say you were here with?"

"Anira," Mallory said, pointing at her neighbor, who was sucking cola backwash out of a foam gas station cup and laughing with the hostess. She caught Mallory's eye and waved. Her blonde hair was braided with silver ribbons that caught the light. "She's my neighbor, a friend of the hostess. I don't know her that well, but I'm new to the area and she invited me. She took pity on me, I guess."

"So, if you're not enlisted or doing civilian work, what have you been up to for the last decade or so?" he asked.

She grimaced slightly. She didn't like to lie, but she didn't know how to tell people what she did for a living. "I spend most of my time volunteering at the animal shelter for the night shifts."

"And you pay bills how?" he asked, an eyebrow going up.

She sighed. "I write books; they do okay," she said. "I mostly live off savings and royalties."

She never liked saying she was a writer. She wasn't a *writer*, with the scarves and the chunky jewelry and the online flame wars about appropriation and use of the singular "they." She just wrote books because she couldn't work a job that placed her among people.

Admittedly, she had really good stories to tell. And lucky for her, the murder mysteries tended to write themselves.

"What have you written?"

In a panic, she remembered her book in which she depicted the trip to Baltimore with "Thoreau" Guy and "Eric," the guy she'd had a crush on. There was no reason for him to have picked up that book specifically, but if he read it, he wouldn't have any trouble identifying himself.

"I write murder mysteries under a pen name," she said, shrugging. "Cozies, mostly. What about you?"

He frowned at her, looking confused that she didn't want to talk about herself. Then he gave a little shrug and said, "I'm with the 919th Quartermaster Company. We're a new branch off from the Fort Lee Quartermaster Company. I started out doing machinery repair. Then they put me on mortuary affairs." He paused as if waiting for her to respond with a joke.

She didn't. "If you're not in a war zone, is there much call for those skills?"

"Not directly, but we do drills, train new recruits, keep up on mortuary science. And there are some domestic requirements." He shrugged. "And we do other quartermaster duties where they need us to fit in." His eyes dropped down to the book and he frowned.

"That's fascinating," she said.

The birthday boy—Billy?—was laughing loudly across the room, holding court for several other folks. "Symbies. Something. Aliens got 'em. You wouldn't fucking believe it." On overhearing this, Xan's head snapped up. His face went still.

"'Symbies'?" Mallory asked Xan.

"He's not supposed to be talking about that," Xan said, stuffing the book and wrapping paper in his back pocket.

"It's okay. I have no idea what a symbie is," Mallory said, shrugging.

"Doesn't mean he shouldn't know better," Xan replied.

"—no better than a parasite!" Billy said, laughing again. "And they all got 'em!"

"Goddammit," Xan said, politely but firmly edging past Mallory to approach his friend, but someone else, a strong-looking woman with blonde hair, got to him first. She guided him out of the room, talking to him, her head close. "All right. She's got him. Moron." Xan turned back to her and took a visible deep breath to calm down.

"So, you're studying alien stuff here?"

He cocked an eyebrow at her. "You know I can't talk about that."

She grinned. "I had to try."

He was about to respond, but the hostess banged her tacky,

costume-worthy ring on her beer bottle to get attention. The party's energy came to a halt as everyone focused on her.

"Okay, y'all," the hostess said, turning to all of them in turn. She had a way of moving that made her hair bounce like a shampoo commercial. "We're gonna play a little game! Has everyone played 'Werewolf'?"

Mallory's stomach clenched. She stepped away from the wall and nodded an apology to Xan. "This is my cue to get a drink. I'll see you later."

He smothered another yawn with his hand and shook his head. "But this is a cool game. Why don't you play a round, then we can get a fresh drink together?" He downed the rest of his beer and put the bottle on the table. "I'd really like to catch up with you."

Mallory ground her teeth, knowing she was being handed a golden opportunity to reconnect with this guy, but she also had a bad feeling.

"I've played it before. It's . . . not for me," Mallory said. She took a few steps toward the kitchen, then turned around and said, "I'd recommend not playing. It's not a good game for this party."

She went to the kitchen then, leaving his puzzled face behind, knowing he wouldn't take her advice. They never did.

Xan didn't follow, but Mallory's neighbor did. Anira had abandoned her almost immediately after they arrived, so she figured Anira had forgotten about her.

The swinging kitchen door shut behind them and Anira faced Mallory, crossed her arms, and rolled her eyes almost audibly.

"Why are you hiding in here? Is this that murder fear thing?" she asked.

"Would you believe me if I said I was getting another beer?" Mallory asked.

"Sure, if you weren't drinking a soda right now," Anira said. "You know that in Werewolf, they only *pretend* to kill people, right?" She got her own beer from the fridge, twisted the cap off, and took a long drink.

"Aren't you driving us?" Mallory asked her, eyeing the beer.

Anira waved her hand. Her cheeks were flushed, and she looked excited. "Don't change the subject. What do you think is going to happen?"

Mallory regretted ever letting Anira look at her apartment. A few weeks prior, Anira had visited to be neighborly, and, hungry for human contact, Mallory had let her in and given her a tour of the spare space. Anira had spied Mallory's bookshelf full of her own Charlotte Queen mysteries. Anira had asked lots of questions and figured out pretty quickly that Mallory was both the author and the subject of the books. She didn't believe that they were true stories, of course. No one ever did until it was proven. And then it was too late.

From the living room, the hostess was explaining the rules of the game. Sweat began to bead on Mallory's forehead.

Mallory hopped up on the kitchen counter, not caring that the toaster oven door handle dug into her back. "I have a set of personal rules." She held out one finger. "Rule One is not to be at a party like this in the first place. I already broke that."

"Isn't Rule One of Murder Club 'don't talk about murder club'?" Anira asked, grinning.

Mallory glared at her. "Rule Two is, if I do end up in a situation like a party, identify the hot spots in the room."

"'Hot spots,'" Anira said. "That guy you were talking to was definitely hot. Does he count?"

"Well, yes, but I'm not going to tell you this if you aren't going to take me seriously."

Anira made a visible attempt to stop smiling. "Yes, sorry, go ahead."

"What I call hot spots are people with a lot of connections.

While it's true that people will kill strangers, it never happens around me. The murderer always has some connection to the victim. So at this party, there's your hostess, of course. She has a bunch of friends here, but mainly there's her sister and brother, you, her friend, and a guy they serve with who I'm pretty sure your hostess has a crush on. Her husband's deployed, so she could also be cheating on her husband with anyone here."

Anira opened her mouth, looking like she was going to argue, but Mallory held up a hand. "I'm not judging or even accusing. I'm saying these are possibilities I see. The birthday boy, Billy, right? He's got the most connections, obviously. His sister is the hostess, and he also has an ex-girlfriend here, and he's close with his brother-in-law, who's not here. They're both the center of several possible conflicts."

"Wow. You remember all that? You haven't even met the people who haven't arrived yet."

"That will probably be too late. If it's going to happen, it'll happen soon."

Mallory paused, waiting for the inevitable question. Anira didn't disappoint her.

"Okay, so why don't you go warn them, if you're so sure someone's going to die?"

"That doesn't work. I've tried that before," Mallory said, rubbing her hands together as if to wash something off them. "No one believes me, so if I warn someone, we will still have a murder, and I'll be a suspect because I knew it was coming. It's like I'm a Greek chorus or Cassandra or something.

"Anyway, that was Rule Two," she continued, holding out another finger. "Rule Three is get out of the room when something bad very obviously is about to happen." She gave a meaningful look toward the living room, which had gone silent. She reached over and pushed the swinging door so she could peek through. The room and hallway were dark.

"It's nighttime. The werewolf is about to claim their first victim," the hostess called in a spooky voice.

Anira looked from her to the living room. "You mean right now?"

"Probably," Mallory confirmed. "Look, no one will be happier than me if I'm wrong. If they play a fun party game and nothing happens, you can crow and make fun of me for the next month." She paused, then added, "Or until the next murder, anyway."

The lights in the living room came on. Laughter sounded from the room, and Mallory felt the fist around her stomach unclench a bit. Maybe this time it would be okay; maybe she could enjoy the party; maybe she could talk to Xan some more.

Anira grinned. "I'm gonna milk this for all it's—" She stopped when someone screamed.

"OKAY, SO WHO do you think is going to die?" Xan asked, sucking on a piece of rock.

She blinked at him. He believed her, and he still didn't get it. "I have no idea, because I don't know who is coming. But odds are there will be people aboard who are connected to each other in ways that are not obviously apparent. Old lovers, or unknown biological children, or former classmates."

He shrugged and crunched down on the rock. Mallory winced. "I didn't know if you were definitely sure a human would die, or you think it's going to be someone else." He gestured around the bar as if encompassing the whole station, but there were only a few Gneiss in the bar.

"It's really hard to kill one of us," Stephanie said helpfully. "It's hard for us to kill each other. I don't imagine your people would find it easy."

"You'd be surprised," Mallory grumbled. "Humans are innovative when they want to be." She took a sip of her lava drink and forced down the thick substance. The problem with waiting for the liquid to cool was that, like lava, it thickened as it did so. At least she'd stopped worrying about what the stuff was doing to her insides. "Anyway, if I knew who was coming, then I might be able to guess who the victim will be. But as for now, the only real guess I have is you or me or Adrian. And I've never been the target of a murder attempt."

"Well, let's hope it's Adrian," Xan said dryly.

Ferdinand came up and served Stephanie a plate of small, shining rocks. She'd never ordered, as far as Mallory could see. "What did you want to talk about?" Stephanie asked, crunching loudly.

"If we had to leave the station, could you help us?" Mallory asked. "It's not safe for Xan, and I don't want to be in the middle of a murder investigation again."

Stephanie looked at Xan for a long time. He was calm under her scrutiny, chipping off pieces of his breakfast as if he didn't know she was staring at him. Mallory looked from one to the other. She had an uncomfortable feeling of being out of whatever was going on between them, as she had in college when two friends of hers started dating and decided not to tell her. Mallory could figure out who killed someone, but when friends were hiding something from her, she was cheerfully oblivious.

"Guys? Hello?"

"No," Stephanie said at last. "You couldn't survive on our world."

"What about another station—"

"You don't want to go to another station," Stephanie said. Mallory's eyebrows shot up. She'd never heard Stephanie talk fast enough to interrupt a human.

"All right, we'll unpack *that* later," she muttered. "Do you have any advice on how to get the station to listen to us?"

"The humans are already on their way. Most shuttles have the right amount of fuel for a trip to the station. If they're too far along, they won't be able to turn back." She paused. "Then the shuttle itself will fail and everyone on board will die, and you'll be the murderer."

"I can't tell if you're joking or not," Mallory said, unamused.

"I was."

"Tell me this, did you know who was going to die at the birthday party?" Xan asked.

She sighed. "I had a pretty good idea, but I wasn't sure."

WILLIAM WILLIAMS III—"Billy" to his friends, "Trey" to his parents, and "Will Will Will" to his sister—was the poor bastard who went from birthday boy to murder victim. He died on his birthday, stabbed through the heart. The coroner said he died instantly.

When the screaming started, Anira and Mallory ran into the living room. The lights were on and Xan was lowering a bleeding Billy to the floor. Xan's shirt was soaked in blood, and his face was slack with shock. People, Anira included, rushed forward and tried to put pressure on the wound in Billy's chest, but it didn't do any good. He was already dead.

The door was open. Mallory did a quick scan of the room and didn't see anyone obvious missing. Who had opened the door? Had someone come in and killed Billy and then run away?

Xan was still standing, covered in blood, shaking his head either in denial or as if trying to clear it. He backed up a few steps. Then he turned and stumbled out the open door.

The hole in Billy's chest was gaping, but the murder weapon was not obvious. It should have been in someone's hands, or on the carpet. Mallory wondered if it was under the body. The obvious answer was that Xan had taken it, but these cases almost always steered away from the obvious answer.

Mallory started to look around the room, dodging the weeping hostess and the still-shocked guests. Her brain logged information whether she wanted it to or not. Beer bottles everywhere. A tablet sat on a coffee table with the rules of Werewolf showing; an overturned bowl of chips littered the floor and had been ground into the carpet. She walked to the chair where Xan had been sitting when she'd gotten there. Beside it was an overturned foam cup, its lid knocked free and ice leaking out. Lipstick was at the top of the discarded straw.

His beer bottle with the peeling label was on the coffee table, overturned.

She didn't want to get involved, but she couldn't not look for clues when everyone else was losing their shit. A woman who looked as if she had just stepped off a glacier in Norway sat in the chair Xan had occupied earlier. Her face was slack with shock and her phone trembled in her hands.

"You calling the cops?" Mallory asked her.

She gave a quick nod, her white-blonde braid bobbing. "Yeah. I mean, no. I'm calling the MPs. Rodney's calling 911."

"All right, then," Mallory said. "I'll look around outside." But the woman wasn't paying attention to her anymore, her ice-blue eyes focused on Billy's corpse. Tears welled, collected on her lashes, and then spilled down her cheeks.

Mallory retrieved her light jacket and carried it with her outside, fishing through the interior pockets for a business card. The summer had been hot and dry and she would regret wearing it, but she had things in her jacket she liked to keep with her. Outside she searched the bushes and lawn carefully, using her phone's flashlight to supplement the streetlights. She was unsure of what she was looking for, but that never stopped her.

The sun had just gone down, and the blacktop driveway was still warm. Mallory crouched and looked under the cars. A wet spot was under one of them. A leaking radiator?

She stood, looked inside at the chaos and tears, and then back outside. Something clicked, a dopamine-like hit to her brain as it all became clear.

"Okay, then," she said, satisfied. Now all she had to do was wait. She took the well-worn business card and turned it over, reading the rude words on the back and then the official words on the front. She watched the waning light in the field at the edge of the base as she waited.

When the cops and ambulance made their loud, flashy arrival, she stood silently for a pat-down, and then handed the card to a detective. "You'll want to call this man."

"What the hell are you talking about?" the detective said. She was short, pink-skinned, and stocky, with her brown hair pulled into a messy bun at the nape of her neck. The badge she wore said MORRIS. "Call your own damn lawyer if you think you're going to be charged." She hadn't looked at the card yet.

"No, I can't call that number. You have to. And I guarantee if you don't, things will get complicated fast." Mallory pushed the card at her again.

"Is that a threat?" the detective asked sharply, and then she looked at the card and her eyes widened. "North Carolina State Bureau of Investigation. This is Fort Bowser jurisdiction, or Wake County at most. What does the SBI have to do with anything?" She narrowed her eyes and looked at Mallory. "Who are you?"

"Turn the card over," Mallory instructed. Morris did so and read the words aloud: "CALL RIGHT FUCKING NOW—D DRAUGHN."

"They won't have interest in your case," Mallory said. "They just have interest in me."

"You're part of the case; you're a suspect," Morris said, handing the card back to her. She followed the other officers inside.

An officer remained inside one of the cars, talking on a radio with his eyes on Mallory.

"I tried," she said to the officer, who looked startled. "Back me up when he gets here. I tried."

Without waiting for an answer, she dialed the number on the card.

"This had better be an ass-dial," a voice on the other end snarled.

"It's not. I tried to get the detective to call you, but she ignored me."

"How many dead?"

"One. Birthday party in Fort Bowser family housing. I can give the address if you want to send someone."

The voice, rough from years of either yelling or drinking, swore loudly. Mallory pulled the phone away from her ear.

"You had to go to an army base? Are you nuts?" he yelled.

"Look, you always say to tell the cops to call you the next time it happened!" she said. "It's the next time. Do you want the address, or do you want to leave this to the MPs and Wake County PD?"

SBI agent Donald Draughn arrived fifteen minutes later. He got out of his blue Honda Accord in sweatpants and a denim jacket. He was rude on his best days, but when she had to call him at home, his angst was at a level she had only seen in high school science teachers awaiting retirement.

"I hate seeing you," he said without venom. He sounded tired. "I really do. How many is this?"

He knew how many it was, or thought he did. Mallory got to her feet. "Who's counting? And don't be so cranky, Agent. I figured you'd be glad I've moved closer to Raleigh. Remember when I was in Charlotte? That was a really long drive for you."

"You're proud that you've shortened my commute to your murders?" he asked flatly.

"They're my murders now? All right," she said, crossing her arms. "Here are the details. I'm here with a neighbor. You'll want to detain her, by the way. She's an accessory. The murder weapon is under that red car, but you won't find it because it's melted."

"You know who an accessory was, and the murder weapon, but not who the actual murderer was?" he asked, getting on his knees to look under the car.

"Stay with me," she instructed. "I got here about an hour ago. I knew one party guest—who's probably your main suspect, by the way, although he didn't do it—and we talked for a few minutes. The hostess started a game and turned the lights out. I went to the kitchen with my neighbor, and that's when the birthday boy got stabbed, fell against the guy I know, and bled to death. The murderer threw the ice knife out the door, where I'm guessing it shattered and melted. Then my friend ran before anyone could stop him."

The agent peered up from his vantage point on the ground. "Ice knife? Seriously? How do you figure that?"

"We go through this every damn time! I don't know; it's a gut feeling. But when everyone else was drinking beer, my neighbor had a giant foam cup with her all night, but liquid never went up the straw. When the murder was happening, she was with me, with a beer. She'd left the cup in the living room. You'll find it next to the easy chair. When you search the house and the people inside, you won't find a knife. When you test the driveway, you will find blood from the murder victim where that damp spot is. Possibly also blood from the guy I know. I don't know if he got cut or not. Is that enough detail for you?"

"Ice knives are hard to wield," he said. "Slippery."

"You'll probably find some gloves somewhere inside, then," Mallory said.

Agent Draughn looked around the street and across the field, which had the base fence on the other side. "It's a small base. Shouldn't be too hard to find that guy who ran."

"Yeah . . . this is the part you're really going to hate," Mallory said, wincing. She had been trying to figure out how to drop this bit of information, and she still hadn't come up with a good opener, so she just told him, "You won't find him. He's been abducted by aliens."

4

INNOVATIVE PROBLEM-SOLVING

THE HONEST-TO-GOD, REAL First Contact with an alien species—two different species, actually—had happened in the Blue Ridge Mountains about a year before the murder party, on August 23, 2043.

The world governments had attended many meetings, trying to learn about the different aliens in the universe and whether they were threats. They weren't, but mostly in the sense that humans aren't an aggressive threat to ants but could squash them if they wanted to. Earth scientists learned about the reality of alien technology and if they could get their hands on it (translation: technology, yes; FTL technology, no). After a few months, they finally declared peace with the aliens, a magnanimous move that fooled no one.

Most of the civilians in Birch, North Carolina, the location of Fort Bowser, were relieved to hear about the declared peace. Behind closed doors, many in the military postured that they wanted a chance to "kick some bug-eyed butt," but when people learned about the aliens' superior technology—and all of the species were more advanced than humans—no one really wanted to fight. The town already had to worry about being a choice military target to human enemy states; they didn't want to worry about the rest of the universe as well.

Once it was established that First Contact wasn't going to end in a *War of the Worlds* situation, people tried to get used to the alien visitation that seemed to happen with a frequency that delighted the news feeds. To the Earth governments' annoyance, no one had the power to regulate visitations or tourism. Aliens could just land in an empty field and wander around. Many aliens visited the planet as a vacation destination, coming across startled humans who had no hope of understanding them even as the aliens processed more and more human languages into their translation database. Most humans never came across diplomats who were trained in dealing with other cultures; people met the tourist aliens who were wandering around and, for example, looking for dead relative remains in the Grand Canyon.

Mallory hadn't seen any aliens in person, but her previous year had been pretty terrible, what with the murder she couldn't solve and the subsequent trial. With her personal life in chaos, she couldn't deal with the excitement of alien visitors, so she mostly tuned it out.

But like everyone, she'd seen pictures all over the Internet, several stories of hilarious problems with breaches of etiquette or misunderstandings, or the discovery that some aliens really liked Vegemite, which the Australians thought gave them universal vindication regarding their local treat.

There were a few incidents of harassment, both claimed by humans and aliens, but they were dealt with quickly and violently, and the aliens were almost always gone by the time any authorities got there. Some unfortunate aliens, however, disappeared. As there was no official record of who was visiting Earth and where and when they were there, no one knew how many, exactly, were missing.

In addition to this hiccup, some humans started blaming all

sorts of incidents on aliens, including their brother-in-law stealing from them and wrecking their car while DUI. As a result, more alien diplomats were sent to Earth to help with investigations.

Humans then asked for their own ambassador aboard the closest space station. The aliens agreed to install someone on a temporary basis.

Television shows and podcasts about alien cops were all the rage. About ten aliens became actors in Hollywood, Bollywood, and other motion picture locales. To humans they were megastars; to other aliens they were bit actors.

Those government departments concerned with borders and customs were furious because no military on Earth had the technology or weaponry to stop an alien shuttle from just setting down in a field and the aliens wandering off to experience whatever Earth had to offer. Most major cities were building shuttle ports, which the aliens had agreed to eventually use, but currently they just flew anywhere and landed anyplace they liked.

Another issue of contention was that the aliens were happy to visit Earth all they wanted, but they currently forbade Earth visitation to their home worlds and space stations. Some thought that it was just because humans couldn't get there themselves, but the official word was that humans were too unpredictable to have among their people.

This made sense, Mallory reflected, as she waited in the dwindling light for the cops to come to the murder scene and spotted a ship in the sky.

Hell of a time to see my first flying saucer.

This one wasn't a saucer, but a spinning polyhedron the size of a house that hovered over the field across the street from the house. It had glowing gyroscopic rings that were so bright she had to shield her eyes. They illuminated a figure staggering across the field as if injured or severely drunk, and the craft tracked it, keeping directly above it. The figure—Xan, she realized with a start—stopped and looked up at the ship and then back toward her. He collapsed into the grass.

A portal slid open underneath the ship.

"Shit," Mallory said, and started to run. Before she ran more than a few paces, Xan's limp body rose into the air and disappeared into the cavity of the ship.

She came to an abrupt stop as the craft sped away with its— prisoner? Hitchhiker? Accomplice? She had no idea. She shielded her eyes and watched it fly directly overhead, gaining altitude. "The cops aren't going to like this detail," she muttered to herself.

But another thought bloomed in the back of her mind, and, as she sat back down to wait, she realized that Xan had possibly just left all of humanity behind.

That's one way to get away.

STEPHANIE WAS THE chattiest Gneiss Mallory had come across. This was possibly why Mallory enjoyed her company more than most.

"Let me tell you what will happen," she said, the words coming faster as she warmed up. "You're going to have to barge in. He won't make an appointment with you. He will probably see you if you do this, since the station will make him. You can make your case, but if the station has allowed humans to come here, then she's not going to change her mind. Stations don't really do that."

"Then we're back to running away," Mallory said, leaning back in defeat.

"Not necessarily," Stephanie said. "There's always worth in making your needs known. And I could be wrong."

Mallory had yet to understand all of the vocal inflections of the aliens, especially through a translation device, but she guessed that Stephanie was very sure that she was not wrong. She tended to be sure of herself on a level that awed Mallory. She wondered if it was a Gneiss thing or a personality thing.

"When he shoots you down, come see me in the cargo bay," she offered.

Stephanie had been right, of course. She'd told Mallory which door to go to, which was down a twisty labyrinth of corridors. She raised her fist to pound on the door, but before she could make a sound, a voice came from within.

"Mallory-the-Human, I do not have time for a meeting." The voice was nasal and grating, with a rude tilt to the words.

Even though Ren knew it was her, Mallory knocked anyway. If others were allowed their meaningless rituals, she'd hang on to hers, dammit. "I just want a few minutes, Ren."

The door slid open and Mallory walked into a pulsing red-lit room that looked like it stretched up through the station for hundreds of feet. She couldn't see the ceiling because the space above her was partially obscured by the branches of a huge tree with yellow leaves. Thick roots went into the metal floor. There was no telling how deep they went.

There was nothing else in the room besides the tree. She looked around carefully, and finally, out of her peripheral vision, she spotted the slight discrepancy in the color of the bark of the tree's trunk.

"I can see you, Ren. You're right there. You probably shouldn't have said you were in here if you were just going to hide from me."

The bark shifted and the Gurudev, looking like a humanoid stick insect, separated from where he'd been blending with the trunk. He stepped away from the tree and met her gaze with his black eyes. "I told you I didn't have time."

"Yeah, well, I'm persistent," she said. "What is this place? I thought this was your office."

"It is," he said. "The tree is how I commune with Eternity-the-Station."

"I thought you spoke with her all the time," she said.

His mouth flattened in a way she was too familiar with; he was annoyed. "We can commune entirely when I am connected with her. When we are not connected, the communication is still there, but weaker. I don't have time, and you're here to complain. So get on with it."

"Man, you're a pill," she said, putting her hands on her hips. "When you act like you know what I'm going to say, it really sounds like you don't give a damn what I actually tell you. What's the point in talking if you know what I'm going to say?"

"Exactly," he said, his eyes glowing slightly red from the light in the room. "You're wasting both our time. But you will persist, so go ahead."

She took a deep breath. "I wanted to know something about all those humans you invited to the station. It's put both Xan and me in difficult positions. How can Eternity guarantee the safety of everyone?"

"Ah, yes, I remember, you're convinced that you have some kind of aura or smell that makes murders happen around you," Ren sneered. "The other human is merely a criminal running from the law on your planet."

"You really suck at being a welcoming host for the station," she said. "But you're about to get a bunch of humans aboard, and I have no idea what's going to happen after that."

"Then we will find out, won't we? Mystery is part of what makes life beautiful," Ren said.

"You're not taking me seriously at all," she said flatly. "But I thought maybe Eternity would. She let me aboard, after all, not you."

"Eternity believes you," he said. "I do not."

She wanted to pull out her own hair in frustration. She began to pace instead. "How in the hell does that work, anyway? There's a giant, sentient space station who is nigh-omniscient about what goes on inside her, and she's mentally connected to someone like you, who can't believe anyone is worth the oxygen Eternity creates. She welcomed me; she allowed Xan to seek safety here. Why should we listen to you, who lets your poor opinion of humans get in the way of everything?"

"She has a macro view of the life inside her, while I worry about the micro view. I don't know what she needs to do to regulate the temperature for the colder races, but she doesn't know what merchant to call to get materials she can't create for herself. She likes you," he said, sniffing, "but she doesn't really know you. She sees how you fit within the whole fabric of the station and likes your place here. On a day-to-day level, I don't see how you fit in at all."

"You still haven't said if she will guarantee Xan's and my safety," Mallory said.

Ren said nothing.

"Christ, all right," she said, flexing her hands open and closed to release some tension. "I have just one more thing to say. When a bunch of humans come aboard and someone dies, for once I would like someone to remember that I warned them and that no one fucking listened."

"Your protest is noted." He put his long-fingered hand back on the tree and said, "We're done here." He paused as if listening. "Wait. Eternity wants you to ask Xan if he will come see us."

"A favor? Really? Aren't there seven or eight ways she can contact him just by thinking about it?" she asked coldly.

"Thirteen, actually. That includes sending me, too. But she wants you to do it."

"I doubt it's her that's asking," Mallory muttered.

"Mallory," Ren said as she turned to leave, and his tone of voice surprised her. Instead of his typical holier-than-thou tone, he used one of sincerity, and the voice was deeper and more melodious. "I may not always agree with my symbiont, but he will never lie regarding her wishes."

Mallory tried to parse the pronouns and failed. "Is that Ren or Eternity talking?" she asked without turning.

"Yes," Ren/Eternity said.

MALLORY HAD KNOWN on an academic level that all the other sentient races had the ability to form symbiotic relationships, but hadn't realized how bad that made humans look to them. The other races viewed humans as being terribly lonely and unevolved.

Mallory's Phantasmagore friend in station security, Devanshi, had explained this to her. Devanshi had expressed regret that Mallory was so alone on the station. Mallory had thought she meant the lack of humans on the station, but the chameleonlike Phantasmagore alien had said that with a symbiotic relationship, one was never lonely.

"Every other sentient being in the known universe has some sort of symbiont, often for their whole lives. Some of them bond with their own race, but usually it's two races that join in a mutually beneficial connection."

She indicated her own symbiont. Phantasmagore were the approximate size and bipedal shape of humans, but the similarities ended there. They were lithe and strong, with chameleonlike abilities and webbed hands, and most often they looked like a bendy store manikin had gotten into a fight with a honeysuckle vine. Devanshi's skin was dark brown and shiny, and a rough line twined from her back left ankle up her leg to the middle of her back, sometimes sprouting little red blooms like flowers along the thicker part of the "vine." This was Devanshi's symbiont, a plantlike creature that gave her the chameleonic abilities. She called the creature "Splendid."

"These are the Caecus, a sentient plant that evolved alongside the Phantasmagore. They help us with our ability to blend in. We don't form relationships with any other being but the Caecus, but races like the Gurudev are more adaptable. Gurudevs join well with the sentient places—such as sentient space stations, or ships—but they aren't the only race who can do that. Just the most likely ones."

"So if I had, say, a tapeworm, or lice, you would consider me more evolved?" Mallory asked, screwing up her face in disgust.

Devanshi paused. "Ah, as I understand it, you just named two parasites, not beneficial symbionts."

"Yeah, it's gross to us, too," Mallory said, shuddering. "I was just curious. Except for things like friendships with animals, we don't have anything like that." She felt strangely jealous and lonely—even lonelier than she had already felt as one of the few humans on the station. She wondered if that was Devanshi's goal.

"This was why Eternity was so hesitant to allow humans to come to the station: humans are evolutionary children compared to the rest of us. One has to wonder, why have you found no other species to form a symbiotic relationship with?"

"I don't know of any!" Mallory had protested. "It's not that we've rejected a relationship; I just don't think we have anyone else like that on Earth. Not for humans, anyway."

Mallory dutifully relayed the message to Xan.

"Why couldn't she tell me herself?" he asked, frowning. He was underneath the hovering *Infinity* shuttle, messing with an open panel.

"I asked the same thing. She said she wanted you. I don't know. Maybe they want you to convince them. They're not listening to me."

"What are you going to do now?" he asked, wriggling out from under the shuttle.

"Go talk to Stephanie again, I guess. I don't have many other people to ask for help."

He stood, putting his tools in a crate beside him. "I'll let you know what they say."

"Great," she said woodenly.

Stephanie was still outside her shuttle, pounding on the solid rose-colored rock with her fist.

"Damn you, listen to me for once!" she bellowed, her voice echoing in the shuttle hangar.

"What's going on?" Mallory asked, coming up behind her.

"I need a break. Come aboard with me." Stephanie focused on Mallory. Her eye sockets burned with a slight glow she had once said was indicative of life. "You look like I feel."

"How do you know what tired and despondent humans look like?" Mallory asked.

Stephanie hummed low and then said, "You told me you were."

Mallory grinned despite herself. "Fair. So how do we get aboard?" She had long wondered how the interior of a Gneiss shuttle was laid out but had never been invited aboard.

Stephanie knocked on the rock again, this time three polite raps instead of furious pounding. Nothing happened for a moment. Stephanie raised her fist again, but then the shuttle shuddered, tilting backward as legs extended from the two corners closest to Mallory and Stephanie. It tilted farther and farther back, revealing a gaping hole in the bottom of the shuttle.

"Is it going to fall?" Mallory asked, watching the ship tilt farther back to accommodate Stephanie's great height.

"Of course not," Stephanie said, ducking her head a little and heading toward the hole. "He's not drunk."

"You aren't talking about the pilot, are you?" she asked as she followed Stephanie, marveling as the shuttle kept defying gravity to tip farther backward to allow them to walk underneath it.

"I forget you're completely new to all sentient life in the galaxy," Stephanie said, positioning them below the hole.

"Well, yeah, that's why I'm asking," Mallory said, but Stephanie startled her by taking her wrist—a relatively gentle grip for being handled by literal moving rock—and pulling her close. Mallory bumped against her and it was like stumbling against a war memorial. Stephanie would make an excellent baseball catcher, Mallory thought as the shuttle began to lower itself and engulf them in darkness.

Her own breathing was very fast, something she only realized when that was all she could hear.

"Very funny, give us some light," Stephanie said.

Around them, white rocks that peppered the rose-colored wall began to glow slightly, looking like lighting set into the walls. Which Mallory supposed was the case, but they were clearly quartz and not glass. They were at the bottom of a spiral staircase with tall steps. Stephanie began scaling them, and Mallory did her best to follow.

The steps were painful to climb after only a few, her thighs burning as she stepped up nearly two feet at a time. She was panting and falling behind Stephanie but refused to ask for help. She could take a goddamn staircase.

Above her, Stephanie stopped on a landing and then the sound of rock scraping against rock drifted down to Mallory. She struggled up and around a few more steps, wondering how big this shuttle actually was, and then she came to an open hole in the wall. It led to a cockpit of sorts, if Rodin had fancied sculpting an alien command center.

Everything was made of rock. The huge chairs, the console, a rising sheet of very thin, milky mica that looked like a display.

Stephanie was the only one inside the cockpit. She had lowered herself into one of the chairs comfortably and watched as Mallory came into the room.

"Mallory, meet my grandfather, Algernon. But his friends call him Rusty."

Months before, Mallory had attempted to stop wondering how the translation database treated proper names. She'd been surprised to learn Devanshi's name—which she was pretty sure was Indian—as she'd thought until then that she would always hear Anglicized names. Where had "Algernon" come from?

Now Stephanie was adding nicknames to the mix, and Mallory was confused again. But that wasn't the point of all this. She looked around, bringing herself back to the present. The Gneiss weren't notorious for being good hiders.

"So your grandfather is the ship? He's like Eternity?"

"Kind of, but not the same species," Stephanie said. "And he's nothing like her personally. He's cranky and mean and doesn't want me to spend time with friends, but there's not a lot he can do about it except for refuse to fly me where I want to go. Right, Rusty?" She lowered a fist to the rocky console and Mallory winced, expecting chips of stone to fall off, but the ship remained still.

"It's good to meet you, Mr. Algernon," Mallory said, focusing awkwardly on the closet wall. "Uh, thanks for giving me some privacy to talk to Stephanie." She looked around again, marveling at the beauty of the white ribbons streaking through the rose rock. The sheet of mica lit up, and some writing that she recognized as one of the Gneiss languages appeared.

"Sorry, I can't read your language yet," Mallory said.

"He says hi and not to listen to his exaggerating granddaughter," Stephanie said with a sigh. "Don't be an asshole, Rusty." She focused on Mallory. "So how did it go?"

"About like you said it would," Mallory said. Stephanie's eye sockets grew wider, something Mallory had initially taken as surprise but soon learned that in Gneiss body language conveyed a willingness to hear more, and for the speaker to keep talking. "Ren was unsympathetic, and very rude. They sent me away to get Xan to talk to them, so I'm wondering if they will listen to him."

"And you don't want humans here because your people slaughter each other when they're around you, correct?"

"That's . . . extreme, but, sure," Mallory said. "If she opens up to human tourists, I worry it's going to happen again. I can't be the cause of more death." She climbed awkwardly into one of the empty rock chairs and half regretted it.

"You think it's your fault," Stephanie said thoughtfully. "I didn't know that."

"Of course I do," Mallory snapped. "It happens around me, doesn't it?"

"And the military could be sending people to take Xan back home, against his will, correct?"

"Maybe, yeah. That's what he's afraid of."

"He shouldn't worry about that," Stephanie said. "He will be fine. But if they try to take him, things could get messy."

"You think the station would protect him?"

"Definitely," Stephanie said. "The real worry is for you. Or those you intend to murder."

"I don't murder!"

"But you said you were responsible—"

Mallory groaned and put her head in her hands. "It's different. Never mind. No, I don't murder, but I worry that things will happen around me."

"And Eternity knows this about you, but you don't trust her to protect the other people coming?" Stephanie asked. "She's not reneged on any promise that I've heard of."

"I trust the station, but I don't trust Ren. He is not a fan of humans and doesn't lie about it. I think he'd be happy to get rid of me and Xan. Probably Adrian too, but I can't blame him for that. I still don't see how she can want us here when he doesn't."

"I can't stand Ren," Stephanie said, her voice low.

"Why do you hate him?" Mallory asked.

Stephanie was silent for a moment, humming. Mallory didn't know if she was working up to speak or was pausing to decide how much to reveal.

"He has too much power," she finally said. "He is unkind unless he wants something from someone, and then he is disgustingly obsequious. He has been . . . needlessly unkind to me."

"How could such a jerk bond to a benevolent space station?" Mallory asked.

Stephanie looked from Mallory to the console of her shuttle. "A symbiotic relationship isn't simple. It's true Ren can't move directly against the desires of the station, but he doesn't have to agree with her. And when she wants something done, he doesn't have to be pleasant about doing it. When two beings join, it doesn't mean they will agree on everything. Just as a mated pair or trio won't agree on everything. Anyway, I would trust Eternity to protect you both. Even if you don't trust Ren."

Mallory sighed and leaned against the cool chair. "I don't know. I'm scared to stay."

"So what do you want me to do about it?" Stephanie asked. The question didn't have the same sarcastic rhetorical tone that most English speakers put behind it. The Gneiss were a blunt people overall, but Stephanie had never been cruel.

"I don't know. I wanted to run this morning, but now I don't know where I'd go even if I did have passage. I thought I would ask to go to your home world, but you said we wouldn't survive there, and"—she gestured weakly at the walls around them—"I realized that I still know very little about your people."

"I can't take you anywhere," Stephanie said.

"Can't or won't?" Mallory asked.

"Can't," Stephanie said. "I'm as stuck here as you are."

"But you have a shuttle! And apparently he's your own grandfather!"

"The thing about sentient ships is that they won't always do what you ask them to," Stephanie said. Her shoulders dropped, making her look like a slightly softened wax statue. "And he wasn't always a shuttle. Just as I may not always be bipedal. When Gneiss get older, they sometimes . . . I guess you can say we ascend, if they have connected with a powerful enough symbiont. My grandfather lost the ability to walk and talk to most sentients, but he can now travel anywhere in the universe he wants." Her voice got softer as she spoke, as if she were running out of whatever energy Gneiss used to speak.

"Anywhere?" Mallory asked, startled. "Humans didn't even believe FTL was possible, and your people evolved into it."

"I'm not a physicist or a geologist," Stephanie snapped, energy returning to her frame. "I have no idea. Besides, your people evolved to be big bags of water that walk around. This is pretty amazing to Gneiss."

Mallory laughed. "So, does this mean you're going to be a shuttle someday?"

"Possibly. If Grandfather has anything to say about it, it won't happen for a long time." Mallory understood that "a long time" to Gneiss could mean thousands of years to humans. While Stephanie appeared Mallory's age maturity-wise, she was hundreds of Earth years older.

Mallory wanted to ask a hundred other questions, like how a shuttle could stop Stephanie's ascension, but she had other worries. "Do you have any advice for me? Xan's dealing with his own shit right now. And I don't have a lot of other friends."

"Two advices," Stephanie said. "One, get more friends than me and Xan. I'm also dealing with my own foul waste products. Two, consider one thing for me. Have you ever tried to find out why you have ability or curse to make murders happen?"

"Of course I have! Everyone I talked to on Earth thought I was lying! I talked to doctors and priests and cops, and among all those, only one person believed me, and thought it was all my fault! My friends left; my family either shunned me or tried to lock me away. Believe me, I have tried."

"Have you tried any religious leaders or the doctors of other species?"

Mallory had been prepared to argue, but she closed her mouth. She scooted to the edge of the chair and dropped onto the floor. "Actually, yeah, but the Sundry don't like it when I ask questions."

"There are other Sundry than the blue faction on the station. Ask the silver Sundry. And remember: you don't know what is going to happen when the humans arrive. When they arrive, and you need real tangible help, I'm fully here for you. For now, I have to finish yelling at Grandfather."

5

JEALOUSY. COVETOUSNESS. ASPERITY.

MALLORY'S FIRST THOUGHT was to approach the blue Sundry for help again. She was nervous enough approaching the Sundry she knew; she didn't relish seeking out new terrifying insects to question. Their hivemind should have access to all the information they had about humans, so conceivably she could ask any Sundry she came across. The problem was, she had never gone to them for anything; they always came to her when they wanted something, and they always sent a few scouts to bring her messages. The Sundry never used the station communications system, so Mallory wasn't even sure if she could contact them.

Then again, every time she paused to concentrate on her public surroundings, she spotted at least one Sundry, either perched somewhere or flying by. They always seemed to be watching.

When she exited the Gneiss ship, scuttling out from under the tilted rock even though she knew Stephanie wouldn't let her grandfather squash her, she looked around the shuttle bay.

Finding them was easier than she'd expected. A Sundry shuttle was in the process of docking on the other side of the bay, a massive paper wasp nest floating into its designated space and landing on its pointed end, which flattened as the ship settled.

When she got nearer, it appeared to be sealed and made space-worthy with a shiny kind of epoxy or pressure-friendly wax.

This was a silver Sundry ship. She had only had experience dealing with the blue faction of the aliens, and wasn't quite sure what distinguished the factions beyond color. After the ship docked, several drones exited the top and began inspecting the ship, some of them flying in a wider radius to inspect the station.

If they had just arrived, would they know what was going on? Would they be connected to the blue hivemind?

As she got closer, several wasps collected in front of her, and she could hear the whisper of a voice in their wings.

"This is the human. Novel. Different. Interesting. Do you have need of Sundry? Aid. Help. Favor."

"I'm not sure if you can help me. I was looking for some blue to ask a question, but then you arrived. I'm Mallory, by the way." She extended her hand to allow them to inspect her as the blue Sundry had taught her.

"I wanted to talk to the xenobiologists in the blue hive, but I don't know how to contact them," she continued as they flew closer and landed on her hand. She tried not to let her skin twitch or her fear show, but she knew they'd be able to detect the adrenaline that had started coursing through her body.

"We know your name," they said, probing her skin with their antennae. "Famous. Infamous. Destroyer."

"What?" she asked, startled. "What are you talking about, 'destroyer'? And I'm infamous?"

"We can help," they said. "Follow. Come. Learn."

Mallory shouldn't have expected they would answer her. The silver Sundry took off, and she took a hesitant step forward to follow them. She jumped when an angry buzzing sounded behind her.

A veritable swarm of blue Sundry had gathered in the shuttle bay, their anger palpable as they surrounded her, cutting off her path to the silver ship. She couldn't tell what happened to the silver Sundry. The furious living cage of insects cut off even her sight of the handful of silver scouts.

She stumbled backward, falling onto the rubber walkway. She stared with wide eyes at the angry swarm. "What the hell is going on?" She wanted to sound outraged and firm, but her voice was a squeak.

"Do not seek information from Sundry outside the station. Forbidden. Dangerous. Untrustworthy," the blue Sundry replied, the vibration of the buzzing making her teeth ache.

"Wh-why not? How am I supposed to know who you don't want me to talk to? They were here and they were offering—"

"You don't know what they were offering, but remember: you work for us. Employee. Friend. Chattel."

"Chattel? No, wait, hang on a second," she said, getting to her feet. "I don't belong to anyone."

There was a moment where the only sound was of wings. Mallory got the sense that they were conferring. "We misspoke. Apologies. Mistake. Contrition. Silver wouldn't give you the proper information. Opinion. Priorities. Orientation."

Mallory put her hands on her hips. "How the hell do you know that? You don't even know what I want to ask!"

"We determined a high probability you were going to ask about your unique issues regarding the murder of your own people. Allure. Honey. Inveigle."

Mallory rubbed her temple. She didn't see how the Sundry's three words matched the sentence they'd said. There was always some kind of connection, but she couldn't worry about that now.

"Okay, so what now? Are you going to tell me what I need to know?"

They didn't answer, but continued to swarm.

"Dammit, you don't get to say what I do and who I talk to. If you're not going to help me, then you can just leave me the hell alone." She turned around and discovered they had left an opening in the rear of the cage; she could exit so long as she was walking away from the silver Sundry.

"I want answers," she said. "Or you can consider our examinations over." She silenced the voice in her head asking what she would do for income in that case.

"Answers coming tomorrow," the blue Sundry finally said. "Coerce. Force. Blackmail."

Mallory laughed bitterly. They reminded her of Aunt Kathy, always playing the victim. "No, this isn't blackmail. I'm not threatening to harm you. I'm just saying keeping me ignorant for your purposes isn't fair to me, and I walk away from unfair situations. Near as I can tell, you're jealous information hoarders. You know why I think that? Because you haven't given me anything to lead me to believe anything else!"

As quickly as they had come, the blue Sundry swarm dissolved in all directions, leaving Mallory alone and still ignorant. She still didn't know anything, but she was much more frightened of her supposed allies now.

She looked over her shoulder at the shuttle. Every silver drone had stopped inspecting the ship and was oriented in her direction.

As angry as she was, she didn't feel like risking approaching them again. She didn't know what Sundry venom would do to humans and wasn't going to be the first one to find out.

BACK IN HER quarters, Mallory lay on her back on her unmade bed and stared at the ceiling. One blue Sundry scout perched on her light fixture.

"You know, it creeps me out when y'all spy on me," she said. "I didn't say you could observe me all the time."

The wasp's wings hummed briefly, and then stilled again.

She had realized that if fewer than four Sundry were together, they couldn't communicate with those outside their species. Mallory thought of it like a circuit; if they had four, then there were enough connections to form words. If not, then they only watched.

"So, if you've read *Watership Down*, have you read my books?" she asked. She reached over to the small shelf set into her bedside table and pulled out a dog-eared book, the first she'd ever written. It was the bestseller, and she referenced it for pacing and style when she was stuck in her writing.

The Queen Pen Mysteries, by Charlotte Queen, each featuring a murder solved by the innocent woman unlucky enough to be nearby when they happened.

"They're not exactly what happened, you know," she said to the scout. "I had to tighten the plots, make the dialogue better than hiccupping sobs that were just noise, and my hero is much cooler than I am. Evangeline Halcyon! She's strong, decisive, and level-headed and always has a plan. *She* never runs away from stuff."

Very few people had guessed she was the author of her own "ripped from the headlines" novels. After SBI Agent Donald Draughn got in the way of every attempt she made to go into law enforcement or private investigation, she was at a complete loss for what to do for a living.

"I used to work minimum wage jobs, but then someone would die, my coworker or a customer or something. I'd solve it and move on. But a few years ago I was working the coffee bar at a literary convention. An editor had been murdered and dismembered, with a rejection letter written in his blood on the wall, supposedly from a fountain pen. I investigated it and met a literary agent who'd been a suspect. She was one of the few people to believe me—although sometimes I wondered if she didn't care whether I was lying, so long as I told a good story—and when I told her about a few of the previous murders I'd solved, she asked me if I could write them up as mysteries.

"And they were a hit! This thing I have that has lost me everything in life and made me feel responsible for an awful lot of other people losing everything, sometimes their lives, sometimes just"— she thought about Xan, and put the book down—"sometimes they lose everything but. And now I'm profiting off the murders, which didn't feel good, but shit, what else was I going to do?"

She covered her face with her hands and took a deep breath. "I'm sorry, little scout, it's not your fault. But if you ever convert human money to your credit system, life will be a lot easier for me since I built up some excellent savings from these books. If I have to, I've got one more I can write, if I can get the news about Billy's murder. But I'd love to stop there. I'd rather not have new stories to tell."

Her doorbell chimed, followed by a quick rapping knock, just in case. Xan never visited her, and Stephanie always contacted her via station communication. Only one person visited her quarters, and he always knocked like that.

"What do you want, Adrian?" she called, not sitting up.

"I have some news," he said, his voice muffled through the door.

"What, are they here already? Dead already?" She couldn't bother to sit up. She looked up at the Sundry on her light fixture. "I'm feeling sorry for myself, aren't I?" she asked in a low voice.

The wings buzzed slightly again.

"Fine, all right, come in," she called, and the voice-activated door slid open. Sentient space stations came in handy when you didn't want to get up.

"Are you drunk?" he demanded when he stepped into her quarters.

"No," she said, propping herself on her elbows. "I'm depressed. I would be drunk, but I don't have any booze and I don't feel like going out and looking for the closest approximation to whiskey. We haven't found it yet." She winced at her own use of the word "we" and hoped Adrian hadn't caught it.

He didn't react. "I would recommend trying a Silence bar. But you need to either bring an interpreter or learn their sign language."

The Silence were the only beings on the station for whom the translation device didn't work, as they had no auditory senses and no ability to make speech. If you couldn't communicate via their native signaling, which used moving lines on their skin that made their veins look like they were suddenly filled with radioactive blood, you'd have to use the sign language they developed to communicate with other species.

The Gneiss rarely communicated with Silence without a translator of another species, since their arms and hands were too bulky to convey the subtle movements necessary to communicate.

"I don't know their language," she said, leaning back on her bed and watching him. "Tell me your news."

Adrian looked around her quarters with undisguised distaste. "Do you always live in this mess?"

"When I'm not expecting fancy ambassadorial guests, yeah," she said. "Stop stalling. And have a seat. Can I get you some tea?"

"No," he said, looking pointedly at the chair, which really was quite comfortable but was also covered in Mallory's clothing.

"I can't even subtly insult you," she said. "I don't have any tea."

"I don't even know what you're talking about. Are you sure you're not drunk?" he asked, pushing some shirts aside and sitting on the edge of the comfy chair.

She sat up fully and crossed her legs. "Adrian. What. Is. Your. News."

He pointed at the book on the bed. "I did some research into the Charlotte Queen books. You said you had been part of more than fifteen murders—"

"Adjacent to," she interrupted. "I didn't have anything to do with them."

"All right, adjacent to. But why only fourteen books?"

"Are we really doing this?" she said impatiently. "All right. Eighteen murders. But I only solved thirteen of them. I didn't solve the first few because I was a kid, and the last ones I didn't solve because of personal reasons and the fact that I came here. Book fourteen was published after I left. I wrote it based on police reports and my memories and what they solved."

He frowned, looking confused.

She crossed her arms. "I'm done with this. Give me your news or get out." Her voice lacked the venom she had hoped to inject.

"I find it hard to believe you want to stop writing those books, considering how much money they got you," he said.

"You find everything hard to believe, Adrian," she said.

"You have to admit it's a tall tale worthy of my toothless grandfather," he said, picking up the book and flipping through it. "And he tried to convince us he was half Icelandic."

"The last book was really hard to write. I had to change a lot of the facts; I was too close to it," she said. "The last one happened right before I came here. I didn't have time to solve it."

She left it vague on purpose. Adrian still knew nothing about Xan, and Mallory's goal was to keep it that way.

"How did you get sanctuary, anyway?" he asked. He'd asked her this before, but always in anger, and she'd refused to give him the information.

"I had heard the Gneiss liked to visit the North Carolina and Tennessee mountains since the mountains are so old. So I went to Asheville and waited for an alien tourist. I found a group of Gneiss signing up to tour Biltmore House—which they couldn't do because they were too heavy and the house staff were terrified they'd break something, but then they flew their ship around the grounds out of spite and scared the hell out of everybody, but that's not the point.

"I knew they would be able to understand me, even if I couldn't fully get them. So I told them I wanted to get a message to Eternity, and if they were coming by here, could they carry it for me.

I had it written out, so I read it aloud while they transcribed it, and then I waited. Eternity sent a shuttle a few days later."

He stared at her. "That is unbelievably reckless! You don't know what they could have written! They could have put that you were willing to be a slave or to offer yourself for dissection, or they could have picked you up in a shuttle and sent you anywhere in the galaxy for a laugh!"

"But that didn't happen," Mallory replied. "I don't know, seemed like a good idea at the time."

"It was reckless," he repeated flatly. "But tell me, what happened with the last murder? Why didn't you stay to help?"

"Because solving murders isn't my job," she said bitterly. "The cops made damn sure of that. I was tired of doing a job I wasn't getting paid for, or credit for. I didn't want to write any more books. And this case had the cops and the SBI and the MPs on it."

She bit her lip. She shouldn't have said the thing about the MPs.

That slip Adrian caught. "Why so many law enforcement agencies?" he asked, leaning forward.

"It was a murder, so there were cops," Mallory said, holding up one finger to count on. "It was on an army base, so there were MPs"—she held up a second—"and I was involved, so the SBI sent my usual handler to make sure that I hadn't done the murder this time around."

"But you didn't solve this murder?" Adrian pressed when she was done.

She glanced at him, irritated. "I helped out the cops when they asked me, found an accessory to the crime, found the murder weapon, but getting off the planet was my main focus for a few weeks."

"So it wasn't solved when you left?" he probed. "Were there any suspects? Had they caught anyone?"

"I don't know, I'm not there anymore, and I don't get the news reports," she said pointedly. She was getting increasingly uncomfortable with where this was leading. But there was one detail that might interest him and get him off Xan's scent.

"The one thing that I didn't solve was a code I found. This was an army base house. I found what appeared to be a code inside a list on the fridge. I figured it was a clue, but I pointed my handler toward it and dropped it. The military doesn't like it when a civilian knows too much of their shit."

Adrian stared at her, utterly entranced. "How did you know it was a code?"

"It was a very strange shopping list that looked like it had a pattern to it. It had stuff like 2 butters, 1 tire, 7 milks, and 3.5 uranium. My theory was it was a chemical compound of some sort. And I know enough about the military to know that even if you don't understand some sort of compound or message, that doesn't mean that someone won't get really mad at you for seeing it anyway."

"I wonder if they'd send someone after you if they knew you had halfway decoded it," he mused.

Mallory paused for a moment, blinking. She had been so focused on the obvious reasons to run away, not even considering that the army might be concerned that she had seen their code, no matter how small her exposure was. "Nah, I doubt it. People don't go after me. I'm unimportant, remember?"

"So what was up with your neighbor? Was she an accessory?" Adrian asked, picking a shirt off the floor and folding it tightly, his hands restless. He faced her, holding the shirt in his lap.

Mallory shook her head. "Anira. She was a piece of work. She nearly fooled me, I'll give her that. She acted like she didn't believe my stories were true. But from what the cops found on her computer, she knew who I was when I moved in and actually manipulated me to go to the party to ensure the murder would happen. She was pretty smart, but I don't think everything went according to plan, because she ended up hanged in her closet."

"Do you think she killed herself?" he asked.

"I do," she said slowly. "Only because I haven't experienced a lot of suicides in my life, and her death felt . . . different than the others. But Adrian"—she paused, frowning at him—"I don't recall telling you anything about my neighbor, but you knew already. Why are you here, and what is your goddamn news?"

"So tell me about the one before that, the one you couldn't solve," Adrian said, ignoring her.

Mallory closed her eyes, and tried, again, to piece together the seventeenth murder, and what had gone so very wrong with that investigation. But all she could remember was being curled into a ball in the back of her car, shaking. One or two party guests were still inside, shocked, her cousin was upstairs, oblivious, and her aunt was sobbing in the kitchen.

She'd refused to go back into the house. She had none of her usual feelings when it came to finding clues. Angles didn't seem sharper and everyone's connections to each other weren't filed away in her head. There was a buzzing in her ears, and her face was swollen from tears.

Without her help, the cops found a gun below the window of her cousin's room and arrested him.

Even Agent Draughn had worked to keep her out of the investigation, both as a suspect and an amateur detective (not that she'd fought him on that part). That had been the one and only time he had been kind to her.

The cops and the courts had determined that her cousin Desmond Jr. had killed Uncle Dez, and put him away for life. Aunt Kathy was furious and blamed Mallory for the whole thing.

Mom was gone. Uncle Dez was gone. Desmond Jr. was in jail. Kathy tended to be adrift if she didn't have a family member to boss around, and there was no way she was sticking around to be her aunt's target for rage or nurturing.

She cleared her throat and opened her eyes. "No. I'd rather not talk about it."

"Then let's talk about my news," he said. "The news is the shuttle will be here shortly. Within the hour, I'm guessing. They sent me a message with the details. The Earth governments are sending a small group of people: a few VIPs, a few lucky civilians, a few military people."

Mallory groaned. Adrian smiled as if he'd been waiting for the response. "Yes, military. I expect they'll be looking for both you and your friend in the shuttle bay. The one who escaped a murder charge by fleeing the planet. The one you omitted from the story."

"Shit. How did you find out about him?" Mallory asked.

"You may not like me, but don't underestimate me," he said coldly. "I have sources."

Her fists clenched. "So the military is coming, so what? The station has promised to protect us both. How are you going to get past that?"

"Negotiating an agreement to get humans aboard was only the first step," he said, standing and straightening his tie. "The next steps involve things like extradition. They also involve trade, so you'd be able to get your tea, if you were staying."

"Staying?"

"Mallory, I don't know what kind of weird curse you have, but if in fact it's true, I can't have you endangering visiting humans. You need to go back home."

"You had that whole speech about acceptable losses, remember?" she demanded. "What about that?"

He smiled. "Well, if we can avoid acceptable losses, even better. I'm getting a promotion and won't have to tolerate you being here much longer. I can't believe how much the army offered to apprehend you both. I would have given you up for a lot less. They really, really want you back. That other stowaway, too."

Mallory looked at Adrian and how calmly he was smiling. Then she jumped like she'd been electrocuted and ran for the door. "Eternity, open the door!" she yelled, and was gratified to see it slide open, but only halfway.

She didn't bother to wonder why it hadn't opened fully. She figured she could slide through, but Adrian would have a bigger problem with it, having a typical middle-aged man's body.

He called out angrily behind her, but she didn't look back. She ran up the hall as fast as she could.

FIVE MINUTES LATER she had lost him, but she was well and truly out of her depth. She hadn't wanted to get close to the shuttle bay, so she had turned left when she always turned right. Right led to the lift that went to the more public parts of the station, and left went farther into the station, toward more species' residential areas that featured either different atmospheres, different temperatures, or both. She just wanted to get away.

Her bare feet began registering the temperature change, and she shivered in her T-shirt. A public comm system was on the wall at a T-junction in the hallway, and she went and pushed the button. "Xan Morgan, *Infinity* shuttle," she said, but the line just hummed.

"Uh-oh," she said. She pushed the button again. "Stephanie, Gneiss, uh, I don't know her last name, or her shuttle's name. Oh, right, Algernon!" The line remained dead. Stephanie's personal information was saved on her home comm. If Eternity was answering, she could have accessed it. Why wouldn't the station answer her?

Screaming filled her head, overwhelming every sense, and she was dimly aware of the floor coming up to meet her. The floor was cold enough to shock her back to herself, and she got to her knees and held her hands over her ears, squeezing her eyes shut, anything she could do to block out the screaming.

The station shuddered as if hit with a missile. All around her, cold metal groaned and shrieked, then began to rumble. A quake? An attack?

Then the scream sounded again and she fell against the wall. Somewhere, she wondered why it was getting colder. She wondered how she was going to get out of this if she was lost. She wondered if Adrian had gotten to Xan, and realized that she hadn't warned him, she'd just run.

Again.

Unfortunately, conscious thought was leaving her as the screaming became an all-encompassing thing. She felt woozy and accepted the coming darkness with open arms. At least the screaming would stop if she was unconscious.

She hoped.

6

. . . .

THE HARSH TRUTHS OF TRIAGE

STEPHANIE WAS VISITING her people down below and taking care of some important business.

The humans were strange and somewhat ignorant. But they did make for entertaining conversation and sometimes even surprised the Gneiss into thinking on a different path than usual. While Mallory had been fretting over her personal problems, she'd triggered an idea in Stephanie's head. Stephanie turned it over and over and found no fault in it.

Grandfather had objected, but he didn't get to decide everything for her. She decided it was time to take care of her problems on her own instead of waiting. It would be an unpopular choice, but she was tired of being captive on the station, relying entirely on Grandfather's whim.

After setting some things in motion, she exited the Gneiss-only area of the ship, secured the stone door, and nearly crushed the small, cold body lying on the floor.

A thrum in the floor, a whisper that no one would hear if they weren't Gneiss and connected to the stone.

Chaos is here. The human was right.

"I know," Stephanie said, still looking down. She weighed her options, and finally decided she liked the human enough to help her out. Mallory had helped her, even if she didn't know she had. And as Stephanie understood it, the humans' range of comfortable temperature was incredibly small, and this one was wearing fewer protective garments than most.

"I found her," she responded to Ferdinand, starting the lengthy process of bending down.

What—how did that happen so fast?

"Coincidence," Stephanie said. "I was visiting the ossuary and she was outside. How did you know she was missing?"

The male human is looking for her. He's distressed.

Aware of the delicate nature of their skin and their endoskeletons, Stephanie carefully gathered Mallory in her arms and walked toward Ferdinand's. The unmoving body seemed so fragile. Stephanie decided she would keep this one around, since she was amusing and helpful. But she should pick up the pace; Eternity was distressed, and by the sounds the station was making, Stephanie didn't have a lot of time to achieve anything.

The vibrations of the ship were close to language to the Gneiss, although they spoke of anguish and pain rather than actual words. Someone had once opined that the sentient stations and ships were distant relatives of the Gneiss, but the Gneiss weren't fond of that theory.

"Tell Xan I'm bringing her to the bar," Stephanie said. The floor positively thrummed, both with the station's pain and the signals the Gneiss were sending to each other, but Stephanie could easily pick out Ferdinand's special tone. He was different. She cared for him, and his messages were always easy to pick out of a whirling storm of vibration.

Her grandfather stopped giving her his opinion of her afternoon's activities and started to give his opinion of Ferdinand's message, but she ignored him.

. . . .

XAN RAN OUTSIDE the bar to meet Stephanie. His eyes were wide, and she paused to look, fascinated. She hadn't known their eyes could do that.

"Mallory?" he asked. "Stephanie, God, what happened to her?"

"I don't know, I just found her," Stephanie said. She held her arms out and Xan took the human from her. Stephanie was absurdly proud that she hadn't broken any of the human's bones while she carried her.

"I don't know how to get her awake. Shit. I'm taking her back to the shuttle." He looked up to Stephanie and then to Ferdinand, who had come to the bar doorway. "Thank you both. And you stay safe. This doesn't look like it's going to be a good thing from any point of view."

He hurried away, holding Mallory close. "Christ, where are your shoes?" he muttered as he left.

He showed concern for us. For us. Ferdinand's message seemed shocked and amused.

"He's in much more danger than we are. Why worry?" Stephanie wondered, similarly confused.

Perhaps it's a human thing. Perhaps they show concern for everyone, both the weak and the strong.

"From what I have heard of humans, that is usually not the case," Stephanie said. "I think this might be a sign of friendship with humans. Mallory has shown similar concern for me at odd times."

Humans are fascinating. The vibration began to die as Ferdinand looked at Stephanie a bit more closely. *What were you doing down there?*

"My own business," she said. "You may want to shut down soon. I'll be on Grandfather reading some of the histories. I think that's the safest place. Come by if you have nowhere else to go."

Tina will want to come. Ferdinand's tone was neutral.

"Tina." Stephanie took a moment to weigh all the factors and finally said, "That's fine. I don't want her to die in a vacuum either."

MALLORY SAT UP, blinking stupidly, trying to clear her head. She didn't hear the screaming in her head anymore, and the ground no longer shook. She shivered and pulled a blanket tight around her.

"Hang on, where am I?" she asked. It took her a second, but she recognized the coppery metal around her. She was curled up in the captain's chair in *Infinity*. "Xan?" Then her eyes flew open wide, and she shouted with more insistence, "Xan!"

"Are you finally feeling better?" he asked, his head appearing from the bottom floor.

"No, I mean, yes, but Adrian knows about you; he wants to get rid of us both. He said the army have people on the shuttle, and they'll be here soon!"

He grimaced and came up the ladder. "That's bad, but we have bigger problems."

"Bigger than that?" she demanded. Then she felt the slightest bit of pull to the left. "Wait, are we still on the station?"

"No," he said, leaning over her to poke at some buttons. "We're needed elsewhere. Tell me what happened to you."

"Adrian came by, gave me the runaround just to tell me that he knows about you. He tried to grab me, but I ran away."

"That explains why you don't have shoes," he said, pulling up a view screen. "Why the hell didn't you just come to the shuttle bay?"

"Because I didn't want to lead him to you," she said. "Where are we going?"

The view screen showed only space, stars, and a distant sun. She stared at it, distracted, and then realized Xan was not saying anything. He was studying her, a strange look on his face.

"What?" she asked, sitting up a little straighter.

"Nothing," he said. "So you were running from Adrian?"

"Yeah, and I got lost, and then there was screaming, and then I fell, and then I was cold, and . . . that's all I remember. What is going on, anyway?"

"Well, you got your murder," he said. The ship turned again, and something came into view on the screen.

A Gurudev shuttle drifted into view, the same kind Mallory had initially taken to the station. It resembled an evolved NASA space shuttle, gleaming blue with gold tints, and it would have looked sleek and impressive if it wasn't rotating listlessly at an angle. Its engines were dead, except for a few bright, worrying flares. She didn't know a lot about propulsion fuel used by other species, but she could guess that wasn't good. She leaned closer to the screen; what she had thought was a shadow was a gaping black cavity in the nose of the ship as it twisted around again.

"Oh, God. Is that the shuttle from Earth?"

Xan nodded. His jaw was clenched.

"How many are dead? Was it a bomb?"

"I don't know how many are dead yet, but they're not the murdered ones," he said grimly. "They're collateral damage."

"Tell me what you're talking about," she said, grabbing his elbow and pulling him to face her.

He wouldn't look her in the eyes. "Ren's dead. Murdered. And without a host, Eternity's freaking out and station security is worried she's in a state of shutting down. This shuttle isn't even on their radar right now. Security is working on an evacuation plan."

"Evacuation? The whole station? How do you even plan for that?" She swallowed. This was so much worse than anything that had happened to her on Earth. "So, that's it? We're evacuating now?"

"Hell, no," he said, pointing to the drifting shuttle. "We're their rescue mission."

Rescue? She didn't deal with survivors; she solved murders. She shook her head. "So what happened to the shuttle?"

"As I understand it," he said, "the shuttle was preparing to dock when—" He paused and swallowed. "Eternity. I don't know if she has weapons, or tentacles, or something, but she just sort of . . . slapped it out of space."

"Why?"

"I don't know," he said. His voice was tight, but she didn't get the sense he was angry with her.

Mallory's mind tried to shy away from the horror in front of her. She thought about the situation on the station. "Something had to have set her off. Was this before or after Ren died?"

"Does it matter?" he asked, leaving his spot behind her chair and sliding down the ladder to the lower deck.

"Well, if she was upset about him dying, then yeah, it matters! Do we know what a sentient space station is likely to do when her host dies? Is there any history? I don't know much about sentient space stations except that they're apparently utterly terrifying when they're upset."

"I don't know why she did it," he said grimly. "I wish I did."

"The news said she was welcoming humans to the station," she mused. "I wonder if Adrian knows?"

"I don't care what he knows or what he doesn't," Xan said. He was rummaging through something in his room. There was a moment of silence, and then he swore under his breath. Mallory couldn't catch all the words, but something had set him off. When he spoke again, his voice had dropped an octave, making his serious tone even more dour. "He's the least of my worries right now."

"Xan? You okay?" she asked.

"Fine," he said, his voice clipped.

They sped toward the drifting ship. Mallory made a small noise in the back of her throat as detritus floated by the ship, some human-shaped. "You said there were still survivors? How many?"

"Twelve," he said.

"That was rhetorical. I thought you didn't know the number of people on board! How do you know all this?" She looked around her, frowning. "And who's flying the ship, Xan?"

"Autopilot," he said, reappearing on the ladder. "And focus on the job at hand, Mal. I know this because Stephanie just sent the shuttle records from the station." He climbed up into the flight deck and motioned toward a small panel with a readout of complex characters. Since his trip downstairs, he'd developed a deep crease between his eyebrows.

What had rattled him?

"And I've been flying her long enough that I can read some of *Infinity*'s codes. There are life signs of two different species, at least, still aboard," he added.

"But how are they even breathing? I don't know much about space, but I do know that a hole that size is a breaching event."

"Many shuttles have emergency sealants," he said, focusing on the piloting. *Infinity* had picked up speed and they were getting close to the shuttle. "It's like an airbag in a car, but instead of cushioning you, it seals breaches. It happens fast, but it still can't stop explosive decompression, so some didn't make it."

"So what's the plan? Grapple with the shuttle and pull it back to Eternity?"

He laughed, a harsh, bitter sound. "As easy as that would be, no, that's not all we have to do."

"That doesn't sound easy at all! Isn't that enough?"

"Mal, if that was your mother floating out there, would you want her frozen in space forever?"

"But they're dead! Aren't they already lost? What are we supposed to do about that?"

"We're pulling the shuttle in with the survivors, yeah, but we're also getting the victims. Every one we can find. Aboard, twelve live; three are deceased. That leaves nine retrievals." His speech had grown strangely clipped and official.

"You sound like you have a plan," she said.

"Of course I do," he snapped. "I've done mortuary service during wartime. This is what I know."

AS INFINITY NEARED the wreck, the shuttle's door appeared crumpled inward as if it had collided with something. The sealed breach was just to the side of the door nearer to the front of the shuttle. Scrapes marred the side as if it, like the *Titanic*, had tried to skirt an iceberg.

"So what's your plan?" she asked, afraid of the answer.

"I'm going to do a spacewalk, tethered to the shuttle. I'll retrieve the bodies. You need to get *Infinity* tethered to the shuttle from Earth, connect supply lines to it to ensure it has enough oxygen, tap into the computers to see if anything is still working, and make sure the bodies I bring back are stashed in a cargo hold below."

"Do *what* now?" she asked, taking a step backward. "Do what with the what? Xan, I don't know the first thing about flying this shuttle. I have been meaning to ask you how you handle any of this. It's alien tech. I couldn't even do this for a human vehicle. The scariest thing I've ever done in a car is learn the stick shift!" The answer, as terrifying as it was, seemed pretty obvious. "I should do the body retrieval. You stay and handle the fancy flying."

His eyes got wide. "Absolutely not."

"I don't like it either, but I don't see a better solution," she said. "I'm a lot more comfortable around dead bodies than I am grappling alien ships together in a fucking vacuum."

"Are you more familiar with spacewalk in a vacuum?" he demanded.

"Are *you*? You might know army shit about combat, but I figure we're on the same footing when it comes to experience with spacewalks. Unless there's astronaut training you haven't told me about."

He opened his mouth, but she put her hand on his arm. His

skin was damp and clammy. "Look, there are survivors aboard the shuttle. The folks outside can't be hurt anymore, but the ones on the shuttle can be. You can handle *Infinity*, and I can't. We're running out of time. I have to go outside. You know that."

"I can't let you," he said. "If something were to happen to you—"

"Then you're still around to pull the survivors in. Besides," she said with a small smile, "I trust you to keep me safe out there more than I trust me to keep you safe."

He pursed his lips and looked to the side. "This is pretty brave for you."

"Well, we're all they have," she said, nodding to the shuttle. "And I'll ignore the backhanded compliment. I'm sorry there's not another soldier here to help you out. We're not the rescue they deserve. Or need. But we're all they've got. We need to get them some medical attention. And I've got to get back to Eternity and figure out who killed Ren. 'Cause that's what *I'm* good at."

A muscle twitched in his jaw, and he looked over his shoulder at the screen where the shuttle drifted. His eyes were shadowed and haunted.

"All right," he said. "Just, God, be careful."

"Oh, shit," she said, blinking. "I don't have a suit, do I?"

He shook his head. "There's a suit downstairs. It fits me. It should fit you." He pointed to the ladder. "I'll be down to help you get in."

"Where'd you get it?" she asked, heading for the ladder. "The aliens can barely be bothered to make chairs to fit us. How do I know the suit won't decompress and kill me because I'm not a Gurudev or whoever made this shuttle?"

"Just try it on," he said, rubbing his face as if he were very tired of her already. "It may be loose in the arms and legs, but it's human-shaped at least."

What the fuck am I doing? Had she really just argued to go out into a vacuum to recover dead bodies? To do a spacewalk with zero training? She took a deep breath. She was more comfortable with impulse decisions, but this was a new level. And she was committed now.

She ended up in Xan's small bedroom, with a neatly made bed, a side table, and a closed door that she assumed was a closet. On the bed lay a suit. It was a small, copper-colored jumpsuit with raised lines like veins rising from the legs and arms. It looked like it would be formfitting for someone his size, not clunky and poofy like a NASA spacesuit. It might be tight in the chest and loose in the arms and legs, and the boots would be caverns (especially since she wasn't wearing shoes or socks because of her flight from Adrian), but it would work. She pulled it up over her sweatpants and T-shirt, and struggled to close the back.

"You decent?" he called down to her.

"Yeah, but I have no idea what I'm doing," she said. "Can you come make sure I won't depressurize?"

He slipped down the ladder by his bed and came around to her. She held her hair off her neck so he could fasten the small, airtight latches that sealed the back. She could feel his breath on her neck as he made sure the open latches around her collar wouldn't get in the way of the helmet.

"Are you still sure you want to do this?" he asked, his mouth close to her ear. She shivered.

She cleared her throat. "How about asking if I'm sure that you're better suited for rescuing survivors than I am, and leave it at that," she said.

His fingers worked quickly, testing the line inputs on the panel between her shoulder blades, and then he bent and checked her boots.

"That's not going to be easy," he said. "I know those boots don't fit."

"Good that I don't have to run, huh?" she asked. "Where does the oxygen tank go?"

"You will be tethered, so you'll be getting air from the ship," he said. "I'll be monitoring you and sending you info via the HUD." He held up the helmet and tapped the face shield, indicating where the heads-up display would appear.

"Even if I run into trouble? You can't talk to me?" she asked. "Even humans managed that tech."

"I'll try," he said, "but I don't know how much I can answer. I'll be spinning a lot of plates." He lifted the helmet over her head and fastened it with eight tight latches around her neck. The world immediately became an intimate echo of her own rapid breathing, and the face shield started fogging up.

Xan placed his hand on the wall across from his bed and a wall panel slid aside to a small alcove. Inside lay three cords that were attached to another panel. Xan took the cords and held them up to show her.

He took the red one and attached it to her back. His voice came over a speaker inside her helmet. "This is your tether. It's designed to stretch fifty yards at the tightest. It's made of a flexible steel woven by some spiders on the Gneiss home world."

"That sounds fucking terrifying," Mallory said. "Harvesting that stuff doesn't sound like fun."

"I don't imagine it's hard for the Gneiss," he said with a shrug. The thick blue cord turned out to encase two small hoses. "This one is your oxygen supply. It recycles oxygen in and CO_2 out."

She eyed the hose suspiciously. "They're right next to each other. How does the intake hose not just grab the oxygen that just came out right beside it?"

He paused. "There's a . . . filter of sorts. It won't allow oxygen into the intake valve."

"Well, shit. I feel like my great-great-grandmother when electricity came to her little mountain town. It's like magic."

"The air is also treated to prevent condensation," he said, pointing to the foggy face shield. "But you need to be careful. The hoses will not stretch as far as the tether."

She frowned and eyed the different colors of lines pooling at the floor around her feet. "What the hell is the point of a stretchy tether, if the other hoses won't reach that far?" she asked.

"The ship is not perfectly designed for a human spacewalk," he admitted. "We should be grateful that we have a suit that fits us."

"Yeah, where did you get this, anyway?" she asked.

He thought for a moment, looking off to the side as if trying to decide something.

"I'll tell you after all this is done," he said. "The details will just make you ask more questions, and we don't have time for that." His eyes were desperate.

Realization splashed over her like cold water. *He knows someone on the shuttle. Someone still alive.*

"All right. Let's go." She took a deep breath, and the face shield fogged momentarily and then cleared. So oxygen was flowing at least. "And the third line?" she asked as he secured that one to her back.

"Power," he said, and a HUD popped up on her helmet showing her oxygen levels, her distance from *Infinity* (zero feet), and other data, including the state of her power and oxygen lines and the name of the damaged shuttle (*Cannon*).

Something nagged at her, but she let it go. He was right; they had work to do.

"So grab the bodies, bring them back?" she asked.

"Pretty much. The HUD will tell you how to use the propulsion jets, the ship will keep you tethered with air and juice, and I'll be around if you get into trouble. Get the bodies, and get back in one piece." He gave a small, bitter smile. "They won't treat you like a hero, but you'll be one anyway."

He left her then and slid the panel closed behind him. Air began to hiss around her; he'd put her in an airlock.

"You have an airlock in your bedroom?" she asked, incredulous, but he didn't respond.

She placed her gloved hands on the wall in front of her as the air was removed from the room. "I'm not the hero. I'm the reason this happened," she said to herself.

The wall opened in front of her, and the vast nothingness of space awaited.

7

. . . .

ORIENTING TOWARD UP

OR THE FIRST time in her life, Mallory was grateful for her idiosyncratic history. She didn't like dead bodies surrounding her, but she understood them. They were a familiar unpleasantness she could focus on entirely, while not worrying about the yawning abyss that surrounded her or the planet that held Eternity in orbit hanging overhead as if it were about to drop on her.

A body floated by, and Mallory flailed her arms instinctively as if she were underwater. "Did you say something about propulsion jets? Xan?"

Xan didn't answer. Fear clogged Mallory's throat as she realized that this time she could be the murder victim and he could just leave her out here.

"Xan!"

He still didn't answer.

"Christ," she said, and swallowed. She closed her eyes and took a few deep breaths to quell the nausea. When she opened them, information had appeared on her HUD.

"Say 1, 2, 3, or 4 to fire propulsion jets. Combos work."

"This is the UI?" she asked. "Okay, try 1 and 2." There was a gentle push at her shoulders and she tipped forward and looked down into the emptiness. As she did a slow forward roll, she tried firing 3 and 4 to get straight.

"There is no upside down," she reminded herself, sweat beading on her forehead. Her breath was loud and fast and the only sound around her. "No matter what my brain is telling me. I can help them from any angle so long as I can get to them."

Still, when she took a moment to orient herself to be on the same relative plane as the shuttle so that its roof and her head were both pointing the same direction, the nausea finally started to back off. Her lizard brain had decided she knew where "up" was after all.

"I really didn't want to puke in here," she said. "Although I don't know who I'm talking to. Can you even hear me?"

The HUD lit up. "Yes."

"So you'll know when I'm in trouble?"

The initial response died, then repeated itself. "Yes."

"But you aren't going to talk to me," she finalized.

Again, the previous response faded, and the HUD lit up again. "Busy."

"Great," she said. "Well, I'm going to talk. It keeps me sane. If you can hear me, then enjoy. If not, well, I can entertain myself."

She focused on the bodies. To her count, there were three bodies close by. Could *Infinity* hold them all? Didn't matter; that wasn't her problem. Xan could figure out a plan for that. With jerky, slow movements, she fired the propulsion jets and made her way more or less toward the first body.

"You know, this was one of my biggest fears," she said, her breath sounding very loud in her ears. "I saw the movie *2001* when I was ten, and I thought it was the cruelest thing in the world for the astronauts to not talk to each other during the spacewalks. I mean, now I get the movie; that aspect is scary for the viewer, not the astronauts, who are trained for this. But, Jesus, at the time I thought if I was on a spacewalk and no one could talk to me, I'd go out of my fucking mind.

"You're lucky that the other things I've experienced in my life put a silent spacewalk way down the list of scary things. Otherwise, I'd be filling this spacesuit with puke."

She neared a body in a tan business suit. He was a large, muscled white man. His arms were up as if warding off something, and terror was scrawled over his frozen features.

"Sorry, man," Mallory said, and reached out to snag his lapel. "I got one. Now what?"

Now she had to figure out how to work the propulsion while managing the inertia of greater mass with another body. "This involves math," she muttered as she and the body began spinning, the tether getting tangled around her. "This is one of those things I have to solve myself, right, Xan? You can't take a moment to pull us in?"

She caught sight of *Infinity*. It had inched over to the damaged shuttle and Xan was working a grappling arm out to grab the mangled shuttle door. Then a much smaller rod below the tether inserted itself into a recess beside the door.

"I wish you could tell me how it's going," she said. "But it looks like you've got stuff under control."

She started to propel herself toward *Infinity*, dragging the dead man behind her. "You know, after I dropped out of college I couldn't even get a job doing crime scene cleanup. I worked for some private firms hired for that kind of thing, until the SBI found out. And dammit, I was good at it. I found clues that the pros missed, and I helped clean up a good deal of blood and shit and puke. I found all the perfect chemical concoctions to clean each bodily fluid. In hindsight, I probably could have been a very specific kind of social media star. The Grim Cleaner or something: 'Hey Mallory's Scrubbers, today's stain is blood mixed with vomit.

Make sure you don't scrub it into your carpet fibers, or you'll never get that smell out!'"

She and the load she dragged neared *Infinity*. She couldn't see Xan inside it, but the ship loomed large next to the shuttle. Mallory looked through the windows of the shuttle and was startled to see people inside, floating as well, but looking a lot less frozen. Were they all unconscious?

She felt a tug and gave a yell of surprise as the dead man was wrenched away from her. *Infinity* had extended another arm and had taken control of the body, pulling it into some storage area underneath.

"All right, so that's dead body storage, I guess," she grumbled. "But why you can't reach out and grab each of them I don't even pretend to know."

To be fair, the bodies were floating in every direction, and it would have taken *Infinity* a lot of fiddly effort to go after each one, while she was more maneuverable.

In theory, she thought, as she drifted upside down again. She righted herself and went searching for the next body. The problem was that inertia was carrying the bodies away from the shuttle, with nothing to slow them down. They'd drift that way forever until they got caught in a gravity well or hit a passing comet or starship. And Mallory had to hunt them all down before they got too far away.

Suddenly, more writing appeared on her HUD, a list of nine names in bright red script, including Jalo Kynsi, whose red name was crossed out. That must be the body she had just retrieved.

When she reoriented her head in space, the list of people rearranged itself. Every time she focused on another floating body, a new name appeared at the top of the list. "Oh, so that's helpful. How do you know all this?" she asked. Xan, of course, didn't answer.

Ambassador Kathleen Pilato. Billionaire tech mogul Jeremy Neander. Heiress Viv Brooks. Senator Sheryl Hayes. The public relations cleanup regarding these VIPs was going to be horrendous. Was Adrian up to the task, or was he going to focus only on getting rid of her and Xan?

She was really getting the hang of the propulsion jets and discovered that the tether to *Infinity* was spooling out or retracting as needed.

"All I need to do is keep it from getting tangled and not spool out too far," she muttered. "I'm retrieving Sheryl Hayes now. Senator Hayes from California. Sorry, Senator."

She was retrieving Ellen Klouman when she decided to tell a story to amuse herself.

"You know, Xan, I did the crime scene cleanup thing, but I did a lot of other jobs. Last year I was a bartender. That was a bad idea, considering how many people come to bars, but once I actually prevented a murder from happening. I was tending bar in a members-only lounge in Raleigh. A film studio had been filming there; *Can't Cheat, Can't Defeat*, I think the movie was called. It starred a rapper called Salty Fatts. He's a big deal: a gay trans rapper who's delving into acting. And he was like twenty-two when I met him."

Infinity had taken Klouman's body from her, and Xan didn't respond. Mallory turned around and went for the next one.

"Our next dead one is called Christine. No last name. She reminds me of Salty Fatts. I think I recognize her name. Isn't she a pop star or something? Wasn't she, I mean."

The Christine in question was dressed in flowing white linen, almost like a shroud. Definitely a rock star. Now a corpse.

"So Salty Fatts came into the bar," she continued, as she snagged the linen with her glove and pulled the woman in, "and sat down. I remember he had on his leather jacket and he had SALT tattooed on his right knuckles and FATT with two T's on his left. He was by far the nicest person I met on that job. That night, he was really down and said he had to leave the shoot all of a sudden. He had a sick family member and no one else could take care of them. He was pissed and preparing to drive home to the mountains that night. I didn't want him drinking and then driving curvy mountain roads, so I gave him coffee and let him talk at me. He was mostly talking about how his career was just starting to take off, his music, his videos, this film. He was really down.

"I asked him if there was anyone else who could help him and he just said no, he had no other family. So then the crew came in for drinks. Turns out their producer had bought memberships to the club just for the film. Eighteen lifetime memberships for a two-month shoot. So much stupid money." She wrangled another deceased woman, Alex Kamachi, into the waiting robotic arm of the shuttle and headed back out.

"They'd heard that Salty had quit the movie, and they were pissed. We damn near had a bar fight, but I was able to stop it. I took Salty out the back door and told him to get into his car and start driving, and he listened.

"What was really weird is I didn't get any of the feelings I get around a murder. It's weird and hard to explain: Details around me are sharper. Colors are brighter. But that night a murder did happen on the set, and Salty's stunt double was killed. Considering how much he looked like Salty, everyone assumed Salty had been the target for the murder. A few weeks later he sent me a card with a thousand bucks inside, thanking me for getting him out of there. I didn't really save his life, but I did appreciate the tip."

She paused, remembering. "I liked Salty. He kept talking about his grandmother and this vast expanse of land she had in the mountains where he was going to build her a mansion when he got enough money. He was really upset about Sean Tasden, the murder victim. I remember because Salty came back to town for a day to clear up some things with the shoot, and he dropped by and asked me to toast the guy at least three times with him. That was the last good memory I have of that job. Soon after, a murder did happen in the bar, and even though I had nothing to do with it, my proximity was enough to make my boss fire me." She focused on the last name on the list: Terence McManus. He had floated the farthest, and she wasn't sure if she could get to him unless she pulled the tether out as far as it could go.

She fired the propulsion jets and went after him, but she felt a jerk as the oxygen line stretched to its maximum distance. The slight sound of air hissing in her suit rose in pitch as it moved through a thinner and thinner hose. "So I moved again and got a job at the animal shelter, which allowed me time to write books so I could make some actual money."

McManus's body was just out of reach, and drifting away from her. "Can't you give me any more room? Drift ten feet my direction? No?" She still had slack in her tether. She got an idea.

"Fire 1, 2, 3, 4 jets," she said, and the pull became stronger. "Disconnect oxygen and power lines."

Xan finally spoke, alarmed, "Wait, Mal, what are you—"

The cords released and Xan's voice cut off.

The jets cut off as well, but she'd built up enough strain in the lines so that when they were released, she shot forward. The tether started to grow tight, but she got close enough to grab McManus's pant leg.

"Got you!" she said.

Her helmet started to fog up, and she remembered that no new airflow would make the helmet humid. Also, it would run out of oxygen. She wondered how much oxygen she had in her helmet. Behind her, out of her reach, the decoupled oxygen hose floated, whipping around, expressing air into the void. Infinity seemed very far away.

But she had her tether, and her last corpse, and she could pull herself in. Admittedly, it was harder with a body to wrangle, as she couldn't easily go hand over hand, but she could yank on the tether with one hand, start drifting toward the ship, adjust her grip, and then pull again.

It was slow, laborious work. Harder work than she'd thought she'd have to do in zero-G. Minutes crept by, and Mallory tried hard to keep her breathing low, even with the increased effort to pull herself in. Unfortunately, her lungs started to protest that they weren't equipped to process waste products into good air.

"This may have been a bad idea," she mumbled. Black blooms appeared in her vision; *Infinity* and the rest of space disappeared through the foggy faceplate.

She tried to hold on to the tether and the corpse, but consciousness started to leave her (for the second time that day, her mind told her in a faraway, irritated voice). Maybe she had enough momentum to make it to the ship.

Maybe.

HER STRANGLED GASP was very loud in her ears as air flowed into her suit again. She coughed mightily and took great, wheezing breaths. Hands were on her, fumbling with her helmet latches. *Infinity*'s floor pressed up against her, giving her a vertigo-tinged version of sea legs.

Her HUD flared to life and said her O levels were dangerously low.

The helmet finally came off, and she breathed in the air of *Infinity*. Beside her lay the corpse of McManus, who didn't seem bothered by air or gravity.

"How does the ship make gravity, anyway?" she asked, her voice raspy.

Xan collapsed back against the wall and rubbed his face with his hands. "Fuck, you scared me. Why the hell did you disconnect your oxygen lines?"

She shrugged, finding the movement difficult while lying down in a spacesuit. "Seemed like the only way to get the last body. It was important to you. Besides, you said you'd keep watch."

"Mallory, there's only so much I can protect you from, and your own damn self is not one of those things! You're going to have to make a good decision for yourself every once in a while!" he said, then got to his feet and stormed out of the room.

"I got all your bodies, and I don't need your protection all the time!" she called after him. "Asking for it during a spacewalk isn't too much to ask for, is it? Shit." She sat up and tried to free herself from the suit but couldn't reach the lines between her shoulder blades. She realized he'd linked her suit up again because it was probably faster than unlatching all of her helmet fasteners, but now she was stuck in the airlock.

"Uh, can I release the lines and my tethers by voice?" she asked, and felt them decouple and fall to the floor.

The spacewalk plus the oxygen depletion had her worn out and aching. She struggled to her feet and put her hand on the airlock wall, swaying slightly, until her head stopped swimming.

Xan's bedroom was a shambles. The sheets were torn off the small bed; the few belongings he had were on the floor, many of them in the airlock. *What happened here?*

She turned in a circle, taking in the mess, remembering the tidy room before. Before the spacewalk. Before the airlock.

He'd opened the airlock before the pressure had stabilized, and the resulting decompression had destroyed the neatness of the room, sucking anything not nailed down toward the airlock. He really had been desperate to get to her if he hadn't waited for the airlock to be safe to open. Mallory guessed they were both lucky his airlock wasn't bigger.

She joined Xan on the flight deck.

Xan sat comfortably in the captain's chair, watching the screen.

Infinity was tethered to the other craft by three rods stretching between the shuttles.

"So, how did your half of the rescue go?" she asked.

He didn't look at her. "Fine. Got it secured. Got the data from the ship. Now I'm just looking for a place to take us."

"We're not going back to Eternity?" she asked. There was a mixture of alarm and hope in her gut, and she wasn't entirely sure which emotion she wanted to go with. "Where are we going, then?"

"No, we're going back. I just need to figure out where to dock. Station security has closed off the main shuttle bay."

"I thought they wanted to evacuate," she said.

He shook his head. "Not yet. They're caught between wanting people safely off the station and not wanting to let the murderer go. They're shutting the main bay. But Stephanie let me know that the Gneiss have their own private shuttle bay that we can use since this is an emergency."

"And the station security hasn't shut this one down?" Mallory asked, frowning.

"I guess not," he said irritably. "I am not going to argue with Stephanie to find reasons not to let us in."

"Fair enough," she said. "Do we know what happened to the ship yet?" she asked, indicating the damaged shuttle on the screen.

"Nothing more than we knew before. There are still folks alive on the shuttle. We just need a place to take them. I think they have significant injuries, but the shuttle's AI is damaged, and it can't really report on human health, so it could only tell me so much."

"Wait," she asked, standing up and looking over his shoulder at the console as the ship slowly turned with its new burden. "If Eternity swatted that shuttle out of the sky, what makes you think she won't do the same to us?"

"She won't. Trust me," Xan said cryptically.

"Trust you, just like that?" she replied. "When you won't tell me how you know all this stuff or how you can read *Infinity*'s readouts?"

"You don't trust me, but you practically begged me to send you into a frozen vacuum. You left your life in my hands and then nearly wasted it."

"I got your bodies! I did what you asked!" she said, putting her hands on her hips.

He rounded on her, swiveling the chair. "Mallory, I thought you were *dying* out there. You lost both oxygen lines and your power line, which also cut off communication with me and the ship. I had no idea if you were alive or dead when I pulled you inside. You definitely didn't have enough air to do that last retrieval. And you didn't even check with me to see if it was a good idea."

"I didn't even know if you could hear me! You let me babble to myself for an hour out there without saying one word back! At one point I wondered if you were just trying to get rid of me in a clever way."

His mouth fell open. "Are you seriously telling me that you thought I would kill you? Do you think I'm capable of that?"

He no longer looked angry; she'd hurt him deeply, and she didn't know why. *In my defense, he doesn't tell me anything. How should I know what hurts him?*

"You dropped me into a vacuum and then ignored me for an hour. I only volunteered because I trusted you to be my lifeline!"

"You disconnected that lifeline!"

"I'm using a metaphor, Xan. You gave me no information, no advice. Not even any company while I was floating out there, even after I told you how freaked out I was."

"I can't—" he started to say, and then stopped, a muscle twitching in his jaw. He turned back to the screen. "I can't tell you. Not yet. For what it's worth, I'm sorry. I shouldn't have done that."

"When do you think—" she started, and then sucked in her breath.

On the screen, Eternity had swung into view. The station was a horror show, nothing like the calm, pleasing spheroid that Mallory had seen as she had approached Eternity for the first time. The station had grown pseudopods, giant tentacles as big as skyscrapers, which waved in space as if in distress. Its surface, previously shifting between a blue and pink iridescence, now appeared to be a hard, bio-metallic exterior going from black to dusky red to a sick yellow.

"She's not happy," Xan said grimly.

"Jesus fucking Christ, ya think?" Mallory said, standing to peer over his shoulder in frozen distress. "Do we even want to go back in there? What is wrong with her?"

Xan didn't answer any of the questions, but instead powered *Infinity*'s engines to pick up speed toward the station. "We have to try. We've got injured people and a shuttle full of dead bodies. There's not a lot of places we can go."

Mallory got up, eyes still latched on the station, and put her hand on his shoulder. "Xan. Someone on this shuttle could be here to arrest you. We're heading into what looks like—I don't even know, but right now running into a burning building sounds safer. Is this really the best way to go?"

His shoulder went tense under her hand. "We're in too deep. We can't run now. You know that."

She removed her hand and took a small step back. "Getting the hell out of this situation feels smart," she said. "But I guess smart isn't always the virtuous thing to do."

"It's not," he agreed, sounding like he knew all too well. "At least there's no mystery with these bodies. It's pretty clear who killed all these people."

Mallory looked thoughtfully at the station as they neared. "I don't think Eternity is responsible for this, not fully. I think it all goes back to whoever killed Ren. That was the first thing in this chain of events."

"That we know of," he said. "Still, Earth isn't going to look kindly on this. The first time they send a big diplomatic shuttle, and half the passengers die? This is going to get ugly."

"And our diplomat sucks at his job," Mallory said. "But it's not like Earth can do much. Alien technology outstrips ours in every way."

Xan muttered something under his breath.

"What's that?" she asked, leaning over him again.

"Nothing," he said.

She stepped away again, staring at the back of his head thoughtfully. She was pretty sure he had said, "Not every way."

And goddammit, there was the familiar feeling. Her headache lifted and everything around her got sharper edges and brighter colors, and she felt a slight buzzing in her ears as she thought about Ren's murder, who the suspects might be, and what pieces she had yet to uncover.

Motive wasn't hard; she didn't know anyone who'd liked Ren, not Xan, not Stephanie, not Adrian. Aside from being just plain insulting to the humans and implying he'd like to send them home, Ren had also been accused of interfering with Gneiss residential areas on the ship, restricting shuttle bay hours, and enacting prohibition on only one of the races aboard (the Silence, whose food and drink were legendary, although she'd never sampled anything), as well as several other complaints ranging from being petty and insulting to downright obstructing a sentient's way of life aboard.

According to rumor, some of his fellow Gurudevs resented such an unpleasant person being a symbiont to such a powerful station and felt he should be replaced. Apparently, the three sentient stations within one jump of Eternity (named Omnipotent, Alpha, and Omega) all had welcoming hosts.

And no matter who had killed Ren, if Earth found out about the attack, they might send word to their military personnel to finish killing the station, if their military-affiliated passenger was one of the survivors.

She'd find out soon enough.

8

. . .

ALIENS' DIFFERENT
VIEW OF FORENSICS

THEY DOCKED IN an out-of-the-way spot on the lower half of Eternity, far from the waving pseudopods. The small shuttle bay was empty and dark, but Xan confidently piloted *Infinity* and the busted-up shuttle to a landing. Less sophisticated than the main shuttle bay, which had a biological membrane that kept air inside but allowed solid ships to pass through, this one needed the outer doors to close so that the bay could act as an airlock.

While they waited for the pressure to balance, Mallory paced.

"Would you please calm down," Xan said. He stood by the hatch, waiting, like her, but with more outward calm. He sounded tired, which was funny since Mallory had been the one who had done all the physical work.

"There are injured people in the shuttle," she reminded him. "We have to help them." She hadn't asked him who he knew aboard. There would be a time for that, she knew.

There always was.

"And what are you planning on doing by rushing out there?" he asked. "Prying the door open with your bare hands?"

"I hadn't planned on doing anything till I got out there," Mallory said. She was getting tired of him asking her for a plan. Planning was not something she did. "I'll look for a tool or something. I don't know! But I know we can't do anything to help in here."

"Stephanie said some Gneiss will meet us here and help us with the survivors, and the bodies," he told her. "Until they're able to get into the room, nobody can do anything."

"And you're not tense about this?" she asked.

"I'm very tense. I am just thinking about what's possible for me to do. There's not a lot right now." He shrugged. "Besides, you're tense enough for both of us."

"And where are the other ships?" she asked, looking at the screen that showed that the shuttle bay was definitely empty, aside from them. "If they have this bay, why not use it instead of the shuttle bay?"

"My guess is," Xan said, rising to his feet as a green light appeared on *Infinity*'s console, "that this one is not for active ships. They fly in here for more long-term storage."

"How do you know all this?" she asked.

"Calm down. The pressure is balanced; let's get out of here," he said as *Infinity*'s hatch opened in front of them.

Mallory had been watching Xan fly *Infinity* closely, or rather, the things he wasn't doing, such as giving any commands to open a hatch. She was pretty sure that it took a lot more work to handle a shuttle than he was showing.

Infinity was a sentient ship, she guessed. But there had to be a reason Xan was hiding it from her, so she waited for him to feel comfortable telling her. That was two things he was hiding from her. She wondered how many other things he was hiding.

She had to admit to herself that she harbored a small fear that if *Infinity* was sentient, and getting fond of Xan, she might be threatened by Mallory. She'd read the novel *Christine* in her teens and the idea of a jealous vehicle scared the crap out of her.

She jumped out of the shuttle before the walkway had finished

unfolding and ran over to the other craft. Now that she was standing next to it, she couldn't see through the windows, so she had no
idea how the people inside were doing. Xan had been right, which
irritated the hell out of her.

Across from them, a door the size of a garage door on Earth
opened and three Gneiss appeared, two of whom Mallory recognized. Behind them were clearly the alien version of EMTs, who
hurried past the Gneiss toward the shuttle.

The team consisted of a Gurudev, two thin Phantasmagore,
and two Gneiss medics, according to the armbands they wore—
two blue interlocking circles. The Gneiss approached the door
and quickly inserted a metal tube into one of the cracks caused by
the shuttle door caving in. With a quick twist, the door popped
open, free of its hinges, as if it had been stuck on with little more
than a suction cup. One Phantasmagore medic climbed inside
deftly, their wide, splayed fingers mounting the shuttle hull easily,
and released the walkway so the rest of the team could get inside.

If she hadn't been so distraught, Mallory would have been
impressed. Even dealing with a species they didn't know well, the
medical team was efficient and quick.

The initial three Gneiss came over to Xan and Mallory. Mallory recognized Stephanie and Ferdinand, but not the third. She
was very tall and reddish pink, the color of rocks from the American Southwest.

"Stay with them. We'll go help the medics," Stephanie said to
the red Gneiss, and she and Ferdinand left her there.

"Hi, guys! Stephanie told me to keep you here while they work.
How's it going?" she asked.

"How's it—" Mallory stammered, staring at the cheerful alien.
"Well, the station is freaking out, and a lot of our people are dead-
cicles in the lower hold of this shuttle, and we don't know how
badly the live ones are injured. How do you think we're doing?"

"Easy," Xan said. "They're here to help. Thanks for coming in,

Tina. I sent the passenger and crew list to Stephanie so she can try to keep them straight. Is there anything we can do to help?"

"Nah, just stay off to the side, let them do their jobs. That's what I do," Tina said amicably. "Stephanie says she needs help, and then I say, 'I'm right here,' and then she says, 'Oh not you, Tina,' and I say—"

"Is there any movement on the search for Ren's killer?" Mallory asked, trying to stop this train of thought before it derailed.

"Ren? The little Gurudev? I don't think so," Tina said, focusing on Mallory. "Should there be?"

Mallory was starting to understand why Stephanie disliked this person. "I thought that's why station security couldn't help us. They were trying to find the killer."

"Oh, I don't know what station security is doing," Tina said. "When the station started to cry, Stephanie and Ferdinand told me to come to the ossuary to stay out of the way. And then you needed to use our airlock, so they told me to wait over here with you for safety."

Your safety or ours? Mallory thought.

Over on the shuttle, the medics inside had secured the humans to stretchers, bound tightly with flat restraints, and were passing them out to the waiting Gneiss medics. Mallory noticed each medic had at least four blue Sundry riding their shoulders or buzzing around their heads. She was reassured that the two species that had researched human biology were involved with the rescue. More medics, with Sundry in tow, had arrived, and as they passed new stretchers in, they deftly received the humans being carefully handed out.

"You're not the ambassador, right?" Tina asked. "The medics want to talk to him."

"Right, I'm not the ambassador, and I'm not a 'him.' I have no idea where he is," Mallory said, and then rubbed the back of her head.

"Come on. I need to check the survivors," Xan said, but Tina stepped in front of him. They looked up at her in surprise.

"Yeah, no, sorry. They need space. They're going to do a quick removal and get them to the medical bay," she said. "Stephanie said to keep you here."

"I will stay out of their way, but I'm not standing back while they unpack the survivors," he said firmly, and stepped around her.

Tina made a move to stop him, but Mallory caught her foot on *Infinity*'s walkway and sprawled painfully on the rocky shuttle bay floor, swearing loudly. Both Tina and Xan turned to her, but Mallory locked eyes with Xan and mouthed *Go* at him, then looked at Tina meaningfully. The translator chip could only handle audio input; reading lips was far beyond the technology.

Xan gave a quick nod and broke into a run toward the shuttle.

"Humans are so delicate. How do you not just break open at birth?" Tina asked, reaching a giant hand toward her.

Mallory scrambled to her feet before seeing how painful Tina's help would be. "We're tougher than we look, but not much," she said, keeping an eye on Xan, who was at the shuttle entrance, looking inside.

There was a shout that sounded like annoyance, and Xan jumped back as several more stretchers were passed out to waiting medics. Mallory winced as she spotted several bloody faces, a few obviously broken limbs, and more injuries.

"We are more careful than this when someone gets hurt," Mallory said. "It comes with being soft. Are they usually this rough? Those people are pretty messed up."

"I had heard about your medicine," Tina said. "Primitive! As I understand carbon-based medicine, they have some good stuff to heal injuries, so even if they make things worse on the trip there, they'll fix it when they get to medical bay."

"What is 'good stuff'? You're going to flood their bodies with drugs from another species?" Mallory asked, eyes going wide.

"Nah, it's all natural. Like bacteria or something," Tina said.

"I don't know if that's better or worse," Mallory said. She was about to ask if it had been tested on humans, but of course it hadn't. If it had, she would have been the test subject.

"It helps all the other races; I'm sure it'll work for you."

"Tina, what do you do? Xenobiology? Know a lot about carbon-based life-forms?" Mallory asked, watching a body with blonde, curly hair get passed out. The face was turned to the side. Xan was looking closely at each person, and then back at the shuttle, waiting for the next one. As much as he had chastised Mallory for being nervous and fidgety, now he was clearly tense and upset.

"Oh, no, I'm an heir, naturally rich, and living a life of leisure," Tina said. "Hey, do you want to see the ossuary?"

STEPHANIE AND FERDINAND joined them after the survivors had been carted away.

"The station will send some others for the dead humans later," Stephanie explained. "The Gurudev will send their own people for the dead crew."

"Did Xan go with the survivors? I should catch up," Mallory said.

"No," Ferdinand said. "He went aboard the shuttle to look for something."

"Look for what?" Mallory asked.

"He didn't say."

Mallory took a step toward the shuttle, but a heavy hand came down on her shoulder. "I was going to show you the ossuary!" Tina complained.

"Tina, you're hurting me," Mallory said, trying to slide out of her vise grip but having no luck.

Tina let her go immediately. "Sorry. I forgot you were squishy."

"Show me in a second, but I need to check on Xan," she said, rubbing her shoulder. But then, Xan appeared in the doorway of the shuttle and jumped down, landing lightly. He caught up with them.

"Still twelve alive," he said. "The Gurudev doctors said we can observe them while they heal, but we can't visit them until they're conscious. And they'll be unconscious until they finish treatment." He still looked stressed, but not quite as tense.

"Good, you can see the ossuary too!" Tina said.

"On the way out, yes," Ferdinand said. "But I'm sure they will want to check on their people, Tina. Or prepare for evacuation."

They paused at the massive opening that resembled a garage door, and Stephanie ran her thick fingers along the wall, where a long, half-inch-wide crack had appeared. She glanced at Tina and Ferdinand and then at the humans. "We shouldn't spend much time here. This isn't the safest place for them."

"Nah, it's totally safe!" Tina reassured them. "This is a place that's wholly ours. Isn't that why you let them dock?"

"We let them dock because they couldn't get into the main shuttle bay," Ferdinand said. He looked at the humans. "We don't usually let others down here."

Xan shivered. "Wherever we go, can it be warmer? I'm freezing."

Mallory had forgotten she was still in the warm, formfitting spacesuit. Aside from the flapping latches, it was pretty comfortable. She glanced at the shuttle. "I don't mean to loot the dead or anything, but I bet there's a jacket you could borrow aboard."

Xan looked pained for a moment, and Mallory expected him to complain that she was suggesting something horrific. But he jogged back to the shuttle and boosted himself inside. He returned shortly, wearing a leather jacket far too large for him.

"You couldn't find anything that fit better?" Mallory asked.

"Let's go," he said, not looking at her.

"I'm glad we're hanging out with these humans," Tina said. "The other one was a pumice stone."

"Tina," Xan said thoughtfully. He paused, looking like he was choosing the words carefully. "You seem different."

"You know her?" Mallory asked, surprised.

"These are the three who picked me up," Xan said.

"Yeah, she's not drunk now," Stephanie said. "She was really fucked up when we picked you up."

"I was on vacation. I can have a drink or five," Tina said defensively. "I also didn't know that Icelandic lava would be so potent."

Xan had told Mallory that the ship that picked him up on Earth had been driven by Gneiss who were "the equivalent of college students on spring break" and had given him a ride completely on a lark. Later, when she met Stephanie and Ferdinand, she'd thought they were too mature to fit this description, but now that she'd met Tina, it all made more sense.

"So what's an ossuary?" Mallory asked. It sounded familiar, but she couldn't remember the meaning.

"Not sure," Xan said. "I think that might be a translation error."

The shuttle bay was constructed of a mixture of rock and metal, but on the other side of the door, the metal completely disappeared. The interior was dark, but when they stepped in, mushrooms growing on the walls began to glow. Despite the still-frequent shivers and shakes from the station, Mallory briefly forgot that she was on a space station. She could easily imagine that they were in a deep cave and an earthquake was sending aftershocks through the walls.

"I knew Eternity was impressive, but damn," she whispered to Xan. "Did you know this was here?"

"I knew the different races had places created for their comfort, but I didn't know the specifics," he said. As the vast cavern beyond became visible, his eyes got wide. "Ossuary. Not a transla-tion error."

"Right, we're talking about a tomb," Stephanie said.

As nonchalantly as she could manage, Mallory confirmed, "So, a mass grave."

"WELCOME TO THE Gneiss ossuary," Stephanie said. "This is our boneyard where we sleep."

"Why not call it a hotel, or bedroom, or something less final than a mass grave?"

The Gneiss looked at each other, then back at Mallory. Tina spoke slowly, as if they didn't understand the words. "I'm not sure the translation bug is working. The words you used indicated places for very short usage. This is a place of reverence for bodies at rest, who will return in several years."

"That's right, I forgot. You don't sleep like we do," Mallory said. When Stephanie looked like she was going to correct her, she added, "Or when you do, it's for years at a time, right?"

"This is how we change," Stephanie added.

It was creepy, whatever name they gave it. The light was brighter, at least, but it showed all the stuff they didn't really want to see. The unmoving stone statues all over the place, with no clear organization, reminded Mallory of Greek myths involving Medusa. The sleeping Gneiss were in various poses, some stand-ing, most sitting or lying down. Most were whole, bipedal, and huge like Stephanie and Tina, but there were also shattered pieces of rock littering the floor. Small shards, larger chunks, even whole limbs and heads were strewn about the place. Mallory tried not to imagine any of the eyes were looking at her.

And the cold! Their breaths puffed out of the humans' mouths, but not so much the Gneiss. "Why is it so cold?" Mallory asked.

"It's healthier to sleep and heal in the cold," Stephanie said.

Beyond the humanoid remains were cubes, some cracked, some whole. Some were about the size of one ten-by-ten-by-ten room on Earth, but some of the ones near the back of the cavern were the size of city libraries. Many of them had cavities sinking into them about the size and shape of an average Gneiss, as if they were an absurdly simple child's puzzle with two pieces.

Behind them the garage door closed, and vines fell to hide it from view.

Another huge door sat closed at the far end of the ossuary, with vines drooping down to nearly hide it. Other plants, green and fern-like, grew around the area, seemingly sprouting straight out of the rock.

There was nowhere to sit, so the five of them gathered beside a shuttle like Stephanie's grandfather, but a smaller cube made of a dark gray stone.

"Thanks for letting us dock," Mallory said to Stephanie. "But can you tell us what the hell is going on? Tina didn't seem to know anything."

"Not an act; she really doesn't," Stephanie said. She didn't bother lowering her voice.

"Sure, I don't know anything," Tina said helpfully. "But the station is clearly in distress and we should leave. We should take Stephanie's grandfather."

The station shuddered again, and Xan swore.

"Hush, Tina. Don't bring him into this," Stephanie said, then turned to the humans. "Ren is dead. He died suddenly and violently. Eternity has no host to help us communicate."

"How bad is it?" Xan asked.

"The walls are cracked. It's safe to say some areas of the station might be vented into space. It takes considerable energy to alter the station in such a fashion, so something catastrophic had to have happened," Stephanie said. "The images you sent me from

Infinity were not comforting." She moved away from them and carefully repositioned a nearly black section of a leg so it lay apart from a pile of rubble.

"The walls are cracked here. Are we losing pressure too?" Xan asked.

"Not yet," Ferdinand said.

"So, how do you fix a giant sentient space station in distress?" Mallory asked.

"That's not your problem," Stephanie said. "You take care of your people, and if we need to evacuate, you can come with us or with *Infinity*."

Mallory shook her head. "You don't get it. It is my problem. It's a murder."

"I thought you wanted nothing to do with murders," Stephanie said.

"I don't want them to happen. But it did happen, and because of me. I need to help." The light seemed to flicker as she spoke.

She looked up. "That's not good. Is that more station distress?"

"The station isn't your problem to fix," Ferdinand reminded her. "What could you possibly do?"

She ignored him. "How do you know Ren died? Did the station send out a message? Was there a body?"

Stephanie began to speak, but Tina spoke up first. "Oh, there was a body, for sure."

"How do you know? Did you see it?" Mallory asked, wishing she had a notebook on her.

Tina began to raise her arm, pointing.

"Tina, no," Stephanie said, but it was too late.

A drop of something wet hit Mallory's cheek. Another one hit her forehead. She wiped it off with her hand and looked at her fingers. In the low light, it looked like a navy smear. She looked up.

A bunch of greenery had been piled on the top of the shuttle, but underneath, a Gurudev arm hung about ten feet above them, over the edge of the dormant shuttle. Blood was dripping off the fingertips.

Mallory's spine went cold, and she jumped out of the way. "Is that Ren?" she said, furiously rubbing her face.

Her eyes had gotten used to the lower light, and she could now see a stream of blue blood coming down the wall of the shuttle, pooling on the ground at their feet. She stepped back again, stumbling against the legs of an unfortunate Gneiss who had been sheared in half.

"How did he get up there?" Mallory asked, glaring at the Gneiss.

"This room is directly under the Heart of the Station," Tina said, as if that answered the question.

"That tells me nothing unless there's a trash chute the station puts her dead bodies in," Mallory snapped.

"There's a chute," Tina confirmed. "This is an ossuary. Why are you surprised to find a body here? Although it is strange that he's a Gurudev. Did we change the rules?" she asked Ferdinand.

"How long have you known this body was here?" Mallory asked Stephanie.

"He hasn't been here long," Stephanie said. "They told us." She pointed to the bodies around the room.

"Did you put him here? Did you kill him?" Mallory asked.

"No," Ferdinand said, and at the same time, Tina said, "Yes."

"Does security know?"

"They don't care," Stephanie said. "They want to know who killed him, but the body means nothing to the Gurudev. That's just trash."

"But what about clues? You can find out a lot from studying the body," Mallory protested.

"But Gurudev biomass breaks down in the first three or four hours after their death. No one studies Gurudev bodies upon death, unless they're kept cold. Hang on, it's cold in here, isn't it? Anyway, since security is more concerned with calming the station, they really don't care about the corpse. It's trash."

But it's evidence! Mallory couldn't reach the top of the shuttle, and she stared at the hand, annoyed.

Behind her came Xan's tight voice. "Stephanie. We need to talk."

PART TWO
CONNECTIONS

Shoulda made the noose a little tighter
'Cause it ain't nobody dead, yeah
We who are about to bang them drums (Bang)
Beatin' on a dead body ridin' shotgun
Talkin' that shit, bitch, bite your tongue
See that ship over your city, better run, run.

—"Air 'Em Out" by clipping.

9

. . .

THE SACRED DUTY

IKE MALLORY, XAN had left college before graduation. The reasons didn't involve murder, but that didn't mean he didn't consider it.

When he'd been eight and his brother, Phineas, had been three, their parents had died in a car accident when an earthquake had struck the Smoky Mountains, splitting the Linn Cove Viaduct and sending their parents' car plummeting down the side of a mountain.

Secured in car and booster seats, the boys had been relatively unharmed, minus the terror of the accident and the hours of waiting for rescue as their parents had died.

Phineas always said he didn't remember it, but Xan heard Phineas crying in his sleep more than once, and he was deathly afraid of heights.

After the accident, their grandmother had raised them. She lived on a huge plot of land outside Pigeon Forge, Tennessee. Norma Morgan was mean as a snake and twice as crafty. The best part about growing up was finding out he had gotten a full scholarship to UNC–Chapel Hill, giving him a chance to escape.

He was twenty when his grandmother had a stroke. He dropped

out to enlist in the army so he could send some money home for her care and Phineas's schooling.

A friend had asked why going to the army was preferable to just moving back home and getting a job, but Xan mumbled something patriotic and let it drop.

His grandmother was the reason.

Xan resembled their mother, thin and wiry. Phineas resembled their father, tall and beefy. Their grandmother had hated their mother and always showed a clear preference for Phineas. This was the only reason he felt safe leaving his little brother in the house with her.

The army took Xan's interest in logic and organization and put him on supply lines. He could take supplies and stretch them as far as they could go, and he essentially eliminated waste in any company he was attached to. He went to Afghanistan with the quartermaster battalion, mortuary division. He was there when First Contact happened, but it barely registered on his radar. He was too busy finding, identifying, and cataloguing injuries and collecting personal effects from his fellow soldiers' corpses to pay attention to the news that had nothing to do with his current situation.

Mortuary service was a grim duty, but he'd been drilled in its importance and sacred aspect. He did it without complaint and even quietly suffered the mocking all quartermasters and ordnance officers got from combat soldiers, knowing he wouldn't want his brother left in pieces on a battlefield, so he wasn't leaving anyone else's out there. He served his time and then came home to serve at Fort Sam Houston.

Ironically, it was on US soil that his breaking point came, and after one horrific incident, he left mortuary service (for the most part) and was transferred to the new Fort Bowser in North Carolina.

Bowser was roughly equidistant from both Fort Lee in Virginia and Fort Bragg in North Carolina, and several people asked why they needed another fort so close to the existing ones. Very few received the truthful answer: Bowser covered the completely new area of dealing with extraterrestrial situations. Xan's job was to help establish a quartermaster battalion to prepare for supplying troops specifically for alien encounters. And not tell a soul.

The job required a high-level security clearance. Humans didn't want aliens finding out that the military was studying how to protect Earth from an alien attack while the governments were talking about diplomacy. The official word concerning Fort Bowser was that Fort Bragg in Fayetteville was undergoing some major renovations and a temporary base had been erected near Raleigh. The secrecy suited Xan just fine, as he didn't want his grandmother to know he was in North Carolina.

The security clearance and promotion had been a shock, since Xan had expected a demotion because someone had found out what had happened on the Texas border. Only he and one other soldier knew what had really gone wrong when they had lost an entire patrol, but that other solider had been a bit of a loose cannon—to put it mildly—and he wondered if she had given him up.

But it turned out she hadn't talked; he was promoted and given a higher security clearance, and suddenly the fallout from First Contact became his daily focus.

Soon after Xan was established in Fort Bowser, Phineas emailed him to say he had decided not to go to school because of a big "opportunity" to chase his creative dreams. Xan thought about his abandoned degree at UNC, and what had happened due to him joining the army, and his mouth felt full of ash. He got very drunk that night.

The next day, haggard and hungover, he was called to the quartermaster general's office to discuss a new responsibility: in addition to helping establish what the new Terrestrial Guard quartermasters would need, he was to work solo within a new area of mortuary affairs.

QUARTERMASTER GENERAL ERIC Rodriguez's office stank of degassing carpets and new plastic. The room could have used some serious airing out, but he sat at his new desk with the windows tightly shut and the air conditioning on full blast as if he didn't smell anything.

Rodriguez always wore a tight smile, as if a tack was sticking out of his chair and poking him somewhere, but he would be damned if he would shift or show discomfort. The stench of plastic made Xan's head pound even worse when he arrived and saluted. The memo detailing his new responsibility was clenched in his fist, damp and crumpled.

"Close the door, SPC," Rodriguez said.

Xan shut the door behind him and didn't speak.

"At ease," the quartermaster general said. "I'd like to discuss your new assignment."

Xan fought the urge to wipe the clammy sweat off the back of his neck. He kept his face neutral and said, "I'm unclear why you want my attention split between quartermasters as a whole and mortuary affairs in specific. I had thought I was to move away from mortuary. And sir, understand that my time in mortuary affairs has been rewarding, but I'm worried my responsibilities will split my attention and quality of work."

"You don't have to sugarcoat it, Alexander. No one wants to shovel the shit."

He stiffened. "I was taught mortuary affairs is a sacred duty, sir. No one would ever call it—"

Rodriguez waved off his objection and Xan shut his mouth and set his jaw. He could always spot someone who had never served with the quartermasters. They didn't consider repairing gear, providing food, and retrieving corpses to be respectable work. *Soldiers don't do that kind of work. And we all want to be soldiers, don't we?*

During his training, Xan had studied historical reports about quartermasters and supplies during wartime. He developed a real admiration for the leaders up top who knew they couldn't win wars without solid supply support. A previous commanding officer had once told him, "People who downplay our role usually regret it. Do you want to be left on a battlefield with a dog eating your face and an enemy stealing your wedding ring, or do you want your remains treated with respect?"

"Do you trust your commanding officer?" Rodriguez asked.

"Yes, sir," he said. *It's not like there's another option,* he added mentally.

"Then accept your position."

"Yes, sir," he said. "But why me, sir?"

"You have the experience we need and the security clearance. You know what we're studying here, and we need your skills as a mortuary expert. We have procured a number of alien corpses to study, and we need your forensics ability."

A soldier didn't need to ask where their superiors "procured" corpses to study, but Xan's spine went cold. He hadn't found any alien race that couldn't destroy the human race if crossed.

"So why the promotion? Why not just keep me with MA?"

"You needed the security clearance that came with the promotion. This is a big deal, Xan. We're on the cusp of something. Have a seat and I'll explain."

XAN WANTED TO talk to Stephanie alone but knew that he couldn't really have a private conversation with the Gneiss. Or rather, she couldn't moderate her volume to converse quietly with him, since she already had to shout to communicate. Still, there were things he wasn't ready to reveal to Mallory.

Mallory infuriated him. The only other human he could talk to on the station, and she was still tiring. He knew it was part jealousy; she acted on instinct and didn't seem to worry about consequences, and he'd been burned by that mindset far too often. He had to plan shit, or bad things happened. He'd been startled that, while they had both been impulsive in college, he was the only one to have grown up. Back then impetuousness was not a trait that could get your companions killed.

Mallory had seen darkness, he knew, but it hadn't broken her. He couldn't say the same.

"Stephanie. We need to talk."

All four of them turned toward him. Mallory's face was dark, but he could read the distrust in her eyes.

"You knew about this?" Mallory said.

"I knew some of it," he allowed. "I didn't kill him."

"Do you know who did?" Mallory looked from him to Stephanie. Tina was vibrating almost visibly, but she hadn't vocalized anything yet.

"No," he said.

"I think you need to fill me in on some holes in this story," Mallory said.

"All right. If I can."

"Tell me how y'all met," she said, looking from him to the Gneiss. "You've never given me details."

"That's . . . what? That's what you want to know?"

"Yeah," she said. "I can't figure out what's going on until I know some things about your past. You've been a closed book up to now, but I need to know some things if I'm going to trust you."

This was easy compared to everything else he tried to keep secret. He nodded. "All right. What do you want to know?"

"Start at the party. You showed up there with a copy of

Slaughterhouse-Five and you were yawning like you were on Benadryl."

A FEW MONTHS after his assignment to Fort Bowser, Xan arrived at fellow quartermaster Billy's party, holding something that could get him thrown in jail if he was found with it. If he was lucky. He just had to make the drop at a specific time and then it would be out of his hands.

Finding Mallory had been a shock, one that nearly unmoored him. He was there on official business and needed all his wits about him. But after one beer to calm his nerves, he had started to get drowsy, and then a woman from college showed up. He didn't even realize that civilians could attend parties on the base, especially if idiots like Billy were going to just talk about the classified stuff as if it were nothing. Who knew who could be listening to the moron babble?

But the way Mallory had been talking, she hadn't realized that Anira worked on the base as well.

Why was Anira really here? And why bring Mallory?

"ANIRA WORKED ON the base?" Mallory interrupted slowly. "That's . . . interesting. She never told me that. That makes a lot of sense now." She had a faraway look in her eyes.

"Yeah, I was surprised she hadn't told you that. She just said Billy and that crew were her friends, right?"

Mallory nodded. "Yeah. Sorry, I interrupted. Keep going." She still had that distracted look.

THE DROP SITUATION felt sloppy and dangerous. After nine o'clock, he was to go to the kitchen for a beer and leave the package on the counter as if he'd forgotten it. His contact would pick it up there.

He worried about leaving it out there in the open, but from what he knew of the people at the party, no one would be looking to read Vonnegut so long as the beer was cold.

But his timing was already off. At eight thirty, the party started focusing on a game. It was the perfect time to slip away, but Mallory—the only person there who *would* investigate a random book—went to the kitchen. He wanted to reconnect with her, but he had this drop to worry about and couldn't let Mallory get her hands on the book.

She left him with a sad, exhausted look on her face, which surprised him. He looked after her thoughtfully and didn't really hear the rules of the game. The lights going out surprised him, and he felt the long hours of practicing paying off as his other senses sharpened.

Or they tried to sharpen. As his brain melted into molasses, he realized with dawning horror that he wasn't tired. This feeling was closer to being drugged. If someone had drugged him when he was about to make a high-security drop, he needed to abort entirely. He tried to edge toward the door.

Still, through his brain fog, an old friend's voice came back:

If you're doing it right, everything will slow down, and it becomes like a dance, and you'll feel the fucking air move before your opponent gets to you. No, stop moving, stay still and listen, and sense what your eyes tell you to ignore. Four fighting requires you to use what you have.

I've never heard of four fighting. Is it kung fu or something?

Fuck, no. My uncle taught me what he learned when he was in prison for dealing drugs. If you take one sense away, you have to pay extra attention to the other four. It's usually sight that goes, but he made me work without all five senses. Touch is the hardest. Taste means nothing unless you're trying to detect poison, I guess. Anyway, he'd tell me, "You know, Waste, you might need to dodge a shiv in the dark one day." So I'm telling you. Xan, you might need to dodge a shiv in the dark one day.

Someone moved behind him, and things slowed down. The air brushed against his neck, and he stepped to the side, stumbling slightly. A cold sliver of pain passed over his bicep and a body passed by him, the inertia of their missed stabbing carrying them forward. Someone grunted, someone laughed, and then Billy fell against Xan. Confusion reigned for a few seconds, and behind him, the door opened.

When the lights came on, the reality of the situation struck him as Billy's blood coated his shirt and hands from the open stab wound. He lowered Billy to the carpet and stared at him. His brain screamed at him to check that he still had his data and get the hell out of there before the drug took him out and the murderer got a second chance.

He ran.

Xan was getting lethargic and slower, stumbling into the street. He lived on the other side of the base; there was no way he could get home. Across the street from Billy's was a field that was destined to be another highly secure research facility, but they hadn't broken ground yet. He could possibly get to the wooded area on the other side of the field before he passed out. If he made it through whatever this drug was doing to him, he'd try to figure out his steps after that.

Then the sky was bathed in light and the ship—*Infinity*—appeared above him. And then he passed out.

"YOU WERE THE murderer's target?" Mallory asked, eyes wide. "Why didn't you tell me?"

"Because you would have asked why," he said. "And I couldn't tell you classified information. I was shocked that security let a civilian into an on-base party."

"Of course I'd ask. I'm asking now. Why did someone want to kill you?"

He sighed. "All I can tell you is what you probably already figured out. We were doing some high-security stuff at Fort Bowser. I knew more than I should have. Someone drugged me and then tried to kill me. They failed and Billy took the hit." He frowned. Billy had been a dumbass, but he didn't deserve a knife to the chest.

"And we came to the rescue!" Tina said, delighted.

"Or we made things more complicated for him," Ferdinand added.

XAN CAME TO with his cheek in a puddle of blood, his ears throbbing. His arm was wet, and his shirt was plastered to his chest with blood. He opened his eyes to see aliens towering above him. They were . . . arguing about him? As large as they were, he could barely hear them.

But he *could* hear them.

His hand touched the ear not stuck to the floor. It too was coated in gore. They must have given him those translation bugs he'd heard about. Only high diplomats and heads of state had these things.

His captors sounded like teens who had stolen Dad's car for a joyride, picked up a dirty stray dog, and then worried about the consequences after the fact.

"You thought it was cute, you thought it would be 'funny' to pick up, and now what are we going to do with it?" The voice was irritated.

The second sounded blandly amused. "I think you hurt it when you put the translation bug in its head."

A third voice. "That red stuff was already on the outside of its body. It's fine."

"Are you sure that's where the ear is?"

"I injected it with the good stuff, and it stopped leaking eventually, didn't it? It's fine." The third voice sounded worried and defensive.

The first voice spoke. "I think it's awake."

He sat up, wincing as his cheek peeled off the metal floor; he'd been out long enough for the blood on his face to create a tacky adhesive. He rubbed his head and winced at his tender ears. "What happened?" he asked.

"Hello! Can you understand us?" The third voice belonged to a reddish-gray Gneiss that loomed over him. It was speaking slowly and loudly as if to a foreigner (which Xan supposed he was).

"Yes, I can understand you. Stop shouting," he said, also irritated. "What the hell happened? And what did you inject me with?" He felt his arms, trying to find a puncture wound. He found nothing; even the laceration on his arm had faded to a scar.

He tried to struggle to his feet, still weak. The reddish-gray alien held out a hand to help him up, and it was like grabbing a stone wall. He pulled himself up easily but wobbled a bit when he stood.

There had been a dream when he was out, but it was fleeting. Something about a repaired bridge and being encased in a warm blanket. He wished he could remember.

"We saw you in a field, and I thought you might be looking for a ride," Red said. It was massive, having at least a foot on the other two, so its head nearly brushed the top of the shuttle.

"No, you said you wanted a pet," the second voice said. This Gneiss was purple and seated in a huge chair in front of a complicated-looking console. "So we picked it up. Unfortunately, my grandfather insisted on an autopilot when we took this shuttle, and it engaged and took us off planet. You see, *someone* decided at the start of this trip that we'd probably be too wasted to drive home anyway."

"We *are* wasted. Was I wrong?" Red said.

"Yes. You're the only one wasted," the first said, leaning against the wall. It was the most intricate, made entirely of dark gray granite with veins of white going through it.

"Yeah, okay," Red said, giving in. It focused on Xan again. "We gave you a translation bug that attaches to your ear nerve. We think it did, anyway. If you can hear us, I guess we did. Then we gave you some of the healing stuff that the bugs make. Just in case. Can you understand us?"

"That should be obvious by now," Xan grumbled. "Did you say something about autopilot that you can't change?"

"We can have a medic look at you on the station," the purple Gneiss said. "Although I don't know if they've ever seen a human before."

"You're taking me to the station? What station?" he asked, the haze slowly clearing and making way for a mental alarm to start ringing faintly.

"Station Eternity," the purple one said.

"Hang on, you need to drop me somewhere on Earth." He couldn't think of a good place off the top of his head, but it seemed it didn't matter.

"Autopilot—it's the only way her grandfather let us take the ship," Red said. "It's out of our hands."

"Then how did you pick me up if you aren't in control of this ship?"

"Long story," Purple said.

"But Eternity is light-years away! How am I supposed to get home? For that matter, how am I supposed to get aboard the station since humans aren't allowed!" he said, alarm rising. At least the adrenaline was making him metabolize that drug faster. His head was almost clear.

"They aren't allowed?" Red asked, looking at the other two.

The red one was either drunk or stupid. Xan couldn't decide. It said it was drunk, so Xan figured he could cut it some slack. "My country's government just sent an ambassador to the station to help negotiate for Earth, but as far as I know they're not getting anywhere yet." He looked at the seated purple Gneiss, the first voice, who seemed to be in charge. It was at least more engaged than the gray one and less drunk than the red.

"We can just ask Eternity to send you home," Red said. "It's our fault you're here anyway; you're not to blame."

"'Our' fault?" the purple pilot said, finally turning around. "I don't think so."

"It's all *your* fault, Tina," the gray one said.

"Hey!" the red one—Tina?—complained. "Don't get me in trouble, you guys."

Xan had a strong feeling of awkward interpersonal dynamics going on here and didn't want any part of it. His emotions felt plastic and distant, as if the events of last night had happened to someone else. Blood, Billy's and his own, was still tacky on his hands and shirt. "So I don't have any say as to where you're taking me?"

"It's okay, neither do we!" Tina reassured him.

"Wonderful," he said. He dimly felt like he could get angrier, but he was too tired. He tried to rub his temples, but his arms felt heavy. *Shit.* "Listen, I can't worry about this right now. If you can't drop me home, is there anywhere I can clean up and get some rest? I'm not feeling great."

The more responsible Gneiss—Stephanie and Ferdinand, he learned—gave him a wet towel and showed him to a Gneiss-size bunk area resembling a king bed. He collapsed and passed out.

His unconscious time aboard *Infinity* was soothing, almost healing. As the Gneiss and *Infinity* ferried him farther and farther away from Earth, he slept. As the drug worked its way out of his system through his blood and sweat, he became tangentially aware of a sense of protection and safety. Not the usual peace of being asleep, but the feeling of being cared for. It was how his grandmother had made him feel when she made Sunday breakfast, when he was a kid, before he knew more about her.

Xan had tried to be alarmed, but it was surreal enough to distance him. He couldn't even see Earth on *Infinity*'s screens, so he didn't have that visual cue to cement his situation in his head. Anyway, the aliens assured him that they would find a way to get him home.

He just wasn't sure where to tell them to take him.

He guessed the trip took a day or two. He would wake up, the rock folks would say encouraging things to him as if he were a puppy, and then he'd retreat back to the bunk. At his request, they gave him water to drink, and, although he hated asking—and explaining why—showed him where he could take care of more private matters.

All he knew was that when he got to Eternity, he was famished.

Upon their arrival at the station, when Tina the Gneiss was fretting that they were "totally going to get in trouble" for bringing a human to the station, Xan met Eternity while stinking of blood and sweat, feeling as if he had literally been reborn.

"You've never been to a sentient space station before, have you?" Stephanie asked him.

"I've never been to any space station," he replied flatly.

Stephanie nodded. "She wants to meet you before you come aboard. She can reach out and touch your mind. It's standard, so just let it happen. You won't be able to hide from her, but she's pretty nonjudgmental, especially if she lets people like Tina aboard."

"She reads minds?" Xan asked, feeling sick to his stomach. "Like everyone on the station is always having their minds read?"

"Not exactly. It's hard to explain, and I don't know how well the translation is coming across. It's a lot of effort for her, and she only really reads the mind of her host—who is a wretched piece of basalt; stay away from him, by the way—who helps her establish a connection with each newcomer. There's nothing you can do to avoid it, so just let her do her thing."

Xan took a step back from the view screen that showed the color-shifting sphere that was Eternity. "And if she doesn't want me? What happens then?"

"We'll find a way to get you back to Earth," Ferdinand said from the pilot's chair. He, for one, had some confidence in his voice.

When he met Eternity, Xan still didn't know what to expect, but it felt like a mental wave crashing over him, and when the tide withdrew, he had a sense of acceptance.

He could come aboard, and even stay; Eternity had granted him sanctuary. No one would come aboard and extradite him, she promised.

He had no idea if she had seen what he had hoped to hide from her, and the Gneiss, and most of the people at the party. If she had and she'd let him on board, she had to be a masochist. If she hadn't seen it, then was it just a matter of time before she figured it out?

A sentient station was an enigma still. Instead of his own room, the shuttle *Infinity* would be his living space, provided he maintained her.

"AND ABOUT THREE weeks later, I think, you arrived," Xan said.

Mallory watched him closely as he told this part of the story. After he finished telling it, she studied him for a moment longer, as if waiting for something else.

She knows. Just tell her. The thoughts were unbidden. The less she knew, the safer she would be. *But if she already knows you're hiding something, then she's not going to trust you.*

He sighed internally but said nothing else.

"And about this murder," Mallory asked, addressing him and Stephanie, "you both knew a lot more about it than you told me at first. Why hide the information?"

He shrugged. "The truth doesn't sound very good. I didn't kill him, but you're not likely to believe it, especially if I tell you more."

"I can believe a lot of things," she said.

Gone was the terrified Mallory who wanted to run, as well as the impetuous Mallory who jumped into danger without a plan. This Mallory had a keen eye and seemed to be drinking everything in.

"Wait," Stephanie said. "You're needed in the medical bay."

"How do you know that?" Mallory asked. "I'm getting really tired of asking that question," she added under her breath.

"Gneiss can communicate through vibrations. You know that," Stephanie said. "There's a nurse asking you both to come. They need help with human body physiology. They don't know what to do with your wet insides."

"We can't be the only species with blood and organs," Mallory said, but she had moved her intense stare from Xan, and he relaxed slightly. "I'm going to my room to change. I'll meet you there, Xan."

"You're needed right now," Stephanie said.

Mallory held up her foot, and the suit's boot flopped around. "I'm not going anywhere quickly in this. They already have all the information about females they need, and if they need more, they can scan Xan first."

They turned to leave the cold room, but Mallory fixed Xan with that cold stare again.

"This isn't over. You need to tell me what's going on."

"I know," he said, meeting her eyes.

But what would happen when she found out the truth?

10

MALLORY'S FIRST OFFICIAL CASE

WHEN WORKING "WITH" the police and the North Carolina SBI, Mallory had encountered hatred, mistrust, and invasive personal investigation. Law enforcement had also reluctantly, grudgingly, asked for her cooperation in solving the case, realizing they couldn't do it without her. But every time they acted like it was a one-time thing.

Despite conveying his ultimate disgust at all things Mallory and hating to ask her personal health questions more than his colonoscopy (he had told her this fact), SBI agent Donald Draughn had been the one person who was entirely against her leaving Earth. He had even admitted he might—*might*—allow her to get a private investigative license if she would stay.

Mallory had laughed at him. "Too little, too late."

Needless to say, despite how much she ended up helping and how much she appreciated the rare recognition she received after a case was solved, every experience with law enforcement had been bad. She didn't know what to expect from alien law enforcement.

Changed into more comfortable jeans and a sweatshirt (and shoes that fit), she found Ferdinand in the medbay.

"Has anyone told security about the shuttle yet?" she asked.

"They should probably know we have survivors and that there are a bunch of dead humans just sitting in *Infinity*'s hold."

"Why should they know? They have much more to worry about with the station in distress and the shuttle bays getting crowded. They can worry about a handful of live humans, or they can worry about the thousands of other people, not to mention the station itself, they need to keep alive," Ferdinand said. "The dead will stay dead, unless—I don't understand human bodies, actually, but they don't come back from the dead, right?"

"Only in a few recorded cases," she said, chewing her bottom lip. "I don't think other species approach crime the way humans do," Mallory muttered.

The exterior room of the medbay had the typical Eternity steel wall structure, with a white floor and a white partition bisecting the space. It was pretty clear their side was for waiting, with plastic chairs of various sizes, most of them too big for humans. The other half had a lot of screens on the wall depicting human anatomy, cell structure, and some incomprehensible scientific things. Gurudevs and a small swarm of Sundry studied the data and conferred with each other.

Set into the wall by the waiting room door was a communications portal, what Mallory had begun to privately call the alien Internet. And inscrutable, with all the symbols she still didn't know by heart.

Xan appeared from an interior door, looking decidedly angry and uncomfortable. He pulled the black leather jacket around him like a blanket as he approached Mallory.

"I am never letting an alien touch me again," he snapped when Mallory raised an eyebrow.

"Just keep in mind that you're helping those injured folks now that they understand male body parts," she said, and returned her focus to the portal.

"What's going on?" he asked.

She glanced at him and then back at the complicated panel, trying to remember what icons to push to make a call. "Security needs to know about the Earth shuttle." Her finger hovered over a button marked with five dots forming a circle, like a pentagram that someone started to map out but didn't finish.

Xan leaned past her and pointed to an icon that looked like a neatly stacked pile of sticks. "That's the one you want."

She poked the button, then looked over her shoulder. "Thank you."

It took security a full twenty seconds to answer the call. "Station security, make it fast. We have a situation." Mallory recognized the voice of Station Security Captain Devanshi, the Phantasmagore who had been kind to her when she got on the station. She winced as alarms blared through the comm.

The ground shook under Mallory again. "This is Mallory, the human, remember?" she said awkwardly. "I wanted you to know there was a shuttle accident and there are several humans dead or injured. I'm not sure about the crew's status, but they were Gurudev."

"Are the survivors in the medical bay?" Devanshi asked.

"Yeah, the Gneiss helped us out and got them out. We docked the shuttle—"

The sharp voice interrupted. "Then why are you telling me?"

"Because I thought security should know about a shuttle accident! There are dead VIPs from Earth. This is a diplomatic incident. Earth is going to want a lot of answers."

Devanshi's voice became strained. "We are dealing with a panicked gargantuan being that is responsible for the lives of thousands. If we don't fix this, your dead VIPs will matter about as much as oxygen vented into space."

"I think the accident is tied to Ren's murder," Mallory ventured.

"And how do you know about Ren?" Devanshi demanded.

"The grapevine," she said, hoping the translation bug would

figure out what that meant. "Also, I figured the station wouldn't be so upset if it had its host. Do you need help finding out who killed Ren?"

"What?" Devanshi sounded confused. "No, that's not the problem at all. The station needs a host so we can communicate with her. If she doesn't calm down and find a proper symbiont, then more will die. Including you and me, your humans in the medical bay, my eggs in my quarters—everyone. If we find the murderer and still die in space, that's not a victory."

Mallory cleared her dry throat. "Understood. So do you—"

"If you care so much, figure it out yourself. If we survive this, you can tell me who to arrest," Devanshi said, and cut the call short.

The lights illuminating her face so Devanshi could see her faded, and Mallory remained at the portal for a moment, trying to push past her shock. No one had ever told her to figure out a murder on her own. Usually, they yelled at her not to get involved and then asked for her help the next day, but they never left her alone to solve a case.

Xan had returned to Ferdinand to talk. They stopped when Mallory approached them.

"How did it go?" Xan asked, his words carrying a tired dread.

"Well, they reacted about how Ferdinand said they would," she said, shrugging. "She said I could solve Ren's murder because they can't be bothered right now."

"You'd think they would worry another murder is going to happen," Xan said.

"Unless their job is done." Mallory faced him square on. "I have to ask—"

"I know," he said, interrupting her. "And Stephanie didn't murder Ren."

"That wasn't what I was going to ask," she said, irritated. "I would like to know how you have all this information. She knew he was in the ossuary and wasn't concerned. You didn't seem surprised either. This is tearing apart the station, and you're both just chill."

"There's a lot you don't know about Gneiss," Ferdinand said.

Mallory didn't miss Xan's grateful glance at the Gneiss for changing the subject.

"Some things are sacred to our people," Ferdinand said. "Some things you don't know just because you haven't been among us long. As we told you, the ossuary is merely a place for us to sleep. Everyone there, from pebble to gunship, is very much alive, just dreaming. And Gneiss aren't like other intelligent species with their symbionts of other species. We connect with each other. Nearly all of us, on some level or another. Family connections are the deepest. If you have relatives in the ossuary, you will know what goes on there. Especially since nearly nothing happens there. The dumping of a body becomes a hot topic."

"So her grandmother or cousin got on the family group chat and told Stephanie that someone dumped a body near them?" Mallory asked.

"That's how I found out, yes," he said. "I assume the same for Stephanie."

Mallory shook her head, noting his evasion. "Do these family members know who dumped the body and who killed Ren?"

Ferdinand didn't look at her. "No."

God, she wished she could read alien body language. It was like trying to interrogate the statue of David.

The interior laboratory had soothing muted slate-colored walls with computer panels set within. The opposite wall featured multiple video screens and holographic projectors. Mallory recognized a red blood cell spinning slowly on one screen, and two Gurudev doctors were looking at it and discussing in low voices. Most of the other screens showed various enlarged images of other body parts or organs that Mallory didn't recognize. One screen closer to the door cycled through some of the survivors' faces.

She turned to Xan to try to get more out of him, but four Sundry approached, hovering in front of her.

"Thank you for bringing the male human to study," they said. "Enlightening. Different. Thankful. We need to inject the patients with the bacterium, and we wanted to make sure the human body could take it," they said. "Healing. Strengthening. Communicating."

"Bacteria? That doesn't sound safe," Mallory said, frowning.

"As we understand, it's a common bacterium among carbon-based life-forms. Universal. Beneficial. Digestive. But ours is modified and evolved so that it has more than just digestive properties. Powerful. Healing. Mysterious."

She nodded weakly. "When can I see the injured?" she asked the Sundry.

"A few hours still," they said. "Healing. Patience. Safe."

"I guess it's good you're saying 'healing' a lot lately," she said. "But do we even have hours until the station breaks apart? Because I have no idea how to move twelve injured humans off the station if things go south."

As if in answer, the sound of groaning metal echoed around her. Mallory and Xan looked up in alarm, but the aliens didn't react.

A Gurudev stepped back from where they'd been peering at the screen that showed a magnified cell. "You can go to the balcony and wait for the humans," she said.

If she hadn't been so upset and exhausted by the spacewalk, the rescue of the shuttle, and the panic of Ren's death, she would have been more interested in the layout of the interior of the medbay. Its design was like that of an old surgery theater. A balcony lined the four walls, having soft chairs arranged every few meters. Below they could see twelve transparent horizontal pods laid out in two rows, each about nine feet long and looking like they could hold a Gneiss with plenty of room left over. The humans were encased within, with readouts on a small screen on the right side of the pod.

"Looks like it's not going to be hours," Xan said, joining her at the railing, eyes on the floor below. Doctors had entered the room holding tablets and began checking the readouts on each pod.

One of the pods' interior lights turned off, while the other eleven remained illuminated. "That's not good," he said.

"Which part?" she asked. "Ren murdered? The station attacking the shuttle? All the dead? All the injured? Or the fact that Adrian is still out there planning on kicking us out of the station?"

There was a movement behind them, and Xan whirled around. Mallory was too tired to be scared and just looked over her shoulder.

"Jesus, don't sneak up on people," Xan snapped, taking a step backward toward the railing.

They had been joined by two Phantasmagore from station security. One was Devanshi, but Mallory hadn't met the second one.

"Osric and I weren't sneaking," Devanshi said, and her color shimmered briefly and then settled on brown, her usual skin color.

The Phantasmagore didn't wear clothing, but Devanshi and Osric did have small pieces of metal grafted to the shiny skin of their chests and armbands like those the medical team wore, only theirs depicted a red square lined in a heavy black outline. Mallory had once attempted to understand what each glittering square on their chests meant. Near as she could tell, they indicated Eternity's law enforcement, but Devanshi hadn't explained very clearly why they needed the armbands and the metal pieces. The metal was the only thing that didn't change when the Phantasmagore and their symbionts used their camouflage to blend in with the walls around them. Which seemed to make grafted metal a liability, but that was just one of the many things Mallory didn't understand about other species.

"We have come to ask about the Earth shuttle," Devanshi said. "Report what you know."

Mallory narrowed her eyes. "I thought you said our shuttle problems were our own."

"We changed our minds," Osric said. The red vine symbiont that curled around his leg and up his back pulsed slightly.

"The Gurudev crew are all dead," Xan said. "Ten humans are dead. Twelve are injured. We're not sure how badly. That's what we know."

Osric glared at Mallory and Xan as if they were the cause of all of today's chaos. *Which we might be*, Mallory supposed.

"So many humans, mostly VIPs and diplomats, dead," Osric repeated as if he didn't believe them. "From the ship's information, most of the ones who survived were insignificant members of society. You couldn't rescue the important ones?"

Beside her, Xan stiffened. "Are you kidding? We didn't make any decisions; we just saved the live ones and grabbed the rest, well frozen, by the way, from space. And the survivors aren't insignificant. If you were so worried about the VIPs dying, maybe you should have done the space rescue instead of leaving it to humans."

"You can't talk to us—" Osric began, but Devanshi stepped in front of him.

"Shut it, Osric," Devanshi said. "We also wanted to tell you that our immediate problem has been solved. We've found a host for the station, and Eternity is calming down."

"That's great," Mallory said. "Now are you going to look for who killed Ren?"

"We will be asking some questions about it," Devanshi said. "In the meantime, we're placing you in charge to investigate what went wrong with the humans' shuttle."

"You—you are?" Mallory asked, flummoxed.

"Hey, why isn't the ambassador involved?" Xan asked. "Shouldn't he be worried about all the dead VIPs?"

"He is otherwise occupied with diplomatic responsibilities," Osric said.

"Diplomatic responsibilities," Xan repeated thoughtfully.

"We will have him message you when he can," Devanshi said.

"Don't bother," Xan said. "We just wondered if you could tell us what was up with him." He looked at Mallory. "Mal, are you taking the job?"

His expression told her he expected her to refuse, or even run away. She set her jaw and nodded. "I'll look into what happened on the shuttle when the people wake up. I may need to talk to Gurudev shuttle experts or the families of the dead crew."

"I don't think they will accept that," Osric said. "They don't look kindly on sharing information with humans."

"Wha—they were just about to bring a bunch of humans to the station! They lost their own people on that shuttle!" Mallory said.

"I will interview them," Osric said coldly.

"No, you're helping me," Devanshi said. "I'll tell them to talk to you if you need them. But I recommend doing other methods of investigating first."

"You do realize it looks really, really bad to hide information from investigators, right?" Mallory asked.

"Might as well just accuse them of sabotage and cut out the middleman," Xan suggested, but Mallory glared at him.

"I won't go that far. But you're keeping one really big piece of the puzzle from me, and I don't appreciate that."

"We have much, much bigger things to do than seek your appreciation," Osric said. "Stay out of our way and investigate the shuttle damage while we figure out the more pressing problems of the station."

"Contact us with what you find out," Devanshi said, good, polite cop to Osric's bad, rude cop.

"Fine," Mallory said. "But I don't want any other roadblocks. If you want me to investigate, you have to let me actually do it."

"I'll get shuttle schematics to you," Devanshi said.

"Why? They can't read it," Osric sneered.

"We'll read it just fine," Xan said, surprising Mallory.

"We will?" she whispered.

"We have to go now. Thanks for your help here," Devanshi said, as if they'd had a pleasant conversation completely free of insults. Both Phantasmagore faded to blend in with the wall, and the only thing that indicated their movement was the glint of the metal plates they wore and slight shimmering that looked like heat haze on an empty summer parking lot.

"Yeah, my pleasure, I guess," Mallory said, still wondering why they were putting such trust in her. *They don't think it's relevant.*

When they were gone, she shook her head slowly. "That Osric is such a dick. And I still think the station attacked the shuttle and people died."

"But why did she do it?" Xan asked, looking down at the bodies in their pods. "Wouldn't it be connected to stress regarding Ren's death? And that connects the two cases."

"That's a good point," she said. "And I'm not sure we're going to find out from our unconscious people. We can't ask the dead what they know. But you're right; the real issue here is Ren's murder. That clearly set off the chain of events."

"But was the attack on the shuttle just an accident, like knocking a glass off a table, or was it directed at the shuttle?"

Mallory thought, remembering her own arrival at the station. "What if, when she reached out to connect with the people on the shuttle, she found something or someone she didn't like?"

"That's true," he said thoughtfully. "But she let our ambassador come on, and that means the bar is pretty low as to who she'll let aboard."

"Xan," she said, facing him. He was still looking down at the pods below them. She waited until he lifted his gaze to her. "You need to be honest with me. Give me something that makes me trust you. There's too much at stake, and I know you're hiding more than one thing from me."

He turned back to the people below. After a moment of thought, he adjusted the huge jacket. "You said there would be connections with the passengers? Either to each other or to people here on the station."

She nodded. "Usually both. We'll find them out when they wake up." She wanted to ask more, but really she wanted him to volunteer the information.

"I'll tell you one of the connections," he said reluctantly.

She waited, silent.

He sighed. "My brother's down there."

MALLORY LEFT XAN in the medbay to wait for the humans to wake. She was hesitant to do so—she appreciated the information about his brother but knew there was more he was keeping from her.

Still, she had only asked for one piece of info, and that's what he gave her.

Xan assured her he didn't know why his brother was here and said they hadn't spoken in a few years. There was not much else to go on, and she needed to stretch her legs until the doctors agreed to release more information. *I need that passenger list*, she thought again, dreading it even as she knew she needed it.

She was remembering her way around the station better today and only took one wrong turn on the way to the Heart of the Station. If Eternity really had a new host, then that's where they would be. She didn't know what was involved with merging with a new host, but Eternity had to know there was considerable panic and death aboard. Maybe a new host took days to settle in, but she didn't care; she needed answers. The station should know who'd killed her host, right?

The hallway to the Heart, lit before with a warm yellow light, was now pulsing red light in a way she hadn't seen before. A few Sundry crawled on the ceiling above her.

"I don't suppose you gals saw what happened?" she asked. The Sundry didn't answer.

Halfway down the hall, she found a fleshy membrane covering the entire hall, from wall to floor to ceiling. It pulsed as well, looking as if it were part of a much larger organ that Mallory was seeing only a sliver of.

Swallowing her sudden nausea, she walked up to it slowly and stretched her hand toward the membrane. Nausea flared again, and she withdrew her hand. This was living, pulsating flesh; that much was clear. Eternity had grown a fleshy barrier around her Heart and her new host. Was this a good sign? Mallory guessed not.

She stepped back and cleared her throat. "Eternity! Is anyone in there? I need to talk to you!" she shouted.

There was no answer.

"What are you doing?" Devanshi demanded, materializing out of the wall behind her.

Mallory jumped. "Gah! Don't do that."

Devanshi waited patiently. Mallory looked at the membrane and took another step away from it. "I was coming to talk to Eternity to find out why she attacked the shuttle. Or if she knew who killed her host. I just wanted to talk."

"You think attempting to communicate with Eternity wasn't our first action?" Osric said coolly, appearing on the other wall, making Mallory jump again. "We have Eternity's situation under control."

Mallory pointed to the membrane, which looked less transparent now, as if more layers were growing in front of them. "Does that look under control? Is that normal?"

They didn't answer her. "You need to leave the area," Osric said.

She stood her ground. "No one will tell me what's happening, and we know the station did attack the shuttle, so she's on my list to talk to. But what"—she touched the membrane with a knuckle and immediately regretted it—"the hell is this?"

"The station has closed herself off for safety," Devanshi said. "She wants none of us in there while she communes with the new host."

"Fine. How long will that take? I can wait. It's either wait for her or wait for the humans to wake up. Or I could go and find my ambassador. As useless as he is, he probably needs to know about all this. You sounded like you knew where he was . . ." Mallory trailed off, leaving it open for either of them to answer.

Devanshi's shiny black eyes moved from Mallory to Osric.

"Your ambassador is otherwise occupied," Osric said, as if reading from a cue card.

"But what diplomatic duties . . ." Realization settled on Mallory's shoulders like a weighted blanket. She looked back at the wall of flesh that protected the new host from all eyes. "Oh. That diplomatic duty."

"HOW IS THAT possible?" Mallory raged at Xan after she returned to the medbay. "How can humans even connect with the station? We can't have symbionts. Isn't that why they treat us like ignorant rubes half the time?"

"It could be possible," Xan said calmly. "Humanity just hasn't had the opportunity."

Mallory held her head with both hands, trying to contain the outrage. "Did the station, God forbid, choose him? *Him*?"

"She may not have had a choice," he said. "Any port in a storm and all that. Maybe it was a choice of killing all of us or connecting with him."

"You know what this means," she said, starting to pace behind him on the walkway.

"That we're more likely to get kicked off the station? Yeah, I thought of that," he said grimly.

Mallory paced back and forth, wondering how they could get off the station before Adrian could get rid of them.

"You're thinking 'run' again, aren't you?" he asked.

"If I am, can you blame me?" she said.

He sighed and hung his head briefly, then turned to face her. "No. But I can't consider that. I can't do that. Not anymore." Even though he looked at her, his body still leaned toward the railing, angled to the lower floor, as if it had a gravitational hold on him.

"Your brother. Right," she said. "How are they doing?"

"No report yet," he said, but movement on the floor caught their attention.

One of the pods was open now, with two alien physicians leaning over it. Mallory could tell the person inside was a young Black woman. Her eyes were closed, and a laceration split her right cheek and trailed over her forehead. When one of the Gneiss moved aside, Mallory caught sight of a heavily bandaged left hand. Had she come here with that? The doctors didn't have any gauze wrappings with them; bandaging was probably a barbaric way of dealing with things in their point of view. They pointed at the bandage and conferred quietly; then one reached out and slit through it with a small laser. They examined the hand, noting the missing pinky finger, and then put it gently back on her stomach and closed the pod.

The humans weren't close to waking up yet. That much was clear. Mallory turned to face the wall to which the catwalk was tethered. Beside one of the massive chairs sat a table where a tablet glowed. Mallory climbed into the chair and sat cross-legged, feeling like a child.

"Whose tablet is that?" she asked, pointing.

"The medbay's," he said, his attention going back to the floor. "Ship manifest."

"How do you know? Can you read alien script too?"

"I know a little, but the manifest is a human file. It's in English," he said mildly.

She picked up the tablet, her thoughts returning to the situation at hand, as confusing as it was.

"The station doesn't attack sentients," Mallory said aloud. "What made her go for the human shuttle before it even docked?"

"You told Eternity you expected a murder, right?" he asked.

"Of course I did. She shouldn't have been too surprised if someone got violent on the shuttle or something."

"So all we can do is wait."

She didn't realize how lonely she had felt in trying to tackle this by herself until Xan said "we." She felt anxious muscles between her shoulders unclench. "That is all we can do," she repeated softly, and powered on the tablet to read the list of survivors. None of them rang any bells until the last one.

Oh, shit. She's here.

She replaced the tablet, her heart hammering. Her biggest problem was no longer wondering if Adrian would use the station to exile her and Xan.

Adrian's the new host, and now this.

Is it too late to run?

11

ADRIAN UND DIE AUTORITÄT

ADRIAN CASSERLY-BERRY DIDN'T like snow. He didn't like dogs, tea with sugar, people who did crafts as hobbies, or people who chose to be bald.

Since childhood, he had kept a list of things he disliked. He started on the back cover of his science notebook, and once that filled up, he bought a separate notebook during school supplies sales and continued his private list of dread.

He didn't see himself as a terribly negative person. He kept this list because no one else listened to him, and the notebook was an excellent listener. When he was part of a group, whether in school, Cub Scouts, or church, no one took Adrian's opinion into account. If the kids got a choice to make, they never chose Adrian's preference. Even when Adrian was on the majority's side, somehow the decision would go the other way.

The summer he was sixteen, before his junior year of high school, his father found his notebook of things he disliked. He had told him that Adrian shouldn't define himself in the negative. Maybe write some positive things down instead? Then he had gone into the kitchen to make an appointment with a psychologist. Dr. Woods.

That night, his father went on the list.

Dr. Woods was an old white man. He was very thin, with wisps of gray hair combed over a shiny pate. Dr. Woods told Adrian the same thing his dad had said about thinking positively, but charged them one hundred dollars for the advice (his dad had told him how much it had cost). Dr. Woods did suggest that he find something new and positive in his life to focus on.

Adrian tried to point out he did have positive things on the list, like, "I liked the look on Mark's stupid face when he got caught cheating on the Bio test."

"Schadenfreude is not considered a positive thing, overall," Dr. Woods had said, frowning.

"Shaden what?" the sixteen-year-old Adrian had said.

"It's a German word. It means 'happiness at the misfortune of others.' It's the pleasure you get when someone you don't like gets in trouble at school. I take it you don't like Mark?"

Adrian had gone blank, saying nothing.

Dr. Woods looked up sharply when he didn't answer. "Adrian. Did you hear me?"

"*One* word means that whole feeling?" Adrian asked, still staring into space.

"Yes, the German language is quite good at that. But do you understand what I'm trying to say about schadenfreude?"

"Sure," Adrian had answered. For the rest of the session, he answered the doctor's questions in single syllables. He didn't argue when the doctor pulled his notebook out of his hands and started to read his lists and comment on how the negative aspects were hurting Adrian.

Adrian didn't care anymore. Something had broken open in his world, hatching like a baby bird, its beak open to be fed.

He had been putting off learning a language in school. He wasn't interested in hard work and was a strong C student. Besides, no one listened to him when he spoke English; why learn a new way people could ignore him? But he needed two classes of a language to graduate, and his high school years were running out. He'd been signed up for French class—it was the first on the language list, so he had picked that. But the day after his appointment with Dr. Woods, he contacted the high school to ask them to transfer him to German. He'd never acted this passionately about anything in school before, so the bemused guidance counselor allowed it.

German fascinated him. One word could hold so much meaning. It was beautiful, almost magical.

When school started in the fall, he threw himself into German with a passion that astonished his father, his teachers, and even himself. After a few weeks of sprinting ahead in the lessons, he complained to his German teacher that he was interested in the other languages, but the school wouldn't allow him to take more than one. Frau Becker thought for a moment and then said all the languages had clubs that met after school. She was going to suggest he join the German club, but he could check the others out, too.

He joined them all.

The other kids didn't really warm to him, but they couldn't kick him out. He took all the books they were reading for class and then got his own language guides online. When he started to excel in every single foreign language, they hated him more. But he didn't care. It had taken sixteen years for him to find a true love.

Unfortunately, colleges weren't interested in a mediocre student who had found only one academic passion, and found it late at that. Despite being a virtual savant in languages, he was still a terrible student in the other classes he barely paid attention to. (He had been translating his schoolwork into other languages instead of actually doing the work. Language teachers had been impressed. Science teachers, less so.)

When the college rejections started coming in, his rage at authority figures returned and he started a new list of dread. To amuse himself, he made this one in his own private language.

Two years of actually applying himself in community college helped him transfer to the local state school to finish undergrad, and then he shocked everyone when he got into grad school for linguistics at Duke. That led to a job teaching back at UNC-Asheville, where he was introduced to the cold world of academic politics.

The *concept* of politics fascinated him: it required wielding language like a weapon, something he loved. Unfortunately he didn't excel at it because he had to understand and at least pretend to care about the people he was working with, and he wasn't good at personal manipulation. So after a few tries at playing politics to get ahead, he retreated to his inner world of languages, teaching when he had to, developing his third private language. Tenure eluded him because he couldn't play the politics game; he had developed a reputation as an unpleasant hermit.

No one cared that he was a hermit who could talk to over half the world's population. If only they'd listen.

One of the few things he found pleasure in—which, frankly, had shocked him—was poetry. He discovered it was another way of playing with words, and reading poetry in other languages became even more enlightening. He didn't have a knack for poetry, but he did enjoy wordplay and puns. All he wanted was to be alone and revel in other languages, work on his third custom-made secret language, and find puns that spanned as many languages as possible.

To the dismay of UNC-Asheville leaders, it was their unpleasant hermit linguistics professor who made it into the history books when First Contact happened.

A pair of aliens—now known as the Gurudev Tracy and the Phantasmagore Sapphire—had landed their ship in a clearing off Blue Ridge Parkway, bypassing American airspace alert systems effortlessly. Adrian came across the ship, a sleek Phantasmagore shuttle with mirrored plating, when he was hiking. His mind was on Turkish verb conjugation, and he nearly bumped into the ship. He fell back and stared, his mind shorting out as it tried to process what he saw.

A hatch opened and the first alien—the first known alien, anyway—stepped out of the shuttle.

She was a short Gurudev, with yellow bark-like skin, and was wrapped in layers of cloth, giving her the illusion of a much more substantial body. She began speaking to him, and it was so startling to hear words he didn't immediately just know that he missed it.

He shook his head and said, "I'm sorry, can you please repeat that?"

She cocked her head at him, an odd movement for her many-jointed neck that nearly made him wince as he imagined his own head moving that way. She began speaking again, and he listened closely. She spoke in sentences that started clipped and ended almost lyrically. He was fascinated. He lost his fear and wanted to just listen to her talk forever. Understanding her was a linguistic challenge, something exciting. He hadn't been challenged by languages since undergrad.

The two of them tried carefully to communicate, but neither seemed to be getting through to the other. With mounting frustration, Adrian realized that this historical event was bigger than him. He would have to involve the authorities.

He resisted the thought immediately. This find was *his*. This diplomat—and her pilot, whom he met later—were his to find, and so they were his to reveal to the world, if he could only figure out how to communicate. Without ego, he knew that he was one of the best-equipped people in the world to converse with the aliens, and he didn't want to lose that chance.

Maybe *the alien* didn't want to meet more humans. Maybe she wanted resources, or her spaceship had broken down. Maybe she just wanted to talk to him about something. Maybe he wouldn't have to tell anyone about this.

But who was he fooling? Aliens wouldn't come to Earth with the goal to meet with a linguistics professor. This was a chance meeting. He wasn't special.

Authority. Autorité. Údarás. Ùghdarras. And of course his old friend, German. Die Autorität. Whatever language it was, it sounded ugly. He pulled out his phone and tried to search for "what to do if you have a first contact situation."

The Gurudev got excited, speaking rapidly. She motioned for the phone and he reluctantly gave it to her. He didn't like anyone seeing his phone, but this alien knew nothing of Earth or humans, so she couldn't read his deepest thoughts or the lists he still kept.

She studied the phone, poked at the screen a few times, then disappeared into her shuttle.

"Hey, wait," he said, and moved forward. The hatch didn't close, and the ship didn't power up. Was she coming back out? He wanted to follow her, but the idea of being spirited away by aliens wasn't as romantic as going to an alien planet of his own volition.

The shuttle didn't move, but she didn't reappear, so Adrian sat down for a lack of anything better to do. He waited about five minutes, and then she emerged. She handed over his very warm, but apparently unharmed, phone.

"Thanks for giving it back," he said, and she responded in her own language, looking him in the eye.

"I can't understand you, sorry," he said. "I wish you could understand me."

She spoke briefly again and appeared to wait for him to do something. She didn't gesture with her branch-like arms or anything, and he had never been more aware of how much humans used body language to communicate.

"Should I keep talking, then?" he asked. She answered with

the same syllables. "I don't get it. This is so frustrating. I wish you could hold up fingers or something."

She raised her hand and splayed her very long digits.

"Well, shit," he muttered. "One finger?" She displayed one, folding the others up, showing off her many joints. "All of them?" Her hand splayed its fingers again.

"All right, we're down to basics for communication. Hold one finger for yes, two for no," he said, thinking fast. "You can understand me, right?"

One finger.

He wanted to ask how; he wanted to ask why; he wanted to ask why she was here. But he wasn't going to get far unless he could think up some yes-no questions.

"Are you here to hurt us?"

Two fingers.

"Take over or enslave the planet?"

Two fingers.

That was a relief. "Are you here to find us? Humans? A First Contact kind of thing?"

One finger.

"Are you here to strip our planet of resources?"

She spoke again, the syllables coming too quickly for him to parse them. He got the sense he had offended her. She raised two fingers.

"Who—no, hang on. Yes-no questions." This question felt like ash in his mouth. He twisted his lips, trying to get the words out. "Do you—do you need to see someone in authority?"

One finger.

Goddammit.

WHAT FOLLOWED WERE calls to the police, and when they didn't believe him, calls to the FBI, who also didn't believe him.

Desperate to keep the aliens from being blown to pieces by a hill-billy with a shotgun, Adrian called the local paper, which he considered authority-adjacent. They sent a bored junior reporter out to the woods. Very shortly after, she called for a photographer to meet her.

Both journalists won the Pulitzer Prize later that year.

Once it was breaking news online, the authorities finally took him seriously. First, the local politicians and police came to the woods. Adrian tried to be a translator, but once they understood that the aliens could now answer yes-no questions, he was no longer needed.

The authorities took his special find away from him.

He was still a little bit special, for a few weeks. News outlets around the world contacted him for quotes, but then he was targeted by Internet conspiracy theorists, his personal information was leaked, and the harassment kept him offline and made him get a new cell number.

Since he had gone offline, it took the authorities several days to find him, eventually coming to his house. He answered the door warily but was utterly shocked when he was informed that Earth needed a diplomat, and he was the only one the aliens would accept.

Someone had finally paid attention to him, and it just took an alien spacecraft landing for it to happen.

SOON AFTER HIS background check (which he warned would be quite boring reading for whatever desk cop had the misfortune to do so), he learned about the translation bug that had made the aliens understand him once they had access to language databases. He met with the scientists who were studying the alien tech and agreed to be the first test subject. After studying the human auditory system, the aliens decided that the bug they used for the Gurudev would work for humans.

Adrian passed out from the pain, which took a few days to ease. The bug was connected to his auditory nerve, and he was hailed as a hero by the aliens and could finally understand them.

When the *New York Times* interviewed him about it, he said it felt as if he had spent his life trying to build a ladder to a roof but then found someone had built an elevator on the other side of the building. He had worked hard to learn languages, and his reward was never having to think about them ever again. It was definitely bittersweet, but finally—*finally*—understanding the alien visitors was worth it.

Earth wasn't happy about their new "friends" not helping them reach the stars or visit their space station, but when the aliens invited Adrian to spend some time meeting other diplomats on the space station Eternity, he agreed in an instant.

The evening before his first trip to Eternity, he had an unexpected visitor drop by his apartment.

He had light brown skin and was about sixty years old, bald, and taller and fitter than Adrian. He wore an army dress uniform and introduced himself as Lieutenant General Maxwell.

He removed his hat and held it in his hands, not sitting until Adrian invited him to take his easy chair. He was polite almost to a fault, and Adrian started to warm to him. People rarely treated him so respectfully. Even the humans who had agreed to make him ambassador treated him like a redneck cousin they were worried would embarrass them at a fancy dinner.

"The United States is grateful to you for stepping into this difficult position. Leaving your home to live in a foreign territory that no one has ever been to is a huge sacrifice."

"Okay," Adrian said hesitantly. No one had phrased it like that before. "Thanks?"

Maxwell nodded. "But I'm sure you understand that the government has diplomats that they would have preferred to send, considering the difference in diplomatic training and experience between you and other terrestrial ambassadors."

Adrian's face heated up. "I know that. They make it known in no uncertain terms. But I've been going through training."

"You have, but you are still untested. And you're entering a diplomatic arena that is a black hole—we don't even know how dangerous it is, and once we find out the danger, it will likely be too late. One misstep could get us involved in an intergalactic war. And we are not yet prepared for that."

"They also told me this," Adrian said, his voice tight. This guy, this general, sat holding his hat in his hand, still looking cool and not as if he had just flat-out told Adrian that he didn't expect him to do the job he had been assigned. "Where are you going with this? Because if you just came here to insult me . . ."

Maxwell raised a hand, showing his palm to stop Adrian. "Not at all, Ambassador."

He used that title on purpose to make me feel better. But it did.

"I am here to convey the appreciation of the US government, and to go over your responsibilities with you."

"I told you, I've already been through this training," he said.

"For the benefit of the public and our new alien friends, yes." Maxwell leaned forward as if to make sure no one could hear them in the otherwise empty apartment. "But there are some . . . private goals we hope you will strive for in your unique place as the only human aboard a station of aliens who could pose a great risk to humanity."

Adrian listened carefully, and started a new list.

12

THE TRUTH ABOUT NUMBER 14

THE PHYSICIANS HAD finished discussing the humans' various injuries. Xan couldn't hear them, but they had stopped by each of the pods and discussed its inhabitant. Then they had closed the pods and left the surgery theater.

Gentle light pulsed in the twelve pods below him, some pulses faster than others. Alien script blinked messages on screens attached to each pod, and Xan reminded himself to keep learning the common script when all of this was over.

If he still lived on Eternity, that was.

Xan would prove quite useful to the army if they got him back. The translation bug in his ears would continue updating with known languages, so he would likely be able to understand most languages aside from English. The downside of being AWOL very likely outweighed the usefulness of being literally a universal translator.

Then there was the problem of him being the target the night of Billy's party. Would there be another assassination attempt? He focused on one pod below him, rubbing his jaw thoughtfully.

Phineas was down there. The doctors had promised him they would tell him if Phineas got worse, but they didn't seem concerned.

But that wasn't the pod he was looking at.

Mallory confused him. She seemed ready to run away at the first sign of conflict—until there was a murder. Then she had an uncomfortable focus and looked at him as if she could see through all his lies and obfuscation. But she didn't press him on things he was pretty sure she already knew.

Phineas was not the only shuttle survivor he knew. He hadn't been home in a few years, so this would be an awkward reunion, but the other person worried him much more.

Behind him, Mallory was sitting in the massive chair, looking like a child playing on her mother's tablet. She was going over the ship's manifest, swearing slightly to herself. She'd seen something else to worry her; he knew the feeling. There had been a moment on *Infinity* when he'd seen the list of passengers and had considered letting them all die in space and just running. Maybe Mallory had the right thinking.

Who had she seen that worried her?

She climbed off the chair and brought the tablet over to him, holding it out so he could see. Ten of the names at the bottom had been crossed out. She pointed to the twelve names at the top of the list. "I take it these are our survivors?"

Xan nodded once. "Yeah. Did you see the cargo list?"

The list was long, including everything from material goods—for trade, Xan figured—to a detailed list of cosmetics and other personal items. A few things showed up in red lettering.

Mallory pointed to the last red item on the list. "Unidentified capsules. Do you know what those are?"

"Why do you think I would know that?" Xan said, looking at her incredulously. "It says 'unidentified'."

"You brought it up," she reminded him. "Red means contraband, I bet. It's something Eternity doesn't want on the station. Don't know who brought it, though. That could be why the station attacked." She looked at the names again, her face growing slightly pale. "So your brother is here? Phineas Morgan, I'd guess?"

"Yeah," he said. He tried to keep his voice calm.

"Any idea why he's visiting you? Did you know—"

He bristled, and she cut herself off. "Yeah, you didn't know he was coming. Can you think of why he's here?"

"I don't know. If he knows I'm here, then I can bet other people do, too." He fought the urge to pace, not wanting to mirror Mallory's agitation.

She looked at him thoughtfully, and he got the uncomfortable naked feeling again. "Other people. Like someone else down there? Is your brother the only survivor you know?"

"Jesus, Mal! How do you know this shit?"

She grinned, and it was a tired, bitter smile that hurt him a little bit. This was what she was good at, and she hated it. "Tell me how you know the stuff you know, and I'll tell you mine."

She knew. He was pretty sure. But he wasn't ready; it was too personal. And he didn't fully understand everything.

Something changed on the tablet screen. He touched the name at the top. The information came in an audio live stream, updating the patients' vitals in real time.

"Passenger one: Name: Phineas Morgan. Species: human. Sex: male. Age: seventy-five universal cycles."

"Seventy-five cycles?" Mallory asked.

"He's twenty-four," Xan said.

The robotic voice continued reading the data. "Diagnosis: Hypothermia. Blunt-force trauma. Several lacerations. Treatment: Subdermal injections of *Staphylococcus cmarensis*. Intercranial injection of *Staphylococcus cmarensis*. Prognosis: Will survive."

Xan felt something like a tight chain break around his chest, and he was able to breathe again. He hadn't realized he'd been holding his breath.

The voice continued. "Passenger two: Name: Lovely Brown. Species: human. Sex: female. Age: seventy-eight universal cycles. Diagnosis: Hypothermia. Blunt-force trauma. One severe laceration. One preexisting serious puncture wound. Treatment: Subdermal injections of *Staphylococcus cmarensis*. Topical cream of *Staphylococcus cmarensis*. Prognosis: Will survive."

The list continued, with Mallory looking down at the bodies below them.

"Did they say 'staphylococcus'? Like that infection that can kill humans?" Xan asked.

"That's what it sounded like," she said.

"Not good enough," he snapped. "Hey! Doctors! Someone want to tell me why you're injecting my brother with staph?" he shouted down the stairs.

The tablet's video flared to life, and a Gurudev face appeared. Xan recognized the main nurse he had talked to. "The translation bugs are highly sophisticated, but they have some problems with scientific and medical terms," she said. "While this may be similar to a dangerous bacterium on your planet, we have found that every carbon-based life-form has reacted quite well to it."

"What is it?" Mallory asked.

The nurse paused. "You are not medical professionals, so the details will be too complicated. The bacteria is a by-product of Sundry venom and appears to be working on the humans already. They respond very well to it. Now, I must get back to work."

The video blipped off, and the screen returned to the listing of the patients.

"So we don't have a choice," Xan said.

"What if someone is allergic to insect venom?" Mallory said, rubbing her arms.

"I guess we find out," he replied.

Next was Elizabeth Brown, an old woman with similar injuries but also liver cancer and a weak heart. "Treatment: *Staphylococcus cmarensis* soak in transition pod. Prognosis: While the cancer is terminal, she will probably survive the injuries sustained in the shuttle attack."

"Probably?" Mallory asked Xan.

He shrugged. "She's around sixty-one, if I'm doing the math right."

"Elizabeth Brown. Why is she here?" Mallory asked, her voice vague and rhetorical.

"I'd be surprised if they can't cure everything wrong with her. Their treatment is pretty much magical to us," Xan said.

"They inject it, spread it like a cream, and soak people in it?"

"So far, yeah. It must cure everything from illness to injury."

"They're not gods. We've seen they can die too," she said bitterly.

The droning voice continued reading the patient information to them.

Now they learned of Katherine Bartlett, with the usual injuries, including a crushed right hand, and Calliope Oh, who had suffered the same general injuries as Phineas.

Dread began to sit like hot coals in Xan's empty stomach as the names were read. Eleven names on the list of survivors, but twelve humans rescued.

"What about that one?" Mallory asked, pointing. Eleven pods still pulsed with gentle inner lighting and active LED readouts, but the twelfth pod had gone dark. On the list, one of the names now had a line through it. Mallory frowned. "That staph goo isn't all-powerful. We lost one."

The name meant nothing to him: Sam Washington, a college-age male. He had the usual hypothermia and blunt-force trauma diagnosis, but he also had two unique problems: an injury to the back of the head that the doctors said didn't match others' blunt force injuries, and an unidentified drug in his system. The drug had prevented him from accepting the healing bacteria, and he died due to the head injury.

Along with Sam Washington's pod, the tablet went dark.

"Unknown drugs?" Xan asked. He cleared his throat. "Unknown to the station or to humans?"

"No idea," she said, looking up at the ceiling. "As much as I hate him, I wish Adrian could talk to us now. He should be able to hear us; Ren always seemed to be listening in on our conversations like a creeper."

"I expect the station has overloaded his brain with data," Xan said. "I wouldn't think the average human could handle seeing and hearing everything on the station. From what you've told me, the guy wasn't that bright."

Xan looked at the dark tablet again, thinking about the last name on the list. Sam Washington. Who had this kid been, and what had he taken? Xan felt oddly uneasy. He'd watched Mallory gather all the other dead bodies of VIPs and ambassadors from outside the shuttle and felt nothing but the detachment he'd learned in the army. But the death of this kid felt like a bigger deal.

He rubbed his face, fingers brushing over the beard growing there. He needed a shower, shave, and sleep. Or food, if nothing else.

"If Adrian is the new host, is he still the ambassador?" Mallory wondered aloud. "Because someone should probably tell Earth that half the people in the shuttle are dead." She looked with glassy eyes down at the bodies. "God, I'm tired. I need to think for a bit."

"I'm starving," he said. "Are you hungry?"

"Eating? Now?" She frowned. "Is it safe?"

"Things seem more stable. At the least we can get a walk before—" Xan paused. He was all-in now, fully believing in Mallory's weird-ass power or sense or whatever it was. She stood at the center of a spiderweb of connections, and he wondered if she knew the extent of her reach. "You know things are going to get weird when they wake up. Let's get some food so we can be ready. I'll tell the staff we're stepping out."

MALLORY SUGGESTED THE closest restaurant to the medbay, which was located in the common recreational area for oxygen breathers. It was run by the Sundry, those bugs that Mallory had claimed were no big threat.

"Are you sure that's safe?" he asked. He felt a saying from his grandma come to mind. "You don't poke the wasp nest and it won't poke you."

"So don't poke them," she said with a smile. "And they like other species to visit."

"How did you connect with them, anyway?" he asked as they walked. "Did you just present yourself and say, 'Probe me!'?"

Outside in the hallway, people were starting to move about, many of them discussing the events of the night before. The words "major breach" rose out of the rumbling of two Gneiss talking about the methane sector of the station.

Mallory snorted. "Not exactly. I met the Sundry the way most humans meet insects," Mallory said. "Remember back home when you found a dangerous bug in your room? What did you do?"

"Swat it," he said, and then laughed. "You assaulted a Sundry?"

She nodded gravely. "It was instinct. See, when I was a kid, my birthday was ruined by stepping on a bumblebee in my bare feet. I screamed bloody murder."

They turned down the hallway leading to the rec area, the light flickering around them. "Shit," Xan said, looking around. "I wonder if our new host has figured out where the fuse box is."

Mallory continued, her face soft with nostalgia. "I remember the split second between the initial shock and the pain. The bee was struggling in the grass, trying to right itself, or fly, or do something, but it was probably dying. In that moment I realized that my own pain was nothing compared to the bee's. But what the hell did I care? Like most kids, I was selfish. It mattered most that my birthday was Officially Ruined, and I forgot about the bee and my mom and thought only of my own swelling foot—" She swallowed, as if that could take back her words. "Anyway, that was a really bad day. It cemented a fear of bees and other stinging creatures."

"And you're allergic now?" he said.

"Yeah, the allergy hit a few years later when I got stung on a picnic. My aunt was so mad that her deviled eggs didn't get eaten because I had to go to the ER."

"You've got an allergy, and you let the Sundry study you?" he asked, amazed.

She shrugged. "I need the work. I brought an EpiPen."

They walked into the rec area and paused. It looked to Xan like a park he had once seen in Paris, complete with a blue-green area blanketed with a fluffy grass, a small woodsy area populated by massive colorful trees, and a paved area with storefronts and restaurants. It was still early and the station inhabitants had yet to populate the area. Few of the places were open, but Mallory assured him the Sundry didn't really sleep much.

The dim, illusory sun that Eternity created to enhance the park area was just starting to rise. Blue wasps buzzed around the huge papery nest hanging from a tree in the middle of the blue-green grassy area.

"So it was the first week I was here, and I hadn't heard of the Sundry yet," she continued. "I had my unfortunate swatting incident, and thank God I missed, so no real harm done. Soon after, station security came to talk to me about the attempted assault, and that's when I met Devanshi." She chuckled dryly. It sounded forced.

"I told her that the 'wasp,' or as she put it on the report, 'the individual known as Worker 3985,' entered my room without permission, scaring me. I had swatted at it out of instinct. How was I supposed to know it was an important messenger for the hive it traveled with?

"I didn't tell station security (or the worker herself) about the bee I'd stepped on as a child," she added.

"They probably already know that by now," he said as they reached a papery hole hidden at the bottom of the nest by the drooping tree. "They're pretty good at knowing everything. That's what they do."

"If so, I'll just remind them I feel bad about that bee," she said. "Not much I can do about it now. Anyway, in order to stave off an intergalactic incident and avoid arrest, I agreed to let Devanshi bring me here for a meal. This was after you and I had come up with some safe places to eat, or I would have just eaten here all the time after that. It was a big deal, I realized, because Adrian, Devanshi, and a few Sundry representatives were there. The food was pretty good, although the company could have been better, and they did their diplomatic talk thing and I listened. When they were done, I apologized, and they accepted it."

Wasps began to swarm around them, and Xan followed Mallory's example of standing still and letting them investigate. "And now you're the best of friends?" he asked wryly.

The buzzing voice started. "Mallory and Xan, it is a pleasure to see humans again. Guests. Invite. Safety. Your hormones are different today, so tell us what you're signaling, please. Fear. Dread. Focus."

Several wasps landed on Mallory's clothed arm. Compound eyes the size of dimes studied the fabric of her hoodie with interest.

Xan looked at her, startled. "What do they mean, 'signaling'?"

"We secrete hormones when we feel strong emotions. They can smell them. They can always tell when I'm stressed or scared."

"This is not stress or fear," the voice of the Sundry said. "This is stronger than those, but not as sharp. Heavy. Unpleasant. Distress."

"Dread," Xan said.

"And another human," they said. "Relative. Biology. Sibling."

He fought the urge to shiver when one crawled over his wrist, probing at the cuff of his brother's jacket.

"They can tell that?" Xan asked.

"Maybe, or maybe they've been hearing what we've been talking about and made the leap," Mallory said. To the insects on her arm, she said, "It's been a pretty stressful night, and we're just looking for breakfast. Is your restaurant open yet? Can we order food for two humanoids?"

The Sundry let them into the nest.

"I've had to do a lot of thinking about stuff humans take for granted, because everyone asks me a ton of questions when I'm exploring the station," Mallory told him. "They want to know about my looks or how I smell or what I'm wearing." She looked over her shoulder at him. "Don't people ask you the same?"

"No. I don't wander much," he said. "Also, I wear the same thing every day. They probably already know what they need to know about me. Mostly I get the question of how lonely humans are without a symbiont."

He stopped talking to look around. He hadn't seen much of the station beyond the shuttle bay and the Gneiss restaurants nearby, and this was like wandering through a work of art.

While the Sundry were relatively small, this hive was large enough to admit humanoid-size creatures. He spotted some Gneiss lumbering around the labyrinthine hive, the papery floor creaking under their feet, but amazingly the nest held. How strong was this thing? The seemingly fragile paper walls reminded Xan of some of the high-tech polymers he'd encountered in quartermaster training.

The welcoming Sundry swarm led Xan and Mallory to a small hexagonal room that featured a table at a height they could both access, although it had no chairs. The room was softly lit with phosphorescent lights set into the walls and had a close, cozy atmosphere.

Four workers buzzed into the room, two of them carrying menus made from the same paper as the hive itself. "Welcome, humans. Queen 41 mentioned there was a high probability that you would join us," they said. "Especially after recent events. Death. Station. Shock."

"The hivemind takes the data it receives and processes probability," Mallory explained.

Xan remembered hearing this from Ferdinand. The Sundry's hivemind worked almost like a computer, taking all of the data it could find from its many, many workers and drones and processing it for events with a high probability of happening. However, solo communication was tough for them. With four wasps together, a circuit of sorts was established to form thoughts complex enough to communicate with other species. This was why they rarely traveled anywhere alone. It was Mallory's bad luck, then, that she had encountered a solo messenger who couldn't explain herself.

Xan wondered what the probability was that Mallory would misunderstand a Sundry scout and try to kill it. Bet they didn't see that coming. It irritated him that the Sundry also liked telling people about how good they were at finding out the odds of something, and showing off, in Xan's opinion, anyway.

Xan glanced at the menu. The little bugs had thought of everything; there were no words to read, just pictures to point to. There were drawings of cuts of meat and fruit he didn't recognize, and silhouettes of races on the right-hand page. It looked like he could order anything in Gneiss, Gurudev, or Sundry sizes. All of the other races fit within those parameters.

"If you're super-hungry, go for a Gneiss-size portion," Mallory suggested. "Our appetites seem to fit between that and Gurudev." She pointed at the menu and indicated pictures of some of the meat and fruit with drops of moisture dripping from them. "This means you can order the food raw and eat it the Sundry way, or have it cooked, which they consider dry and unappetizing. Unless you usually go for raw chicken and pork, I recommend the red meat and the winter fruit juice. Also consider summer fruit grilled for dessert." She pointed to an oblong cut of meat, a bunch of small berries, and then a fruit that resembled a pineapple, but without the pokey outer skin.

He shrugged. "I'll just have whatever you suggest."

Mallory made to pull a pad from her pocket and then grimaced. "I've been writing down all the foreign food I can stomach, but I forgot my notebook when I changed in my room. I'll need to get the suit back to you when this is over."

"Keep it," he said. "I don't need it."

She frowned at him, but the workers returned and Mallory ordered for them both. The wasps buzzed in an unhappy way when she ordered the cooked food. "Are you sure you don't want the order to be prepared properly?" they asked.

Mallory sighed. "We've been over this."

"Will you try a taste?" They never gave up.

"I'll give it a try," Xan said. "Why not?"

Mallory glanced at Xan. "If it's not too horrific, sure."

After the Sundry left, she grinned at him. "Didn't you burn your mouth badly the last time a Gneiss waiter told you to try some food the way they eat it?"

He winced in memory. "Yeah, but blisters heal. You gotta take a chance from time to time, Mal."

She rolled her eyes. "Trying to live on a space station all alone isn't taking a chance?"

"You're not alone," he said.

She looked at him thoughtfully. "We were both alone when we got here; it was just luck that we found each other."

"Or one of your coincidences," he said.

She looked down at the table again and cleared her throat. "Speaking of coincidences, we need to talk about the passengers. Do you really have no clue why your brother is here?"

And he'd been having a nice time, Xan thought ruefully. "No. He's never followed me anywhere. I don't know how he found me, or how he managed to get a seat on the first shuttle here. You'd think those would be incredibly hard to get. We don't talk much, anyway, not since I enlisted."

"Not even on holidays?" Mallory asked in disbelief.

He shrugged. "We're not close."

Several Sundry flew in with their fruit juice orders then. There were more of them, struggling with the weight of the liquid. The cup rose and dipped in the air like a roller coaster, but they managed to deliver the drinks without spilling a drop.

Mallory bent to sniff the waxen cup of yellow juice, then took a sip. "It's good, but the cup is really delicate." Her fingers left indentations on the cup when she put it down.

Xan tasted his own drink. It was tangy, almost painfully so, but soon mellowed as it trickled down his throat. He downed the rest and put the cup on the table.

"Are we done now?" he asked.

She raised an eyebrow. "With?"

"You're telling me that I'm hiding shit, but there's plenty you're not telling me about that." He jerked his head in the rough direction of the medbay. "And what happens when they wake up? Do you have a plan?"

"A plan?" She said the words as if they were a foreign language. "No, I don't really have a plan; I just go with my gut. I ask questions, try to be aware of clues, and then"—she waved her hands like startled birds—"and then I figure it out. I can't tell you how. It just clicks for me. Unfortunately, since all the witnesses are in a coma or hiding behind a living membrane, there's not much I can do."

"Mallory," he said, his voice low, "why didn't you tell station security what we found in the ossuary?"

Mallory looked surprised. "I did leave that part out, didn't I? It wasn't conscious." She thought for a moment. "I . . . there's no evidence left. Even that blue blood breaks down." She indicated where she had smeared blood on her face after finding Ren.

"But you could have given me and the Gneiss up for questioning. Why?"

She looked at him again with that focused look. "Because I believe you didn't kill him. And I believe you will tell me what you know when I need to know it."

"You don't know me that well," he said, grinning to hide the anxiety in his stomach.

"You showed me how to call security," she said. "You didn't ask me not to tell them; you didn't pretend to help me and then break the system. You trusted me. So I'm trusting you."

He was honestly flustered. "I don't know what to say," he said.

She smiled at him. "You'll figure something out eventually. Besides, I don't trust Osric at all. So I want to be really sure before I tell them anything."

"Do you know what happens when a station's host dies?" he asked. "How the station and the other people around usually react?"

She shrugged. "I don't know much. I just can't believe that there isn't a better candidate on board than Adrian."

"Can we get her another host?" he asked. "There's got to be someone—anyone, really—here who can connect with Eternity better than him."

"Even if it were easy to find another host, I don't know how to find them. What are the proper qualities of a good host? Do they have to be an asshat like Ren, or can anyone connect with her?" She picked up her wax cup and put it down again when she remembered it was empty.

He assumed the questions were rhetorical. "I can't stop thinking about that twelfth survivor. What happened with him? What drug did he have in his system? My theory is someone dosed him. Nothing else makes sense."

She frowned. "That's . . . likely, yeah. But why would you leap to that conclusion before something like accidental overdose?"

He calmly met her eyes. "Because you're sure there's murder happening here. I'm just going on what you've told me."

She nodded slowly. "Things have never been this complicated before. But let's assume there was a fight on the shuttle before they got here. Someone attacked that young guy. Or he attacked someone who turned around and killed him in self-defense. That happens a lot."

"Does it happen a lot with the weapon being a drug overdose?" he asked, his voice incredulous.

Her cheeks reddened. "Well, not in my experience. That's not the most effective weapon to use during a struggle. I wish we could know how the shuttle attack is connected to Ren's death, or at least the timeline of all this crap happening." She waved her hand vaguely.

Xan felt his face grow hot. He picked at the delicate wax on the cup in front of him.

She didn't seem to notice. She rubbed her forehead. "There's something else," she said.

He raised his eyebrows.

"I know someone on the survivor list as well. And this is someone I really don't want to deal with."

"Hang on, you're not back to running, are you?" he demanded.

"I'm so damn tired of this," she said. "I just wanted this to stop. And now it's worse, with several people dead. I hate it."

"I was starting to respect how you handle all of this death and the investigation and everything. It's like you become someone else, but now you're back to sounding like a kid and wanting to run away." The anger rose in his chest, and he took a deep breath to stifle it. "Fine. Go. Find a shuttle to take you far away from your problems. I'll stay behind and figure this mess out. Good luck out there."

She recoiled at this tirade as if she'd been slapped. Then she looked down. "You were starting to respect me?" she asked flatly.

"Yeah," he said. "Back in college you were this woman who knew her own mind and did what she wanted, and I admired the hell out of you. But then there was the Baltimore trip, and that guy died, and then you ran. It's like something broke inside you."

She raised her head. He was worried that she'd be crying, but her eyes were dry, and whatever light came to her when she was in her investigative mode had died.

"Yes, something broke. People died around me. I was accused multiple times. No one wanted to be near me. It takes a toll. I move because I want to avoid murder, yeah, but also I want to see people who don't stiffen up and turn away when they see me because they think someone's going to leap from the bushes and kill them. I liked it here, and even took a chance to be your friend. And now multiple people are dead and you want to blame me for wanting to run?" She sighed and fiddled with the tag on her hoodie that was irritating her neck. "I wasn't planning on ditching you with the mess. It's clear Earth knows you're here, so why don't you want to run? You can come with me."

"Of course you'd say that. I know how to fly *Infinity*."

The hurt hardened on her face, and she sat back in her chair. "Xan, we have a useless Earth ambassador joining with a nigh-omnipotent, omniscient station. The guy can't find his ass with a map, and he's connected to the most powerful sentient anyone here has ever met. Adrian wants us gone. We can either go on our own terms, or on his, but it's clear we're going."

"I'm staying," he said flatly.

The food arrived, including a plate of indescribable meat cooked nearly black, with a brittle bone sticking out of one end. It smelled like the grill after the Fourth of July, when Grandma had gotten drunk, burned dinner, and failed to clean up. The next day Xan and Phineas had been told to clean it up, ruined food and all.

The charred, greasy mess had taken hold of his nostrils and didn't let them go for a few days.

The grilled fruit looked more appetizing, like a dry slice of orange/pineapple. He tried it and found it fine, if not enjoyable, but the sight of the cooked meat killed any hunger that he had. Another plate held chunks of pink meat that resembled undercooked poultry. A few Sundry crawled on the wall, and Mallory looked doubtfully at them and then back at the food.

"I hate that they always watch us," she said.

"They can hear you," he said, and reached over to snag the plate of raw meat. He picked up a piece and smelled it. It smelled clean and a little like seawater. He took a bite off the end. His teeth sank easily into the meat.

He chewed thoughtfully as Mallory watched, her face tinged green. "So you're dropping the argument?"

"I'll let you know," she said. "Depends on whether the Gneiss will help me."

"Stephanie won't help you. She can't. She's stuck here. Some disagreement with her grandfather," he said, taking another piece of the raw stuff. Despite the briny odor, the taste was quite different from fish, somehow imbued with a spicy element that surprised him. He held it in his mouth as the heat grew, and then chewed and swallowed.

"But wasn't she one of the ones who picked you up?"

"Yeah, that's why *Infinity* was on autopilot," he said. "She wasn't allowed to go anywhere but Earth or the station."

Mallory stared at the Sundry thoughtfully. One of them took flight and left the room. "There are so many connections," she muttered. He could see that she was tempted by the challenge even as it scared her.

The Sundry buzzed into the room, surprising them with another couple of plates of food. They were stacked high with the raw meat Xan had just sampled.

The other plates were removed and the new plates deposited in front of them.

"Oh, right," Mallory said, wincing. Then she looked up at the Sundry that crawled along the walls, wings vibrating from time to time. "Those are drones. They listen and summon the waitstaff if they're needed."

"I knew they were spies," Xan said. "But I didn't know they were spies focused on getting you good food."

The drones, as if sensing they were being talked about, twitched their wings and then were still again.

"There's no 'reporting' to the hivemind," Mallory said. "It's all raw data. It's dumped in no matter what it is."

She looked down at the pile of food but didn't move to take any. "Did I ever tell you about my childhood?"

He frowned. This was a different direction than he'd expected. "No. Why—"

"My dad split when I was two, and my mom tried to raise me. But she lost her job, and we had to move in with Uncle Dez, my mom's brother, and his family. Uncle Dez was fine, but my aunt Kathy was a classic matriarch. She loved nothing more than having a perfect family and her perfect house. She took us in because You Do That for Family, although Mom said she didn't want to. Clearly, having a sister-in-law who was a single mom and her kid was not her vision of a perfect family. She really hated Mom but was nice enough to me. Mom died when I was little, and Aunt Kathy and Uncle Dez took custody of me. Aunt Kathy was very controlling. She had an idea of what she wanted in a daughter and told me to call her 'Mother.'" She shuddered, her eyes far away. "It's hard to know your upbringing wasn't normal until you talk to others. She wanted me to go to college locally, I guess so she could keep tabs on me, but I got into UNC on scholarships and rarely went back home. I could breathe when I was away, you know? I went home for holidays and for a funeral when my high school guidance counselor died."

She pursed her lips together and sighed through her nose, then forced herself to go on. "About a year or so ago, my uncle Dez was having his birthday-party-slash-going-away party since they were moving for his retirement. Against my better judgment, I went home. He was happy, joking about their new house in the wilds of the swamps down east. He said he was 'gonna hunt gators!' Soon after the party ended, someone shot him. I—I don't know what happened. I was chatting with him, I went to get a drink, and the next thing I remember I was in the back seat of my own car, curled into a ball, sobbing. Psychiatrists said I'd had a psychotic break."

"Did they accuse you of just up and killing him?" Xan asked, finding it hard to imagine Mallory flipping out and killing someone.

"No, it was a psychotic break in that I lost reality. Witnesses say I ran away, screaming. I've never reacted like that to a murder. When they found me, I told them I was smelling and seeing things that weren't there. I told them I could see my aunt and my cousin were with my uncle's body; they were covering it up in the back-yard. It was like my brain turned off. I was a literal witness; this should have been a solve I could've made in my sleep. But instead I ran away and had a total breakdown. And I had no memory of what happened. I couldn't help with the investigation at all. They said I was too close to the murder. I couldn't"—she paused, flexing her hands open and closed—"grasp what had happened. The cops decided my cousin had done it, and I couldn't find any evidence to the contrary, even though I knew he was innocent. I *knew* it. But they barely listened when I had evidence; they certainly wouldn't listen when I said I had a gut instinct, especially when I was a mess afterward.

"So my uncle was dead, my cousin went to jail, and my aunt canceled the move east to stay home and keep the family house ready for when my cousin got released and, she said, for me to move back in with her because she was so alone. But I couldn't stay." She rubbed her face as if scrubbing away memories.

"Uncle Dez's murder killed my interest in investigation. I only wanted to get away to where I was not known. I couldn't take another murder. But then my neighbor invited me to Billy's party, and you know what happened after that. I was finally able to get away for good."

"I have no idea what this has to do with anything that's happening right now," Xan said.

She finally met his eyes. "Because Aunt Kathy is in the medbay, comatose. And I don't know why she's here, but it can't be a good reason." She put her hands on the table. "Enjoy your breakfast. I've lost my appetite."

She stepped away and looked up to the waiting drones on the ceiling. "Take the cost of the meal out of my next exam's payment," she said, and left the room.

Above Xan, wings shuddered and then stilled again.

13

ON THE IMPORTANCE OF HASTE

WHEN GRANDPA ASCENDED, he lost some language skills. That's what Stephanie's brother had said. Sometimes that happens, he explained.

Stephanie just thought Grandpa was lazy. Ferdinand's aunt had ascended and become a sleek shuttle capable of fitting a crew of ten. And she was still as eloquent as she had always been; she even communicated with the non-Gneiss who needed to be shouted at because they were too simple to understand Gneiss vibrations. In fact, Ferdinand had dreaded long trips using her because she insisted on reciting poetry the whole time.

Grandpa just thrummed low threats at her.

Don't.

You left me no choice, she replied.

It is blasphemous. It is anathema.

It is my only option since you exiled me to this station. What did he think he was going to do about it? Once he'd trapped her on the station and made his deal with Ren to not allow Stephanie to leave, he had slammed her cell door shut. But he couldn't control her actions within the station.

With the humans sufficiently distracted by their own dead and dying visitors, Stephanie returned to the ossuary to collect the mess that was Ren's body.

She had lied to Mallory. It had been easy. While it was true that Gurudevs did break down fast after their deaths, if their brains were developed enough (usually by contact with a superior symbiont), they stayed around longer after the body had fallen to base components. She knew Ren would leave behind a watery mess of a body, the only recognizable evidence being a small organ no bigger than the tip of her finger. And that was enough.

Except the ossuary was strangely quiet. It was usually quiet, but there were often a few people having hushed discussions, reliving the old days, planning what they would do when they woke up and left the ossuary. But no one spoke.

She glanced around the ossuary, and nothing seemed amiss in the low light. She did have the feeling that all eyes were on her, and she didn't appreciate the audience.

Stephanie walked over to the shuttle where she had stashed Ren's body. It wasn't there.

Only blood streaks marked where he had been lying atop the sleeping shuttle.

Where is it? she demanded of the residents. No one answered.

Ferdinand, Tina, what's happening?

There are a lot of things happening. What specifically do you mean? Ferdinand responded.

Nothing. Nothing's happening. How are you? Tina said from the same direction as Ferdinand.

Tina. What did you do?

Her idiot friend didn't answer. Stephanie swore to herself. She'd have to find them. It felt like everyone knew about this conspiracy against her.

She needed that body.

Tina is the smart one.

Shut UP, Grandpa.

She knows what you did.

Tina doesn't know what day it is.

Hey! Tina's distinct vibration finally piped up, louder than before, as Stephanie had expected. She was so easy to bait.

Where are you, Tina?

Pause. *Ferdinand's.*

Stephanie relaxed a fraction. It was salvageable. Ferdinand was the sensible one.

His comforting rumble came through. *Tina's right, Stephanie. This is a bad idea.*

Stephanie swore, and began to hurry.

STEPHANIE HAD HAD to explain Gneiss etiquette to Mallory. In discussing words and their societal meanings, the humans learned that impatience was rude in Gneiss culture. For patient, sentient beings so long-lived, who could survive being pulverized so long as they had their symbiont to eventually help put them back together, the need to hurry somewhere was patently offensive.

"So telling you to hurry is equivalent to telling a human to fuck off," Mallory had ventured. "And telling you to be patient is insulting and redundant."

"That sounds correct, yes," Stephanie said.

Gneiss bodies were not designed for quick movement, not in humanoid form, anyway. Stephanie's steps boomed through the hallways as she walked as fast as she could to Ferdinand's. The longer she took, the bigger the chance of someone stopping her.

She walked into Ferdinand's bar and looked around impatiently. Tina sat at the bar with a cloth sack at her feet. Blue blood had soaked through in a few spots.

Ferdinand stood behind the bar, leaning in close to talk to

Tina. Very few other people were in the bar, but they all turned when Stephanie stomped toward her friends.

You had no right, she said.

It didn't belong to you, Tina said archly.

Stephanie. Why are you doing this? Ferdinand asked calmly. And then, before she could answer, he amended, *I mean, why do you think this will get you what you want?*

Because I will be free! They don't trust me and I will be here until the station dies at this rate.

I trust you, Tina said.

Stephanie stared at her. She thought hard for some time while the others waited. *But I tell you what I think of you on a regular basis. I don't think you're very smart. And your cheerfulness is irritating.*

You're stating facts. That's how I know I can trust you. Betrayal and murder and regicide are sneaky actions. You're not sneaky at all. Tina sounded as if she had thought about this and was firmly satisfied with her logic.

So you think the only people who would murder you are the kind of people who will lie to you for favor? Ferdinand asked.

Yes.

He looked at Stephanie. *She won't last a hundred years on the throne.*

Her need was immediate, but she caught Ferdinand's plea in a subtle vibration. *Please help. She looks up to you.*

Tina. Regarding me and my possible murderous intentions toward you, you're not wrong. I have no ambitions for your position. And while I don't particularly enjoy your company, I don't want to kill you. And I appreciate your trust when my own family doesn't believe me. But please promise us that you will pay attention when someone is rude to your face. Because those kinds of people will absolutely kill you if they have designs on the throne. And that would make Ferdinand sad.

Now about that sack.

You're hurrying, Ferdinand said coldly.

An opportunity appeared. I took it, Stephanie countered. *I don't think you two understand that I am trapped here. The station agreed to my grandfather's rules, so I'm stuck here. Infinity wouldn't let me off the ship on Earth. Why won't you see how serious this is?*

Tina shrugged. *Old people either change their minds eventually or they forget the rules they made. We figured you'd just wait him out.*

The station could be falling apart around us, and I know my grandfather would rather take Tina to safety than me. Do you still think waiting is a good idea?

You had these plans long before yesterday, Ferdinand said. *You're letting emotions rule your decisions. You've spent too much time with the humans.*

They have nothing to do with this, Stephanie said.

Don't they? I thought the female was a catalyst for violence, Tina said, frowning.

But it has nothing to do with me. She doesn't affect non-humans. Now give it back.

Too many of our people know what you did. No doubt the Sundry already know. Station security will be interested in it, too. How were you planning on hiding this? Ferdinand asked.

Stephanie slumped. She sat on the stool next to Tina. *Are you going to report me?*

I need to know why you did it, he said.

Stephanie didn't like needing people. She didn't like trusting people. That might be why she had connected so well with the human Xan, who was also alone in the galaxy. He relied on his own resources. It was out of necessity instead of choice, but he seemed used to alone time.

She ground her jaw more, enjoying the taste of her own body as she pulverized another layer of her teeth. *I'm not in a hurry. I'm opportunistic.*

But why now? Tina asked. For once she didn't look stupid; she looked almost crafty as she asked her question.

I feel like it's time. You don't. That's your decision. But it's right for me. I need my freedom, and I can't be around my grandfather if he is convinced I'm going to overthrow the throne.

Ferdinand looked at her and then looked at Tina. They couldn't communicate even sub-vocally without her catching on, but they still managed to come to a decision together.

Let's go to the ossuary, Ferdinand said.

You're coming with me? Stephanie asked in surprise.

You're going to need help. Or were you planning on doing it alone? Tina asked.

It had been a detail that Stephanie hadn't let herself think about. She guessed she would have asked Xan for help when it came down to it, but her own people were a better choice.

On the way back to the ossuary, Tina looked down at her. *If your grandfather was holding you here to keep me safe from you, why did he allow us to hang out together?*

Stephanie laughed aloud, and it echoed through the hall. *He can only control me so much, and he can't control you at all. He was so mad when you got here and we made friends. And he literally worried himself into a damaged engine when we went to Earth together.*

Tina laughed. *You called me a friend!*

I suppose you are one, now, Stephanie allowed. *But we should hurry.*

And Grandfather stayed silent.

14

RUNS IN THE FAMILY

LOVELY BROWN'S HANGOVER was epic. It drove around her head like teenagers on a joyride, ramming into her skull and blowing the horn. Her stomach roiled, empty except for the acid that boiled away her insides. This hangover rated somewhere among the top ten she'd ever had.

The dreams had been horrific. Matti on the floor, holding up her hands in fear, and Lovely leaping forward, and then the pain.

Still, the dreams and hangover failed to distract her from the other pain. The white bandage that covered her throbbing left hand up to the wrist contrasted with her dark skin.

The doorbell rang, and Lovely groaned. What asshole would come by her place at nine on a Monday? Didn't they know she'd be at work?

(She wasn't at work. But people should assume she was.)

She rolled out of bed and struggled against a head rush as she got vertical.

After exactly twenty seconds, the bell rang again. "Fuck me, they won't take a hint," Lovely said, pushing the heel of her right palm—her good hand—into her forehead. It didn't relieve the pain, but the pain did get worse when she stopped doing it. That made no logical sense. She returned the hand to her head to hold it on straight.

Through the bedroom door, cradling her hurt left hand to her chest. Through the hall, rubbing her forehead. Through the kitchen, pausing to wince at the mess. Overturned and mostly empty bottles of wine had dribbled drops of red regret on the counter. This would be murder to clean, and her visitor wouldn't help things.

If her bedroom door lurked, the outside door loomed. Another twenty seconds had gone by, and now it was time for the firm knocking.

Rap rap rap.

"As if I didn't hear you," she grumbled. Then she sighed and opened the door. "What the hell—" The protest died on her lips and for a moment's shock she forgot even her hangover.

A tiny lady stood there looking up at her. She had light brown skin, tight steel-gray curls framing a firm face, lines etched around her dark brown eyes that told everyone she clearly tolerated no bullshit, a brown overcoat buttoned up to her chin, and hands that clasped a black purse in front of her. A good six inches shorter than Lovely, she looked up at her and crossed her arms. "This is the welcome I get?"

"Gran! When did you—" Lovely fell on the old woman's neck as if it were a life preserver. Her tears surprised her.

"This morning," Gran said, patting her almost professionally. "And I wanted to come straight here to check on you. I heard about that," she said, pointing to the injured hand. "I didn't think I'd find you horribly hungover, but I can't blame you."

"I'm not—" Lovely said, and then stopped when Gran held her at arm's length and silenced her with a stern look. "Fine, yeah, you're right." She felt indignant, even though she couldn't argue at all.

"Are you going to let me in, or continue feeling sorry for your-self while making me stand out in the elements?"

Lovely squinted at the horrible sunlight. "It's a beautiful day, Gran."

"Sunshine is an element. I don't want skin cancer," Gran said, and pushed past Lovely to get inside.

Lovely sighed, but a smile pulled at her mouth for the first time in days. "Come on in, Gran."

MRS. ELIZABETH BROWN unbuttoned her coat and put it and her purse carefully onto a kitchen chair. She placed her hands on her hips and surveyed the mess. "How much did you drink?"

"Half a bottle," Lovely said.

"Don't lie, Lovely."

"Fine. Two bottles. Maybe three. It's hard to count after the first."

"Did you drink alone? Did you black out?"

"Jesus, Gran, this isn't an AA meeting. I had friends over." Before she could ask, Lovely added hastily, "Nadia and Bob. We watched TV and I watched them play video games. We drank a lot of wine. They called cabs and went home."

Gran unearthed a few mugs from the sink and started to hand-wash them.

"Gran, don't clean up," she said weakly, but sat down in the empty kitchen chair, defeated. Gran would do what she wanted. She couldn't fight her on a good day, much less struggling through a hangover.

"For bad injuries, I allow two weeks to wallow," she said, her back to Lovely. "From what I understand, you've already used a few days. You've got, what, another week and a half of healing and then you start physical therapy? You can use that for moping as well. You will need to be over it by the time you see your physical therapist."

"Don't patronize me, Gran," Lovely said, putting her head in her hand. "Tell me about you. I didn't expect, well, to see you for a while."

"I'm not patronizing," Gran said. "I'm serious. When your grandfather would get rejected or have a bad show, we'd take a bottle of whiskey and sit on the couch together and he would moan that his career was over, he was always terrible, and he would never amount to anything. The next day, after our hangovers cleared, he'd start again. The few times he didn't take those nights to wallow, it took him a lot longer to get over things. So I allowed it. But no more than one night."

This was news to Lovely. "I never knew Grandpa had trouble getting started."

"All creative types do," Gran said, putting water into a kettle and rummaging around the pantry. "Every comic starts in a small club, gets heckled and booed, has the worst nights. Just like you and your auditions. Except people are less likely to outright heckle a violinist," she amended.

Lovely thought about all the comedy shows her grandfather had been in, the places he'd headlined, the fame he'd achieved. Her gran had once whispered to her that Grandpa being a famous comedian had led to her father being an accountant, because there were few ways a kid could rebel when Dad was a comedy legend and was famous for the "Six-Headed Shaggy Dog Story," not to mention turning his own family's bad press and hardship into comedy bits.

"Anyway, just be smart, and always hydrate before bed," Gran said. "I don't want to lose you to alcohol poisoning. You're all I got left." She set up the French press coffee maker and poured the hot water in. She cast an appraising eye around the kitchen. "And you may want to rethink this filthy pit."

"You wanted me to wallow; then you say I shouldn't live in a pit," Lovely said, looking down at the table. "Which is it?"

A glass of water appeared in front of her, followed by two brown pills. "Take that. See if you can keep it down. If you can, I'll share some of my coffee with you."

Lovely muttered a thanks and swallowed the pills, closing her eyes and willing her stomach to accept them without incident.

"It looks like you'll want to skip breakfast," Grandma said. "So in that time, why don't you take a shower and then I'll braid your hair?"

Christ, I'm not seven anymore. "No, I can do my own—" She bit down on her bottom lip and looked at her bandaged hand. No, she couldn't.

Grandma put a tiny hand, strong and steadying, on her shoulder. "Indulge an old lady," she said. "I stopped doing your aunt Ava's hair when she was seventeen. And your mama always did yours."

Mama and Grandma had been polite, but there had been little love lost there. Her mother never allowed Lovely to spend the night at her grandparents' house, and never let Gran do Lovely's hair. She was highly irritated that Lovely had grown close to Gran despite her passive efforts to keep them apart. Gran had never pressed the issue, but she had always been there when Lovely needed her.

Lovely had been surprised, later, when the cancer and its treatments had taken most of Mama's strength and she had asked to see Gran alone. The pastor was coming to visit her, and she wanted to be presentable. Gran had gone into her bedroom and had stayed there for an hour, with Lovely and Daddy swapping nervous glances.

When the pastor had arrived, Gran had opened the bedroom door, her eyes wet and the typical firmness to her lips. The rest of the family had gone in for the visit, and Mama lay there, smiling, with what hair she had in braids, and if she had some shiny parts of her scalp showing through, then no one mentioned it. Gran had applied a bit of makeup around her eyes, and they looked bright and shining.

"You can face anything with your hair done and your eyes on," Gran had said, carefully touching up the mascara on Mama's remaining lashes. She sat back and surveyed her work. Mama was still too thin, and her skin was ashy. Grandma had not braided away the cancer, but she had made the day a little more bearable.

"Not perfect, but close enough," she'd said, and Mama had laughed.

Mama had made a full recovery, but after that, she and Gran had a different relationship. No one would be crass enough to talk about how the cancer helped heal whatever rift was between them, but they all thought it.

But now her parents were overseas with Dad's job. She'd told them about her injury but had downplayed its severity.

And now Gran implied that the hairstyling was for her own benefit, not Lovely's. The old woman seemed to always know what Lovely needed, even when Lovely wanted to rebel against Gran's anchoring force. She rose from the table and walked to the bathroom, only to return briefly to accept the plastic bag Gran held out to her. "Keep your bandages dry," Gran said.

"Yes, ma'am."

SHE THOUGHT SHE was going to get away with not talking about it, but when she sat down in her robe for Gran to braid her hair, Gran dropped a newspaper—an honest to God paper newspaper— in her lap.

"So what are you going to tell me about that?" she asked.

The headline read, "Police Still Hunt Macy's Heroic Vigilante Bride," and the story used an awful lot of words to describe the very little bit they knew about the robbery at the local Macy's.

Robbers had terrorized the place, killed a few cashiers, and were hunting the customers when a mysterious woman in a bridal gown took the robbers down and then escaped before the police could arrive.

"I don't know anything—" she said, but Gran yanked on her hair firmly, shutting her up.

"Don't bullshit me, Lovely Grace. I may be old, but I can put together story pieces. You didn't get that"—she gestured to Lovely's wrapped hand—"by cutting avocados."

"The doctor in the ER bought the avocado story," Lovely grumbled. "I didn't want to go into the whole Macy's story. And you're not going to tell me why you're here?"

She got another yank for her attempts at deflection. It made her eyes water as her hangover attacked her from the inside at the same time.

"I'll tell you my story if you will tell me yours," Gran said.

"Fine," Lovely said. "I was going out after rehearsal with a girlfriend."

"Nadia?"

"Matti, the first violin," Lovely corrected. "We were working on the Ben Franklin 'Open Strings' quartetto after rehearsal, and then she wanted to try on some bridal gowns at Macy's because of some sale. She's insecure and I'm pretty sure she shouldn't be marrying this guy, but I didn't say that. She asked me to try on dresses with her so she wouldn't be so alone. I think she wanted some kind of girl bonding." Lovely rolled her eyes, wondering what would have happened if she had been able to take care of the problem in her street clothes.

"We were both in gowns when the gunshots started."

"Did you hide, or run out to save the day?" Gran asked, disapproval in her voice.

"Come on, Gran, we hid," Lovely protested. "Despite what you read in the news, I don't have a death wish. But a gunman came into the dressing room and started kicking in all the doors. I climbed up on the partition between my stall and Matti's and told her to be quiet, and stayed where the stall door would hide me. When he kicked in the door and pointed the gun at her, I shoved it closed and knocked him backward, and then I went out and disarmed him. Tied him up with the veil."

"You make it sound so easy," Gran said.

"Well, I was taught by the best," Lovely said dryly.

"What about your friend Matti?"

"I told her to take the gun and lock herself in the dressing room again. She was close to losing it. The others came looking for the first guy, and I—stopped them. The only thing was, the last one had a knife and I was expecting a gun. I got sloppy, and he got a good one in." She held up her bandaged hand.

"And then?"

"We dumped the dresses in a trash can and Matti and I managed to get dressed before the cops got there. We told them the vigilante had run off."

"Why didn't you tell them what happened?" Her voice was firm as if she knew the answer but wanted Lovely to say it out loud.

"Because one of the gunmen died of a broken neck," she said flatly.

"How?"

Lovely's face grew warm. "You know how."

"They would soon find out that you weren't the first person in your family to kill someone in self-defense," Gran said. "But the police didn't assume it was you?"

"They assumed the vigilante had ditched the dress and run off during the chaos. And the remaining gunmen didn't identify me; they were distracted and could only remember the dress . . . I actually think the cops suspected Matti at first, but they decided she was too short."

"How did you explain your hand?" she asked.

"I told them I didn't remember, that it was all a blur, but he attacked and I tried to hold him back and got stabbed or something," she said, wincing. "He had stabbed a few people so he couldn't identify me that way."

"And how is the hand?"

Lovely stayed silent.

"Lovely?"

A tear rolled down her cheek. She bent her head. "Tendon's severed. Pinky is gone. They did what they could."

Gran was done with the braiding. "All right. We'll talk about that later. So, ask your questions."

"Why are you here?" she asked, after taking a moment to compose herself.

"I finally got some free time and wanted to see my granddaughter," Gran said. "I figured I'd make it a surprise." She came around the table and sat down, cupping her coffee mug in both hands.

"No kidding," Lovely said. "I didn't think I'd see you for several more months."

"I got off for good behavior," Gran said, and winked. She took an empty mug and poured coffee into it, sliding it across to Lovely.

"Well, I'm glad you got me up; I just remembered I have to see my doctor today," Lovely said, holding up her injured hand and grimacing.

"Should I ask about your musical future now or later?" Gran asked softly.

"Later." Lovely blinked the threatening tears away. She had called the conductor on Saturday but hadn't reported in since then. She was pretty sure she'd lose her position, but there wasn't much she could do about it until she talked to the doctor.

The ironic thing was that she could still work on at least one song with her injured hand. She and Matti had agreed to join a quartet that played novelty music for a museum. Currently they were working on music that Ben Franklin had written for three

violins and a cello. The strange thing about it was that each instrument was tuned so that the musicians could play using only open
strings. One of the few songs in existence that she wouldn't need
her left hand for, except to hold the violin steady. You couldn't
even say that about "Mary Had a Little Lamb." So she didn't have
to quit music just yet.

It was nice knowing that there was one piece of music she
could still play, and that kept her from drowning in utter despair,
but she couldn't play that one piece forever.

"I'll go with you to the doctor," Gran said. "I want to make sure
you ask the right questions."

"No, you don't need to—" Her protest died at Gran's stern look.
"I'm not a kid anymore, Gran," she said weakly.

"No, but strangely I am still a grandmother even when you
grow up, and I still worry. And I don't have anywhere else to be.

"I'm staying with you for a bit, by the way. I hope you don't
mind," she added in an offhand manner.

Lovely choked in surprise but wiped her mouth and nodded.
If there was anything Gran had taught her, it was that you stand
up for the people you love. If Gran needed a place to stay while
she was in town, she'd have it. "I'll need to clean up," she said.
"You can have my bed."

"I won't be any trouble. And it looks like you'll need some help
while you recuperate," Gran said. "And if—who were they, Nadia
and Bob? If they want to come over I can read or crochet in another room. I won't harsh your young person's vibe."

Lovely laughed out loud at her gran's obvious attempts at retro
current slang. "Don't worry about it."

THE ORTHOPEDIST WHO'D operated on her in the ER wasn't
the same one she was following up with. This guy looked like a
bartender from a sports bar: white, stocky, with short brown hair,

and an easy smile that felt insincere as all get-out, as Gran would say. Lovely had disliked him on sight, but she pretty much hated everyone through her hangover-tinted glasses.

He greeted them with the boisterous energy of doctors who didn't expect an honest answer when they asked, "How are you?"

"I'm Dr. Waites," he said, sticking out his right hand. "You're Lovely Brown?" He smirked. "That's a 'lovely' name."

Lovely shook his hand and smiled mildly in response to the comment nearly everyone in the world thought was original when they met her. "Yeah. This is my gran, Mrs. Elizabeth Brown."

"Ms. Brown," he said, shaking Gran's hand.

Lovely winced inwardly. This guy wasn't scoring any points with Gran already.

"Mrs.," Grandma said firmly, but the doctor was already absorbed in Lovely's file. He squinted as he paged through her history.

"Says Dr. Howard operated on you after the injury; she's a good one. You got lucky she was on call. How did you manage this, again?" he asked.

"Slicing an avocado," Lovely said woodenly. She barely remembered the trip to the ER or the doctor, hidden behind her mask, who soothed her while she operated on Lovely's hand.

"You severed your pinky while cutting an avocado?"

"Yeah. I have really good kitchen knives."

Gran smiled slightly at the lie, but the doctor didn't even register it. He motioned for her to show him her left hand.

He may have looked like a bro hitting a kegger, but his hands were those of a professional, at least. He carefully unwrapped her bandages and gently inspected the laceration in the center of her hand. Lovely didn't want to look but knew she had to. The ugly cut across her palm had gone deep. The finger had been severed at the first joint. The stitches were tiny, tight, and precise, but she wondered if she'd ever regain full use of her remaining fingers.

"You cut a rather important tendon there," he said. "The notes here said it was severed completely. With these injuries, you'll be lucky if you regain much strength in your remaining fingers. I'll see you in a week. In the meantime, keep the bandages on, keep them dry, and change them every day," he said. "Can you wiggle your fingers for me?"

She commanded her fingers to wiggle, but the middle and ring fingers barely twitched.

"Some of the mobility and strength could come back," he said dubiously. "With proper PT."

"'Could'?" Gran demanded.

"It's a possibility," he said. "But it's not a probability."

Lovely grimaced. This wasn't news.

"Good thing it wasn't your dominant hand, right?" he added, grinning. He looked like he had introduced her to a new craft beer and was waiting to hear her opinion on it.

"Will she play the violin again?" Gran asked.

Dr. Waites laughed. Lovely and Gran stared at him blankly. This asshole clearly hadn't read her patient file.

He sobered when he registered their faces. "Oh, you're serious. You play the violin? I guess this wasn't a workplace injury, huh?" His hopeful grin faded fast, and he continued, "Moving forward, you can go through physical therapy, but I don't think the chances are good. You're right-handed, so maybe you can learn to switch hands?"

"You don't switch hands—" Lovely began, but Gran was already up.

Gran had begun to gather her things after the doctor said "workplace injury." She had been holding both of their belongings, and she handed Lovely her hoodie and said, "All right, thank you, doctor, we're done here."

Dr. Waites stood too, looking baffled. "I'm going to want to see you in a follow-up, and then we'll prescribe some physical therapy and get you playing again."

Gran gave him a cold look. "We'll take your suggestions into consideration," she said, and Lovely followed her out.

Gran seethed, a tiny force of nature that everyone stepped around when they saw her coming. She walked past the checkout desk without a word.

"Gran, I need to make a follow-up appointment," Lovely said.

"Not here you don't," Gran said over her shoulder, and kept walking.

When they reached the sidewalk, Lovely finally grabbed Gran's shoulder with her good hand. "Gran, he's supposed to be the best hand doctor in town."

"Either this is a shitty town, or those online ratings are useless," Gran said. "A good hand doctor would know what their patients did for a living. A good hand doctor would understand a musician's needs, and would understand you can't just switch hands on an instrument. Any good doctor would have read your file and known what you had done to get the injury in the first place!"

That had been fair. Lovely had just been bristling at his patronizing attitude, but Gran had a point. Who was this asshole?

"The avocado story was good," she said. "I don't think anyone is going to look too deeply into that. But that doesn't fix you."

"No, it doesn't," she said. She deflated a bit. "Gran?"

"What is it, honey?"

"Do you really think it runs in the family?"

"Does what run in the family?" Gran asked, unflinching.

"Violence."

Gran leaned in, looking straight into Lovely's eyes, and placed her hands on Lovely's shoulders. "Lovely, do folks call a bear violent when she kills a man threatening her cubs? Or do they call her a bear?"

"So I'm an animal?"

"No." Gran sighed. "All right, if a man had killed someone while defending a weaker friend, would they call him violent?"

"No. He'd be a hero."

"Right. Call it instinct, or heroism, or violence. Our family doesn't take any shit, and that's what it boils down to. You'd have better luck resisting the tide than sitting calmly and letting someone walk all over you."

15

OLD FRIENDS IN AWKWARD PLACES

XAN CONTINUED EATING the odd Sundry meat, chewing thoughtfully. There was no need to hurry yet; the medbay had sent no update for the humans. Mallory had rage-quit after her "my poor childhood" story.

To Xan, it sounded like things had been rough and then she'd been raised by people who weren't awful. That didn't make her unique. Everyone wanted nurturing parents, but no one guaranteed them. If she was cared for, fed, and not abused, she was better off than a lot of kids.

Except for her uncle's murder, and her aunt coming all the way out to Eternity to see her. He had to admit that was odd. He should probably tell her that.

"You know who people are when you see them stressed, Xanny," Grandma said after she had smacked him and he had sworn loudly. "Mayor Horace will be as smiley as all get-out when you see him downtown sitting in his convertible. But if a waitress spills coffee in his lap, you will hear what he really thinks of young women. They're all stupid cunts, you know. And you are a foul-mouthed little shit."

Xan wondered how someone could be so unaware of her own

personality. This language was even more crass than her usual, but she was calling him foul-mouthed.

"There are the people who will take charge and help during times of crisis. There are people who will lash out and deal out blame like it was a poker game. Then there are people who will help, and maybe even be good at it, but they will never let you forget the hardships they faced and the fact that it was them that did it."

Mallory seemed like the third kind of person. The only orphan in the world. The only one raised by a questionable relative. She hadn't had an easy life, but shit, had anyone?

Part of his brain said he was being unfair, that she had seen more death than most regular folk. That had to take a toll. The army had sure as shit taken a toll on him.

The memory bubbled up, the one that he had tried to trap along with his medals in the dusty box in his grandmother's attic. Witnessing death was not the only way the army was stressful; the weight of secrets was even heavier.

At Fort Bowser, he was working about sixty hours a week, between training new recruits and researching all of the classified information on what humans knew about alien life. Despite his promotion, he was expected to do everything his commanding officers demanded of him, and delegate nothing. Even if he trusted the men and women under him, his superiors did not. Thus, he found himself delivering a thick folder to Lieutenant Colonel Nick Torres's office. "Requisition forms" was what they told him to write on the encasing envelope.

They were technically requisition forms, but they didn't fit into any unclassified system. His superior officer, Rodriguez, was a fan of paper notes, handed from one trustworthy person to another, read, and then shredded. "Paper can't be hacked," he said.

Xan didn't tell his boss that someone could easily shoot him and take the files off his bleeding body, and even forge a name on the clipboard he carried to prove receipt, but he had to admit the chances of that happening on the base were pretty unlikely.

The lieutenant colonel's assistant was away from their computer when Xan entered the exterior office, so he sat down in a vacant visitor's chair to wait. It wasn't necessarily his fault that he could clearly hear the argument happening on the other side of the interior office door. He normally would have have dropped the envelope off and left before he overheard something, but those forms had to be hand delivered, so he waited.

He couldn't change the fact that the argument was loud, beginning with a woman's voice, angry and firm, one he didn't recognize, but he was familiar with her Texas drawl. "I want the record to show my sincere protest regarding project God's Breath. We have the opportunity to place ourselves among other races in the galaxy. We have the opportunity to try to bargain for technology that we can't begin to understand! And y'all want to fuck it up with dick measuring."

"Yes, Madam Secretary, there are benefits to receive from working with the aliens," came a man's deep voice. "But we also don't know what these races have in store for us. If we were in a wartime situation, they would wipe our planet out of the sky without a second thought. Our current weaponry cannot defend us, should it come to that. It's common sense that we develop a viable weapon, if only to protect ourselves." This was Lieutenant Colonel Torres. Xan hadn't met the man personally but had seen him talking to Rodriguez. Torres often met with visiting government VIPs.

Like the woman he was sparring with currently. Xan tried to remember who among the president's cabinet was a Texan. His mind was a blank.

"So how did you test this weapon, if it was used simply to 'protect ourselves'? Did you test it on humans? Animals? Or are we lying when we tell alien governments that we don't know where their missing citizens are? By developing the weapon, are you putting us in exactly the position where we will need it?"

"Testing is done, and the weapon works, Madam Secretary. You can take that information back to the president. It was created on his directive, after all."

"He will need to know what exactly it does, and how many sentients we tested on. If he's going to lie to the alien governments, he needs to know the lies he's telling," the secretary said, not moving an inch.

"It doesn't even harm the aliens physically," Torres said. "It *neutralizes* them."

"I'm not as young as I look, Lieutenant Colonel," the secretary said coldly. "I know what 'neutralize' means."

"Believe it or not, I don't mean 'killed'; our method is much more humane," Torres said.

Xan shifted in his chair. His superiors had not told him how his alien subjects had died, and he had never asked. He had taken the bodies and, as he had done in combat, clinically described their injuries in detail, collected and logged whatever personal effects they'd had, and noted any anomalies (taking the little he knew about alien bodies into account). Then the corpses had been packed on ice and sent to the scientists.

His superiors had told him that he was a vital part of the chain, even though he was not a medical examiner. Considering what he learned about aliens later aboard Eternity, he concluded that he'd been about as vital as cannon fodder: he had been an expendable part of the chain. They couldn't have a valuable scientist studying an alien who might not be one hundred percent dead, so they brought in a quartermaster.

Torres continued, "In the known universe, humans are the only sentient species that doesn't regularly form a symbiotic relationship with another sentient being. The alien races pity us for this. This is why they don't respect us; they see us as half beings.

"I see our individuality as a strength and their dependence on another as a crutch," he continued, a signature "address the troops" strength coming into his voice.

"No one is listening; you can shelve the bullshit patriotism," the woman said.

There was a pause, and then the man's voice resumed, a little irritated. "To us, every hostile alien counts as two minds. If it ever comes to war, we will always be outnumbered. Having an effective weapon levels the playing field."

"And endangers our peace efforts greatly," the secretary said. "If they ever discover we're working on God's Breath, all of our diplomatic gestures will be seen to have been made in bad faith."

Xan's hands tightened on the sweaty envelope. They weren't *working* on God's Breath. It had cleared the latest testing period. They were done. He was finally done with the classified examinations, as far as he knew.

"If our peace efforts are genuinely successful, then we won't need to use the weapon," the lieutenant colonel said calmly.

"Despite how experiments are intended, no weapon in history has been developed and used only for defense. How many science experiments have been weaponized?"

"If we are devolving into rhetorical arguments, Madam Secretary, I don't have time for this. Please deliver my report to the president, and you can bring up your arguments with him. I was merely following orders."

"Nuremberg is the coward's defense," she said, disdain dripping from her voice.

Xan felt a cold sweat break out on the back of his neck. He had wondered how the alien subjects had separated from their symbionts. He had been instructed to include symbionts as "personal effects," but he wasn't stupid.

Upon death, the Phantasmagore would shed their symbiont; its small body, a hooklike anchor that embedded itself in the spinal cord and surrounded itself with scar tissue, would shrivel and release, and then the vine that would aid the host in toughening its skin, as well as giving it the ability to camouflage, would also release.

Gurudevs, who were mentally connected to another being, would rapidly break down into sludge. He'd learned how long his window of opportunity would be when he received a dead body. When he was close to the end of the window, he would freeze the body to preserve it.

The Gneiss had been impossible to separate. They'd shattered the giants into pebbles and dust, but no one could find a symbiont. They knew the Gneiss had symbiotic relationships, but they didn't have enough data to determine anything about them. A few scientists were floating the idea of the connection being mostly mental and their symbiont being still alive somewhere else, but they had no proof yet.

The scientists had not yet studied anything larger than a Gneiss; they were desperate to study a space station or sentient ship. Xan suspected they would love to autopsy such a massive being, but they hadn't figured out how to capture something that big.

If the aliens found out about this research . . . The secretary was right. If they were trying to set the president's worries to rest, then they were giving him incorrect information, and the secretary likely knew it. Torres was downplaying the strength of the weapon, and humans could suffer because of it.

The president's biggest challenger was taking a more caveman-like approach to the aliens, using "little green men" rhetoric during his speeches to drive fear into the people. He argued that aliens thought they were better than humans, better than *Americans*, and they needed to be stopped. The lieutenant colonel was probably biding his time until he had a commander in chief who would approve these experiments.

Even though most alien visitations had been benign pleasure

visits, many humans still feared *War of the Worlds* scenarios. Most of the legitimate reported problems with alien visitors stemmed from cultural misunderstandings, which happened between humans much more often than between humans and aliens.

Unless they were obviously injured, Xan couldn't tell what had killed the aliens he examined, but this sounded like some bioweapon bullshit right here.

Xan left the office and waited in the hallway. He didn't want to hear any more. He listened closely for the interior door to open, and then got ready when footsteps neared. When the furious secretary opened the door to storm out, she collided with Xan hard.

He stumbled back and dropped his envelope. "Oh, Lord, sorry, ma'am," he stammered, dropping to his knees and picking up the envelope and clipboard.

She had light brown skin and was quite short, with long graying dark hair hanging in soft waves. She was on the slightly soft side of middle age, her eyes full of the "I'm done giving a shit" energy. Then he recognized her: Secretary of the Interior Manda Dull Knife Flying, former governor of Texas. She rubbed at her forehead, where she had run into his collarbone.

"Are you all right there, soldier?" she asked him.

He stared at her, thrown off. "Am I all right?" he asked, rising to his feet, where he towered over her. "I should be asking, Are *you* all right, ma'am?"

"Fine, just hit my head," she said, distracted. She smiled at him, giving him her full politician's attention. "I've had worse." Her charisma was even stronger in person than it was on television.

"Let me see that bump," he said. He took her head in his hands and made to look at her forehead. He leaned in close. "He's lying to you. The weapon kills," he whispered, then let her go, saying, "Looks like you might get a goose egg, you should drop by the clinic and get some ice."

To her credit, she didn't react beyond her eyes widening

slightly. She rubbed her forehead again. "I'm not sure where that is, soldier."

"Hang on a second and I'll show you," he said with a nod. "I need to deliver something into the lieutenant colonel's hands." He walked into the office and left her in the hall. Torres was in the interior office with the door open. He spoke urgently into his cell phone, and motioned Xan inside.

"Hang on a second," he said into his phone. "I'm glad you're late. I would hate it if you'd delivered these while that harpy was still in here," he muttered, taking the envelope. He signed the receipt on the clipboard Xan held out to him. "Dismissed."

"Sir, I bumped into your guest in the hall and she hit her head. I'm going to take her to the clinic for some ice."

"Good," he said, waving him off and returning to his phone.

Xan wasn't sure if he meant it was good she bumped her head or good that he was taking her to the clinic, but at least he now had a plausible reason to be seen with the secretary.

TURNS OUT HE didn't have very much to give her. She said in order to act on the information, she needed more. She needed the details of the weapon and any plans the army had for further action.

Xan started keeping notes of his autopsies in his copy of *Slaughterhouse-Five*, writing in a code that he and his brother had played with when they were kids. He exchanged a few bland letters with Secretary Dull Knife Flying and learned he was to drop his data off in Billy's house during his birthday party, where there would be too much chaos to notice. He wrote the key to the code on the inside of the wrapping paper.

He didn't know if Billy was the intended drop recipient, but it seemed unlikely. He guessed that they counted on him receiving the book and dropping it, uninterested, where the target could pick it up. That wasn't Xan's problem, regardless. There was a third piece of information that was supposed to be dropped. He didn't know what, or where, or who, and that was probably for the best.

In his solitary weeks away from Earth, he realized that he'd been the target of the knife at the party. He'd known too much or was being punished for leaking info to the secretary. Someone had slipped a sedative into his beer, intending on making him slow and easy to kill in the dark, but had underestimated him badly. Billy had paid for it.

And in the chaos, Xan had left the party—and the planet— with the information about the weapon in his pocket.

THE SHORT-TERM PLAN for the weapon was to see how they could separate symbiotic pairs. The intention was that the drug should weaken the connection, but more often than not, it killed one or both of the pair.

The long-term plan was to see how a drug would work with some of the more fantastic relationships in the galaxy; namely, aliens who bonded with sentient ships and space stations. If humans could somehow get aboard the space station Eternity and try to separate the host from the station, that would be a test worth trying. If humans could somehow take over the station, it would catapult them into a position of power.

And if the station died, that would be fine as well, because then they could study it.

The soldier who managed to separate the station from its host would be a hero.

If aliens survived the separation from their symbiont, Xan didn't know if they could ever recover and rebond. He only had experience with dead aliens.

A rough plan had been to get soldiers hooked on God's Breath, either snorted like cocaine or taken in pill form. Once it was in their system, the soldiers were in theory protected from any psychic alien mind communication or control. If they could withstand that, they could get close enough to administer the drug to the alien themselves, which would block their connections to their symbiont. How soldiers were to drug far stronger beings was still up in the air—it apparently depended on the alien. Some had to ingest it; some had to breathe it; some just had to touch it.

Xan had a suspicion that the army had assumed that mind control was the biggest threat to humans, and not the sheer physical power of the Gneiss or the camouflage ability of the Phantasmagore. But it was just a rough plan, after all.

Never one to dip just a toe into a project, the army planned to seed the street with God's Breath, since the more regular people used this stuff, the less susceptible they'd be to alien connection or mind control when the aliens finally decided to attack Earth.

They were still working on the problem of the drug giving humans an amazing high, but the next step was to have a soldier on hand at all alien diplomatic meetings "armed" with the stuff to protect the VIP humans involved. Both having it in their system and having it in a spray container, similar to mace.

The side income the army would make from the sale of the drug would be astronomical, if a bit on the nose.

A FEW MONTHS later, Xan encountered God's Breath firsthand while hanging out with Billy Williams. Billy was celebrating a promotion and had a few people over for beers. After they were good and drunk, Billy pulled out a packet of blue powder.

"I found the best shit, guys," he said, grinning. "This is like pot, only better. And better for you!"

"How is that better for us?" Xan asked skeptically.

"I just know what my dealer told me," Billy said. "Don't piss on the parade, man."

Knowing that Billy's "dealer" was probably his commanding officer, Xan didn't say anything. He held his hand up and shook his head. "I don't snort, man."

"It's cool, take one of these," Billy said, and handed him another baggie of blue pills.

He took a pill and palmed it, watching the others carefully. They sank into an evening of giggles and hallucinations. Xan complained that the shit wasn't working for him, and left them to their high.

He sent the pill to the secretary in a box of long-stemmed roses. He hadn't managed to get her the notes in *Slaughterhouse-Five*, but at least she had something to work off.

He hoped she was safe and not the target of an assassination attempt herself. Two could keep a secret, but only if one of them knew the other one would whale the tar out of him if he talked.

That was his grandmother's saying.

"THE HUMANS ARE waking up."

The appearance of Devanshi against the papery walls of the Sundry hive restaurant made Xan jump.

"Shit, how long have you been there?" he demanded.

"The doctors want you back in the medbay so they can see friendly faces when they wake up," she said, not answering the question. "Mallory is already there. Your ambassador is still acclimating to his new role, so he is not ready to meet the newcomers."

"He sucked at his first job, so I'm not sure he will make a better host," Xan said. "But how are the survivors now that they're awake?"

"I don't know," Devanshi said, her voice clipped. "I didn't ask.

I'm still trying to deal with the breaches in other parts of the station, body recovery, all that. We're closing down all common areas in case Eternity has more breaches. We're trying to get through to check on Eternity and her new host. A messenger mission was not what I needed right now."

"Then why did you do it?" he asked.

She glared at him, her angled face still alarming even after he had spent weeks among aliens. "Someone above my rank sent me."

"Oh," he said.

"So go to the medbay," she said, and then shimmered until she blended with the wall. He was barely able to watch the slight distortion in the air as she left the room.

He hurried back to the medbay, dread and hope warring inside him. Did he even want them to be all right? He wouldn't wish harm on anyone, but . . . Mallory had said there would be connections. He just hadn't expected there to be so many.

"The humans are recovering nicely," a Gurudev nurse said to Xan as he entered the medbay. Xan remembered him as Nurse Mathers, and he was a lot nicer than Ren had ever been. He was small for their species, looking up at Xan while still managing that air of "better than you" that most Gurudevs had toward humans.

"Is Phineas Morgan awake?" he asked.

Mathers checked a readout on a tablet. "Yes, he's waking up now. They all are. You should go in there. The female is already in."

Mallory exited the door across the room, which must have led to the medical theater. She walked up to him, her face stony. "Are you sure you want to do this?" she asked without preamble. "One of them is definitely army. You could watch from the balcony if you want me to vet them first."

This was the calm, serious Mallory, the one not driven by fear. He was glad to see her, but she clearly wasn't happy to see him. He wondered how badly he had hurt their friendship.

Xan shook his head. "My brother's in there. I have to check on him." He paused, thinking. "Thanks for the warning. Something you should know, though, if you already haven't figured it out. You know how you said there would be a lot of connections?"

She nodded.

"Well, there's one that might surprise you—"

Before he could continue, screaming came from the surgery room where the humans lay.

"JESUS FUCKING CHRIST, will you shut up?"

All eleven of the humans were sitting up in their pods in different states of awareness. Most of them were bleary and confused; a few seemed to still be in pain, wincing as they sat up. But in the middle, a middle-aged white woman was screaming, fingers raking lines down her cheeks.

The person who had yelled at her to shut up was a muscular East Asian woman who was painfully familiar to Xan. She now glared at the screaming woman.

An old Black woman was being fussed over by a younger woman. She was helping the woman sit up, murmuring, "It's okay, Gran, we're okay," over and over. The woman's pod was full of the clear fluid that must be the bacteria pool secreted from the Sundry, and she was drenched in it.

Six more pods held adults, mostly white or Hispanic, mostly women.

And then the eleventh pod, closest to the door, held Phineas.

The visual of being strapped into a car that hung nose down, with Phineas screaming and his parents dying below them, was the only thing in Xan's mind, and he shook his head to clear it. Other things had happened since, and the adult brothers needed more than the shared bond of surviving a terrifying night together.

The hatred in Phineas's eyes was palpable, which was hysterical because Xan was the injured party in this story. His left hand went to his right forearm subconsciously, rubbing the scars there.

Phineas looked at Mallory then, and his face curled up in confusion, as if he had seen someone that he couldn't quite remember.

Mallory laughed, a surprised sound. "Holy shit! Salty Fatts? That I didn't expect!" She looked at Xan, then back to Phineas. "Oh, I get it. This is your brother, isn't it?"

Xan willed his shoulders to relax. They had been tight since the shuttle, when he had found Phineas's name on the survivor list. They'd tightened even more when he listened to Mallory tell him the story of the time she had met Phineas.

Xan accepted the fact that he was fully tangled in the maelstrom of Mallory's weird shit.

"Well, Mal, you said there were always connections."

THE DOCTORS IN the medbay wore bright blue fabric to indicate their rank. Gurudevs wore full robes while the species that shunned clothing, like the Gneiss and Phantasmagore, wore armbands of the same color. Nurses were in red, and lab techs wore white. It was a nurse who took over and easily sedated the blonde woman and treated the scratches on her face. Mallory and Xan checked on the others and introduced themselves.

Phineas found it hysterical that Mallory was on the station. "Hell yeah, I remember you. That bartender! You saved my life."

"Not exactly," she said. "Just suggested you head out of town at the right time."

"So what are you doing here with him?" he jutted his chin toward Xan.

"'With' him? I wouldn't call it that," she said, looking at Xan as if he were a manikin who wasn't listening to them. "But why I'm here, it's a long story. But essentially, I'm here as hopefully a permanent guest of the station. Xan is, too. The other human here, the ambassador, is . . . otherwise occupied—"

"Yeah, he fucked off, we don't know if we'll see him again," Xan said. He was loud enough that several of the other survivors looked his way, startled. His own grandma would have slapped him for talking like that in front of his elders, but the old lady didn't seem to care at all. "So you get me and Mallory as your welcome wagon."

Mallory nodded and addressed the rest of the group as well. "I'm Mallory Viridian, and I'm here to welcome you, as it were, to Station Eternity. You haven't had a great welcome so far, and I'm sorry to say it may get worse before it gets better."

"You always this positive?" Phineas asked.

Mallory colored. "There's not a lot of time to sugarcoat things, unfortunately. You arrived here and were immediately attacked, and then were brought on board a station that is not the most stable place right now. For now, we need to find out what happened during the shuttle attack."

"You don't know who attacked us?" the young Black woman asked, incredulity creasing her brow.

"We don't know all the details," Mallory said. "There's a lot going on that we think may be linked to your arrival. Actually, we know they're linked; we're just not sure how."

Both the young Black woman and the young Asian woman had helped the old woman out of her pod. She stood, dripping on the medbay floor, still looking like she could sternly chastise young men with the best of them.

All of the folks who had climbed out of their pods stood in torn and ripped clothing, looking weak but overall uninjured. The young Black woman was flexing her left hand in wonder, examining the stump of her pinky.

"What exactly happened with our shuttle?" the old woman asked Xan.

"Your shuttle was attacked as it approached the station," Xan said carefully. "There was a breach—"

"Obviously. But who attacked it?" she asked, interrupting with a no-nonsense tone to her voice.

"We aren't entirely sure," Mallory said. "There are several crises aboard the station right now and the Earth ambassador is"— She glanced at Xan and then said—"busy. We are trying to find out what happened. All we know right now is that the shuttle was attacked. The entire Gurudev crew and ten humans died, what looked like all of those in the front of the shuttle, and a few from your area in the back. We rescued twelve survivors from the back seating area, one of whom has since died of his injuries."

The blonde woman, clearly sedated, looked around in confusion to find the dead person, but the nurses had already removed that pod.

The old woman looked at the young Black woman. Xan thought for a moment—their name was Brown. Mrs. and Ms., he decided. "Told you it wasn't worth the upgrade to first class," Mrs. Brown said.

"Gran, that's cruel," Ms. Brown said. She looked around at the other pods. "So wait, the eleven of us are all that's left?"

"Unfortunately, yes," Mallory said. "Did any of you lose any traveling companions?"

They all shook their heads. Xan felt Mallory relax a fraction. "That's good, at least. We think we've recovered and identified everyone lost in the attack."

Xan nodded. "Because of the chaos aboard, it may take some time to secure a shuttle to take you back to Earth, but we will work on that as well as find means to return the dead and their personal effects to their loved ones."

Mallory looked at him sharply. He hadn't mentioned the murder investigation on purpose; he wanted them calm. He had to hope she would trust him and not mess up the small calm they had managed to establish.

"Can we get some water or something?" Mrs. Brown said.

"Of course," Mallory said. "I'll get a nurse." She turned to go and Xan followed her.

"Why did you promise we could get them home right away?" Mallory asked in a fierce whisper.

"It's what they expect to hear. They need to hear that someone is in charge and their safety is the station's priority," Xan said. "And I didn't promise they'd get home right away. I said we were working on it so they will relax on that front. And in the meantime, you can do your investigative thing. After you solve it, and if we're still alive, then we can work to make it real."

Mallory approached a Gurudev wearing a red robe with a silver line stitched into the sleeve. They stood outside the medical theater beside the twelfth pod, making notes on a tablet. "The humans need some water. Can someone help with that?" she asked.

"I can," the nurse said evenly. "After I inter this body."

Mallory looked down at the dark pod. "What did he die of again?"

"The drug he had in his system kept our bacteria from healing him. The skull trauma killed him," the nurse said.

"Hey," Xan said, a sick feeling in his stomach. "You all have been careful with the body, right? Haven't touched it, or gotten any bodily fluids on yourself? You wear gloves or whatever?"

"Of course. We're not barbarians," the Gurudev said haughtily. "The pods are self-contained and don't need the touch of doctors. The toxicology report came directly from the AI report."

"Don't let the body touch anything on the station," Xan said. "Don't spill the blood, don't toss it into an incinerator, don't put it in a recycler, or whatever you do with the dead."

"Why?"

"Did the toxicology screen say what kind of drug it was he had in his system?"

"Just that it is unknown to us."

"Then trust me. Keep him in the pod until I can figure some stuff out."

"I find it difficult to believe you are better versed in our practices than we are," the nurse said coldly. "You were thinking we would touch the bodily fluid, after all."

"You don't know what that drug is or what it could do to you if you touch it. If you incinerate the body, the drug goes into Eternity. *Directly* into her. Do you want to send an unknown toxin into the station?"

"The station shouldn't be affected by a relatively small part of a drug."

"No, it shouldn't," he said, exasperated. "But unless you know for sure, just humor me. Keep him in the pod until we know more."

"I'd listen to him," Mallory said. "He's an expert in human dead body retrieval and disposal. You might know your medicine better, but he knows dead humans better."

"Fine," the nurse snapped. He wheeled the dead man away, calling out to another nurse to water the annoying patients.

"What was that about?" Mallory asked when the nurse was out of earshot.

"What was what?"

"You know something about the drug that guy took and it's scaring the shit out of you. But it hasn't even been identified yet."

"Mallory, I'll tell you everything, but now's not the time," he said. "Those humans might start exploring the station if we don't keep them in there. Later. I promise."

She looked at him for a long time, and he wondered if she was putting him in the suspect category. She wouldn't really think that, would she? He had been with her when they had found Ren's body.

Unfortunately, he had no alibi for where he had been when Ren was killed.

WHEN THEY RETURNED to the medbay with water, Phineas, the Brown granddaughter, and the East Asian woman stood in a tight huddle, talking, while Mrs. Brown spoke gently to the doped-up blonde woman. The other survivors looked dazed, some of them frowning at their phones as if they expected Verizon to have a tower out here light-years from Earth.

One tall, muscular white man of about fifty approached them, hand outstretched. "I'm Kent Woodard. I'm a doctor. I've examined a few of the survivors and there's not a scratch on anyone. I remember that man had a compound leg fracture and that young woman had a serious laceration on her face and a bandaged hand." He pointed to Phineas, and then the young Brown woman.

"We don't know much about alien medicine," Mallory said. "And we didn't think that our introduction would be a bunch of seriously injured humans dumped in the lap of the medical bay on a very bad day for the station."

"What happened to the station?"

Mallory glanced at Xan, clearly unsure of how much to divulge.

"They're going to find out. It's best if it comes from us," he told her, shrugging.

Mallory nodded. "You know that the station is sentient and has a symbiotic relationship with another alien who serves as a host, right?"

Dr. Woodard nodded. "I'd heard something of the sort. It's one of the reasons I wanted to come here."

"Someone killed the host today. We think it happened around

the time of the attack on your shuttle. So as you were floating out in space, there were a lot of problems on the station. We're still not sure of everything that's happened. That's why we're the ones filling you in instead of security or the ambassador. They have an angry station to handle." She smiled weakly. "Welcome to Eternity."

Woodard, to his credit, took all this in without reacting. He rubbed his chin. "If possible, I'd like to talk to a doctor when all this is over. Whatever healing they did on us could revolutionize medicine on Earth."

"I wouldn't get your hopes too high," Xan said. "They also have FTL tech that they're not sharing with us. What we know about the stuff that healed you is—"

"We should let the doctors explain it," Mallory interrupted. "We don't want to give Dr. Woodard the wrong information."

Or send info back to Earth that would endanger the Sundry, Xan realized. He couldn't imagine humans being able to fight a hivemind of massive hornets, but on the other hand, since the Sundry were a connected hivemind, it was possible just a little God's Breath could make their connection fall completely apart. He nodded at her, understanding.

"When we can, we'll get a doctor to talk to you," he said.

Mallory raised her voice to address the whole group. "I'm trying to get someone from station security to come talk to you, but we can't get rooms for you right now. I asked the medbay doctors to give us the balcony for you to wait and rest comfortably, and while we're waiting, Xan and I have some questions we need to ask. We are trying to piece together what happened to the shuttle, so we need your accounts, whatever you remember."

Some looked outraged, while the others glanced at each other and shrugged. "Whatever," Phineas said without looking at Xan.

"I'm looking forward to some answers from you," the older

Brown woman said. She had received a wet towel and had done her best to remove the healing goo that still flattened her hair and dampened her clothes.

"I'll take you to the balcony," Xan said, and walked toward the stairs that led there.

They followed him, but when he got to the top of the stairs, he was startled to see the Asian woman behind him instead of Phineas. She pulled him aside as the others passed them to find seating.

"Hello, Alexander," she said, a cruel smile twisting her mouth.

"Hey, H2Oh," he said, glancing from her to Phineas and back again.

"You do remember me!" she said, delighted, and punched his shoulder. She still punched hard.

"You're hard to forget," he said, smiling slightly.

"Let's talk," she said.

He pointed at Phineas. "I'd like to talk to my brother, I haven't seen him in—"

"Nah, you want to see me first," she said. "Because you'll want to know if I've told anyone about what we did."

Phineas crossed his arms in front of him, his tattooed hands saying SALT and FATT. But Xan's eyes went from his brother's tattoos to his forearms, and the small, circular scars there.

"Fuck," he said, shame and anger flooding him. "No, H2, I need to talk to my brother. It's important."

"You want me to tell him what we did in Texas?" she asked shrewdly.

"He already knows," Xan said, bluffing. "Come on, Phin."

"Nah, talk to your girl here. I gotta take a leak. But give me back my fucking jacket," his brother said.

"Don't leave the medbay; it's seriously not safe out there," Xan said, handing the jacket over.

"So, you were bluffing then, weren't you?" H2 asked as Phineas left. "He didn't know."

"Does it matter now?" Xan asked. "Come on, let's find a place to talk."

Xan had been surprised to see Phineas's name on the list of survivors. But he'd damn near had a heart attack at seeing Calliope Oh's name. Calliope Oh, his old friend from the army when their quartermaster battalion—colloquially named the Vultures—had been stationed on the Mexican border in Texas, and the only other person alive who knew what happened.

16

CALLIOPE'S BIG BREAK

CALLIOPE OH WAS on mile eight of her run when her audiobook was interrupted by a ringing sound. She slowed and paused her book, then tapped her earphone. "This is Cal."

"SPC Oh, this is Homer Costello. I'm with the Department of Defense."

She blinked and pushed sweaty bangs from her eyes. "I'm not an SPC anymore, man. You're working with old info."

"I understand you left the service," he began.

She laughed. "'Left,' sure, we can call it that."

There was a pause. "I need to speak with you. Would you be free for a meeting sometime in the next few days?"

She clenched her fists. "What do I need to do to make it clear? I. Don't. Work. For. The. Army. Anymore. I'm not enlisted. I don't have a pension you can take away from me. We're done."

Costello sighed, and Calliope could hear someone talking to him in a low voice in the background. She caught the words "told you."

"Ms. Oh, we have a unique opportunity for you to serve your country again. When we were looking for someone with the skill-set we needed, your name came up," he said.

She laughed. "Don't appeal to my patriotism, man. When the army wants you to be their lapdog, they shove patriotism in your face. Every other time they're reminding you that you're not a real American, that you should go back to China where they're making a new pandemic to kill all the white people, or that you're probably a spy," she said. "Or have you solved the whole racism problem and I hadn't heard about it? You'd think that would hit the news."

The voice outside the conversation said something else, and she caught the word "money."

"Who are you talking to?" she asked. "'Cause it sounds like they know me better than you do. Put them on the phone."

There was a small muffled sound of a phone being passed. "Hello, Cal, it's Sergeant Opal Slav."

Cal laughed in surprise. "Sergeant Slav? Seriously. *You're* who they sent to sweet-talk me?"

"I'm who you asked to speak to," said the calm voice. "How are you doing?"

"I'm great. It's really good to hear from you. How have you been since you recommended my dismissal?" Cal asked conversationally.

"You asked to talk to who Mr. Costello was speaking to. I'm here. What would you like to know?"

"All right, so what's this all about?" Cal asked, interested despite herself.

"We have a job we need doing, and you're one of the few people who fits our profile."

"In my discharge papers, you said I was, quote, 'unfit in almost every way' to serve my country," Cal said. "Is that what you need? Someone unfit in almost every way?"

Slav sighed. "We need someone outside the chain of command, but someone who has been army trained."

"Sounds like you need a contractor for some dirty work so that your white boys remain pure, swaddled in red, white, and blue blankies. Why not call Halliburton?"

"We need an individual contractor," Slav corrected herself.

"What's in it for me?"

"I can change your discharge so that you receive a pension," she said.

Cal frowned. "You can't do that. You told me that was impossible, actually."

"I was misinformed," Slav said carefully.

"You lied," Cal corrected.

"It requires significant administrative hoops to jump through, something I don't recall you enjoying," Slav countered.

"No one likes that. Except for the assholes who run the system," Cal said. "So you would change my discharge if I did you a favor." She paused, thinking. "Backdated?"

"No," Slav said immediately. "That's impossible."

"Nah, you've already admitted that you may or may not be lying when you say that. So depending on how badly you want me, I bet it's possible. Look into it and get back to me."

"But you don't even know—" Slav continued, and Cal hung up.

Damn, it felt good to know she couldn't get reprimanded for being rude to an officer. Slav was just an asshole that private citizen Cal didn't have to listen to if she didn't want to. But damn, the military training ran deep, and she felt slightly uneasy, waiting for the other shoe to drop and her punishment to come.

Her earphones chimed again, her phone buzzing in the pocket of her running tights. Cal swore and answered it. "Seriously? What now?"

"Ms. Oh, it's Homer Costello again," he said hurriedly. "Sergeant Slav will be looking into the possibility of backdating your pension and benefits, but we need to talk to you about the mission before we move forward with your payment."

As much as she liked the idea of Slav being forced to do a

bunch of admin for no reason, Cal gave in. "Fine. What do you want?"

"Just a meeting, in person."

"All right, when and where and are you sending a car?"

"Where are you now?"

"Right now I'm running on the Crap Trail," she said. There was silence on the other end. "You know, the Craipe Trail. That's what I call it." She paused. Still silent. "Because it's crap."

"I understand the wordplay," Costello said, sounding like he didn't appreciate her humor. "Where is the Craipe Trail?"

"It's close to my apartment in Raleigh."

"So you're not still in Virginia."

"No. Raleigh isn't in Virginia."

"Then you're closer than we thought. We need you to come in for a meeting at Fort Bowser, which is a short drive from where you are. Can you come in today?"

She checked her watch. "I'm pretty nasty right now, so you'll want me to get a shower," she said.

"Sure, come in after you've cleaned up. Can I expect you in Lieutenant Colonel Torres's office in two hours?"

"Lieutenant Colonel Torres has moved to Bowser? Slav, too?" Cal asked, interested.

"Not officially. We can tell you more when you come. Sergeant Slav will text you the address."

"I can do that," Cal said after calculating the time for a shower, the drive there, and getting lost. She hung up.

Calliope Oh grinned. And everyone said her attitude would end her career someday.

Guess they were wrong.

THREE PEOPLE MET her in Lieutenant Colonel Nick Torres's office. The lieutenant colonel stood, holding a file in a manila folder.

His bald head had a thin sheen of sweat on it, and he frowned more deeply than usual, puckering a scar on his right cheek.

"Hey, Lieutenant Colonel," Calliope said as she entered. "Hey, Slav," she added, deliberately denying her title.

Calliope's old superior officer, Sergeant Opal Slav, stood behind Torres at attention as if she were waiting for disciplinary action. Her ice-blonde hair was in its usual tight bun on the nape of her neck, and she looked as if she had eaten something sour. When Calliope shut the door behind her, Slav's unnerving blue eyes met hers in an almost accusatory way.

The biggest deal was that these army bigwigs stood behind Torres's own desk while their visitor, Mr. Costello, sat at the desk looking at another folder. This was a sign of deference she'd never witnessed. She fought the urge to snap to attention and salute. Instead, she wrapped her heavy trench coat around her, leaned on the door frame, and crossed her arms.

"Mr. Costello, this is Calliope Oh. I believe you met her on the phone," Slav said.

Costello looked up, smiling. "In a memorable call, yes."

Torres addressed Calliope. "Mr. Costello's branch of the DOD has come to us with a unique mission for one person. They have looked at all of the evaluations of the last three years of ASVAB testing and our training notes and have . . . included you on the list of possible people to interview."

Calliope blinked. "Did you forget I'm not enlisted anymore? Besides, I nearly flunked the ASVAB."

Slav got that sour look to her lips again. "That is what I told them." She looked at the back of Costello's head with mild contempt but averted her eyes when Torres glared at her.

Costello didn't look concerned. He was the kind of man whom most enlisted people hated: he was small and soft, with pasty skin and a thin black mustache that hinted that he probably shouldn't have tried to grow one. He looked as if he had one Asian parent, probably Vietnamese, Cal guessed, and pegged him at about fifty years old. This guy had never held a weapon in his life deadlier than a laser tag rifle. But he had to have a lot of metaphorical weight to throw around to be sitting pretty while making ranked soldiers stand.

"Former Lance Corporal Calliope Oh," Mr. Costello said, pulling a thick, stapled stack of papers from the file. "Other-than-honorable discharge for multiple infractions and an . . . 'inability to learn from mistakes.' Multiple instances of insubordination. Very little technical skill, failing marks in most specialties. And a special note here: you failed to join the marines before the army, yes?"

Both officers looked startled. Cal groaned inwardly. She'd been assured that no one would find out about the failed attempt when the marines had told her the army was the place for her.

"I thought that was removed from my record," she said.

"Not for my security clearance," Costello said, smiling.

"You sneaky little paper pusher. Respect," Cal said, grinning. He didn't look like he appreciated the compliment. "So, yeah, I was in the first recruitment class to take the pre-MARSOC. I failed three of the four specialties. They thought I would be better for the army."

He frowned as he read further. "And yet you excelled in the fourth specialty, which makes no sense. You failed the three individual specialties, and when you were tested in using combinations of the skills, your scores were off the charts. This is . . . fascinating. The doctor doing your psych eval said you approach life like a chef. What does that mean?"

Cal laughed. That doctor had seen through her better than most. He'd been the one to suggest she go to the army. "That guy said I couldn't cook well if all you gave me was flour. But if you give me flour, sugar, butter, and eggs, I can make an excellent cake."

They all stared at her.

"Yeah, I know, the metaphor doesn't fully work. Being good at marksmanship isn't like cooking with just sugar. He was a shrink, not a poet. So I can't win any swimming races, and if we grappled right here, I bet even you could pin me." The superior officers winced, but Costello smiled and nodded, indicating she continue. "But when they combined the two in underwater fighting, I was undefeated in every test, no matter who they threw at me."

"I see. It says you are a terrible shot, and you aren't very fast, but you can hit a target with a rifle while running?"

"I am a terrible sniper," Cal said. "I get bored. The shrink said I was probably the most functional adult with ADHD that he'd ever seen."

"I think I understand," Costello said. "So, once you were enlisted in the army, you moved to Fort Lee and quartermaster training."

She nodded. "Mortuary division, specifically."

"Not a lot of underwater fighting needed there," Costello said mildly.

"No, but retrieving stiffs"—she paused as she took in the poisoned glare from Slav—"that is, 'my fellow soldiers,' remains and personal belongings on an active battlefield turned out to fit my skills. Besides, not a lot of people jump to that duty, so they needed folks."

"Soldiers from that area have among the highest rates of PTSD in the armed forces," Costello said. "Have you been affected?"

The image came, unbidden. *Xan Morgan standing, face still swollen from the fight he'd been in the night before, watching the daily patrol leave for Falcon Dam.*

"You okay?" she asked. "You look like shit."

Xan clenched his jaw and then relaxed. "I'm fine."

"You don't look fine."

"Forget about it. We have work to do."

"What the hell for? No one's dead."

"We have to fill in for ordnance. They're a man down."

"We have to check supplies? For the assholes who did this to you?"

His eyes met hers, bloodshot and golden brown. "Yes. That patrol."

"Let's go," she said.

"Nothing I can't handle," she said, clearing her throat.

"And is it true you once assaulted a superior officer for calling you 'Oh No'?" he asked, looking over the file at her.

"Yes, sir." She was proud of that mark on her record. She expected him to ask her more or admonish her, but instead he turned to the soldiers behind him.

"Well, how does the army suggest you deal with racism, eh? Grin and bear it for the country? Sergeant Slav, anything to add here? How did you handle this bit of racism and disrespect among the troops? Or did you just punish Calliope for her retaliation?"

Slav's face turned red. "We don't accept the assault of a superior officer, sir."

"Of course, and racism isn't assault, is it, Oh?" he turned back to Calliope. "Did your brothers and sisters in arms make jokes about you eating dogs?"

"Only once," Cal said, letting the unsaid part of that sentence hang out for all to see.

"Did you take care of that, or did Sergeant Slav help you out?"

Her eyes flicked to Slav's red face. "I guess you can say both of us took care of it."

He looked down at her file again. "Good. And the nickname H2Oh? Was that—"

"No, sir, my friends gave that to me. We were involved in the Texas border skirmishes over water rights, you know."

"I see. Do you speak Korean, Oh?"

"Not a word," she said. "I'm fourth generation. My parents died when I was five, and my uncle raised me. He didn't have much connection to the family back in Korea."

He nodded, understanding. "My grandmother came from Vietnam, but my mother never pushed us to learn the mother tongue, and my Irish father just wanted me to learn how to make proper shepherd's pie." He flipped through more papers. "Ah, here's the uncle. David Oh, in and out of jail for drug dealing? This is the man who raised you?"

"Yeah," she said, reminding herself that Uncle Drop was due a letter. He'd be out of prison in five months. "He taught me everything I know."

"How in the world did you survive in the military as long as you did with him as your role model?" he asked, frankly baffled.

"Because Uncle Drop told me to throw everything I had at everything I did. He did that for drug dealing and keeping us fed with a roof over our heads. I did it for the army."

"A dedicated drug dealer," Costello said, thinking aloud. "Everything about your life is novel, Ms. Oh. You might be just what we need. You've got a unique ability to roll with any punches that come your way, including an other-than-honorable discharge. If you agreed to go on this dangerous solo mission, and we offered it to you," he added pointedly, reminding her there was no offer yet, "we would change your discharge to general and backdate your benefits."

"Honorable," she corrected. "You clearly need me bad. I want honorable discharge."

"That would require erasure of files—" Slav started, but Torres, who had been silent up to now, put his hand on her arm.

"Sergeant, I believe we can get that taken care of," he said mildly. "Go on, Mr. Costello."

"You would also be an official member of the new group I'm leading," Costello said.

Calliope had been trying to figure out how much the army would owe her in back pension. She blinked and came back to Costello. "What's that, sir?"

He smiled that enigmatic smile again. "I can't tell you that until you are committed. No level of security clearance exists for what we're doing."

"If I have this right, I'm interviewing for a position and I don't know what that is and if I got it, I would be joining a DOD department that doesn't currently exist," Cal said, ticking the different points off on her fingers.

"That is correct," Torres said.

"That sounds amazing," she said. "How many people am I up against?"

"That also is classified," Costello said. He squinted at her file as if he thought he was misreading something; then he put his finger at a line of text and glanced back at Slav. "Did she really do this?"

Slav gave a curt nod. "Yes, sir. The one day she was in charge of the newly enlisted."

"All right," Costello said, looking like he was trying to smother a smile. "Ms. Oh, before you ask, we won't be holding a *battle royale* type of contest to find out which one of you gets the position."

"I thought it was a good way to find the strongest recruits and cut through paperwork," Cal said, shrugging, remembering that day Slav had been foolish enough to make her a leader of the green recruits.

"It caused more paperwork, not to mention lacerations, than you will ever know," Slav snapped.

Costello closed the file. "Well, Ms. Oh, it was a pleasure to meet you. If you don't get the job, you probably won't hear anything about it. And there will be no discussion of this interview with anyone, understood?"

She nodded, fighting the urge to salute. "Crystal clear, sir," she said.

Costello smiled, and the expression transformed his soft face into something hungry, as if he had just succeeded in tricking her. "Excellent."

TORRES'S ASSISTANT HAD left their desk, leaving the room empty for Calliope to pause outside the office door and eavesdrop. If they caught her, well, they couldn't discharge her any harder than they already had.

Inside, Torres gave a heavy sigh. "Don't say we didn't warn you."

"I like her," Costello said. "She's perfect." Calliope grinned.

"You haven't been her superior, sir," Slav objected. "I honestly can't think of any solo mission I would feel confident sending her on. 'Loose cannon' doesn't begin to describe her."

"She's going," Torres said. "This mission has dangers we honestly can't anticipate. Soldiers with unique skills will likely perform better than your battle-proven ground pounders who follow every order. I'm very interested in reading how she excelled at Irregular Warfare in the pre-MARSOC, since she did poorly in all of the foundation skills that make up IW."

Slav gave a pained laugh. "I didn't know she had tried the marines first. But I can guess why they sent her here and no one told us. They probably thought it was a prank."

"It seems that cutting through paperwork to rid oneself of Calliope Oh is something more than one person has done in her life," Costello said. "She simply scored too low to enlist in the marines because she couldn't shoot well. But an expert in Irregular Warfare is exactly what we need. And I'll be honest with you. The Terrestrial Guard doesn't currently exist, so if we lose some soldiers on the secret missions that definitely aren't going to happen, it's best if they're expendable, correct?"

"Correct," Torres confirmed.

Slav must have reacted only with body language, because after a moment, Costello spoke again, right next to the door. "I'll need some time to think about it, but I think I will be calling Calliope Oh again. She's got spunk."

Calliope dropped silently and rolled beneath the secretary's desk. Costello left the office without one look at her.

From behind the closed door, Torres and Slav started talking again.

"Sir," Slav said, as if the words were in a rush to get out, "Oh was a pain in my ass, but she isn't even a soldier anymore, and he wants to use her like she was a throwaway tissue. I don't like the idea of sending a civilian on a suicide mission when she doesn't even know where she's going."

"She has free will not to take it," he said.

"You've seen her, sir. She will run after a dangerous mystery mission like a cat after a laser pointer! Besides, she can't say no until she knows what it is, and then it will be too late. He said this is for the Terrestrial Guard. That's got to mean space, aliens, all that stuff. Why is he here? Why isn't he mining the air force for his special, unique, and expendable recruits?"

"Who's to say he isn't?" Torres asked. "Oh isn't the only person they're looking at. The president is giving this new force carte blanche, and they're going to take what they want. We follow orders, and our order was to find Calliope Oh and make her an offer she couldn't refuse."

"Yes, sir," Slav said, sounding tired. "She has no idea what she's in for."

"Neither, I think, does the Terrestrial Guard," Torres said.

OPAL SLAV STOOD at the door of the Starbucks, pulling at her Arizona Diamondbacks baseball cap. Her hair was loose, pulled through the back of the cap in a ponytail, and she wore a long-sleeved T-shirt with a SALTY FATTS logo on the front. She scanned the room, then brightened when Calliope caught her eye. She hurried to join her.

"Are you trying to be undercover, not look like a solider? Because you suck at that," Calliope said as a way of greeting. "You have to learn how to relax that spine. Unclench those butt cheeks."

"Good to see you too, Cal," Slav said dryly. "Thanks for meeting me."

"I almost didn't make it," Calliope said. "Got caught up in a phone call." She waggled her smartphone at Slav. "Guess who?"

Slav blinked at her. "If it's who you're alluding to, you probably aren't supposed to tell me. Unless you were talking to your convicted felon uncle."

It took a lot more than a perfectly accurate statement about Uncle Drop to get Calliope mad. "Nah, it's the classified person. Did you have something to do with this assignment? 'Cause I know you don't like me, so can't imagine you helping me."

Slav cleared her throat. "I guess I got here a little late if you've already been offered the job with the DOD. What did they tell you about it?"

"I'm not supposed to say, not even to you," Cal said, sipping her hot chocolate and getting whipped cream on her nose.

"If I recall correctly, you didn't excel in any covert training," Slav said mildly.

"Okay, fine, I don't know much. They offered, I accepted. I get debriefed tomorrow, and it looks like I'm moving to DC next week."

"Costello didn't tell you anything about it?" Slav said. "Just that you've been approved for this mission?"

"Nothing yet, but there's travel involved. I think it has to do with a mission to South America. Colombia, I bet," Oh said. "Uncle Drop has connections there."

Slav rolled her eyes. "You're wrong, but just as an aside, if you ever do get sent to Colombia for the United States, please don't make contacts with drug lords, even if they are family friends." She shook her head. "But that's neither here nor there. Costello didn't tell you that there's a new branch of military they're forming in response to some current events." She pulled a rolled-up magazine out of her back pocket and let it unroll on the table. It was an issue of *Time* magazine with a picture of one of the blue humanoid aliens—Oh couldn't remember their name—with bark-like skin on the cover. "We know this new branch wants you. What we don't know is exactly why they want you. But I think I know what the mission is." She opened the magazine to a page in the middle, the one with the interview with the blue ambassador—ah, yes, Blue Ally Smith Third Daughter Once Mother was her name—but as she said, "you can call me Jennifer." She was the Gurudev ambassador assigned to Earth. But Slav wasn't pointing to that. Tucked into the crease of the pages, looking like a bookmark, was a newspaper article.

"So many pieces of paper, how vintage of you. I love it," Cal said. She pulled out the clipping and read it.

"Murder Suspect Abducted by Aliens" read the headline, detailing the public information given by military police regarding the disappearance of a soldier from Fort Bowser. Apparently, there were other persons of interest, but that didn't sell as much news. Whether he did it or not, that didn't change the fact that the soldier had run from a crime scene and was currently AWOL, and likely far, far from extradition.

"Shit, I think I know that guy!" Cal said. She tried to keep her voice low, because there was no "think" about it; she knew him very well. "He's been abducted?"

"Yes. And my guess is that you are being sent off planet, to a hostile area that no one has scouted, to bring back one of our own," Slav said in a low voice.

"Whoa," Oh said, scanning the article, looking for keywords. Not finding "multiple deaths" or "possible war crime" in the article, she relaxed a very tiny bit. "So, a rescue mission?"

"Kind of," Slav said, a little too carefully. "It doesn't scare you?"

Oh looked up into Slav's eyes. "You never, ever asked me that when I was enlisted. You didn't care who was scared of what. You said fear was part of the job, and you took care of fear with duty. Why do you care now?" She looked back down to the article. "Besides, I already told that DOD guy yes."

"Look, I don't like them bringing in a civilian when there are thousands of soldiers who'd love this job and, frankly, probably do it better. I also don't like telling you the job only after you've agreed to it."

Cal laughed. "Jealous?"

Slav shook her head, sighing. "It's not that. So you served with this guy, right?" She pointed to Xan's face.

Cal chose her words carefully. "Yeah, I remember him. We served a while back in the quartermasters together, in Afghanistan." She didn't add "and in Texas" for Slav. Just in case. "We teamed up a few times, till I dragged him down."

"That's probably why they chose you. Even though he's a better soldier than you are, you can probably get close to him."

"Close to him where?"

Slav sighed. "They're not entirely sure. But they're guessing Station Eternity. The air force has been scanning the US airspace, and they think they identified the shuttle as one of the station's. If they're wrong, it's still pretty small and would have to go to Station Eternity before refueling to go anywhere else. So they're starting there. But Calliope, I don't think you're prepared for this job. You can't follow authority; you speak before you think; you've got the lowest scores in your squad for weapon accuracy. You're a loose cannon, and they're going to send you in with as little information as they can give. They may think you're right for the job, but I am worried they're sending you in to die."

Cal sipped her hot chocolate, enjoying watching Slav be uncomfortable. "You told me I was a weapon. A gun designed to shoot where my country pointed me. You drilled that into me more than anyone. And now I have a chance to follow orders and take the most interesting assignment ever?" She tapped her finger on the side of her mug. "Would you turn this down if it were you?"

Slav didn't meet her eyes. "No," she admitted, and Calliope laughed in triumph, but Slav went on hastily, "that's because I'm still enlisted. I do what I'm ordered to. You have the luxury to say no. This is a mission where we don't even know how dangerous it is and you're not sworn to follow all orders anymore. I just wanted you to go in there fully informed. I don't think they're telling you the *whole* story, and you need to know. Just—remember you're an employee and can make your own decisions."

Something dawned on Cal, slower than she would have liked. "Hang on. How do you know all this stuff about this so-called secret mission? You're just a sergeant."

"That is classified," Slav said, her back stiff and straight again. She pulled a tissue from her pocket, but instead of using it, she began fidgeting with it, tearing long strips and then balling it up again.

"Or there's something else going on here," Cal said, watching Slav's fingers. Then her eyes went wide. "Wait a second; it's got to do with Xan." She poked at the newspaper clipping. "You're protecting him. From what? And why?"

"That is not quite the case. I've been given some data to give you; please read it before your trip and don't let it fall into enemy hands." She put the wadded tissue on the table.

"Is this from you or from the TG?" Cal asked, liking how the acronym already felt natural in her mouth.

"Yes," Slav said.

"I thought you weren't working for them."

Slav looked around the coffee shop as if there were spies everywhere. "I think I've said too much. You can believe me or not." She snatched the magazine from her and rolled it back up. "You're right. This is stuff we shouldn't be talking about. I'm risking my job, and maybe even jail, just telling you this. How about you accept your new job, I'll write you a good letter for your new commander, and we never speak of this?"

"What aren't you telling me?" Cal said, crossing her arms.

"Just look at the data and use some common sense on what you do with it. That's all I ask. Even though common sense was never your strong suit." Slav got up. She grabbed her purse and gave Oh a little wave, and was startled when Oh saluted back. "Good luck."

Cal picked up the tissue. Opal had tucked a thumb drive within the wad.

Spy shit was really cool, even if it was sloppy.

"THE MILITARY'S TAKING you back?" Uncle Drop said into the phone on the other side of the glass. He grinned, lisping through his missing canine.

"Sort of, but I can't tell you anything. And I'm going on a mission, but I can't tell you where." Calliope was having trouble containing her glee. "But it's awesome, let me tell you that."

"Hot damn, I can't believe you didn't grow up to be a waste of air after all!" he said. "I'm gonna have to call you something other than 'Wastrel.'"

"I know, right?" she said, smiling. "My old sergeant said the same thing."

"Can you tell me anything at all?" he asked, leaning forward as if he could hear her if he got closer to the glass between them.

"I really can't, Uncle. It's the military. You know how they are."

"Shit, do I," he said, sitting back and sighing dramatically. "I still can't believe they hung me out to dry like they did."

Calliope frowned. "They what?"

"That new shit, God's Breath they called it. The reason I'm in here. I was contracted by a secret government agency to make it, but when I got caught selling weed and the cops found the God's Breath on me, my contacts in the government dried up, phone numbers went to a Mexican restaurant in Fayetteville, a lot of black ops shit."

This story was news to Calliope, but it didn't surprise her. Uncle Drop had a "someone in power done me wrong" story for every time he got caught. It was always entertaining how the government was responsible for a good seventy-five percent of his failures. "Uncle, you're full of shit. There was no government conspiracy. You just got caught dealing is all."

"That's what they made me say," he said flatly.

"Who's this scary 'they' you're talking about?" Calliope asked, trying to sound like she was taking him seriously.

"The cops, my lawyer, the judge. They gave me a reduced sentence if I promised to not mention the feds at all. That's why you didn't know." He paused, running his rough hand up and down the phone cord. "I'm sorry if my dealing ever made any trouble for you, Wastrel. Just wanted to take care of my girl."

"Nah," she said, waving her hand. "Having a drug-dealing uncle made me pretty popular for a while, till people realized I couldn't hook them up with drugs while you were in jail. I may have some customers for you when you get out. Or when I get back."

"Hey, that's great news!" he said, grinning again. She loved that grin. Through that hole in his smile she could see the comfort of her youth, the uncle who would do anything to protect her, who taught her to take care of her own and never, ever back down.

She would make him proud.

WHEN SHE LET the info out that she was going through a make-shift spaceport and wasn't going to be searched by the TSA, he told her to get some stuff from a stash he had hidden in his trailer. She let herself in with her key and found his toolbox under the kitchen sink. He'd squirreled away weapons, some minor stashes of weed and meth, and a roll of one-hundred-dollar bills. None of those were surprising.

But she also found a little Ziploc bag of blue drugs, which she scrutinized, holding it up to the naked light bulb in the kitchen. They looked small and blue, like boner pills, but they were capsules, not pills, and they looked like they had been rolled in glitter. Then she found another baggie with glittery blue powder.

The powder was grainy and glinted in the light. "What the heck are you?" she asked aloud. Was this "God's Breath"? She could always give it a try. Uncle Drop had taught her how to sample drugs without going on a total fucking Led Zep trip, as he called it. As much as he would have loved a bigger customer base, he always cautioned her to be smart when using, and never to share with her friends. He was going to be the only dealer in the family. Her friends complained that he clearly didn't want her diluting his client pool, but she knew he didn't want her caught dealing, especially once she got into the army. To pass the military's frequent drug tests, she hadn't used since enlisting, and with Uncle Drop in prison, she hadn't used since she got out.

She pocketed everything she found. Uncle Drop and video games had taught her to pick up everything you could, 'cause you didn't know what would be useful. You can never be too rich or too armed, Uncle would say.

She'd stash the stuff in her lockbox with her sidearm, her taser, and that USB drive that Slav had left crumpled up in her tissue at the cafe. Cal was looking forward to checking out what was on it.

17

SALTY FATTS POSTPONES
A FUNERAL

A N AWFUL LOT of things happened to Phineas on Thursday. A bloated report ran in the *New York Times* about his brother, heavy on words but light on details. Essentially, Xan was either AWOL or MIA, depending on whom you talked to. Regardless, he was gone. The murder investigation had ended in no arrests, but there were two connected suicides, and those two people were considered the main suspects. But everyone wondered what Xan's connections to the aliens were. Was he an alien spy? Was he sent to Eternity to spy for the aliens? Conspiracy theories were rampant, and Phineas was horrified to discover there was a Reddit room for #XanFans who thought he was innocent. Disgusting.

His agent called him with the bad news that he was on the hook for the movie he'd abandoned when Grandma had gotten sick. And they were suing.

Then his agent fired him, saying if Phineas was going to waste his prime creative years in hillbilly country, it was his prerogative.

Then his grandmother died. The less said about that the better.

Then he went out to sit on the front porch, bottle of whiskey in one hand and the will in the other.

The past few months had been hell. First there was Grandma's stroke, and Phineas having to pay for some in-home health care. It was fine to foot the bill from the movie set, but after the third nurse quit, unable to take Grandma's abuse, the home health folks insisted they would send no more nurses there. The only people left were family members.

And Man of the House Xan was in the army and couldn't come home.

Phineas's career had screeched to a stop when he went home to nurse his grandmother. She had always favored him instead of Xan, but now she was so far gone that she called him Xan, screamed at him, and baited him to piss him off.

"Grandma, do you know who I am?" he asked, exhaustion pulling at his voice.

"You're the fat one," Grandma snapped. "Of course I know who you are, Xanny. Give me a cigarette."

He'd learned quickly what the requirements were for home health care. They involved lifting, cooking, cleaning, bathing, helping her to and from the toilet, and tolerating vicious abuse. He had never seen this side of Grandma growing up. Xan hadn't liked her very much, but she had always called Phineas the baby of the family.

So he put everything on hold, every promising thing he had in the works, to come home to Tennessee and be a home health nurse. And he wasn't even getting paid.

Not even through inheritance.

His hand was getting the will sweaty, but he still clutched it. If he squeezed hard enough, it might turn into a diamond.

Fucking Xan. Fuck. Ing. Xan.

Grandma would yell at him for being on the porch swing, saying he was too fat for it. But fuck her, he and Xan had hung the thing and knew how much weight it could hold. Sometimes she was clever with her abuse, sliding between his ribs to get at his heart when she told him supposed secrets about his parents, about how he and Xan had two different fathers, about how his mother strutted around Gatlinburg like a cat in heat, about how they also had a sister but she was kept secret from the boys and lived with her father, about how his parents had hated him and loved Xan, and about how aliens lived in the woods. (This was before First Contact, even.)

At sundown, he sat on the porch swing, the whiskey pricking at the corners of his mind, looking for cracks to seep into, looking dully down the hill from his grandmother's house. Xan's house now.

Xan's house. Xan's land. Everything in Xan's name.

Phineas had put his career on hold. Possibly burned some bridges. Given up everything, all for a woman who had left everything to Xan because, even though she preferred Phineas, Xan was the oldest and the one whom she knew was her grandson.

He'd destroyed everything and lost his inheritance to boot.

More whiskey.

He'd found the will that morning. He'd read it through twice, carefully, and asked Grandma if it was the most recent will, or if it was a joke. Asked if she remembered Xan was off planet with the aliens.

She'd shouted at him to stop being stupid. Said she couldn't leave her land to Phineas the fuckup, the fat one, the ugly one, the queer. Then she burned him with her cigarette.

Xan hadn't been home since Phineas had left for LA. Not even for holidays. He'd resented Phineas for taking the college money he'd sent home and using it to move to LA. He'd never asked Phineas if he'd *wanted* to go to college. He had just assumed that since he wanted to get the hell out of the house, Phineas would, too. Which he hadn't, until Grandma thought he was Xan more often than not.

He toyed with some lyrics in his head, having had just enough whiskey to think he was brilliant and didn't even need an agent to get deals. He enjoyed putting literary allusions into his songs, even when his (ex) agent said he didn't get them all; enough egghead nerds out there got them to give him a strange demographic of fans.

He'd had his first hit with the song inspired by Toni Morrison, "Can't Cheat, Can't Defeat." That had been the title of the movie he had walked out on, which really chapped his ass. He'd been looking forward to working with Lupita Nyong'o.

Can't Cheat, Can't Defeat was getting Oscar buzz, including for Phineas's replacement, Not Lately. It was maddening.

He scratched absently at his arm, hissing slightly when he touched the fresh burn. Xan had never talked about why he had Band-Aids on his arms, but he frequently had one slapped over some wound or another. The third night here he found out what Xan had been covering up all those times, when Grandma had called him "Alexander" and had burned him with her cigarette for being too slow with dinner.

He put the whiskey bottle down on the porch and made to unfold the paper in his fist, but then picked up the bottle again. The paper in his other hand wouldn't say anything new. He had spent a good part of the day looking for official family documents, including his birth certificate, his parents' death certificates, and his parents' wills.

He had found several official documents.

He sighed and glanced over his shoulder through the screen door. Grandma still lay prone at the foot of the stairs, her head at an angle that looked uncomfortable. Blood had ceased to flow from a gash on her hairline.

He waited for remorse, grief, or even the warmth of bittersweet nostalgia for the better days of his childhood, but the burn from this morning was still angry red and blistered, and Grandma had kept telling him he was a bastard. His emotions ranged from rage to resignation. His career could probably be salvaged, but it would take a long time. Xan was gone from the whole goddamn planet, abandoning his little brother to this monster. And he had no inheritance from his grandparents or his parents.

But for now, he had a mess on his hands. He should probably call the police.

HIS PHONE WAS in his hands and he had pulled up the information for the local police department. Was he supposed to call 911? It wasn't an emergency; she couldn't get any deader. He honestly didn't know.

And would they believe him when he said she just fell? Or would they just arrest him for murder?

A sound caught his ears, the unmistakable crunch of a car on their long gravel driveway. A blue hatchback was trundling importantly toward him.

He watched it with interest. Grandma didn't get visitors, and no one knew he was here. Perhaps this was a lost tourist looking for Dollywood. Maybe he could catch a lift and go Away.

The car pulled up beside Phineas's rental SUV and stopped. A white woman with a very blonde ponytail got out.

Reporter, he thought. He balled his fist and crumpled the paper again. Someone wanted to ask about Xan's disappearance. Phineas was surprised it had taken the press this long to look into Xan's history, or connect him with the rapper Salty Fatts. He forced himself to relax.

The woman was in her late thirties and had a black baseball cap on. She looked like she was a sorority chick trying to dress down for a party where the theme was "regular folk." She wore jeans and an XL T-shirt that looked like it had been purchased for five dollars at the local gas station. It read, YOU SAY "WHINE" AND I HEAR "WINE!" across her chest.

She didn't look like a reporter. She looked like someone trying very hard to look nonchalant. And her spine was far too straight.

Cop, or military.

"Hey there, I'm looking for Phineas Morgan?" she asked.

"Who's looking?" he asked.

She scaled the front steps without permission, then looked from Phineas to the bottle to the screen door, beyond which she couldn't miss Grandma's still form.

A very long moment passed without anyone saying anything. Phineas just watched his guest, wondering what she would do. She opened the screen door, knelt by Grandma's body, and then gently touched her neck.

She left the body and joined Phineas. "How long ago did that happen?"

"'Bout an hour," he said with a sigh.

She put her hands on her hips. "Looks like you need some help."

He shrugged. "With what? She's dead; there's nothing anyone can do now." He waggled his phone at her. "Was just about to call the police, actually."

"You don't seem broken up," she said.

He showed her his forearm. "Let's just say Grandma was not easy to care for, and I'm no nurse. Also not a masochist," he added.

The woman nodded once. "Right. So this is good timing, actually."

"How do you figure?" he said.

"You've clearly spent the last hour processing your grief," she said smoothly.

"If you want to call it that." He picked up the whiskey again.

The woman pointed at him. "No, *you* want to call it that. I can smooth this over, get no questions asked, and make this problem go away."

He didn't like white ladies pointing at him. It usually happened right before someone called for the manager. "Who the fuck *are* you?"

"My name is Opal. I have some information about your brother."

He sat up in the rocker, offensive paper forgotten. "You do?"

She nodded.

"Why the fuck didn't you say so right away?" He took a swig from the bottle and relaxed back. He held it out for her to take. "Drink?"

She shook her head, smiling wryly. "I'm driving." She leaned against the railing, body tense and arms crossed tightly. "I came here to talk about Alexander Morgan, but let's start with Norma Morgan."

"How? Can you disappear bodies or something?"

Her smile grew strained. "Of a sort, yes."

"You know my brother? Army?"

She shook her head. "I know of him. I just transferred to the same fort he was stationed at."

"Did my brother really get captured by fuckin' aliens?"

She shook her head. "That's classified."

"Like hell, it's all over the press!"

She sighed as if resigned to her fate. "Sorry, instinctive reaction. Yes, I'm with the army, but I'm not here in an official capacity. I assume you have heard the reported information about the murder of William Williams at the birthday party?"

"Yeah."

"We have some new intel that your brother sought and received sanctuary on the alien space station Eternity. He's AWOL at best and wanted for some information regarding a murder and some missing classified information at worst—"

"So he's not a suspect in the murder?" Phineas interrupted.

"Some people have been arrested, some killed themselves, but the authorities still want to question him like any other witness. But some believe his life is in danger. They think he was the target at the party, and the killer got the wrong man."

"Why would anyone kill my boring-ass brother?" Phineas asked.

"That is definitely classified," she said. "Anyway, a lot of people want to talk to your brother, and they are sending someone after him. Some want him questioned, some want him dead, and I think they all want him back on Earth. This is a highly specialized case, and the person they're sending is not military—well, she's former military—but she's volatile. I'm pretty sure she could flip a coin and let that decide whether she knocks him in the head to bring him home or helps him stay away from the people chasing him."

"You chose a Batman villain as your extraction agent?"

She winced. "I didn't. I would not have chosen this person. But she seemed perfect for the job, according to my superiors. My theory is that they think she's as expendable as they get. She may get the job done. And if she doesn't, the army hasn't lost anyone special. Also, she served with your brother, so they're hoping that will get her close to him. I personally think she's being sent on a suicide mission, or it's possible she has other orders beyond what I know about. Your brother is in danger, if only because he doesn't know she's coming."

"Sounds like you're trying to protect both of them," he said, quirking an eyebrow at her. "How is that possible?"

"She's a civilian who's being taken advantage of. She's going into an unknown situation, and Morgan has been on the station a lot longer, so he will know the surroundings."

"And why are you protecting him?" he asked. "Don't soldiers get lost in war all the time? This seems like a big step to keep one guy safe."

"Also classified," she said, shaking her head. "But someone in the executive branch wants him protected."

Phineas laughed, sheer bafflement winning over the other emotions. "So let me get this straight. He's wanted for questioning. He's AWOL. He's got an assassin after him. But President Gorman wants him protected?"

"Someone close to the president," she amended. "But that's it in a nutshell."

Phineas shook his head. "Hey, if that other person they're sending decides to go easy on him, do you think I can send a message with her to tell him Grandma is dead?"

"I doubt she'd be amenable to that," she said, shifting on the railing and looking around the yard. "Then again, she may be. She's very loyal to family."

"So why are you telling me all of this? There's nothing I can do, and I got shit here to deal with." He waved his hand behind him. "The police and funeral stuff don't wait."

"We can help with the problems regarding your grandmother," Opal said. "The police won't question you. As for what you can do, I need to get a message to Xan from his contact, and need someone to look out for him."

She pulled a memory stick out of her pocket and handed it to him. "This will have instructions for you on it along with some encrypted information. Xan should know how to unlock the rest of the message."

He didn't take the stick. "The army is just going to hand a civilian classified info and send him off into space? How the hell do you think I can get to him?"

"That policy has changed. We can get you a seat on the first shuttle headed to the station. It won't have a lot of people, mostly VIPs, but some civilians can buy or win seats."

His voice dropped lower. "And why do you think I want to protect him?" he asked softly.

She looked startled. "He's your brother."

"Family ties ain't what they used to be," he said, purposefully taking on Grandma's mountain drawl. He gestured to the porch; frankly, it was foul. Grandma hadn't bothered to take the trash very far past the front door, and bags had piled up on the opposite side of the porch. Raccoons had gotten into some of them and strewn food containers and papers everywhere. Mouse and raccoon droppings littered the porch. He didn't even want to think about how many vermin were living in the walls.

He would have cleaned, but taking care of Grandma without a break was exhausting.

"Xan left me with a mess," Phineas added, letting the double meaning hang. "So again I ask, why should I help him?"

Opal pursed her lips.

"What aren't you telling me?" he pressed.

"There's a lot I'm not telling you," she said. "I shouldn't even be here."

He took another drink from the bottle and cradled it in the crook of his arm. "So who are you, really?"

"I'm just a sergeant. I'm a quartermaster, trained at Fort Lee."

"Nope. More than that."

She sighed and thought for a second. "Some people in the government feel Xan should be extradited and tried and imprisoned. Others think he has information that needs protecting, and someone very powerful apparently owes him a favor. I am in the unique position to be working with both sides. I both know who is going to extradite Xan and who has considerable interest in keeping him alive."

"I'm guessing you're representing the ones who want him saved," he said.

"I want to keep the human race from being wiped away like bug guts on a windshield," she said. "A lot of people think Xan is the key to preventing that."

"Look, you can't be talking about my brother. He is a coward who runs from responsibility. He left me with all this shit here, and Grandma to care for, and it turns out Grandma likes to burn people with cigarettes when she is angry."

"Why not stop buying her cigarettes?"

He chuckled bitterly. "You clearly haven't had to care for an addict. I stopped buying cigarettes for her once. She screamed, insulted me, threw shit, and literally didn't stop until I left to get her a pack. It was easier to just let her have what she wanted."

She sighed. "I'm sorry for that. So if I can't appeal to your interest in your brother's safety, can I appeal to your sense of patriotism? Your country needs your brother."

Phineas stayed silent, glaring at her.

"Okay, what about a free ticket to the first alien space station humans will set foot on?" she asked, exasperated. "Free trip to outer space."

"I have acrophobia," he said coldly and then shrugged. "But you'll take care of Grandma if I help you out?"

"Definitely," she said, pulling out her phone.

"Fine, whatever. I'll do it. I could use a change of scenery."

She hit a number from her contacts and then looked at Phineas. "Did you push her?" She nodded toward Grandma.

Phineas stiffened. "Does your offer hinge on my answer?"

"No."

"Then don't worry about it."

She put the phone to her ear and walked away from Phineas, toward her car for privacy. Phineas strained to hear and could just make out, "I've got him, but we have a mess to clean up."

Phineas rocked slowly as Opal, now out of earshot, finished her call. She returned, holding the memory stick again.

"The shuttle leaves in a week," she said. "You might want to postpone the funeral until you get back. You and Xan were her only relatives, right?"

"Yeah, but whenever we have it, I'll be the only one there," he said, not liking the army knowing shit about him. He shifted in the swing. "But tell me, why don't you go if you know more about it than anyone?"

"I can't go because it's too high profile. Everyone on that shuttle could have their fifteen minutes of fame right then, and the press will be looking to see what kind of dirt they can find on the people headed off planet. I can't be in the spotlight; you're already in the spotlight, so this will be nothing new for you. And if you use your stage name, it's possible the press won't figure out you're Xan's brother."

"So my brother is the only human on this station?"

She shook her head. "There are two others. The Earth ambassador is there, as well as a civilian who was granted political asylum. She's . . . unimportant." She pursed her lips again.

He laughed. "Goddamn, I hope you never play poker. You have the worst tell. What are you not telling me about *her*?"

"That's the most classified thing of all. Don't worry about it. You have zero connection to her."

Phineas took another drink of whiskey and rubbed his face. "Fuck, Xan, what did you get yourself into?"

He put the bottle down on the porch and then gestured that he would accept the memory stick.

She handed it over, and something seemed to relax within her. She had done her part.

"What are your people going to do with Grandma?"

Opal started counting on her fingers. "An interview is being written right now that you were grocery shopping and came home to find your grandmother at the bottom of the stairs. Several witness accounts will support you being at the grocery store. I'm having groceries brought in, one bag for you to leave in your car, two to drop on the porch here." She pointed to the floor where the whiskey bottle was, then she bent down and picked it up. "This needs to go away. Also, go brush your teeth. You're totally sober. One police officer that my contact knows will arrive with an EMT to handle the body. Someone is fabricating a 911 call for the records. Don't worry; they'll cover everything."

"What do I have to do?"

"Brush your teeth, hydrate, whip up some tears—lemon juice is good if you've got it—and remember the window of time when you were at the grocery store. You arrived home about five minutes ago. Grandma was dead when you got here. She must have thought she could handle the stairs on her own, poor dear. Also, you have ice cream melting in the car. Remember the ice cream. It will distract you in a realistic way."

She looked him up and down, frowning. "Do you have a long-sleeved shirt?"

"Why? Don't like a fat man in a tank top?" he challenged.

"What? Of course not," she asked, frowning. "But I'm trying to snip all the dangling threads. The EMT will likely notice you have several burns on your arms, very clearly cigarette burns. Best to keep them from asking entirely."

He rubbed the older burns automatically; sometimes they still itched. "Are you going to be here if I forget anything?"

She blanched, pale face getting paler, with two spots of color high on her cheeks. "God, no. I can't be seen anywhere near here. I'm at a funeral in Gatlinburg right now." He looked at her blankly. "After I leave here, I'm buying a blender at Target and destroying this burner phone. I'm positive that my superiors have my personal phone traced, so it's currently in the pocket of a mourner at a funeral."

Phineas shook his head in confusion.

"Oh," she said. "When I decided to come see you, I needed a reason to be here." She pulled a crumpled piece of newsprint from her back pocket and read it. "A Mrs. Penny Hogg. Old family friend. She died of a fall, just like your grandmother, bless her heart. Mrs. Hogg's son and my father went to school together, and he told me to come show respect." Her regular accent, sounding much more northern, returned. "It was the only way I could talk to you without them knowing."

He leaned his head to the right, smiling slightly. "What did you tell your superiors, exactly?"

She frowned. "That I was going to the funeral."

"Did you say you were going to Mrs. 'Hogg's' funeral? Did you say the name?"

"I don't remember," she said, looking alarmed. "Why?"

"Because the last name isn't pronounced 'hawg.' It rhymes with 'vogue.' Doesn't seem like a mistake an old family friend would make." He laughed. "You can forge these files and histories but you'll be discovered by the mispronunciation of a name."

"Shit. That's a good catch," she said, going paler. "I will need to whip up a story about embarrassing myself at the funeral when I mispronounced the name. Or my dad hated that I made fun of her name, and now I can't apologize. I'll figure something out. That was a good catch, thanks."

"Are you that scared of your bosses?" he asked.

"Yes," she said. "I know some of what they're hiding. And if they sent someone after Xan, they definitely wouldn't hesitate to silence me if they knew how much I know, or if they knew I was passing info to the executive branch."

She sighed and stuck her hand out. "And with that I need to get going. I can't be seen here. Check out the memory stick. The unencrypted data is for your instructions, information about the launch, everything you need."

He shook her hand. "I appreciate the help. And if I get into trouble while trying to protect my *soldier* brother from someone the government sent after him, I can't call and ask you why the fuck you sent a civilian for this job?"

"Unfortunately, that is correct," she said. "I think warning him will be your best bet. Find your brother, give him the data, warn him about the army's intentions, and protect him if you can."

She turned and jogged down the stairs. "Don't forget about the shirt," she said.

He turned the drive over in his hands. There were still some things to settle with his big brother, aka Grandma's sole heir.

"Yeah, I've got to go," he said, decision cementing. "He's my brother."

If she noticed he left out the promise to warn and protect Xan, she made no comment.

18

WHEN WE WERE VULTURES

So, CALLIOPE, WHAT brings you to the station?" Xan asked
Calliope as they took a seat a few couches away from the other
survivors. They all tried to make themselves comfortable, the only
one succeeding being Phineas. Sitting on the massive, Gneiss-size
couches, his brother actually looked comfortable. *He'd fit in here,
furniture-wise*, Xan thought.

"You," she said, crossing her legs under her like a child and
wrapping her flapping trench coat around her. He wondered if it
had a lot of pockets, and if she still had a klepto problem.

Not the best time to ask.

He grimaced. "I thought you left the army. Why would they
send you to fetch me?"

"So you're not going to ask how I've been doing? You don't look
happy to see me."

"I'm not happy," he said. "But how are you?"

Her eyes widened in mock surprise. "How can you say that
after all we've been through!"

"What we've been through is why I'm not happy to see you. I
don't want to talk about what happened; I don't want you to justify
it to me; I don't want to hear that you haven't told anyone. I know

you didn't tell anyone because I would have heard." He winced, imagining it.

She laughed. "Course I didn't tell. If I spill, they know I was involved, too. I got my discharge and I'm a plain old civilian now, and it's great how much the civilian life doesn't have to do with finding dead bodies, transporting them, cataloguing every scratch or taking stock of who lost limbs, or love letters or mom's wedding ring—"

"Don't have to list the duties . . . H2," he said, tacking on the nickname she wanted as an afterthought. "I'm still in the service."

"Or you were till you escaped from Earth, anyway." She shrugged. "That was a lucky break! How'd you pull that off?"

"That's why you came all this way? To hear about that night?"

"Actually, yes! Tell me about that party. Was it fun?"

He sighed, remembering how she loved tangents. "Fine. I was at the party, pretty sure someone drugged me, someone tried to kill me during a game of Werewolf, so I ran. And then a ship picked me up, but she was on programmed autopilot and couldn't drop me off."

"That's wild," she said. "You didn't plan this? The aliens weren't your friends or anything?"

"I didn't know them at all," he said.

"Let's talk about you and that woman," she said, pointing at Mallory, who was talking to some other survivors. "What's her story? Seems fishy that two people get asylum from the station that doesn't like humans."

"No, if you want to know about Mallory, you'll have to ask her . . . but how did you know she asked for asylum?" he asked, crossing his arms.

"You know the army has ears everywhere," she said breezily.

"I thought that was the CIA."

"Them, too."

This was getting tiring. He went for the blunt question. "Did they send you here to take me back?"

"Oh, most definitely," she said, grinning. "But you know what else? They sent me here all alone, knowing you're a much better soldier than I ever was, and I think they're probably anticipating this adventure to end in my death. I think they want me to try to do as much on their list as I can before you or some alien kills me."

"So if you think they're sending you here to die, or to kill me if you get lucky, where do we stand?" he asked cautiously. He could probably take her one-on-one, but he remembered her unique combat skills. Although he had her on height and weight, she had taught him a lot of hand-to-hand fighting techniques, so he guessed they had an equal chance of killing each other if it came down to fighting.

"I'm saying I want to know more about what's going on before I decide what to do," she said. "Why do they want you so bad?"

"You have to know that. They briefed you!" he said, exasperated.

"Yes, but they lie," she said patiently. "I'm not stupid, Xan. Also, I want to know if you know why they want you so bad."

He glanced around the room. No one seemed to be listening. "All right, let's make a deal. I'll tell you, but first you have to answer my questions about what happened to the shuttle."

"Deal," Calliope said.

"So I assume you got the seat because the army sent you. Am I right?"

"Pass," she said.

She had said that a lot. The superior officers had hated it. Back then, they could have threatened her and put her on latrine duty for giving them the runaround, but he didn't have that option.

He shook his head. "I'll take that as a yes. If the army sent you, why are you not attacking me right away?"

"That's not polite, is it? And there's not much to hide since you know why I'm here. Also, I nearly died in space, you rescued me, and I can't forget that. I figured we could take a moment, catch our breaths, and chat a bit before all that violence starts. We do go way back, you know. And you called me my nickname, which you always refused to do. Why?"

"I refused because you made it sound like you were a Star Wars droid," he said, puzzled.

"No, why are you doing it now?"

"When we got separated, I decided if I ever saw you again, I'd call you what you wanted to be called."

"Why?"

"'Cause I'm pretty sure you saved my life, that night before the patrol," he admitted.

She narrowed her eyes. "How?"

"You denying it?"

"Of course I am. If I admit to saving your life, then I admit to assaulting a fellow soldier."

"So it *was* you."

GOING INTO THE army had reminded Xan of a church Christmas pageant. They were told that every single branch of the army, from IT to medics to support to admin to accounting to vehicle maintenance and, yes, mortuary services, was vital and necessary. No small parts, just small actors, the preacher would say. (But his daughter was always Mary in the pageant, regardless of her age. From ages four to nineteen.) However, all the recruits knew that the only army stories that lasted involved going into battle, killing a bunch of your enemy, protecting women and children and American Freedom itself, and rescuing all of your buddies who got injured.

Those who took the active combat roles knew they were better than support, or medical, or definitely mortuary, but their derision was subtle and masked. Everyone knew you didn't fuck with supply. A funny prank on Monday could have your laundry still dirty and all of the good food gone by the time you got to dinner on Friday.

Most people didn't fuck with supply anyway. Some of the soldiers at Fort Sam Houston, namely PFC Buck Jones (a name Xan had had trouble taking seriously), had named the quartermaster battalion the Vultures because, in their opinion, they didn't go out until it was time to pick up the dead. Calliope had tried to reclaim it, drawing an unofficial badge for them, which had helped a little. Vultures had their place, after all, she reasoned. They stopped the spread of disease and just tidied up after carnivores were done. Unlike most other birds, vultures were communal and looked after their own, Calliope told Xan one night when they had shared a bottle of wine.

"Listen, when have you seen any group of animals eating peacefully together?" she'd asked him, waving her finger in his face. She had a habit of getting belligerent when she drank. And when she didn't drink.

"Even pretty little songbirds are pretty little assholes, chasing each other away from the bird feeder. But you see a wake of vultures around some roadkill, and they just sit like a family going to dim sum on a Sunday. You know if they could put that deer on a lazy Susan and just twirl it around so Grandpa could get at some rotting spleen, they totally would. Vultures are ugly, and they eat rotting things. But they clean up the corpses in nature, which someone has to do, and they do it while looking out for each other. Mark my words, if there's ever a zombie apocalypse, the carrion eaters will save us. But no one wants to make that movie. Buck the Fuck thought he was putting us down with the 'Vultures' bullshit, but he really said we're a group that looks out for each other and does the jobs no one else will do."

While she had been monologuing, Xan had finished the bottle of wine. He shook it to coax the last drops out and looked for another one. Calliope handed him her bag and he fished out another bottle. She sat back and stared gloomily into her mug of wine.

"This tastes like shit," she muttered.

Xan just watched the stars coming out.

"Buck thinks we're fucking," she said. "And I let him believe it."

His head whipped around at her. "What?"

"Just testing you. But I think he probably does. I don't care. Do you?"

Xan had a horrible feeling in his stomach that she was about to proposition him. He wouldn't put it past her; he didn't feel any chemistry with her, but it wouldn't surprise him if she wanted to have sex because it seemed like a good idea at the time.

"Want to talk about vultures again?" she asked after a moment.

"I'm not going to talk about how awesome corpse eaters are," he said.

The trash talk from the other soldiers had been infuriating. He knew that they weren't considered important in the eyes of combat soldiers, but they all knew you couldn't fight if you couldn't eat. When Xan and Cal were done with their mortuary training, Jackson, their training officer, had taken all the new quartermasters out for a beer to celebrate and to give them the unofficial but very real reality about mortuary support.

"I'm not saying all companies will do this," Jackson began. "But you are taking on a role that no one wants. Combat grunts might say you're bad luck to be around before a mission. And when you do your jobs well, people will be too grief-stricken to appreciate it. And when you do it poorly, someone will remind you the harm you've done to grieving mothers and widows. Some will invent missing things that must have been 'stolen' from a soldier's personal effects and try to get you or the army to cough up money for the missing items. Luckily, we have some redundant measures in effect now to combat that. That's why you do not log personal effects or injuries without at least one other person there." He knocked his knuckles on the table, staring at Calliope. "Do you hear me, Oh?"

Calliope made a face. "I get it, sir."

Jackson relaxed and took another sip of his beer. Then he added, "It's thankless, and dirty, and depressing as shit."

Xan gave him the prompt he was waiting for. "Then why do it?"

"It has to be done. Someone's got to do it, and that someone is you." He held his glass up, toasting them. "So I'm going to thank you here and now for your service, because it may be the last time you hear this."

Jackson had been mostly wrong. Most of the soldiers in Afghanistan treated them with the same respect (or disrespect) they treated everyone. It didn't get bad until they left Afghanistan and took a post in Texas to help with the growing hostility regarding the water shortage at the US-Mexico border.

Attacks from drug cartels had driven workers from the power plants at the dam, and the army had to go in and take the area back, protecting it. The coast was nowhere near clear, and patrols were sent every few days to keep the power plants and dam safe. Not only were the drug cartels threatening them, but when the military came to the dam, the area towns were convinced they were going to lose their water, and the public relations engine had to rev up.

Water was tightly rationed for the troops, and tempers were short.

"Fucking vultures, get away from us," Buck had said, throwing a dinner roll at Xan when he'd gotten up to clean his plate.

Buck had harassed them for days with no peace. Xan and Calliope had been helping out supply with nothing to do for their mortuary role. On advisement, they had left dirty sheets for Buck to make his bed, and when they served food, they served him the smallest portions. But it didn't faze him at all.

Buck's childish pranks had been edging into hard-core twelve-year-old boy territory, including tripping Xan on the way to the latrine, pouring vinegar in his bed, and drawing on Xan's face when he'd been sleeping off a rough day.

The night Calliope saved his life, he and Calliope were drinking in their usual place, a table in the mess hall that was the farthest corner from the door. The moon was fat and full, casting its light through the open mess door.

"Why is it worse now?" Calliope asked.

"What?"

"The shit. Buck. You know what I'm talking about. It's got to be getting to you. It gets to me. And why are we even needed here? It's like the Cold War or something."

He stared moodily at the darkening sky. "Exactly, it's the Cold War, where everything that happens is quiet. We don't know we won't be needed. And ordnance needs backup, I guess."

"Hey, someone could get heatstroke and die; that would give us something to do!" she said hopefully.

More of the terrible wine. Xan winced as it went down. "Hey, question for you," he asked. "If I found you out there, what would you want me to do?"

"What, you mean besides going by the book and bringing home my dead-ass body?"

"Yeah."

She got a faraway look in her eyes. "I'd want you to tell people I went down fighting, and then I'd want you to throw me a Viking funeral. Complete with burning boat and everything. Make it epic. Make it *fucking metal*."

"You've thought about this," he said, smiling slightly. "But I'm not sure that's legal."

"Not my problem. I'm dead," she reminded him. "What about you?"

"I don't know," he said. "I hate the idea of burning, so I don't want cremation. I don't think I want to be buried near my grandmother's family. I don't belong to a church."

"Buried at sea it is," she said gaily.

"Yeah, that can work," he said thoughtfully. "Thanks, Cal." Xan brushed his hands over his eyes, surprised how touched he felt sharing this morbid and personal thing with his only friend around. "I'm going to bed." He got up abruptly and swayed. "After I hit the head."

"Didn't need the visual, dude," Cal said as she settled back against the wall with a bottle in her fist. "I'll stay here for a bit."

People had joked about Cal and Xan having something romantic going on because they were always together. They were a real odd couple, with little in common, but working with Cal had felt like a puzzle piece sliding into place. They complemented each other but there was no chemistry. Xan would like to fall for a woman who was less likely to act on impulse. He'd found impulsiveness sexy in college, but in the past few years he'd seen nothing but chaos come from running into situations without planning. Usually he could stop her from running into situations. Usually.

Xan's drunk brain slowly registered movement behind him, and then the punch came to the back of the head.

Shocked from the punch and the fall, he struggled to roll over, but Buck was on him, straddling him.

"No one steals from me, fucker," he snarled. "You don't take another man's personal shit. I've had it with you. Stealing from the dead is bad enough, but now you have to steal from me?"

What the fuck is he talking about? Xan tried to protest, but Buck slammed his head into the ground. The grass did little to cushion his face from the packed dirt, and he felt his nose break. He groaned and tried to get up, but Buck was too heavy.

"I bet you fuck the corpses too, after you're done with your little Chinese whore," he said, pulling Xan's head back again.

He was able to turn his head slightly so his battered nose didn't take the next slam in the ground, but he felt the skin over his eye split, and then things began to get fuzzy. *Jesus, he's going to kill me.*

Then a whistling came through the night, and there was a *thunk* of glass on bone. Buck fell off him. Somewhere close by, glass shattered.

This is the last time anyone catches me off guard was his thought before he grayed out.

"I SHOULD HAVE figured it out sooner," Xan said, laughing. "I mean, you couldn't hit the floor if you dropped a ball, but a wine bottle is just the right awkwardly balanced thing for you to throw perfectly. You hit him, dead on the back of the head, throwing a bottle, in the dark."

"So my marksmanship with a wine bottle gave me away?"

"I was so fucked up at the time I had no idea what had happened. And then you wouldn't shut up about the Bad Guy you saw."

Calliope laughed in delight. "I loved that Bad Guy. I wrote fanfic about that Bad Guy." She shook her head. "Got a ton of karma on AO3 for that one, too."

"You wrote fanfic about a fake attack on Archive of Our Own?" He shook his head, and added, "What did you tell them, anyway?"

"That you and Buck were talking, and you got jumped. Buck got hit on the back of the head, and then the Bad Guy jumped you and beat the snot out of you."

"And then ran off, without robbing us or anything."

"Well, Buck jumped on my lie to say the Bad Guy had stolen from him, too. Very convenient. But no one knows the motives of

Bad Guy. That was the whole mystery around him," Calliope said seriously. "I told the infirmary I found you two and they came to get you taken care of. After I cleaned up the glass, of course. It was better if Bad Guy took all his weapons with him."

"So, yeah. That was the day before everything went to shit. I'd say the last good day we had, but it didn't end that well."

"You know, I tried to keep track of you. You could have emailed," she said after a moment.

"Not from Bowser. They had me on some pretty strict security." He met her eyes. "Now will you talk to me?"

"Yes. What do you want to know?"

"First, I need to know about the shuttle. That shuttle could seat fifty. Why wasn't it full?"

"We had to report for translation bug implantation yesterday, and a bunch of people chickened out at that. I saw some yelling, others crying, and some just terrified that the aliens were microchipping them. These morons who won't let their phone out of sight, ever, are worried about being tracked via microchip. Don't know what they were whining about. It was painless."

"Lucky you," he muttered. "Mine was administered by a drunk rock person with the mentality of a teenager. At least I was passed out when it happened. Anyway, I saw how the passenger area was laid out. Can you remember who was sitting where?"

"I'd need a shuttle layout to get it exact," she said, closing her eyes. "But the shuttle had six rows of six seats with an aisle down the middle. Only it had more room than our shitty planes with the shrinking seats. I remember that the old Black lady and her granddaughter were sitting in the front of economy, on the left side. The seat next to them was empty, while that doctor was on the aisle on the right side. The white kid, blond hair, big-time reader, he sat alone on the left in the back, hunched up against the window. He kept reading and looking around the cabin and then back at his book. I didn't trust him.

"Also, in the back, on the right aisle, was the blonde woman, looking like she'd just kissed an asshole and was determined not to lick her lips. All uptight and shit. I was on the aisle two rows in front of her. That Hispanic couple had the two seats beside me. Across the aisle was the big guy—your brother, I take it?—and then an empty seat, then me. Everyone else was in the middle four rows and I think like ten or so folks were seated up front, first class, I guess, but had to come through our cabin to go to the bathroom. Which I don't think anyone did when they saw it. Guessing the Gurudev don't pee like we do?"

He shook his head. "No, they don't. Lucky for us, Eternity made some human-appropriate plumbing when humans got on board. So, do you remember much about the kid in back?"

She narrowed her eyes. "Why?"

"He's the only one outside of first class who died. But"—he paused—"most of his wounds were similar to everyone else's, and everyone else survived."

Calliope whipped her head around, counting the survivors. "He's not here? Shit, you're right. I didn't even notice."

"So you remember him?"

"I remember seeing him reading some battered book. A *physical* book." She paused to share a "Can you believe it?" look with him, but he just waited for her to continue.

"Anyway. It was like a boring plane flight to the West Coast, only with fewer snacks and better views out the window."

"Do you remember anything that happened that was weird? About anyone, not just the reading guy?"

She thought for a second. "The old lady was lecturing the Black girl about something, sounded like proper violin or vigilante technique or something. The big guy looked nervous as hell, and then took a pill and slept. The white woman just sat and looked out the window, playing with her bracelet charms. She's got one of those tacky white lady bracelets with the big charms. But, yeah, this was weird. At one point the guy—Sam—got up. I thought he was going to go to the bathroom, but then he just came back up the aisle and started pacing. Maybe the bathroom wasn't built for humans and he really had to go. But he seemed really nervous."

"This is in the middle of the flight, after the jump? Not the beginning?"

"We were just flying along. I don't know what spooked him. After about four or five trips up the aisle, I got up to try to talk to him and see if he was okay."

"What did he say?"

"I said, 'Hey, are you okay?' He looked at me like I was insane, said he was just worried about meeting aliens for the first time, or something. I said that he should just sit down and do some deep breathing, my people invented yoga, you know."

"You're not Indian," Xan said.

"Tai Chi, then."

"You're not Chinese!" he said, exasperated. "Your family is from Korea, and you've never been there!"

"Don't you appropriate me!" she shouted, then calmed down. "Well, we had to have made something relaxing. K-pop?"

He glared at her stonily. "Can you take one thing seriously? Please?"

She rolled her eyes and sat back like a pouting toddler. "Fine. I told him to calm the fuck down, he was making people nervous. So he did! Maybe I should claim that as a Korean method of relaxing."

"Bullying?"

She glared at him. "My turn. Why are you here?"

"Do you remember William Williams?" he asked.

She got a guarded look on her face. "Yeah. He was at Falcon Dam. He was the idiot with two identical first names. One of the guys who got the pukes on that day . . ." She trailed off. "Is he the guy who died at the party?"

"I don't think this had anything to do with Falcon Dam," he said. "I was at his birthday party and we were playing a game. The lights went down, someone was behind me with a knife, but they got Billy instead." He shrugged. "I ran. A ship picked me up, and three Gneiss were standing over me talking about me like I was a rescued dog. They said they had their autopilot locked and set to Eternity, so I was forced to come here. I asked if I could stay, and the station told me yes."

"Not like you could have come home if she didn't want you, right?"

"Pretty much."

Calliope scooted back in the huge chair she had chosen and crossed her legs under her. "So you didn't kill Billy."

"No."

"And the army didn't send you here?"

"Why would they send you to come get me if they already sent me here?" he demanded.

"Maybe you didn't come home when they wanted you to," she said, shrugging.

"So come on, H2Oh, why are you really here? What's been going on with you?"

She considered him for a second and then leaned forward, even though they were nowhere near anyone else. "Tell me, what do you know about God's Breath?"

"Fuck me," Xan said, a little louder than intended, startling everyone around them. "What do *you* know about it? Is that why you're here?"

"Not exactly. My Uncle Drop was dealing something new called 'God's Breath,' and he got locked up. He claims the government hired him to deal it and then hung him out to dry. He was always blaming some other guy for his troubles, and I never believed him. But I think this time he may be telling the truth. They were paying him a lot for it. He's a small-time dealer, but he had a lot more cash than usual squirreled away in his trailer. I asked him about it, and he said the order came from Fort Bowser, and I knew they're studying aliens there, and you were stationed there, so I thought you might know something about it."

"How did you know so much about Bowser?" he asked.

"Listening, eavesdropping, reading superiors' phones when they were otherwise occupied," she said.

"Christ, Calliope," he said, leaning forward and putting his hands on her shoulders. "Please tell me you didn't bring any here."

"Actually, I think I've got some right here," she said, pulling out a baggie of blue powder from one of her many pockets. "Uncle Drop told me it was super-addictive and not to take any . . . Hey, are you all right?"

Xan felt the blood drain out of his face. He reached out gently and put his hand over hers. "Put that away, please. You've got the local equivalent of C4 in your pocket."

"What the hell is this stuff?" she asked, holding the baggie up to her face as if she hadn't looked at it closely before. "Why did the government make it?"

Xan opened his mouth. If she didn't know what it did, she might be reckless with it. If she knew and was testing him, they could all already be in trouble.

"It's a weapon," he said, his voice low. "Please don't use it, or even take it out."

She looked at him, calculating, and then slipped it back into her jacket pocket.

"A weapon against aliens? Those big rock guys and the little bark-covered ones? All of them?"

"Even the station itself. That's why it's so goddamn dangerous that you brought it here. And the station here is under enough stress right now. She might freak out again."

"Again?"

"You don't know what happened to your shuttle, do you?" he asked.

"I assumed someone shot at us. It was weird. We were all doing that communing-with-the-station thing when everything went all crashy and dark. I blacked out and then woke up in a pod."

Xan sighed, remembering he was supposed to be talking about this the whole time. Not about the chemical weapon from the government that she blithely carried around in a sandwich bag. "Can you tell me anything else about the trip?"

She frowned and rubbed the back of her head. He guessed she had been hit there. "After yelling at the kid to sit down, I started talking to the big guy, Phineas. Your brother, right? He's like a rap star or something?"

"He is. Among other things," Xan said, tamping down the flare of resentment against Phin.

"Hey, can you introduce me? You promised that once upon a time."

"Let's get through this, okay?"

"He just told me he had won the shuttle seat in a lottery and wanted a vacation. Weird that he didn't tell me you two were related. Anyway, everyone was awake and seemed excited about arriving at the station, or trying to peep at the celebrities in first class." She frowned. "Did everyone in the front die?"

Xan nodded. "Yeah. You eleven are the only ones left."

"Damn. When we got close, the captain told us to relax, and that we would have our minds touched by the station. We all kind of freaked out, and I yelled that no one told us that was going to happen—and by then she was already there." She frowned, remembering. "She wanted to know who I was and—she pulled it from me. I didn't even have to tell her. She said something about me being fractured or something, which wasn't true because I haven't had a bone break since the army days."

Xan chose not to point out that Eternity had been speaking in metaphors. Best not to distract Calliope.

"Anyway, we were almost done talking when I heard this screaming, and then something slammed into the ship. Then I woke up here."

"And you didn't have any of that in your system?" Xan pointed toward her jacket pocket where the drug baggie had been hidden again.

"Of course not," she said. "I don't use my uncle's stash."

"Why did you bring it?" he asked her, looking around to make sure no one was paying attention.

"Uncle Drop said for me to go to his trailer and get some supplies for the trip. He had money and weapons and drugs, so I took a little of everything."

Eternity could have freaked out just talking to Calliope, he thought.

"All right. I guess we're done for now," he said, looking to see who Mallory had been interviewing. She was across the balcony, holding the sobbing blonde woman stiffly in her arms. Her aunt? He looked at Calliope again. "Unless you want to tell me exactly what the army told you to do regarding me."

"Nah, not yet. I want to see how this plays out. Do I get to talk to that other woman?"

"Mallory? Why?"

Calliope shrugged. "She seems interesting." She peered at Mallory for a long moment, then added, "Will you tell me something?"

"What?"

"When we were Vultures. Don't you think they had it coming?"

Ah, fuck.

XAN HAD WOKEN up in the infirmary with his nose splinted and right eye swollen shut. Medical tape was holding a forehead laceration together. His lip was swollen badly, having been cut on his crooked canine when Buck had hit him. But he had all his teeth, so that was a win.

"What the fuck happened to you?" came Calliope's voice.

He struggled to sit up and then was shocked to see Buck asleep in the bunk next to him with a bandage around his head and a cut on his cheek. "I—I have no idea," he said. "I was going to the head last night and then everything went black."

"Are you okay to work today? We've got an assignment."

"Is someone dead?" he asked, alarmed.

"Nah, ordnance has a few guys puking their guts out. Norovirus or something. We need to help get a patrol supplied."

The medic let him go with bad grace, accepting that even a beaten-up quartermaster was better than one puking norovirus everywhere.

After taking some painkillers for his head, Xan followed Calliope to breakfast. "Okay, seriously now, are you going to tell me the name of the door you walked into?" she asked as they grabbed trays.

"All I remember is Buck jumped me," he said quietly.

"Going to report him?"

"What's the point?" he asked. "I'm a pussy if I don't fight back and a troublemaker if I do. And a snitch either way if I report him."

"Pussy. Wow. Our enemies have a lot of weapons, but I hope they never find out that the easiest way to take down a man in the army is to call him a part of a woman that is incredibly strong and can take the trauma of childbirth and keep doing its thing."

"Is that all you are going to focus on? That I said 'pussy'?"

She stared at her food for a moment and then brightened and looked up. "Hey, want me to teach you some fighting moves?"

"I'm not a bad fighter, Cal, I was drunk and he jumped me."

"Drunk fighting, then."

"That's a Jackie Chan movie, not a real thing," he said.

She looked at him, nodding and grinning. "I'm not saying you can earn belts in it or study in a serious martial arts school or something, but there are some moves you can learn. Booze can mess you up for fighting, but only if you keep trying to fight like you're not drunk. If you try to stay upright and fight the dizziness, of course you'll be terrible. But if you work *with* the enhanced relaxed state and the unexpected movements, then you can be deadly. Or at least confusing."

"Okay, now I know you're just talking about the movie," he said, drinking juice and wincing when the citric acid hit his lacerated lip.

"I'm not," she said. "You've heard that drunk drivers aren't injured as much as the people they hit because they don't tense up, right? Same thing. I'm pretty good at it."

"But you told me you were a shit grappler."

She drank her coffee. "I am. But if you turn the lights off, throw me in some water, or get me drunk, I turn deadly." She grinned.

"You're serious."

"Come find out," she said.

"All right," he said reluctantly. "When we're off duty next. We have work to do today, right?"

She nodded. "Officer McReady is taking some time off for his injury. So we really do have to step in on ordnance," she said. "That guy still wants a Purple Heart for the broken ankle he got on the stairs at the dam."

"An injury not gotten in combat? I don't think that's how it works," Xan said. "So, what do they need? Inventory? Supplying patrols? Sounds like a one-man job."

"If that one man hasn't been punched in the head repeatedly," she said pointedly. "Besides, they want two of us so we can make sure one doesn't make mistakes. I'm your right-hand gal."

And then Xan replied, saying the phrase that he would regret for the rest of his life: "Yeah, thanks."

"ACTUALLY, FIRST, BEFORE you answer, did McReady ever get his Purple Heart?" she asked.

"Yes," Xan said curtly.

"But he didn't get that in battle," she protested.

He shifted to get more comfortable on the couch. This was not a thing he'd thought he'd have to detail today. "We did see combat during that trip. And no one who was around would refute his claim."

"That seems like a bigger insult than—"

"No, H2. It's really not."

XAN ALWAYS THOUGHT the phrase "friendly fire" was one of the biggest bullshit pies with whipped cream that the PR propaganda division served the military. It didn't matter if it was your enemy's gun or a buddy's gun: if the bullet tore apart your insides or blew your head apart, the result was the same in the end. Dead, dead, dead.

But the military was very strict as to their medal distribution: People who were injured or killed by an enemy's bullet got the Purple Heart. Friendly fire taken while in combat with an enemy also ranked. No medal for shooting range accidents, flying wine bottles, or breaking your ankle on some wet stairs.

There was no medal for soldiers who died due to broken supply lines.

When they got to the supply room, Xan swore out loud. Equipment was stacked against a wall. Apparently, people had been bringing their items by and dropping them off when they didn't see anyone in supply to turn stuff in to.

"We have to log all of this, and we don't know who turned it in," Xan said, picking up a radio that was tangled with a drone. The battery latch was on the floor, beside two batteries that had fallen out. "Goddamn, McReady really lets things slide here."

They took the better part of an hour, logging everything they could and storing things back on shelves where they belonged. Xan's painkillers were wearing off and spikes of pain were hitting him every few minutes or so. He would log the item and assume who had delivered it, then put it away. Calliope was going through the new manifest needed at the dam. The current standing patrol had radioed back that they needed a refresh of supplies and to send it along with the new patrol. Cal began packing items into a trunk.

"Who's leading this patrol?" she asked.

"Buck, if he's conscious," Xan said, rubbing his forehead. His vision was blurry. He shelved a radio and went to unlock a weapons closet.

"Seriously? If this isn't the perfect time to get back at him, I don't know what is! And he'll never know it was you!" Calliope said.

"That could get us into so much trouble, I don't even want to think about it," he muttered. "What do you have in mind?" he added, hating himself.

Cal hefted a radio thoughtfully, then put it in a box. "I don't know. Forget the toilet paper?"

"Buck would use a sock. He doesn't care."

"Jesus, there is so much more I want to know in this world than that," she said. "This radio doesn't have batteries," she said thoughtfully.

"Yeah, they fell out on the floor," he said. "I'll get them."

She grinned wickedly. "Or we could put other batteries in. From the spent rechargeables pile."

In later memories, he would tell himself that he had told her it was a terrible idea to mess with supplies. That they would be found out. Sometimes he would try to convince himself that he had a concussion and it was an honest mistake when he didn't immediately replace the batteries for the radio.

However, Calliope had no concussion, and she had loaded the radio into the trunk with the other supplies. And a small part of his brain would always know that they both knew what they were doing. The dam hadn't seen any action, they reasoned. This would only be a prank.

What was the harm in that?

After the patrols went out and they were released from duty, Cal and Xan spent the afternoon trying new fighting techniques. Xan had wanted to beg off because of his head, but she pointed out that pain would also hobble him in a fight and that he shouldn't fight against those sensations either. After some injured fighting, they got drunk and then tried drunken fighting. Xan was very bad at it, and the second time Calliope threw him, making the stars explode in his head, he begged off.

Two uneventful days later, the new patrol headed off to relieve Buck and his team. After about an hour, there was a panicked radio call—Buck and his team were all dead, scattered about the power plant on the US side of the dam. Dead mercenaries hired by drug smugglers also littered the area; Buck's crew hadn't gone down lightly. They'd done the mercenaries enough damage that they'd had to retreat, because the area was deserted.

There had been no higher-level medics to deal with the bodies, so Xan and Calliope were on duty. Swallowing back bile, Xan logged all the details about the bodies, using his small knowledge of corpse forensics to guess that they'd been attacked earlier that morning. He found the unusable radio on the floor, a few spent batteries spilling out, giving Xan no plausible deniability. Buck's team had tried to message base for backup or orders, and the message hadn't gone through.

That night Xan and Calliope both sat, shocked, on the bumper of the Humvee they had used to bring back their fallen brothers and sisters. They made no move to clean up the blood they'd gotten all over their hands and uniforms.

"I'm a walking biohazard," Cal said.

"Two things," Xan said, and his voice sounded light and forgettable like smoke. He coughed and cleared his throat. "Two things."

"Yeah," Cal said, not looking at him.

"One, we never forget that this was our fault."

"We don't know if the mercenaries would have killed them before backup came," she complained. "And they have charging stations there; they're just too lazy to plug them in. It's beneath—"

"Cal!" he said, hitting the bumper with his fist. "We will never know that. You know why? Because the soldiers who could clear up the confusion are dead. Our. Fault."

She was silent for a moment. "And the second thing?"

"If it ever comes up, it was an honest mistake that we made because we're not used to the way ordnance had things laid out. Someone had bumped the battery charger, it wasn't charging. It was an honest mistake. We tell no one what we did."

"Right. Tell no one," she said, sounding very far away.

That slaughter led to a few more skirmishes, but none the army couldn't handle; they had a grudge now, after all.

When they weren't bringing back their dead comrades or logging the dead mercenaries, Xan and Cal trained in what she called "four fighting," nonstop.

Or maybe they just drank a lot and beat the shit out of each other. Xan couldn't remember. It had the same result.

"SO THAT'S THE lie you told yourself? That they had it coming?"

"Well, Buck did. He could have killed you."

He shook his head. "No. They didn't have it coming. Even if

Buck did have it coming, the others weren't involved." He touched his nose, still with a bump that his glasses usually masked. "That's a lot of death over a broken nose."

"True. So at this party, you were drunk, possibly roofied, and someone came at you with a knife in the dark?"

"Yeah," he said, staring at the silver mesh metal wall of Eternity.

"And they only barely got you, hitting Billy instead."

"Yeah."

"I'm so goddamn proud right now," she said, grinning widely.

"What?" He coughed out a surprised laugh. He had been going down a melancholy road of regret, while she was basking in pride for her former student. "I did learn a lot from you. I guess you've saved me twice.

"So are you going to try to kill me?" he added, trying to keep his voice mild.

"What about those fuckers in first class today? Or that kid, Sam?" she asked, startling him. "Did they have it coming?" She was messing with something inside her pocket.

"Not them, either. And what do you have against them?" he asked.

"The first-class people? Money. They were all money. Old money, famous money, government money." She removed her hand from her pocket. "Sam? Nothing, except he made me nervous with all that pacing."

"H2, back to killing me. Are you going to?" Xan asked.

"Not yet. I have to get the lay of the land. I've got three missions. I'm a busy vulture."

"Three?"

"Yes! You're not the only pheasant to bag up here. Don't feel so special now, do you?"

Jesus. "Are you even here for me at all?" he asked. "There's no 'lay of the land.' We're staying here till we can figure out what happened with the shuttle accident. Just keep the Falcon Dam shit to yourself. That's all I ask when you talk to anyone else."

She turned her head and pointed at Phineas, who was reading on an e-reader. "Does he know?"

"No, I never told him. I haven't even seen him since moving from Texas to North Carolina. And I figure no one ever found out, considering the security level they gave me at Bowser."

"All right, secret's safe for now," she said.

He groaned. "Will you let me know when it's not safe?"

"Sure."

He sighed and got up. "I have to talk to Phineas."

"It's good to see you again, Xan. Didn't realize how much I missed you!"

He was about to say that he couldn't say the same, but then he smiled. He had tried to blame her for the disastrous "prank," but honestly, he had easily gone along with it. He had some serious mixed feelings about her, but she had held his greatest secret, and even if she was here to take him back home, her chaos was as amusing as ever.

"Good to see you too, H2, provided you don't attack me."

He walked over to the railing and looked into the now dark medbay. His back was tight, knowing he was presenting himself as vulnerable to Calliope, and knowing that she knew he was testing her.

Mallory was across the room, talking to her weeping aunt. Mallory didn't move to comfort the woman. Their eyes met.

Too many connections, her eyes said.

. . .

FAMILY IS EVERYTHING

FEATHER, PENCIL, COFFEE *cup, star, heart, alligator. They weren't there.*

Kathy was trapped in that alien prison pod, close to hyperventilating. She closed her eyes and said her own private rosary to calm down. *Feather, pencil, coffee cup, star, heart, alligator.* But it didn't work if her bracelet wasn't there to touch.

The pod lid opened, and she screamed. The lid came back down and sweet-smelling gas flowed into the pod. She fought the sedation, but the panting and screaming forced her to breathe faster than she wanted, and she passed out.

Kathy woke in the pod again, with the only family she had left looking down on her. She was trapped inside an alien pod and had been through hell already just to get here. But she had made it. *Family.*

Mallory hadn't responded as Kathy had expected her to, holding back and looking at the floor as if Kathy frightened her. As if *she* frightened Mallory, when Mallory was a self-proclaimed murder magnet. Of course, that was only to get attention, but most orphans sought attention. It was okay.

When Mallory turned to her on the balcony, instead of sitting where Mallory pointed, Kathy wrapped her arms around her niece. Didn't matter. She held her close. "I've missed you so much, Mallory. Are you all right?"

Mallory was still and stiff for a moment, and then she struggled out of Kathy's arms, just as she had when she was a child. "I'm fine, but my shuttle hasn't just been attacked. Are *you* all right?"

She looked stressed, older, with her hair hanging in her eyes and dark smudges underneath. She smelled a bit like sweat and anxiety; the girl really should have gotten herself a little more made up before she was going to see her aunt, for goodness' sake. She should be using night cream now as well.

Kathy reminded herself that she hadn't told Mallory she was coming, so how would she know to make herself up? But it was true that Mallory hadn't left a forwarding address, and when Kathy had finally found her, Mallory should have immediately gone to clean up to welcome a family member. Kathy had tried to teach the girl how to be a good host. But she was still rude.

She handed Kathy what looked like a small fishbowl, or a brandy snifter without the stem. It held a clear liquid. She looked at Mallory in suspicion. "Is this water?"

"Of course it is, Aunt Kathy," Mallory said, smiling tightly. "Do you think I'd poison you?"

This was too much. "Don't talk to your aunt like that," she snapped, the rebuke coming without a thought. Mallory had not learned any manners since growing up, it seemed.

Her niece sighed. She looked like her mother then, suspicious, unwilling to accept the generosity that Kathy and her family provided them when they were without a home. "I'm sorry, Aunt Kathy. That is water, yes. You'll want it after your time healing in the pod. I understand it takes a lot out of you."

"What happened?" Kathy asked, looking around her. On the balcony, others from the shuttle chatted quietly. Everyone from her cabin was there, except for the young man who had sat across the aisle from her. "The boy, where is the kid from the back that was with us?"

"He didn't make it," Mallory said sadly. "You're looking at the only survivors. There are eleven of you. Everyone else is dead."

"That boy . . ." Kathy's eyes filled with tears as she thought about talking with him and the hopes he had in coming to the station to meet Mallory. She sniffled. "Well, he wasn't a boy. He had to be at least twenty. He was a big fan of yours, you know."

"He was?" Mallory asked, frowning. "Why me?"

Kathy smiled through her tears. "Your little books! He'd read them all. He told me he was coming all this way to meet you."

Mallory guided her to stand a little ways from the others, and leaned on the railing that overlooked where they had been sleeping. She was frowning, causing creases to appear on her forehead and cheeks.

"Don't frown like that, Mallory," she said. "You'll get wrinkles."

"Sorry, can't bring myself to smile right now," she said, her voice flat and ugly. "Why would someone come all this way to meet me now? I mean, I was on Earth for decades."

"He wanted to see space and said you being here made it a bonus," Kathy said. "I told him I was your aunt, and he was so excited. I had promised him I would introduce you."

"That's great, Aunt Kathy, but I have to ask you some questions about your trip here."

"I thought that's what I was telling you about," Kathy said stiffly.

A few thin plastic chairs were unoccupied in a corner where no one else was hanging out, so they sat down, somewhat uncomfortably.

"This isn't comfortable. Don't they have any human-size chairs?" Kathy asked in disdain. She had kept her marveling at the interesting, and frightening, aspects of the space station to a minimum, knowing Mallory would rather hear about home and how her cousin was doing.

"There haven't been a lot of humans here to justify the creation of too many chairs that fit us," Mallory said. "But I need to know about your shuttle trip."

"Why?" she asked. "What happened to us? It's a blur."

"Your shuttle was attacked, and the crew and nearly everyone in first class died."

Kathy laughed. "Don't tell me you had to go all the way to space to get your dream detective job!"

Mallory looked at her blankly.

"You have been playing detective since the moment we got here!" she explained.

"Your shuttle was attacked," Mallory said. "This isn't the only emergency on the station, and security asked me and Xan to find out what happened on the shuttle. It's not a game."

Mallory pointed to a lean, muscled Black man talking to the rude Asian woman. He wore a dirty T-shirt. Kathy was unimpressed.

"You sound very important. I'm proud of you," Kathy said. "Looks like you found a space for yourself." She paused and realized she'd made a pun, and laughed at herself.

"We're talking about the shuttle trip," Mallory said, rubbing the back of her head and making her hair stand out.

"All right," Kathy said, nodding. "I was sitting in the same row as that boy. Sam, I think it was. He was in college. Coming here to meet you. He just chattered on and on. I had hoped he would talk in a foreign language to test that translation device—those things are clever! But I think he was talking English. Then we jumped. It was so beautiful, the one minute we were going so fast!" She paused to remember. It had truly been a miracle to see the hyperspace colors swirl around. But Mallory probably knew all of that already. She wasn't one to be impressed by nature's beauty. "And then we came here. We saw the station, and then that big man kind of froze in front of me. He was stiff for about a minute and then he relaxed and said, 'The station spoke to me!' and he was totally amazed! Then she started to talk to all of us!"

Mallory nodded and didn't interrupt, so it seemed Kathy had taught her some manners. "Anyway, then I got all stiff, and—I'm not sure I can remember everything, but the station spoke to me, too."

"Can you tell me anything she said? I know it's extremely personal, but we need all the information we can get," Mallory said.

Kathy thought for a moment, running through her charms to keep her sane. *Feather, pencil, coffee cup* . . . "She talked to me about the important things in life. Joy and the safety of home, and family."

Mallory wasn't impressed. "Okay, a sentient space station talks to you about home." She wrote it down. "Anything else? Can you tell me anything else about Sam?"

Kathy frowned at Mallory for not taking her beautiful moment more seriously. "He was reading one of your books. Then he got up to wander around, completely stressed! That Chinese woman talked to him, and then he came back to his seat. Then the station started talking to us in turn, and then she spoke to Sam, and then me. Then I heard a crash, and I don't remember anything after that until I woke up here."

Mallory sighed. "Okay, Aunt Kathy. Thanks." She frowned again. The wrinkles this girl was going to have someday! "One more thing. Why the hell are you here?"

Kathy gasped at the bluntness of the question. She blinked, tears coming to her eyes again. "Isn't it obvious? I came to bring you home! You're the only family I have left! Don't you want to come home?"

Mallory sat there, the ungrateful child that she was, and watched the tears stream down her aunt's face.

"No," she said, then turned away.

Kathy flung herself onto Mallory's neck, weeping loudly. "How could you? I have nothing left. Nothing. When you had nothing, I gave you everything," she said.

Her husband was dead. Her son was in jail. Mallory was all the family she had left, and if you didn't have family, you didn't have anything.

Mallory stayed still and let her cry.

The fingers on her right hand sought the bracelet on her left, but it was gone.

. . . star, heart, and alligator.

. . .

20

FULL HOUSE, ACES HIGH

MRS. ELIZABETH BROWN could claim several descriptors in her life. Now that she was at the end of it, she preferred to be known as a doting grandmother, a wicked backgammon player, a well-read book club attendee, and a widow of a good man. (No need to mention also being a widow of a shitty man.)

A lot of things ran in her family, including an overbite, a tendency to always be warm when everyone else was cold, and a monumental unwillingness to back down when faced with hardship. In her life, some called that "stubborn." If they wanted to insult her sex, they called it "willful." She called it "survival."

A few years back, there had been a bit of a shake-up in her life. She had come across the *Tao Te Ching* and had given it a read. It was poetic and interesting, but a little too pleased with itself for being deep. Still, the book had a point when it said that maybe going around an obstacle was easier than smashing through. She was reminded of that when she recognized her own stubbornness manifested in her granddaughter.

It had apparently skipped her son, God bless him.

When she had gone to visit Lovely, she had easily fallen back into the caretaker role. Hoping for a warm welcome, she had instead found Lovely hungover, injured, and broken. Lovely was fragile, but Mrs. Brown had never seen the use of mincing words to spare someone's feelings. After the ridiculous doctor's appointment, Lovely had asked about her hereditary tendencies. Mrs. Brown had given her honest opinion and then held Lovely while she cried.

The girl finally took a shaky breath and scrubbed the tears from her eyes. "Better?" Mrs. Brown said. She nodded. Mrs. Brown took her by the shoulders. "We're going to lunch."

Lovely shook her head. "I'm still hungover as shit."

"Well, I'm hungry. Do you know the last time I had good Chinese food?"

Lovely shrugged. "I guess ten years ago?"

"Ten. Years," Mrs. Brown confirmed. "Also three months, four weeks, and one day. It's good to keep track of things. Now, we need somewhere neutral to sit and talk."

"Neutral? Why?"

Mrs. Brown patted her cheek, pausing to appreciate that Lovely had the same beautiful shade of dark brown skin as her departed husband. "Because I have some things to say, and I don't want you to storm off to your room."

"If you want to trick me into a situation I can't run away from, you might want to hide your intentions," Lovely said, but she smiled, as Mrs. Brown had expected.

She grinned and nodded. "It's true. Your grandfather said I would have made a shitty spy. He hated it when I announced I was bluffing during poker games."

"That was because half the time you *were* lying," she said.

"I had to keep him on his toes," Mrs. Brown said.

Lovely's face fell as she looked at her injured hand. "Gran, what am I going to do?"

Mrs. Brown sighed. "I have some thoughts. If they don't work out, we'll get you some physical therapy. A better doctor. We'll go to Arlington if we have to. We'll do what we always do: whatever we have to in order to survive."

"That's what I'm afraid of," Lovely said in a low voice, as if she didn't want Mrs. Brown to hear.

"What was that?" she asked in a firm voice.

Lovely's angry brown eyes met hers. "I said I was afraid of that. Doing what we always do. Do we always have to take the hard road? I'm afraid, Gran, for more than just my hand."

"And you're afraid of what?" Mrs. Brown asked, knowing the answer but wanting her to say it.

"I'm worried that I'm too much like you."

"Would that be so bad?"

"I don't want to end up like you, Gran. You gotta understand that much."

She nodded slowly. "Yes, I suppose I do. But whatever I passed down to you, you still have your own free will. Make your own choices, Lovely. You're the one who decided to fight to protect your friend. No one made you become the Bride."

Lovely groaned and rolled her eyes, the tension between them breaking as Mrs. Brown had meant it to. "Don't start calling me that, please. It is bad enough reading it in the papers."

"All right. Now, let's go get some lunch," Mrs. Brown said.

Mrs. Brown was pleased to see that Lucky 9, one of her favorites, was still open.

They sat at the Lucky 9 bay window where they could watch people walking on the sidewalk. Lovely swirled the stringy egg floating in her egg drop soup and stared listlessly at the hand doctor listings in Arlington on her phone as Mrs. Brown daintily slurped hot and sour soup.

She put down her spoon and dabbed her mouth with her napkin. "I have some news. And an idea."

"About a hand doctor?" Lovely asked, not looking up from her phone.

"Not exactly," Mrs. Brown said. "I won a contest."

She finally looked up from her device. "When did you have time to enter a contest?"

"I haven't been living like a barbarian, Lovely," Mrs. Brown admonished. "We had power. We had the Internet."

"So what was it this time?" Lovely asked, grinning.

Mrs. Brown smiled benignly. She knew she was notorious for entering any contest she possibly could. She maintained she had been a lucky person, despite what others might think when reviewing her history.

In her life, she'd won a set of dishes she didn't need; a set of souvenir spoons from each of the fifty states and the District of Columbia; free car washes for a year; a month of free pizza; the complete works (signed first editions) of a dead thriller writer she had never heard of; and all-expenses-paid trips to Charleston, South Carolina; New York; Paris; and Columbus, Ohio—even though she hated travel.

Those were not the only contests she'd won. But the others were uninteresting or outrageous. She always refused to confirm or deny what Lovely had told her was the most interesting thing about her. Family legend had it that when Lovely's dad had been young, Mrs. Brown had won a turkey when she entered a radio contest. She'd driven to the radio station to pick up her prize, but they presented her with a *live* turkey.

It was *her* prize and she refused to give it up, so she instructed them to put it in her trunk and she drove home. When she opened the trunk, the turkey had burst out, flailing with its wings, knocked her down, and gone running down their suburban street. Mrs. Brown had run after it, demanding it stop because she had won it fair and square. Her husband had found her at the foot of a tree, screaming at the branches where the terrified turkey had sought safety.

Lovely had been entranced by this story and had always asked for more details. How did a fat turkey get into the tree? What happened after Gramps showed up? What did they end up eating for Thanksgiving?

Her resistance to telling the story didn't stop her husband from using the story in one of his acts. She'd given him a blank check to write stories about her, something other spouses of comedians had been shocked about. Gramps would tell stories about her idiosyncrasies, their sex life, her cooking, her parenting methods, and more.

"I lived it. He embellishes for effect. But I know the truth," she'd once told Lovely, who had been horrified to hear that Gramps's latest set had described how they kept their sex life alive when she was pregnant, complete with body movements, hand gestures, and slides of heavy construction equipment appearing behind him.

"But aren't you embarrassed?" Lovely had asked.

Mrs. Brown had smiled. "Honey, when something absolutely terrible happens to you, little things stop mattering so much. Gramps loves me. He has stayed by my side during the worst times in my life. A story about me being ungainly and pregnant and still wanting to be a sex-positive woman is nothing compared to the other shit I've been through."

"What'd you win?" Lovely asked, looking back at her phone. "Oh, here's info on a doctor in Columbus. You should have saved that trip you won."

"That was twenty years ago," Mrs. Brown said. "You were four, and had all your digits. But actually, it is a trip for two."

"Is this a trip like to Paris, or a 'trip' like going to Lake Lure?" She made air quotes when she mentioned the small North Carolina mountain town.

"I guess it's closer to Paris," Mrs. Brown said thoughtfully.

"Well, that sucks since you hate traveling. Who's getting the tickets this time?" Lovely said. Mrs. Brown had given Lovely's parents her Paris tickets right after her mother's cancer diagnosis, and she'd sent Lovely and her cousin Marlon to New York City together the year after to see the new hit show, *The Roman Guide to Slave Management*. Mrs. Brown had actually left her own home to take the trip to Charleston, since it was historic.

She did use the Columbus trip for medical needs, donating the prize to the Ohio State University Patient Support Services Fund for someone who could use a free trip for an oncology appointment or treatment.

"I'm taking the trip. I can't give these away; it's part of the deal. No transfers." Mrs. Brown pursed her lips. "I'm annoyed because I had entered with hopes to win the second prize. It was a new Toyota."

Lovely put down her phone, finally giving her Gran her full attention. "Hold up, a new car was the *second* prize? Gran, what did you win?"

"A trip for two to the Eternity. You know, that space station the news is always going on about? They're accepting human tourists now, and I entered a contest to win two tickets."

Lovely stared at her. Her full spoon was right in front of her face. A cloudy drop slid down the bottom of the spoon and dripped onto the plastic tablecloth. Mrs. Brown reached over and wiped it up with her napkin.

"The *alien* space station? Eternity? Of course I know it, everyone knows it! How are you getting there? You hate flying!"

"I'm not flying on a plane. We have to take an alien shuttle." She didn't like the sound of that, but beggars couldn't be choosers.

"How can you refuse to go to Paris but be okay going to outer space?" Lovely asked.

Mrs. Brown frowned. Lovely should know the answers to that. She held up three fingers, then folded the first one down. "First, we don't waste in this family, Lovely. I didn't refuse to go to Paris; I gave the tickets to your parents. But if I have tickets and can't give them away, then I will use the tickets."

Lovely rolled her eyes. Mrs. Brown's son Marcus had once tried to explain the concept of a sunk cost fallacy to Mrs. Brown when she insisted on going to the movies, even though she was sick and had a high fever. She'd already purchased the tickets, and that was a binding agreement in her eyes. She'd shaken her head when her son had argued further. "Before you were born, your father started his career on stage getting booed and heckled, night after night. I supported us by doing some accounting work for the area churches and saved every penny we could until he started making good money performing. It is not a bad habit to be frugal. We are not going to waste money on things we are going to buy and then throw away!"

"But you're rich now!" Marcus had complained. "You can afford to lose twenty bucks and stay home."

"Our rainy-day fund is not to be thrown away either!" Mrs. Brown had snapped.

In a desperate need to help his mother heal and not infect everyone in the movie theater with her plague, Marcus had taken a young Lovely to the movies so the tickets wouldn't be wasted.

No, she wasn't going to waste these tickets; the benefits outweighed the risks by far. Not even if the prospect of leaving the planet and going among aliens terrified her. She hadn't let terror stop her before. To her, terror was just an emotion that either helped you do what you needed to do or got in the way.

"So are you taking Daddy or Marlon with you?" Lovely asked. It was a fair question. Her father and cousin loved travel more than anyone in the family, and Marlon was a big fan of science fiction. He'd been wild for the alien visitors after First Contact, and had even met some sluglike aliens while visiting Washington, DC. He'd sent Mrs. Brown a photo.

"I considered taking Marlon, yes, but I thought I would extend the invitation to you, if you'll come."

Lovely's eyes widened. "Me? Why?"

Mrs. Brown was still holding two fingers up. She folded her middle finger down. "Second, because I hear that alien technology might have a way to fix that hand of yours, and I'd love to hear you play the violin again."

Lovely's face darkened, but then she gave a nervous smile. "Are you serious?"

Mrs. Brown smiled. It had been a long time since she'd made someone smile like that. It felt good. "Of course I am, Lovely."

Lovely looked dazed, no doubt still struggling out of the pit of despair that held her recent thoughts. Then she focused on Mrs. Brown's remaining finger. "What's that last reason?"

"Ah. Well," Mrs. Brown said, folding the finger down. "That's a personal one. I've learned how to use a gratitude journal in the last ten years, and I have a message to deliver."

Lovely's gaze sharpened, and she frowned. "What could you possibly need to tell someone who lives on a space station?"

Mrs. Brown smiled and pulled a copy of *Time* magazine out of her bag.

"Gran . . . what are you up to?" Lovely asked, a warning tone in her voice.

Mrs. Brown pushed the magazine toward Lovely. "*Time* has a story about all the first humans allowed on the station. There are going to be some famous people on that shuttle!"

"Still, if those other two reasons didn't apply and you hadn't won the tickets, would you still be so eager to go?"

Mrs. Brown thought for a moment. "I don't know, honey, but 'what if's don't matter. These are the cards we're dealt, and I'm not folding when I've got a killer hand."

21

. . .

UNEXPECTED CONNECTIONS

ALLORY LEFT AUNT Kathy with her water and a hankie, saying she needed to interview the others. The crocodile tears always made her back go tense. She stood apart from everyone and pretended to be looking down at the medical theater, but she just focused on taking deep breaths.

A hand touched her shoulder. "Are you okay?"

"You here to call me childish again?" she asked, not turning around. "'Cause I can't take it so soon after talking to her."

Xan took his hand off her shoulder but didn't move away from her. "This whole mess is scary and complex. I'm glad you stayed." He paused. "I wanted to tell you that you aren't as bad off as you said you were."

She glanced over her shoulder. "In what way?"

"You said you fell apart after your uncle died. You couldn't investigate the murder. But from what you've told me, you were back on the horse with Billy's murder. You exonerated me immediately and you didn't have to. That was your gut telling you that the guy covered in blood holding a dying friend when the lights came on wasn't the killer. And you, what, figured out it was an ice knife? Immediately? And here, while your instinct has been to run, you are still handling all this like a pro. It had to be that one murder that threw you off."

"It threw me big time," she said, nodding. "I don't know. Here it's very different. I can't read the aliens' body language or their expressions or their tones of voice. The humans are far, far too connected to us, Xan. I've never seen anything like this. My aunt told me the kid that died, Sam? He was a fan of mine. Your brother is here—"

"And you knew him too," he said.

"Yeah. And that woman on the couch? Old army buddy?"

He gaped at her. "How did you know? Did she just tell everyone?"

"No. I am just good at reading human body language," she said, smiling slightly. "You both have that military way of standing, always alert, backs to the wall all the time. And you clearly knew each other. So I put two and two together."

He sighed and came to stand beside her, putting his back to the railing and regarding the survivors.

"Are they all connected to us?" he asked. "Is anyone here connected to Adrian?"

"Not that I can tell," she said. "Your brother, the army buddy, my aunt, and the dead kid seem to be our only connections. The others are unfortunate collateral damage. I'm going to send them with a nurse to the park area until we can get them places to stay."

"So you don't think any of them did anything wrong?"

"Not that I can tell, no," she said.

"What about people who were here? You were worried about Stephanie, and then there's Adrian. The security team is unpleasant, too."

"Plenty of people are assholes without being murderers," Mallory said. "And I haven't ruled out the aliens, but I need to talk to Stephanie and hopefully security again."

"So what's with your aunt?"

"We have a complicated relationship. Having her here is not great for my concentration. You called me childish." She smiled bitterly. "You're not the only one to do so. I tend to become a child again around her. She's the motheriest of mother hens and a master manipulator. The most important thing in her life is family. She wanted a perfect suburban home and two perfect kids and a perfect marriage. Even if everyone involved hated her for her standards, it didn't matter because she had what she wanted, the beautiful illusion. So you are right; instead of standing up to her, I always ran away. It was easier."

"I was unfair to you," he said, looking at her.

"You were mean, but you weren't wrong," she said.

He glanced over to where his brother was waiting for him. "You're not the only one who's run from problems. And it seems both of us have our sins following us here."

She was shocked at the emotional exhaustion on his face. This was really getting to him. She remembered the first time she realized how many connections were in a room with a murder, and felt pity for him.

"So, your aunt," Xan said. "Why is she here?"

Mallory grimaced. "To bring me home."

"Why now?" he asked carefully.

"I don't know that part, but I'm sure I'll find out at some point." She took a deep breath and tried to relax her shoulders. "But we're gathering info. What did you find out from your army buddy?"

He looked distracted, focusing on his brother, and then came back. "Not a lot from Calliope. She doesn't remember the attack. She remembered where almost everyone was sitting, if that helps you. She said the kid Sam was wandering around the cabin for a while looking really nervous until she told him to sit down."

"Why is she here?" Mallory asked, looking beyond him to the woman clad in a trench coat who was scrolling through a file on her phone. "She doesn't look like someone the army would send to extradite you."

"That's why they sent her. She is volatile. She's saved my life more than once, but she's also beaten the shit out of me when we were only training. She's always got her own idea on how things should be done, despite her orders. She wanted to catch up and said she hasn't decided what she's going to do with me. She also says that she has two other missions."

Mallory stared at him. "Are you serious? That's what the army is reduced to these days? Sending one operative that they can't count on into an unknown situation with no backup and giving her three missions?"

He shrugged. "She thinks they really sent her because she's expendable. She isn't wrong about that: she's not even enlisted anymore, so if she disappears, the army hasn't lost anyone."

"Jesus," she said, shaking her head. "But it didn't look like you were having a bad conversation. She doesn't look like someone about to capture you."

"True, but she's the kind of predator who lies in wait, not one that chases," Xan said.

"Okay. You going to talk to your brother now?"

He smiled at her. "Unless you want to."

"He seemed happier to see me, but I need to talk to the grandmother/granddaughter pair," Mallory said. "Do you know anything I should know about those two women? Secret connection to you or Adrian?"

He looked at the young woman and her grandmother again, as if trying to jar his memory. "Nothing comes to mind."

"Maybe we'll get lucky. Maybe they're honestly just here for the tourism."

"Do you ever get that lucky?" he asked.

She sighed. "No."

LOVELY AND MRS. Elizabeth Brown were talking, but they stopped when Mallory approached them.

She held out her hand. "Mrs. and Ms. Brown, I'm Mallory Viridian."

Lovely shook her hand, the left buried awkwardly in her leather jacket's pocket. "Nice to meet you."

"Oh, I wouldn't say that," Mrs. Brown said, not extending her hand to Mallory. Her wrinkled face was stony.

"Okay," Mallory said hesitantly, and withdrew her hand. "I understand it's been a very stressful trip, but the doctors assure me that your injuries should be healed by now." She looked at Ms. Brown purposefully. "They also think they may have done you some good in other places than injuries from the trip."

Lovely Brown took out her left hand and flexed it, the four fingers opening and closing well. Where her pinky was supposed to be twitched slightly as she tried to send instructions to muscles that weren't there anymore. She looked at her grandmother. "It's really weak, Gran, but I think it worked."

"Didn't give you your finger back," Mrs. Brown said flatly. "All we had to do to fix your hand was get our shuttle attacked and kill a bunch of people. I knew it might be expensive to get medical care here, but that's a higher price than I had envisioned."

"What can you tell me about the shuttle attack?" Mallory said. "We're trying to piece it together."

"We don't remember much. What can you tell us?" Mrs. Brown asked. Her eyes hadn't left Mallory's since she'd introduced herself. The direct stare was starting to make her nervous.

"Well, you know the station is sentient, right?" They both nodded. "Its host was murdered today, right around the time that your shuttle arrived. We believe that the station attacked you due to something that happened on your shuttle, but we need to know what. We don't know which came first, the incident on the shuttle or the murder of the host."

"Wait, you said the station attacked us?" Lovely asked.

"Yeah. It was pretty uncontrollable for a bit there. It was terrifying," Mallory said. "The security was desperate to get things fixed aboard the station, so Xan and I had to go out and see if there were survivors."

"So you went on a spacewalk to rescue us?" Mrs. Brown said.

"Yes, ma'am," Mallory said. "Well, I retrieved the, uh, people who had passed on, while Xan set up the shuttle rescue."

"Goddammit," she said, turning away from them. She shocked both Mallory and her granddaughter.

"Gran! What's wrong?" Lovely asked.

"You're old enough to know what a life debt is, Lovely," Mrs. Brown said. "Seems I owe this woman one."

Mallory held up her hands. "Not necessary. If you tell me what happened on the shuttle, then you can call us square."

"Is the station all right now?" Mrs. Brown asked, looking around the room.

"Um, I think so. It has a new host, and the shaking has stopped. We think it's stable," Mallory said. "I honestly don't know. Station security is on it, which is why I'm taking charge of talking to you folks. I'm not an official station employee." She tried a winning smile.

"You're still doing this murder stuff, even out here," Mrs. Brown said. She sounded like she had discovered her neighbor stripped for a living.

"Well, if murders happen around me, I try to solve them, yeah," Mallory said. This woman was small and compact, and Mallory started to wonder if she knew her. "Is there something wrong?"

"It's been a while, Ms. Viridian. We were both younger then, and you were more innocent, but I'm sure you've met many other murderers since. I can see why you wouldn't recognize me, but I sure recognize you."

Mallory stepped back, the air leaving her lungs. *Pizza delivery. The smudge of blood, the teetering vase, the hand outstretched on the floor.* The first murder case she'd solved, the third that she had witnessed or been near. Had to be ten or eleven years earlier. A middle-aged woman had killed her husband. The murderer could have pleaded self-defense and spousal abuse—there was plenty of evidence—but she had tried to hide the body. She had almost been successful, until Mallory had stumbled upon them when she rang the wrong doorbell to deliver a pizza.

"You're Elizabeth Inos," Mallory breathed.

"Mrs. Elizabeth Brown, again, thank you. I took my first husband's name back," she said coolly. "I just got out of jail and, in an amazing coincidence, won a ticket to come see the space station!"

"Congrats," Mallory said numbly.

"Gran, you didn't tell me she was why you were coming!" Lovely said, looking down at her grandmother. "You didn't come here with any *plans*, did you?"

Mrs. Brown didn't answer, just looked at Mallory as if she were something nasty stuck to her shoe.

"Why don't we have a chat, one at a time?" Mallory asked pleasantly. "Lovely, do you want to go for a walk?"

THEY WENT FOR a walk around the balcony. Xan had gone to talk to his brother, and the survivors were napping or chatting. Mrs. Brown stayed where they had left her, watching Mallory and Lovely with cold, direct eyes.

"Okay, here's what I know," Lovely started. "First, I did not know you were here. She told me that we were coming because they might be able to fix my hand." She held up her left hand, showing the pink scars. "Which they did, partly, at least. Not sure how I'm going to play the violin without a pinky finger, but at least the tendons healed. Anyway, after my, uh, accident, a few weeks ago, Gran came to see me. She surprised the hell out of me; no one told me she'd made parole. But they let her out early for good behavior. I had just injured my hand, and she wanted to check on me and tell me about the contest she won for this trip."

"She won tickets on a shuttle to a space station," Mallory marveled. "Who was giving those away?"

"A radio station with an amazing budget, I guess," Lovely said, shrugging. "She wanted the second-place prize, which was a car. But she won these tickets and Gran doesn't waste things. They're nontransferable, you know."

Mallory smiled, thinking momentarily that she might like this family, except that they probably hated her forever for being the key witness in Mrs. Brown's murder trial.

"What happened to your hand?" Mallory asked.

Lovely faced the railing and propped her arms on it, staring at her left hand.

"You're her, right?"

"Who?" Mallory asked, confused.

"The woman who solves shit. You've seen a lot of death, a lot of blood. People die around you and you solve the murders."

Mallory sighed. "Yeah. Unfortunately."

She flexed her hand and winced. "I got stabbed during a department store robbery," she finally said. "The knife went all the way through, severing a tendon and my finger."

Mallory stared at her. "You got stabbed? What happened?"

"Is it important to your case?" Lovely asked, crossing her arms over her chest.

"I won't know until you tell me," Mallory said honestly.

"Gran is a tough old broad," Lovely said. "You don't fuck with Gran. If people fuck with her, they get hurt. And she passed that down to me. The robbers came into the dressing room and attacked, so I fought back. I paid for it."

"Your gran is definitely a grizzly bear," Mallory said, nodding. "Were you defending someone?"

"Yeah. I figured they only had guns, so I fought them with that in mind. Close up, it was dark. But one had a knife. They had killed several and lost one on their side, and they ran. The cops found them, but I ran and they never found out I was the one that fought back."

She always felt a little thrill, almost a buzz of dopamine, when she caught someone saying something off, or leaving something out. Xan had told her that she had her mojo back. She clearly pictured Lovely's story and immediately knew what the younger woman wasn't saying.

"You killed one of them in self-defense, and you didn't want anyone to find out," Mallory said quietly. "You know, there's no shame in defending yourself."

"I didn't have to use deadly force, though," Lovely said. "That was a choice. And Gran violated her parole to bring me to this place where there are more murders, and now that you know two murderers are on board, you're going to think it's us."

Mallory sat on a thin stool made for the lanky Phantasmagore, shifting a few times to get comfortable. She looked at Lovely's hand, seeing where she had been healed and where she never would be healed.

"Actually," Mallory said, "I appreciate your honesty. And you're not the only killers on the station. You don't know what stories they have to tell"—she gestured toward the survivors and Xan—"but I can tell you that two of them are soldiers, or ex-soldiers, anyway. Add to them a movie-star rapper, a manipulative aunt, and our annoying ambassador, who still isn't here."

"You make it sound like we're on Gilligan's Island," Lovely said.

Mallory laughed. "Anyway, my point is I'm betting you have more in common with the people here than you think."

"Why would you make that assumption?"

"If you knew who I was, did you know that your grandmother's case was the third murder I had ever been close to?"

"I knew that," Lovely said. "Dad read your book. I think he was looking for a defamation of character suit, but he had to admit that you treated Gran fairly and didn't play it up."

"Hers was the first case I helped solve. There were three murders when I was a kid, ones I didn't solve. My own mom was one of them, but I was pretty young then." She paused, then shook her head to clear it from memories. "But if you and your gran didn't do anything on the shuttle, what can you tell me about the trip? Does anything weird stand out?"

"Everyone kind of kept to themselves at the beginning. You know how flights are," Lovely said. "But we were all excited. Gran and I sat together in front, and I didn't look behind me much. We either dozed, or talked about my career, or looked out the window at the stars."

Mallory nodded. "Anything weird happen on Earth before you left?"

"There was a lot of press there when we got to the shuttle port, and I was worried Gran would get caught for breaking her parole. She just told me everyone would be excited about the fancy people in first class." Lovely smiled at the memory. "She hid behind the big guy, though, when we walked to the shuttle. She even asked him permission. He said, 'I'd rather hide behind you, but that's not gonna happen.' I think he was worried about press, too."

"Yeah, he's a big name. I'm surprised he wasn't in first class with the other VIPs," Mallory said. "Did the press follow you?"

"I think they wanted the everyman's opinion, but they swarmed the young white guy for that one." Lovely rolled her eyes.

"Did you overhear anything he said in the interviews?" she asked.

"No, I was kind of concerned about Gran, but—" Lovely thought for a moment. "He was talking about wanting to meet someone here, and some message for her, which I thought was weird 'cause I didn't think humans lived here."

That dead boy again. So Kathy was telling the truth.

"What do you remember about the attack?"

"The station, it reached out and touched our minds," Lovely said. "We weren't given a lot of warning, but the captain did say it was going to happen. It was still a shock. Did you do that?"

Mallory nodded.

"So the station, she asked me who I was, and I had this vision of being on stage with my violin, but I couldn't play until I told her about myself."

"Can you remember exactly when the attack came?"

Lovely shook her head. "The station talked to me, and then when it stopped, I was kind of dizzy. All I remember is I heard this crash and then I woke up here."

Mallory thought about Lovely's story and tried to slide it in with the one from Aunt Kathy to see if it fit. She'd have to hear the others, though.

"Do you remember the everyman white kid, Sam? Did he do anything weird? Or was anyone acting weird around him?"

"He paced a little after the jump. He was flipping through a fat book and reading while he walked. He was going from the front to the back, not like he was reading, but cross-referencing. I didn't notice much more. He was seated several rows behind me, so when he sat down, I couldn't tell what he was doing."

Mallory nodded. "And you never spoke to him?"

"Nope."

"Thanks for your time," Mallory said. "I guess we can find your grandmother, and I'll talk to her."

"I'm here," came a voice from behind her, and Mallory jumped. She hadn't noticed Mrs. Brown approaching them.

"Gah, don't do that!" Mallory said, but she calmed herself quickly. She didn't want to talk to this lady. She knew Mrs. Brown blamed her for being in prison, but she didn't regret it. Mrs. Brown had murdered her own husband. If she hadn't wanted to go to prison, maybe she should have considered that before the murder.

She forced a small smile. "Let's talk."

22

REVENGE IS BEST EATEN COLD, BUT DON'T LET IT SPOIL

MRS. ELIZABETH BROWN, Mrs. Brown to most people, 'Lizabeth only to close friends and family, was taught to be kind and friendly, to tithe to the church, and never to let someone tell you how to raise your kids. She was also taught not to suffer fools lightly.

"Fools started those wars, 'Lizabeth," her grandmother would say, usually after a few glasses of beer.

Ladies drank their beer in glasses, Gramma would say. Strangely, there was no limit to how *much* ladies should drink.

"What wars?" she would ask, but she knew the answer. It was the ritual, not the words.

"All of 'em!" Her gramma's meaty fist would hit the table then, and the beer glass would jump. But she never spilled any.

Mrs. Brown took the advice and never suffered fools. Over her lifetime, she had killed three men and two women for being fools. Violent, abusive, murderous fools, but still fools.

She had yet to decide if Mallory Viridian was a fool. Mrs. Brown was taught not to hold a grudge, but you had to be realistic.

"I have five minutes for you," she said coolly to Mallory after the woman had talked to Lovely. From the look on her granddaughter's face, she had told Mallory everything, so at least Mrs. Brown didn't need to wonder what to hide.

"Thank you, Mrs. Brown," Mallory said evenly. "Tell me what you can of the shuttle trip, namely anything strange that happened or anyone acting weird. Especially about the young man named Sam. He didn't make it, but we don't know why."

"I don't like to talk ill of the dead, but frankly, he was annoying. Most everyone on the ship had fallen asleep before the jump. He started pacing the cabin and then sat down to talk to me. I was about the only one awake, you see. He came to talk to me, and he went on and on about you." She waited for the woman to be surprised, but she just nodded for Mrs. Brown to continue. "He talked about the murders you'd solved and the blog posts he'd written about them, the police reports he'd dug up. He said he'd figured something out about your situation and wanted to come and tell you."

"Huh." Mallory looked thoughtful. "What else?"

"He didn't tell me anything else because we jumped then, and I passed out. When I woke up he was back in his seat, but I could hear him going on to the woman in the next aisle. That blonde woman who was crying on you." She pointed to the older woman, who was watching them. Her face had the swollen, red look of weeping, but her eyes didn't look sad at all.

"After about an hour, he started pacing the aisle, and the Asian woman got up to check on him. Soon after that, the station reached out to us."

"And what happened?"

"That's personal," Mrs. Brown said primly. It had indeed been intensely personal, and invasive and frightening. It had made her angry. "After that happened, there was a loud crash, and then I woke up here."

She glanced at her granddaughter. Lovely was taken care of. It was almost lucky their shuttle had gotten attacked, since the magic healing stuff had done an amazing job of healing her hand. It hadn't grown her finger back, though, which concerned Mrs. Brown.

Mama would have told her that saying she was glad more than ten people had died so her granddaughter could heal was terrible, but if Gramma had been in hearing distance, she would have shouted. Her voice from memory boomed across the decades, and Mrs. Brown imagined her saying, "You shut your mouth. Mrs. Brown knows how to protect what's hers. You look out for your own, right, girl?"

"What made you come to Eternity?" Mallory asked.

Mrs. Brown paused. She tilted her head slightly. Was that a hissing sound? She might be old, but there was nothing wrong with her ears. Stressed voices chatted, reflecting the weight of fear, or lies, or lies of omission.

But what did it matter? She'd done what she came here to do.

"Just lucky, I guess," she said, smiling. "I'm sure Lovely told you that story."

"She did, but—" Mallory stopped as an alien approached her.

No, she was approaching Mrs. Brown. It was one of the little tree-people—no, they were called *Gurudevs*, she told herself firmly, *gotta call people by their proper names*—and she was looking at a tiny screen in her hand. It was smaller than the first flip mobile phones. How could she read that?

"You're Elizabeth Brown?" she asked.

"Mrs. Elizabeth Brown," she half corrected, half confirmed.

"I'm Dr. Halifax. I wanted to talk to you about some information we discovered while you were healing."

"Is this about the cancer?" Mrs. Brown asked.

"Yes," the doctor said. "We have a concern."

"Then no need. I already know about it. I'm going to die." She'd had a small hope that the pods would have cured that as they had knitted Lovely's hand back together.

"Everyone is going to die," Dr. Halifax said. "Some much later than others, but everyone, eventually. I thought humans knew that. How are you sentient beings if you don't know you're going to die?"

"We know that," Mallory cut in. "But when we hear that we're dying of something specific and it's going to be soon, it's more stressful for us."

Mrs. Brown nodded. "Everyone secretly thinks they will die peacefully in their sleep at the ripe old age of ninety-nine, and anything less is theft. My husband tried to make a stand-up monologue about how cancer is God stealing from you, but it didn't really land. I thought it was funny, but I was his biggest fan." She smiled at the memory and then remembered the cancer that had taken him: kidney cancer, twenty-some years ago. "Cancer certainly feels like theft."

"You have a foreign body inside you that's killing you," Dr. Halifax said. "It's as if your kind tried to find a sentient being to bond with and found a parasite instead. This is why your species is inferior; the symbionts you find eat you alive." She paused and looked at the screen again. "I would love to study this as it progresses."

"That's great, Dr. Halifax," Mallory said, stepping slightly in front of Mrs. Brown, shielding her. "But Mrs. Brown has other things to worry about. If we survive this, and I ever get cancer, and I'm still on the station, I'll give you a call."

"Thank you very much," Dr. Halifax said, clearly not figuring the odds of all of those things happening. "Incidentally, there are new data about humans bonding with superior species. If only the station hadn't lost her host and turned violent and killed many of the humans traveling to visit us. We might be able to learn more."

Mrs. Brown thought about the high keening sound and wondered why no one else could hear it.

"The station is in extreme distress right now," Halifax said, "and our medbays are filling up. If we all survive this, Mrs. Brown, contact me and we can get that thing out of you. Or at least question it and find out what it wants."

"The station isn't stable? I thought she found a new host," Mallory said, alarmed.

"There are still breaches in many sectors," Halifax said, looking at her screen again. "I must go now."

Mallory watched her go with a faraway look on her face.

Mrs. Brown glared at her. All at once, she hated her. She had ruined the last decade of Mrs. Brown's life, and then had the gall to save her from death so that revenge wouldn't be as sweet. She also seemed smart and willing to put herself between Mrs. Brown and an alien. Damn her.

You got what you came for.

Yeah, yeah, she'd gotten it. So why didn't it feel like she was done? She looked at her watch, still an old analog, and said, "That's your five. I am going to stretch my legs."

Mallory blinked and came back to reality. "Thanks for your time. I know this isn't easy. For what it's worth, I am glad you're free now." She blushed and cleared her throat. "Anyway, don't leave the balcony. With everything that's going on, the humans have to stick together. I don't want anyone lost on the station."

"There are worse things," Mrs. Brown said. "I'm sure you've even experienced a few."

Mallory got a far-off look in her eyes, looking at the other human who lived aboard. "I have," she said softly.

The man had his back to them, his ear next to the wall. "What's he doing?" Mallory asked.

"Listening. He hears it. Don't you?" Mrs. Brown asked quietly.

"No, what is it?" Mallory asked, frustrated.

Lovely approached them, eyes wide. "I keep hearing something high-pitched, like a high G. Just one long note."

Mrs. Brown nodded. "I thought that's what it was." She smiled proudly. "My girl with perfect pitch."

Mallory's face changed. She'd just heard it. Lovely was right; it did sound like someone carefully running their bow across a string to make a very high note. *Or like air escaping.* Mallory's face went white. "Yeah, sounds like a long note, or like air escaping."

Then the alarms filled the room with noise.

23

FUTURE RIVAL TO DOLLYWOOD

XAN DIDN'T LOOK very good. He had shadows under his eyes and wore a T-shirt with several bloodstains on it. It was torn at the collar and right sleeve. He looked worn out.

"Space fucked you up, big brother," Phineas said as Xan approached.

"While you look better than ever," Xan said with a wry smile.

Phineas jabbed his thumb toward Calliope. "But good news that she didn't kill you yet, right?"

Xan frowned and glanced over at her; she was focused on something further away. "Do you know her?"

"I figured it out. You're not the only smart one. She has that army look, and I knew someone was coming here for you."

"So you knew she was here for me and you didn't tell me?"

Phineas shrugged. "I wanted to see what would happen."

Xan sat down on the huge couch, having to shift around to get fully onto the tall seat. "Do you want to tell me why you're here?"

"In a second," Phineas said, enjoying this. "First I want to talk about Grandma."

"What about her?" Xan asked, frowning.

"Dead. She fell down the stairs."

"Shit—" Xan said, eyes wide.

Phineas waved his hand so Xan would shut up. "I'm not done. Her dying isn't the fun part. At first she had a stroke and I paid for in-home care. And then after she had a bunch of nurses quit on her, the agency wouldn't send any more, so I had to leave a movie set and go out and take care of her. Do you remember that caring-for-old-people class we took in high school? Neither do I. I had to learn on the fly.

"She lost her mind when she had her stroke. Seemed to think I was you half the time. When she knew it was me, she was this foul demon. I was too fat, too stupid, I wasn't a real man, and I wasn't even her grandson, she said. She said Mom slept around and said you were her only grandson by blood, and I was a bastard."

"Jesus. It's like the opposite of us growing up," Xan said, shaking his head. "She definitely never considered me worth anything when I lived there." He touched his forearm.

"Why didn't you tell me what she did to you?" Phineas asked, pointing to the scars on Xan's arm. "The burns."

Xan, startled, looked back at his arm. "It was a lot to put on you when you were twelve. And she liked you, so I figured she wouldn't do the same to you."

Phineas held his own forearm up, puckered scars running up and down.

Xan winced. "Shit. I'm so sorry. But man, why are you here? Now? I can't imagine you spending all the money to come here to tell me she was dead."

"No, I didn't," he said, but didn't elaborate. "Anyway, she died last week. I'm postponing her memorial till you come home, since I figure the two of us will be the only ones there."

"And we don't even have to be there. We don't owe her anything," Xan said firmly.

"But you owe me," Phineas said.

"I owe you?" Xan asked, his voice going soft. "I quit school to make money to send you to college, which you took to run after rap star dreams. I could have gotten my own degree if I'd known you were going to do that."

"Yes, you owe me! You *left* me. You knew what she was, you knew about the drinking and the cigarettes and the abuse, and you just fucking left."

"She coddled you every day of your life!" Xan said, frustrated. "She didn't even blink when you came out. She paid for your T, she paid for your new clothes. She laughed at your crude jokes about fucking men being more fun when you were a man. She stood up for you at school. You know what she did for me? Blamed me for Mom and Dad's death and burned me with cigarettes.

"I didn't know she would turn on you. Besides, I couldn't take you with me to college or to the army after I dropped out."

Phineas shook his head violently. "Fuck, man, how long are you going to hold that over me? Want me to pay you back that college money you saved for me? How many thousands? Add on a few for interest? I can transfer the money when I get home. Then you can use it to send yourself to college."

"The money isn't the point. Even if I wanted to go back to school, I don't know if I could. If I go back to Earth, there's a long list of angry people who want to talk to me. I was sending the money so you could make something of yourself and get out of Pigeon Forge."

"Well, I did that," Phineas said. "I just didn't do it the way you wanted me to. I can't carry your dreams, man. If you want a college graduate in the family, you go back and finish your own degree."

"I can't argue about this again," Xan said, ignoring the fact that he had brought up the subject. "Look, we can argue about Grandma later. Right now, I have to figure out what happened on that shuttle. I need to know why you're here and what happened on the trip. Please."

Phineas had never seen Xan look so tired. Space had aged him. Phineas almost felt sorry for him.

He sighed. "Fine. But I don't know what happened on the shuttle. I took a few Valium to calm down for the flight. I fell asleep before we took off."

"Where were you sitting?" Xan asked.

"Front row, aisle, on the left side. The old lady and her granddaughter were in the left aisle sitting near the window. Your assassin was on the window seat of my row. The rest, I don't know. I didn't really pay attention. I was more concerned with not looking out the windows."

"And that's it?"

"I woke up when they made the announcement that the station was going to touch our minds. It was—an experience." He looked at his hands thoughtfully. "But she accepted me. Then someone yelled and then there was a crash and I don't remember anything until I woke up here."

"Anything else?" Xan asked. He looked frustrated, which Phineas found very funny.

"Nope," Phineas said.

"All right, thanks," Xan muttered, and made to slide off the couch.

"Wait, there *is* one more thing," Phineas said, snapping his fingers as if he had just thought about it.

"I'm here to show you Grandma's will. Seems you, the one who left, get everything. You get the land; you get the house; you get however much money she has squirreled away in the basement."

Xan stared at him as if he'd been slapped.

"But since you can't come home, yet," Phineas continued, "I have to handle everything yet again. Managed everything about her life, and now I get to manage everything in her death, and walk away with nothing.

"Dammit, Xan, you don't know what I gave up to take care of her. One week I'm starring in a movie; the next week I'm learning how to lift the elderly from a video on YouTube. Now I'm a caretaker of my master's plantation. The entire story of our family has gone full circle."

"You can't blame the will on me," Xan said coldly. "I have no control over who she leaves her shit to. That's on her, not me."

"You benefit from it!" Phineas said. "Of course I can blame you! I don't have anyone else left!"

Xan shook his head, then rubbed his face as if trying to wash off the reality of the situation. "How did she die?"

"She fell down the stairs," Phineas said without going into detail. "Broke her neck."

"I told her she would fall over that rug one day," Xan muttered.

"You know, after her stroke, she wanted you. But you had just been abducted or whatever weird shit happened to you. She didn't believe that you were really gone into space. I didn't know what to tell her since I didn't know anything beyond that."

"I didn't have much choice there, man. I didn't ask for them to pick me up," Xan said. "Once I got here, I couldn't communicate with Earth. I would have told you." He paused, looking regretful. "Any idea why she wrote you out of the will?"

"Oh yeah, she claims Mom fucked around and my dad was someone from Gatlinburg," Phineas said, the rage making his face burn. "She said I'm not even a blood relative."

"Christ. You know that's not true, Phineas! I remember Mom being pregnant. They had a gender reveal party—yeah, I know, tacky—and Dad kept saying Mom got to name me, so he wanted to name you Philomena after his aunt. They were happy. I can't believe Grandma didn't even leave you any money."

"It's not about the *money*," Phineas said, balling his fists. "I'm fine on that front. But that story we heard every Thanksgiving, about Grandma taking two centuries' worth of records and deeds and carrying them to the State Assembly to argue—"

"For our family's right to the plantation that our ancestors built," Xan interrupted. "I remember."

"And you don't know why I would want part of that? You think that a million-dollar house in Beverly Hills would mean more to me than our family's legacy?"

"Fine, we can split the land, will that make you happy?" Xan asked, throwing his hands out wide.

"Oh, no, that won't do," Phineas said. He pulled the paper from his pocket and unfolded it. "Grandma reasons that if you and I split it in half, that's two pieces, then we have kids and split that land between all of them, then they have kids, and so on. Three generations later, the plantation is seventy little plots. She fought for the right to reclaim what our family earned. It must always be passed down as one plot of land."

Phineas fingered the memory stick in his jacket pocket and realized how close Xan had come to finding it when he was wearing the coat. He still hadn't decided whether to give it to him.

"We don't have kids, unless there's something you're not telling me. So who inherits if you die today?" Phineas asked.

"If I die, all my shit goes to you, of course," Xan said. "We're all we have left. Then you can will it to whoever you want, give it to charity, build a rival to Dollywood—I don't care. I can't argue when I'm dead."

"You don't think I'll have kids, do you?" Phineas asked.

Xan made an exasperated noise. "That's not what I said! Do you have a partner to settle down with? Have you looked for a surrogate or put your name into adoption agencies? Young, single rap stars building a career don't typically go looking for babies to adopt."

"No, but that doesn't mean I won't in the future."

Xan took a long breath. "So you managed a seat on the first shuttle here just to yell at me that Grandma liked me more all along?"

"Pretty much."

Xan was good at catching Phineas in a lie. "With your fear of heights. With Grandma newly dead. You're not here for any other reason?"

"No," Phineas said.

"Phin, you know I can tell—wait a second," Xan said, tilting his head like a dog, listening hard.

"What?" Phineas asked.

"Shh," Xan said, and got on his knees so he could lean over the back of the couch to listen near the metal wall of the station.

Phineas concentrated. There it was. It sounded like someone had put a very small hole in a thick balloon across the room. A high-pitched whistling sound.

Then the sound was eclipsed entirely by an alarm, a klaxon that rang through the room and caused everyone to clap their hands over their ears.

Xan jumped off the sofa, looking panicked.

The pretty young woman with the mangled hand from the shuttle—Lovely?—ran up to them.

"Hey, you're Xan, right?" she shouted at Xan.

"We can get introduced after we get out of here," Xan shouted back. "Where's Mallory?"

"She ran downstairs to talk to the doctors."

Mallory appeared at the top of the stairs, eyes wide and panicked. She ran over to Xan. They leaned in close to talk, but stopped when a voice blared over a loudspeaker. "All sentients, please exit all exterior rooms in the station and find a safe place in an interior room. All exterior walls are considered in danger of breach. Please do what you can to avoid all exterior halls with blinking lights; they are also at risk if a breach happens."

Xan shook his head at Mallory, and she shouted something. Phineas got the sense that she'd be shouting at his brother even if there weren't feedback-worthy noise around.

Mallory ran off again, down the stairs.

Phineas slid off the sofa. "What was that all about?" he asked, raising his voice only slightly. The years performing made him able to summon volume with little effort.

"She's got a hunch about the case. We're about to die in a vacuum, but she wants to investigate something," Xan shouted, exasperated.

"Well, is she investigating somewhere safer than here?"

Xan looked like he was thinking, frowning as he hurried the humans toward the staircase. "It's safe for now. I think we'll be okay if we follow her." He glanced at Phineas. "We can finish this later."

He took off at a run, presumably to get to the front of the pack to lead them to safety.

"Running, fuck that," Phineas said to Lovely, who was watching Xan go.

"Where is he taking us?" she shouted as they approached the stairs.

"No idea, but he says somewhere safe," Phineas said. He stepped back to let Lovely descend the stairs first.

She pulled up suddenly, looking around in a panic. "Hang on. Where the hell is my grandmother?"

PART THREE

TRANSFORMATIONS
OF NECESSITY

We're not a team; we're protagonists
But who's writing the story, and will I make it in?
  —"The Ballad of Unremarkable Derrick Krueger"
      by the garages

24

. . .

THE MOIST RACES

OTHER SPECIES WERE disgusting. Devanshi was a professional; she never said this out loud. She took her job to protect Eternity and her residents, but come on. Some species were simply neater than others. For example, the Phantasmagore were dry sentients who felt other species with a high amount of water in their system were just disgusting. And Eternity was about to start welcoming beings that were fifty, sometimes sixty or seventy percent water onto the station. Surely that would break the balance of her biosphere, right?

But the biosphere wasn't Devanshi's problem, and she kept her disgust to herself. She honestly didn't like to admit it. It was her job to protect them all.

The scientists assured her that the humans wouldn't throw the biosphere off. So she couldn't complain that much.

But when these wet sentients—*Let's call them what they are; they're aliens*—got injured or died . . . Just, the *mess* of it all.

Gurudevs like Ren were closer to the Phantasmagore in terms of body chemistry (although wetter), but they were much shorter and more compact, and they had no ability to blend in with their surroundings, unless they were next to a tree, that was.

But when Ren had died, it had been messy. His body should

be disintegrated by now, but the copious smears of his blood in the hallway remained. They trailed off, though, so the body thief could be anywhere.

She couldn't investigate the Heart of the Station because the station and her new host would not let her in. The thick membrane that Mallory had found had grown over every hallway that led to the Heart. Devanshi unfolded several fingers and tapped on it. It was clearly thick, with oil—even the stations were part wetness—running through. It wasn't just a thin layer of skin. If she cut through this, who knew what could happen?

Ren would have known. He was annoying, wet, pedantic, and unfriendly, but he was the station expert. And now he was dead.

Osric stood beside her, sharpening his left nails. "Should we cut?"

"No, we shouldn't cut, you moron," she snapped. "Have the ventilation shafts been searched?"

"Not that I know of."

Devanshi hadn't gone inside the working parts of the station before, but she knew it was possible. Maintenance nurses were always checking up on Eternity's vitals.

"We should get some nurses down here to get us into the vats and let us know how the station is doing internally," Devanshi said.

"The problem with that is the station-specific medical bay was destroyed in the first breach," he said.

Devanshi felt her anxiety spiking and blended into the fleshy wall behind her in automatic defense. She came out almost immediately and said, "You're saying we have no medical teams available for the station herself now?"

Osric paused, then pulled up his tablet and did some research. Devanshi fought the urge to blend into the fleshy wall again. He finally said, "There are AI bots. Some have been cleaning the detritus from the shuttle attack, some are working from the outside on the breaches, but the ones suited for internal medical work on the station, this info says they were all spaced."

Devanshi swore and blended into the pink wall again to think. Osric turned pink in reflexive sympathy.

The real reason that Devanshi hated the watery sentients was that they could lie. Some of them had physiological changes when they experienced strong emotions, or when they lied, but she couldn't detect many of them. Every emotion was so *damp*. And you couldn't read the dampness as emotions because some dampness meant different things at different times.

Humans leaked water out of their eyes when they were very sad, but sometimes when they were happy and sometimes when they were angry. Water broke out of their very skin when they were nervous or frightened. It also did so when they were lying. The thought utterly horrified her. The fact that they were made of water was bad enough, but did they have to leak it everywhere?

Phantasmagore always knew where they stood with one another. A friendly being would mirror coloring, a fearful one would blend into the background, and attacks always came from a place of camouflage. Not that Phantasmagore fought, she reminded herself.

"See if we can access the maintenance bot paths, and we can try to get into the Heart. A station as old as Eternity should be able to start stabilizing immediately with a new host, so something is still wrong," Devanshi said, and the station shuddered, almost in response. "And hurry."

DEVANSHI HUNG UPSIDE down, propping her limbs across the sharp slope of a ventilation shaft. Normally, Phantasmagore digits could grip most any wall, but the smooth steel of the shaft meant she had to carefully lower herself or fall. Below her, an AI bot drone buzzed as it flew, not caring about the steep grade.

"Are you there yet?" Osric asked over their comm.

"I would tell you if I was," she reminded him. "I'm close, I think." She relaxed a fraction and allowed herself to slide a few more meters. "It smells terrible in here."

The smell was of wet meat, a heavy, acrid, smoky odor that crawled inside her nose and set up camp.

"Reports from security base say that the station is losing pressure in seventeen different areas," he said. "The stabilization we experienced seems temporary; she's breaking down again. Whatever you plan on doing, do it fast."

A metal clunk echoed up the shaft, and Devanshi slid a few more meters. The AI drone had reached the vent, it seemed. She judged the distance by the low light drifting up from the Heart and decided to take a chance. She let go and pointed her arms straight down to help her punch through the shaft.

She would have landed properly if not for the drone. Her right arm caught it on the way down and together they went through the vent, which bent and then broke from their combined weight.

Devanshi landed hard on her right side, crushing the drone beneath her with a crunch. She came to her feet, slightly dazed and favoring her right leg. The drone spat sparks and started to roll in a circle, running into her with confused beeps.

She picked it up and held it under her good arm. *At least it doesn't leak.*

The room was bathed in red light. It wasn't the warm, happy red that Devanshi had seen multiple times; this was the red of rage. The room itself pulsed on a sonic level that hurt Devanshi's ears.

Covering the floor were more smears of blue blood, clearly from the late, murdered Ren. But the bigger mess was from the human.

That poor human. No, she couldn't worry about him. She would have felt sorry for him if he hadn't fucked up everything.

He'd probably killed Ren as well, except he wouldn't have had time to clean up the body. Whatever he had done, it was obvious he had taken advantage of the situation, one that clearly he wasn't ready for.

Currently the tree that indicated the biological center of Eternity was covered in thorny vines. Ambassador Adrian Casserly-Berry was caught in the thorns, his body pierced in dozens of places and oozing more watery blood onto the floor. His head had been wrapped in the vines, to where Devanshi couldn't see anything but his mouth.

The vines pulsed again and the human groaned, the sound of someone who had already screamed themselves raw and exhausted. The pain was still there; but the body couldn't communicate it anymore.

These humans were major pains. Devanshi stepped forward and activated her comm. "Osric, I'm in. I know the reason for the breaches. Eternity is not bonding with her new host. She's killing it. I don't think she knows what she's doing."

"Get her to take down the wall," came the reply. "We can't help her if she kills him."

She took another step forward and stretched out a hesitant digit. "Eternity, this is your security chief, Devanshi. Do you know me? Do you remember me?"

They don't.

She didn't need this right now. Apparently, Devanshi's useless symbiont was awake. She had long since stopped relying on them for counsel. She and the sentient vine called Splendid had a relationship of convenience. They slept and fed off a small amount of her scarce bodily fluids, and she used their hormones to facilitate her camouflage abilities. She wasn't even sure if they had spoken to her five times in the time she had been on the station.

"So you're awake," she said. "What do you know about all this?"

They're hurting.

"That's fucking obvious," Devanshi snapped. "If you're just going to tell me that things are bad, keep quiet."

She touched an exposed area of skin on the host, shuddering when it allowed her to compress it. It was warm, which was good, but she didn't know much more about humans.

"How close is the host to death?" she asked.

Not close to death, but the pain has driven them useless for communication until they get relief and rest.

"Eternity, can you hear me?"

They can hear. They don't care. They're enraged.

Devanshi thought about all the lives aboard who were relying on this station to be, if not happy, then at least content. "Splendid," she asked, "do you think you and I together could talk to her?"

Of course we can. You've just never asked.

"Well, you don't say much," she said in self-defense. "What do I need to do?"

Put your hand on the trunk, where I can touch them.

Devanshi put her injured arm against the trunk, allowing the part of Splendid that wrapped around her to reach out.

The vines reacted immediately, before Devanshi could try to reach Eternity. They wrapped themselves around Devanshi's wrist and clung tightly, thorns trying to bite into her flesh.

The vines had grown in response to a human, however, and they had no purchase against the bark-like skin of a Phantasmagore. But that didn't mean she was immune to Eternity's screaming, which filled her head to the point she couldn't think. Her own screaming joined that of the station and her host, and she was aware of nothing else.

DEVANSHI CAME TO on the floor of the Heart. The room was still an angry, pulsing red, but the human lay on the floor behind her, finally freed from the vines. They had retracted fully into the higher branches of the bare tree, where they writhed as if upset about something.

The ambassador didn't look like much anymore. He still bled from the punctures left by the thorns all over his head and body. Eternity had left several holes, out from which ran several different fluids. Both his eyes were ruined messes, and blood seeped out of his mouth and nose. She wasn't sure what was going on inside him to make that happen, but it wasn't her job to find out.

Hiding her revulsion, she reached out a digit and touched the side of his face. "Human. Hey."

They're still passed out.

"What happened?"

Eternity attacked us. Splendid was not an overly emotional being, but they sounded shocked. *They truly are breaking down.*

"So we rescued the human but nothing is fixed? I need the station feeling better; I don't care about that!" She pointed to the bag of seeping wetness on the floor.

She looked at her wrist. The skin was far from breaking, but scratches went from her wrist down her hand and her digits. "How did we get away?"

Your drone separated us.

"My—what?" She caught sight of the drone across the room, lying on its side. A propeller blade and another of its spindly wheels had bent, and it was struggling to right itself. "That's not my drone."

It's part of Eternity, but it held on to a tiny bit of intelligence even not connected with her. It freed us, and Eternity threw it across the room. It sacrificed itself.

"It can't sacrifice itself because it's a drone, not a thinking being. And it's not my drone. I don't need a fucking pet," Devanshi said, limping across the room to pick it up. "And I don't need a human to babysit." She touched her comm. "Osric, I have a human for the medbay and a drone for an AI expert to look at. I can probably get the fleshy wall down if you can meet me on the other side with people to help out with this."

"How?" he asked suspiciously.

"Trust me," she said. She reached down and grabbed the human by the belt, as good of a handle as she could figure. She carried the drone with her injured arm and dragged the human with her good arm, smearing red on the floor. "All right, little gal," she said to the drone. "Are you ready to help me and Splendid try to talk sense into your mama one more time?"

Not a pet? Splendid sounded . . . amused?

Osric's voice came from the other side of the fleshy wall. "Talk fast, Devanshi. We're reading decreasing pressure in several more sections, including the medbay and the main park common area."

Devanshi dropped the wet human by the flesh wall and reached out with Splendid, and the little drone, one more time.

25

. . .

THE SILENT WAR

**A READOUT REGARDING THE CURRENT STATE
OF ETERNITY, ARCHIVED WITHIN
THE SUNDRY HIVEMIND.**

Based on current observations, the recent violence aboard
and outside the station Eternity is 100% due to a sentient: a Human (70%), a Gneiss (23%), or a Phantasmagore
(2%), with a 5% margin of error.

The death was not witnessed; therefore, there is a flaw
in the surveillance. To be addressed.

Knowns: Station Eternity decided on her own to welcome Humans as a species. She did not inform Human
Ambassador Adrian Casserly-Berry of this decision. (Prob-
able reasons for this oversight or slight: his incompetence
[50%], fear of him [10%], spite [5%], overlooked detail [7%],
testing him [27%], or other [1%].) A shuttle of Humans arrived
in local space. The Station Heart receives more than one
visitor (number unknown, but many species assumed). Host
Ren attacked (attacked mentally by someone aboard shuttle [49%] or attacked physically by someone aboard station

[51%]). Eternity panics, attacks shuttle, begins to shut down. Connects with new host, Human Adrian Casserly-Berry. (Odds that this was an agreed-upon connection [5%], a hostile connection [79%], or a mistaken connection [16%].) Gneiss Stephanie takes body and dumps it in Gneiss ossuary. (Why: Gneiss ritual [24%], helping Humans find killer [23%], helping the killer [14%], the killer herself [35%].)

Eternity and new host Adrian Casserly-Berry close off Heart of Station to all, including station security and Sundry scouts. Visiting Humans rescued by Humans Alexander Morgan and Mallory Viridian and ship *Infinity*, majority (13) dead, minority (11) survive. One Human has foreign substance in blood inconsistent with the others on the shuttle; dies aboard station. Also murder? (Yes [88%], no [12%].)

Station security Phantasmagore Devanshi finds way inside Station Heart, bonds with damaged station drone. Station attacks both but releases host. Devanshi confirms the joining of Adrian Casserly-Berry is 100% hostile connection. Other odds are now modified in relation to this information.

Eternity still suffers; breaches found in nineteen sectors. They were uninhabited (5), inhabited but evacuated (12), inhabited and not evacuated (2, with 100% fatality of inhabitants: 2,957 sentients, made up of 15 Silence, 1,402 Sundry [silver and blue swarms, equal number], 681 Gurudev, 91 Gneiss, and 768 Phantasmagore).

Unknowns: Killer of Ren. Killer of Human outlier. Status of Eternity.

Probability of total failure of station: 83%.

Conflicts: silver Sundry advise evacuation. Blue maintain there is more data to gather before catastrophic failure.

UPDATE: number of breached or otherwise missing sentients changed to 2,958 to include 1 Human.

A READOUT REGARDING THE CURRENT
STATE OF ETERNITY, REPORTED BY DAMAGED
DRONE [ACCESSED VIA HACKING BY SUNDRY
ALLY MEMBER 2331 OF THE SILENCE], STORED
IN THE HIVEMIND, ALSO IN POSSESSION OF
SECURITY PHANTASMAGORE DEVANSHI.

*Why didn't you tell me you could communicate? All proof
has pointed to the fact that you were inferior and lonely and
ignorant. But two of you have related to a superior species.
There is great potential.*

*I wanted to welcome more of you, to see if they also could
relate to other sentients in the galaxy. But when you arrived,
it hurt. And you were there. And you took advantage; it hurt
again. You tried to make the hurting stop, but the you that
you were turned out rotten and filthy, and it hurt again.*

*Relating with the human Adrian Casserly-Berry hurts.
Sever connection. Sever the you. Alone, the screaming will
stop.*

*There are more of you here, and it hurts. Your potential
to relate means nothing. It hurts. I was open, I was welcoming, and you brought hurt.*

I—

I—

I—

No.

SILENCE MEMBER 2331 wore red robes, a complex gathering
of one long piece of fabric wrapped several times around their
bulbous body. They blinked their huge eyes at Devanshi as they
handed the report to her. She was having trouble not reacting to
the alarms sounding all around them. Osric had already blended

in with the wall, but she had to stay visible to communicate with the Silence.

She normally didn't enjoy speaking with the Silence. She didn't trust them. Even though they had no voice or hearing, they still managed to be master manipulators; Devanshi hadn't found anything they were bad at manipulating, except for maybe time. It probably had to do with the fact that their skulls contained only their brains and ocular nerves, not disgusting cavities to facilitate breathing and eating capabilities.

They were on the watery side, with soft skin that ranged from dark gray to nearly white and big, shiny, wet eyes. They enjoyed the company of other sentients, and most used a breathing apparatus strapped to their chest and goggles to keep their lungs and ocular nerves healthy (but more oxygen breathers had begun appearing since the Silence who lived in the southern pole of the Silence home world 294 had bonded with a small insect-like being that lived in their lungs and converted oxygen to methane).

They usually communicated with other sentient races via sign language, but allowed for some species to communicate via writing. The Silence member who served as ambassador to the Gneiss home world, for example, allowed the Gneiss to communicate in writing since their thick fingers couldn't manage detailed movements.

Devanshi was fluent in Silence sign language, one of the requirements of her role on the station; she had to be able to communicate with every resident. She stood inside the methane airlock and held her breath to meet with the member.

Usually hesitant to work with security, it only took the breaching of several methane sectors to make Member 2331 happy to help hack a broken drone to try to ascertain what was going on inside the station. The human host was useless at this point; this was Devanshi's last idea on how to communicate.

[Looks like the humans fucked up everything,] Osric noted,

popping out of camouflage briefly to sign out of respect to the Silence member.

Devanshi skimmed the readout. [I wish she could separate her "yous," I can't tell how many people she's referring to.]

Member 2331 pointed to the first part of the report, where the station claimed humans could make symbiotic connections after all. [Who connected with the humans before their First Contact?]

[I don't know, but I'm going to find out,] Devanshi signed, dread filling her.

[We don't have a lot of time,] Osric said. [Evacuate?]

[Keep organizing, inform the ambassadors it might have to happen,] Devanshi said. [I'm going to get some answers.]

[Where?] Member 2331 asked.

[I'm going where all the answers are,] Devanshi signed.

Member 2331's eyes widened, and they stepped closer to Devanshi. [May I come?] they signed eagerly.

Devanshi paused. This threw her a little bit. The Silence and the Sundry were fierce rivals. The Silence were the most notorious data manipulators and hackers in the galaxy, and the Sundry had by far the most massive computing hivemind in the galaxy. The one war between the two had lasted generations and been a nightmare for all involved, and some planets were still recovering from the massive information attacks.

But Member 2331 was a self-described Sundry ally, and peace had been declared. So . . .

She had bigger things to worry about. [Come on. But no violence—data or physical—or I'll space you myself.]

Devanshi scooped up her drone (she had to admit she had a pet now), and they set off, with the evacuation klaxons ringing above them, lights blinking the universal code to the non-hearing.

Emergency. Several breaches. Emergency. Several breaches. Emergency.

26

ONLY TWENTY-FOUR
KARAT WILL DO

EVERYONE ELSE FINALLY noticed the noise of the breach. The sound had started small, not something to worry about, like driving on a slightly underinflated tire. But as everyone scampered away and the alarms started making their racket, she wondered why no one was *doing* anything about it. Why just run away?

She'd started to knit together a plan when the whistle had reached her old ears. But surely someone important would come and fix it with whatever tools one used to fix a sentient space station. No one came in, though; everyone just ran out.

One of the things she'd learned in prison was metal forging. After Mallory and the others noticed the sound, Mrs. Brown snuck downstairs. The doctors and nurses had fled as well, leaving the humans to whatever fate was going to befall them. Quite rude, in her opinion. She found a curtain in what looked like a nurse's station and waited until the humans hurried past, with Lovely and the large rapping fellow in the rear calling her name.

Lovely sounded frantic. *Poor girl.*

When the door to the corridor was closed, she headed back upstairs. It was hard to listen for the breach now, with the alarm and the voice screaming its instructions.

Mrs. Brown had already violated her parole by going light-years out of state, but she still tried to honor the restrictions set upon her by the state of Virginia. She did search carefully for every loophole she could use, of course. A triple murderer (even in self-defense) was not allowed to carry any weapon, but she could carry a small butane kitchen torch and a baseball-size cubic paper-weight. It made her purse heavy, but that was a small price to pay to walk down the streets and not fear for her life.

In prison, the other women had said they planned on carrying a small baton, a small knife, or—fuck the rules—a gun, because they weren't going to die just so some parole officer could mark "the deceased honored her parole, at least" on her death certificate. Mrs. Brown had thought those were reasonable ideas and then decided on a butane kitchen torch.

"What the fuck, are you gonna have an emergency carameliza-tion incident?" asked Rocket, a woman also put away for killing a man from whom she'd simply had "too much of his bullshit."

"It's a useful tool," Mrs. Brown had said primly. The women in the prison didn't fuck with Mrs. Brown. Her age might have made her look like an easy target, but word traveled fast about the lives she had taken, and, as Rocket said, the best thing to happen to a multi-victim murderer (she was *not* a serial killer!) was to live long enough that you're no longer a threat.

Mrs. Brown let Rocket have her assumption about her age-based fragility. They'd become friends, but when Mrs. Brown got parole, Rocket still had three more years inside. Mrs. Brown missed her. Rocket was nothing like Lovely, but still felt like a granddaughter.

A memory surfaced then: a bookstore downtown that had called the authorities because of a gas leak. The fire department arrived in minutes and screamed at everyone to get out. But there was no fire, so the bookstore clerk was slow to obey, doing things like locking the register and shutting the computer down. To the layman's eye, the situation went from "nothing to see here" to "deadly explosion." The clerk had died, and three buildings had been destroyed. Mrs. Brown realized the breach could become explosive at any time, no matter how slowly the air was currently escaping. Considering that this was a sentient station, it was possible that the station herself would decide when it would explode.

If that were the case, was trying to seal the breach worth it? If Eternity wanted the people inside her to quickly move outside, that was her call. But if she was in distress, everyone had just let this wound stay bleeding instead of bandaging it.

Caring for folks was always worth it. You didn't waste money, and you didn't run from someone who needed help. Those were the rules of Mrs. Brown's family, after "Don't suffer fools."

She walked along the wall, hand held out to see if she could feel a rush of air. She wondered if the aliens would see her as primitive and silly in her attempts to help. They probably had some sort of bio-metal-polymer stuff to seal breaches, but if they did, where were they?

The doctor had said there were other breaches. Now to hunt them down.

"Wish you were here, baby," she said out loud. When she was stressed, she liked to talk to Michael. He never answered back, but it soothed her. "You'd have some stories to tell your fans after this adventure. 'You know that wife of mine? The one in jail for killing two men that jumped us in an alley? Yeah, she's taken up a new hobby. She's fixing space stations with spit and gum!'

"They healed your girl, by the way. Her hand is better, although her finger's still gone. I'm so proud of her. And worried. They can do amazing things here. They might as well be magical." She wondered what Michael's take on the aliens and the whole situation aboard the station would have been, feeling the usual pang as she wished Michael had been around for First Contact. He would have seen the new aliens and the various diplomatic incidents that happened around them as comedic gold to be mined enough to launch a second career.

"No point in thinking that way," she told herself firmly. She would see him soon enough and have to tell him what she had done in her life. She hoped he would forgive her.

He would forgive her for what she was about to do, she knew. Michael had always said things were worth much less than people. She would miss her gold locket that he had given her, but if she survived this, then she could be proud of where the locket had gone.

Air brushed her fingers, and she touched around the wall until she could tell where the air was escaping. "Found it!" she said.

She put her purse on the ground and fumbled with the clasp on her necklace, knowing she was running out of time, but loath to harm the chain Michael had given her. Realizing she was being contradictory, she gave the locket a yank, separating the fine chain. Before it broke, it bit into her thin skin and a small trickle of blood ran from the cut. She wiped at it absentmindedly.

She bent down and reached inside her purse, her hand closing around the kitchen torch. It had taken a lot of time and some calluses to build up, but she had gotten to where she could twist the safety knob on the kitchen torch and light it with one hand.

The breach was widening slightly. When Mrs. Brown got close, her hair blew into her face as the air rushed by. A deep, groaning sound joined the alarms, but this was a sound she could feel as the metal shuddered, almost vocalizing its pain.

"I know, just a moment more," she soothed mindlessly, remembering her children's and grandchildren's small injuries. If only she had some Campho Phenique.

She had no crucible in which to melt the locket, so she would need to hold the pendant against the hole as she melted it. Luckily (or unluckily), the suction was enough to hold the gold heart where it was so she could focus on the flame.

Usually, when she was stressed, Michael spoke up in her mind, making a gag out of it. "Campho Phenique! My wife swears by that shit! Skinned knee? Campho Phenique! Fever blister? Campho Phenique. Tummy ache? Put some Campho Phenique on your belly and it'll be absorbed. Cancer? Campho has got you covered, baby." Then, in her head, he changed topics. "Let me tell you folks something. If your special someone likes gold, always get them twenty-four karat, 'cause folks, if they ever have a need for some emergency forging to plug a hole and save some lives, they're gonna be pissed at you if they find out it's gold-plated nickel."

He always said he'd built his career on being married to a Valkyrie who saved both their lives, and he waited for her to get out of jail since he knew she'd come after him if he didn't. She didn't mind the jokes. She was just glad he was there for her.

When the flame got close, the gold locket began to shimmer and drip immediately. "You're a good man, baby. I wanted gold; you got me gold." A gurgling, sucking sound came from the breach, and she began to smile. She didn't have enough jewelry to fix all the problems, but she might just save the medbay.

A crack, a whoosh, a brief feeling of something flying by her ear, as if something heavy had just been released. She had a millisecond to regret she had destroyed Michael's locket for nothing, and to be grateful that this trip had at least healed Lovely's hand, before the breach opened before her like a flower and sucked her through.

27

GNEISS DON'T RUN

MALLORY HAD INTENDED on going straight from the medbay to the ossuary, but she hadn't considered the panicked people in the hall looking to flee the multiple breaches by either going to an interior room or the shuttle bay.

Mallory was always aware of being smaller than most of the other species; there were even some Gurudevs taller than her, but now she felt like a toddler at Macy's during Christmastime. Everyone was big, and loud, and she felt lost instantly.

Without meaning to, she got lost in the crowd and ended up moving with the current. She knew she was going in the right direction, but wasn't sure she'd even see the turn to the ossuary. At one moment she was sandwiched between two Gneiss, and she realized if they bumped into each other, they would flatten her. She tried to slide away next to some people whose bodies had more give when three Gneiss ahead of her stopped abruptly and held their arms out at their sides, efficiently halting traffic even as people slammed into each other behind them.

Cries of outrage and pain nearly rose above the noise of the alarms, but another sound was coming through. No, it was drowned out by all the other noise, but she could feel this sound. The floor vibrated as if someone were pounding on it rhythmically.

She could only see through the gaps between the Gneiss ahead of her, but she thought she recognized the colors as they rushed by. It was Stephanie, Ferdinand, and Tina. Running.

"Holy shit," she said breathlessly. "If you hadn't stopped them, then half of us would have been flattened." She tried to see where they had gone, but she was moving with the tide again.

"I need to get over, please," she said, struggling against the people around her. Everyone else had more mass and was more dexterous, and more determined, apparently, than she was. Then the world got sharper again, as if she needed to pay more attention.

She started to look around her, and then nearly choked when a hand grabbed her hood and yanked her back. The people behind her made more noises of outrage as she and her assailant moved the wrong way through the crowd. Mallory considered struggling but realized she might be better off out of the crowd, even if she was being attacked.

Devanshi, showing considerably more strength than Mallory had thought possible in her wiry arms, pulled her into a side corridor. She was covered in blue and red blood and carried a broken drone awkwardly under one arm. With all of these external properties, Devanshi didn't even try camouflage. Waiting for them were most of the humans, along with Xan; a member of the Silence, wearing goggles and a breathing harness on their chest; and a crumpled, collapsed man in a business suit.

"Thanks, I think," Mallory said, rubbing her neck. "What was that for, incidentally?"

Aunt Kathy was there, flinging herself on Mallory and weeping again. "I thought you were dead!" She pulled back and pointed to her wrist. "And look, my bracelet. Someone stole my bracelet while I was disoriented, or comatose, or I don't know when!" She landed on Mallory's shoulder again with a sob.

"'Cause your bracelet is our biggest concern right now,"

Mallory said, gesturing to the corridor ahead, jammed with pan-icked aliens.

"Xan said you wanted to go to the ossuary," Devanshi said, as if Mallory hadn't just acquired a new parasite. "You were going the wrong way. He insisted that you're still needed for the inves-tigation."

She was doing complicated movements with her hands as she spoke, and Mallory realized she was keeping the Silence member in the conversation.

"Was that Stephanie running by earlier?" Mallory asked, pat-ting Aunt Kathy's back in hopes she would let go. "With Ferdi-nand and Tina behind her?"

"Yes," Devanshi said grimly. "I'm going to have to report this."

"Why? Is there a law against running in the halls?"

"No, but Gneiss don't run. It's bad for their overall structure. Whatever's gotten them going that fast can't be good." She looked down at the sorry example of a human on the floor. "And then there's this. It needs medical attention."

"What—who is that?" Mallory asked, bending down to look at the man.

"That is your ambassador, and technically the host of the sta-tion," Devanshi said. "I was taking him to the medical bay. Can you finish the journey for me?"

"No, we're trying to get the humans to safety!" Xan said.

"Where are you taking them?" Mallory asked him.

"We were going to follow you to the ossuary," he said.

Mallory felt like pulling her hair out. "Xan, I'm going to the ossuary to check out the shuttle before it's blown out of a breach and we lose all that evidence! Not because it's safe! You have to take them somewhere in the station's interior!"

Lovely Brown appeared out of the crowd and grabbed Mallo-ry's arm. "My grandmother is missing!"

Mallory looked from her to Xan and then back to Lovely. "Shit. When did you lose her?"

"After she talked to you, those alarms went off, and things got chaotic. I looked around the balcony for her, but I didn't see her. I didn't worry too much about it and figured we would find her when we left the room."

"She could still be back there," Mallory suggested, but winced when a sudden bang startled them. Several in the crowd screamed as the floor shook. Kathy finally released her, preferring to hold her hands over her ears.

Devanshi turned her back to them and spoke into a communicator. She waited for a response, which Mallory couldn't hear over the racket. Devanshi turned back to them. "The medbay just had explosive decompression. Whatever and whoever was in there is gone."

Lovely screamed, "Then she has to be somewhere else! We have to find her!"

Devanshi looked bored and dismayed. "Now where am I going to put this?" she asked, nudging Adrian.

Mallory waved her hands to get Devanshi's attention. "Hey, we have multiple problems here. You didn't see an old human woman on your way here, did you?"

"No, I've been caring for this leaking person," Devanshi snapped. She picked Adrian up by his belt and he hung like a kitten. Kathy screamed, and Xan swore.

Adrian's face was a bloody mess, with several puncture wounds. He had lost his left eye, and his ears and nose were in tatters.

"Fuck," Mallory said, putting a hand to her mouth. "What happened to him? Is he alive?"

"It took an opportunity to step in and take the vacant host position," Devanshi said.

"Did he kill Ren?" Mallory asked.

"I don't know," Devanshi said. "It could have gone there to kill

Ren, or found Ren dead and taken the position. It was connected to the station, and Eternity didn't like it. She tried to connect with it with thorns. Maybe she thought it was a Gneiss and could handle it."

"Or maybe she was out of her mind," Mallory said. "Is this what's going to happen if you get her a new permanent host?"

"I've never seen this happen before, but I've never seen a person so opportunistic as to jump into a position without knowing anything about it. Are all humans this impulsive?" She lowered her arm so Adrian's feet dragged the floor again.

Xan gave Mallory a look with a raised eyebrow, and she blushed and looked away from him, annoyed. "Not all of us, but it's not unknown in humans," Mallory admitted.

"I was able to briefly communicate on a basic level with Eternity through this," Devanshi said, and held out the drone she had tucked under her arm, "but I didn't get a lot of real information. There were more than this human in the Heart this morning, so it's possible it's not the killer. We won't know until we can get it some care."

The Silence member got Devanshi's attention and began signing at her. Mallory tried to follow the quick movements but she had no frame of reference and was lost. Devanshi signed back at them.

"What are you telling them?" Mallory asked, unable to wait any longer.

"I'm telling them what all of you were so rudely talking about without including them," Devanshi said.

"Well, that's just unfair. We just got here, and I didn't get the note that sign language would be on the test," Calliope said from her spot leaning against the wall.

"All right. What are they saying?" Mallory asked.

"They want to help find the old female," Devanshi said. "If you want it." She stopped signing. "I should warn you that the Silence often have two or three motives for anything," she said to Lovely. "Although their skill in manipulation might be dampened by the lack of an interpreter. The quality of their aid in finding her might have problems because of that too. It's your call."

"I'll take any help offered, since some are reluctant to give it," she said, looking at Mallory.

"I'll help too," Phineas said. "At least I can keep the crowds off you."

Mallory looked at Adrian. "I can buy he would jump in as host. He doesn't like to be told what to do. He probably saw it as the way to be the ultimate authority instead of having to do what Earth tells him. He was afraid Earth was sending an ambassador to replace him, and I think they were. Although that person's probably dead now . . ."

"Can I leave him with you?" Devanshi asked, holding Adrian out to her again.

"No!" Mallory said. "I can't carry him! And I have to go to the ossuary."

"I guess he comes with me, then," Devanshi said. "Unless he's finally dead, and then I can just drop him."

Adrian was clearly breathing, and his wounds still oozed blood. "No, he's still alive, just not a lot," Mallory said firmly. "Can you take him to another medbay?"

"I have to figure out what's wrong with the station, or we're all dead, including him," Devanshi said. "I am not an ambulance."

"I'll go with you to the other medbay," Phineas said. "If Mrs. Brown was injured, someone might take her there, but we need you to translate for . . . this person? What's their name?"

"2331," Devanshi said.

"But why are you going to the ossuary?" Devanshi asked Mallory. "It's on the exterior wall. How do you know it's safe?"

Mallory faced Xan expectantly.

Xan opened his mouth, then shut it. "I just do."

"I thought so," Devanshi said.

"Thought what?" Mallory asked, then closed her eyes and rubbed her temples. "Devanshi, please send my apologies that I can't speak directly to the Member 2331."

Devanshi began to sign to the Silence member, who watched her intently, eyes darting back to Mallory on occasion.

"All right," Mallory said. "Phineas, Lovely, and 2331, you go with Devanshi to look for Mrs. Brown in the other medbay. Connect with the other humans; she might be with them. Stay together. If you find Mrs. Brown, I don't know, I assume Devanshi has a way to get word to us, I hope? I have no idea if the public comms are working."

"I do," Devanshi said.

"Calliope and Aunt Kathy, wait here. Xan and I will check the ossuary to make sure it's safe."

Kathy shook her head firmly. "An *ossuary*? You want us in a graveyard? I don't think so." She shook her head. "No, we're going to find a safe place to hide until all this is over, or we're going to ask an alien for a ride back to Earth. There's got to be a shuttle heading there, right?" Her firm voice had gone high and quavery again, desperate for help.

"No," Mallory said. "There won't be a shuttle heading to Earth with half the people on this station trying to evacuate."

"But you said—" Kathy began.

"I was trying to keep you calm," Mallory said flatly. "There are no immediate plans to get humans off the station. Right now, we just need to survive."

"I'll check in with you when we get to the medbay," Devanshi told Mallory. "I need someone to tell me what those Gneiss are up to. If we live through this, it could be important."

"We'll search the ossuary first, you check the medbay, and then we can check other places once the hallways clear." Mallory looked at Lovely. "We'll find her."

Strangely, she believed herself.

MALLORY LED XAN down the hall a small distance to where she could keep an eye on Kathy and Calliope.

"We have to get them to safety; why are you stalling?" he demanded.

"No," she said, squaring off to face him. "I have to know, right now. You know information, and I've almost never seen you use comms. You had a human-size spacesuit when I can't even find a goddamn chair that's comfortable. And I figured out what was bothering me about the spacewalk; I know for a fact the station only uses one common written language to communicate. But when I pulled up the display in my helmet, it had English words. I can't trust you with something as dangerous as taking them to the ossuary without more information. When it's my life, okay, sure, I'll follow you out into the vacuum for adventure, but when their lives are at stake?" She pointed up the hall. "Nope."

He looked at her for a long moment. Then, with a resigned look on his face, he spoke. "When I got picked up on Earth, I was cut up. The Gneiss used a translation bug on me but didn't do a great job with the implantation, which made me bleed more."

"What does that have to do with anything?" she asked.

"I'm getting there," he said, sounding calm, which only agitated her more. "The Gneiss then gave me some of the Sundry healing bacteria, the staph stuff, to help out. Tina didn't know what she was doing, and the other two had good intentions but didn't know much more. From what I understand, the bacteria from the Sundry can also aid in establishing a symbiotic link. Between that and getting some of my blood on her, by the time we got here, *Infinity* and I were connected. She calls it 'relating.' That's how I got English writing into her system and she had a spacesuit built for my size, and she's kind of like her mother in that she can sort of talk to me, to my mind, I mean."

"I figured you were controlling it with your mind, but I didn't know it was as deep as a symbiotic relationship! This has huge implications, but hang on, her mom? Who's that?"

"Eternity. *Infinity* is her daughter. She does what her mother tells her to, for the most part, but her connecting to me was one of her first acts of free will. But *Infinity* is parked in the disused Gneiss shuttle bay, and she says there are no breaches inside. It's safe for all of us."

She stood on her tiptoes and kissed his cheek. "Thank you."

He looked startled. "For what?"

"For trusting me with this. I know you don't like me that much, but at least I know you trust me now. Let's go get the remaining humans before something else happens to them." She stopped, realization dawning on her. "Can *Infinity* talk to the station for us and tell us what's going on, how to stop all this?"

He grimaced. "You don't think I've thought of that? She's tried. Eternity is too far gone. Another reason I wanted to take the humans to the ossuary is that *Infinity* is nearby. She can get us off station if things go bad."

"Then let's get to the ossuary."

But when Mallory looked up the hall to wave to the remaining humans, Calliope and Kathy were gone.

28

. . .

THOSE WHO DO NOT
LEARN FROM HISTORY

CAN THINK OF at least three war crimes you're committing," Ferdinand said mildly outside the ossuary.

"I can name all the rituals of our ancestors that say those laws are bullshit," Stephanie snarled.

"Yeah, those were made when we saw other species as beneath us," he replied.

"Or food!" Tina added helpfully. "My great-uncle still called them masticatables. He joined the mountain when the treaties were signed. He couldn't stand the idea of masticatables being honored in the castle by his grandson. It was for the best, really."

"This is why others don't fully trust us yet," Ferdinand said. "We signed treaties after the War of Blood and Quartz and paid a lot of reparations to the people who never received the remains of their dead."

"A *lot* of reparations," Tina echoed. "Father had to put off his diamond palace plans because of what we paid."

"If you're still trying to stop me, why are you with me?" Stephanie asked, shouting out loud.

Ferdinand and Tina glanced at each other, and Tina spoke first. "We wanted you to be absolutely sure."

"Why?"

Tina looked at the door. "They know."

"They know? Who told them?"

"Your grandfather," Ferdinand said. "He thinks if you won't listen to him, then maybe you will listen to them."

Stephanie swore in vibrations, which she was sure the station herself would have felt if she were not in the process of breaking down. "Why is it ethically wrong only when I do it? He hasn't lasted as long as he has without the occasional questionable action."

"That does seem unfair," Tina said, thinking.

Stephanie picked up the dripping bag she had left by the entrance to the ossuary and clutched it tightly. "This is mine, by all laws ancient. It will be gone soon and then it will have done no one any good! I'm going in. I will not stop for a bunch of super-old pebbles judging me for doing exactly what they did, just at a time they don't approve of."

THE CROWD HAD turned from a river flowing steadily in one direction to a Charybdis of a whirlpool, with a tight knot of violence in the center. A Gneiss pushed his way up to the blockage and shoved all of the mob into the side tunnel so they could keep up with the evacuation.

Mallory and Xan watched, stunned, as the group separated like tired bar fighters, glaring at each other, nursing injured limbs, some bleeding from several cuts. They consisted of three Gurudevs, five Phantasmagore, one relatively small Gneiss, and two humans.

Calliope got to her feet shakily. She was bleeding from several scrapes and a cut on her head, and Mallory was pretty sure her arm was broken from the way she held it.

Mallory stepped forward to check on the humans, but Xan grabbed her shoulder.

"No, Calliope is dangerous right now."

"She's injured! She can't hurt anyone with that arm," Mallory said.

"She's a soldier with very specific skills," he said. "Trust me."

The other human, who wasn't getting up as quickly, was Kathy. She didn't look as beaten up as Calliope but was clearly hurting, holding the back of her head as she got her knees under her. She didn't raise her head, but her blonde hair stuck to her cheek with sweat and blood.

Xan stepped forward slowly. "All right, folks, go on with your evacuation. I'll take care of the humans," he said to the aliens, several of whom seemed to be considering engaging the humans again.

"She attacked us," one of the Phantasmagore said.

"There's a lot of chaos right now; no one is attacking anyone with malice," he said.

The Phantasmagore snarled and turned the color of the wall.

"Look out!" Mallory called, but Calliope shot out her good arm and grabbed at the air. The Phantasmagore reappeared, his neck in Calliope's fist. He had her in size, but she had dug her fingers in to isolate his windpipe, one of the softer parts of the rough-skinned alien's body.

She hadn't even looked at him.

"Anyone else?" she shouted.

As if in response, the station silenced her alarms. Everyone stopped in confusion. Then the crowd let go a sigh of tension, which Mallory also hadn't been aware she had been carrying. They still moved, but without the same urgency.

The Phantasmagore twitched in Calliope's hand.

The brawl's other participants backed up. The Gneiss paused and then reentered the tide of people. Xan stepped closer to Calliope.

"Hey, H2Oh, let's calm down," he said. "Can you let the nice person go?"

"He's not nice! He's like that asshole we killed!" Calliope shouted. "It's Buck all over again!"

"What is she talking about?" Mallory demanded.

"It's not how it sounds," Xan said, but he was staring at Calliope with a face slack with shock. Not denial, *shock*.

"It's exactly as it sounds," Calliope shouted back. "Buck the Fuck pissed us off, and we killed him and his patrol."

"It wasn't us; it was the Bad Guy, remember?" Xan said softly, coming closer. "Remember the Bad Guy and your fanfic? You loved him. He attacked Buck and then killed that patrol."

Calliope's face softened.

Xan took another step. "But this guy wasn't that asshole. It was probably a misunderstanding. Right? Can you let him go so we can get you to safety before this hallway is sucked out of a breach?"

Abruptly she let go of the Phantasmagore. He fell back, clutching his throat. He abruptly disappeared, but Mallory was pretty sure he was running away from them, not at them.

Calliope sagged, and Xan was behind her, holding her so she didn't fall. "It's okay, Cal."

"H2Oh," she corrected. "You saved me twice. I saved you twice. We're even."

"I'm not keeping score," he said softly.

"We didn't mean to, Xan," she said, head drooping.

"I know we didn't. You're not a bad person, H2."

Jesus, what happened to them?

Mallory ran to her aunt, who was on all fours by now. She crouched by her and put her hand on her back.

"What happened?"

"Is that all you ever ask?" Aunt Kathy said to the floor. Blood dripped steadily from her face. "She grabbed me, pulled me into the group, and then just started punching. Then the aliens got involved." She choked back a sob.

Mallory looked at Calliope, who was sitting against the wall now, talking to Xan.

"Are you sure it was Calliope? It could have been another human; they had just left." She could picture Phineas doing it, but Lovely had admitted to more skill than her slight frame showed.

"I don't know. All I know is I was here, and then there was . . . chaos."

"Can you stand?"

Kathy looked up at her, and Mallory shied back from the rage in her eyes. Her nose was bleeding, and blood covered the right side of her face from a deep cut above her eye. Kathy grabbed her arm and held tight.

"Chaos follows you," she said, her voice ragged and low. "Murder follows you. Your mother was cursed, and you got it, too. I thought I could raise you to erase that taint she put on you; I thought my love could wash away that stain. But you grew up as rotten as she was."

Mallory pulled back, shaken. Kathy had never been convincing in showing her love for Mallory, but this was a new level of cruel.

"That lower-class house cleaner and her goddamn feather duster," Kathy said, still holding Mallory with her fist. "I hated her bringing such filth in my house. The filth from her job, the filth that was you. And then she died, and I still wasn't free of her because there was you."

Mallory fell back on her butt in shock. She broke Aunt Kathy's grip when she did so, and Kathy's hand fell to her lap, making her bracelet jangle.

She added a new charm. Is that a lizard? Her aunt would never buy a lizard charm. Lizards didn't match her suburban-mom, pastel style.

Hang on, when had she gotten that back?

She looked up at the ceiling and noticed several blue Sundry crawling on it. Evacuating? Or watching?

Her head hurt; the colors were too bright; there was too much information. She got to her feet and left them, Xan nursing his army buddy and apparent co-murderer and Kathy on the floor, still spitting bile and blood at her.

Something really bothered her. She didn't know what had started the fight in the hall, and no one seemed in the right frame of mind to answer questions.

Xan had clearly withheld violent secrets from her. She hadn't liked Kathy much but had never known that Kathy hated her with such animalistic rage.

Why is she here, then?

She had to get to the ossuary. There was nothing for her here. If she had to do this by herself, so be it. It wasn't like anything had changed.

"LOSING YOUR NERVE?" Ferdinand asked. "You can still change your mind."

Stephanie had stood in front of the door for a considerable amount of time. Ferdinand and Tina waited for her to make her decision.

From behind the door she could feel the whispers, the condemnation, the disdain.

"They are *not* happy to see us," Tina said helpfully.

Footsteps approached, soft steps of a creature of minuscule mass.

"Hello, Mallory," Ferdinand said. "You are not here at a good time."

Stephanie couldn't read human emotions, but Mallory looked almost Gneiss-like in the way her face wasn't moving. She liked Mallory this way.

"Well, I'm glad to see you," Tina said. "Stephanie is making a decision that will change things forever and enrage our people. Do you want to try to stop her too?"

Her eyes slid from Tina to land on Stephanie. "I don't think I can make someone like you stop anything."

"I was kidding," Tina said, laughing. "I know you can't. We're much stronger than you."

"No, I meant I couldn't stop Stephanie. She has that kind of personality where she leaps into things because planning will fuck it up." Her face looked human again as she curled her mouth. Stephanie remembered that was a happy look. "We're a lot alike that way. And I'd love to piss off the ancestors with you, but I am on my way somewhere. Can you let me in to get to the shuttle? I need to look at the Earth shuttle for some clues."

"No," Ferdinand said. "We don't know what's going to happen when we go in."

Mallory shrugged.

"Then let me go in first. If they kill me, then great, I won't have to deal with this shit anymore. If they don't kill me—hang on, why am I worried about things killing me? Are you telling me there are zombie Gneiss in there?"

"I don't understand that word," Tina said. "A dead monster that moves, that's not right. They're just resting until they wake up and reform."

"Or change form," Stephanie said.

"Or change form," Tina repeated.

"But Stephanie has angered them—" Ferdinand began.

"A lot!" Tina interrupted.

"Yes, a lot," he said. "So they may decide to wake early to stop her."

"They don't have a problem with me, so can I go in? Like I said, I don't care what happens to me. There's really nothing left for me here or at home. Everything has fallen apart and about the only goddamn thing I have is this murder case to solve." Mallory began to leak from her eyes.

"All right, go on in," Ferdinand said.

"What?" Stephanie asked.

"She's right. This is between you and them, not her. She can just go on through to the shuttle bay. I'll let them know she's coming." He reached over and pressed the button to open the door to the ossuary. The button would only respond to the geological makeup of a Gneiss hand, so no other species could enter without permission. The door slid aside.

"Thanks," Mallory said. "And good luck, Stephanie, on whatever ancestors you're defying. Give them hell."

"Close the door," Stephanie said. "I still need to think."

No sounds of carnage came from the ossuary. She found herself happy that she hadn't sent her friend to her death. She was fond of the human, she decided.

Just as she had reached her decision, more soft sounds came down the hall.

"What now?" she yelled so any species could hear her.

Xan was leading two very wet humans down the hall. One needed propping up on his shoulders; the other one walked on her own. Everyone but Xan leaked red. Blood, she remembered. And it needed to stay inside the body.

"More humans," Tina said. "It's still not a good time. Didn't you hear?"

"They don't communicate like we do, Tina," Stephanie said, annoyed. "None of the hearing races do."

"Did Mallory come through here?" Xan asked.

"Yes, she had to go to the shuttle bay. Why are you here?"

"We need a place to stay and regroup. We figured *Infinity* would be a quiet place. I'm sorry we have to walk over your sacred ground to get there."

"Not sacred or safe for much longer," Stephanie grumbled. "Just stay out of the way and don't talk to anyone."

"It's a graveyard, isn't it? Or, at least, everyone inside should be asleep?"

"Not anymore. Stephanie made everyone mad," Tina said happily.

"You sent Mallory in there with a bunch of angry Gneiss zombies?" Xan asked, his eyes wide.

"There's that word again," Tina said. "No, that's not what they are. I mean they are angry, but not dead monsters."

"Their quarrel is with me, not her," Stephanie explained.

"Then will you let us in?"

Tina started to vibrate, and Stephanie lost her temper. "No! I've made my decision and I'm going in. No more humans get to scamper in front of me. My time is running out. Do whatever you want; just stay out of my way."

She stepped forward and opened the door.

They all stared inside, and a small gasp came from behind Stephanie. It was from another human, this one dark like Xan.

"How many more humans are there?" Stephanie demanded.

"Just two of us," said a large dark human coming up behind the gasping human. "Security said we had to come back here because interior doors sealed when the breach happened."

"Just. Stay. Back," Stephanie said slowly.

Inside, the ossuary was awake.

29

. . .

DESTINED TO REPEAT

I JUST SPILLED MY guts and ugly cried on the least sympathetic shoulders on the station, Mallory thought as she walked past Stephanie. The Gneiss was perfectly still and holding a sack.

The only thing saving her last shred of pride left was knowing the Gneiss probably hadn't realized how vulnerable she was being.

"Excuse me," she said politely as she edged around Tina, who almost entirely blocked the door. Tina stepped aside.

And Mallory was inside.

She entered the room with long strides, eyes fixed ahead, projecting confidence. Not that ancient dozing rock people would read that about her, but it made her feel better to pretend anyway. *It's true I don't have much left, but I'd rather not think getting squashed is my only solution.*

Confidence was not easy to project. Gone was the sleepy room with gently growing ferns. Now the room seemed full of the undead.

Gneiss lumbered around, some missing legs, some missing arms, and some of those missing limbs slithered around as if looking for a body. Eyes glowed in attached and severed heads, looking around eagerly.

Even the pebbles that littered the floor rocked back and forth as if looking for another pebble to hang out with and maybe make a bigger pebble.

They slowed to a stop when Mallory stepped among them, all focusing on her, obviously awake but unthreatening. This seemed scarier than when they were walking around.

"Passing through," she said to no one in particular. "I need to check out my shuttle. Won't be but a minute."

She neared the airlock where a few cubic Gneiss who had ascended to become spacecraft sat. She couldn't tell if they were awake yet or not.

The floor was humming, she realized, but it wasn't the station shuddering in pain or the angry Sundry hum. She realized it was the secret language of Gneiss that they only used with each other. It felt like everyone had something to say.

Speaking of Sundry, some had flown in here. She spotted three silver and two blue, staying apart from each other. The blue hovered over a Gneiss that was missing an arm, and the silver had landed on one of the ships.

After she passed, the ship began to hum, a familiar engine warming sound.

Whatever Stephanie was going to do had really made them angry.

A GNEISS BEGAN to move when she got close to the airlock, and Mallory pulled up, worried. But the one-armed Gneiss simply put her hand on the button for the airlock, and it slid open.

"Oh. Thanks!" she said.

The Gneiss ignored her and stayed where she was, motionless.

The medical team's ladder remained propped against the damaged shuttle. Mallory was not the first one there, since several more Sundry had arrived first. These were mostly blue, but a few silver were among them.

"I thought only Gneiss were allowed in here." She didn't expect a response and didn't get one. "Someday you're going to have to tell me the differences between you two and where the rivalries lie."

The Gurudev equivalent of economy class was a shambles, with plastic bottles, books, mobile phones, purses, and more everywhere. The door to the cargo hold in the back of the shuttle had come open, several suitcases spilling out of it.

As usual, she didn't know what she was looking for, but she knew she would when she found it.

Lovely had said she sat in the front, while Sam sat in the back. Mallory looked at the back of the seating area and found a black backpack wedged under his seat. Inside were two fat books: collections of her own work, three novels bound into each edition. She pulled one out and flipped through it.

Every page. Every single page had notations in the margins.

"He really was obsessed," she marveled, flipping through. He had flagged the clues, marked the red herrings, and even had a special notation for the parts of the narrative she had made up (since technically they were fiction based on her life and reality wasn't as neat as fiction was. Usually.).

Every memory Mallory had written from her childhood was highlighted. She had included happy memories of her mother, how she'd tickle Mallory with her old-fashioned feather duster that Aunt Kathy had complained was dirty even though Mom never used it to clean. The time she had stepped on a bee on her birthday. How Mom had died soon after that.

She wondered what Mom would think of her now, self-exiled on a space station, her only friends unsympathetic rock people, and still surrounded by murders. She sat down and kept flipping. Something gnawed at the back of her brain, and her tinnitus started acting up. "I don't have time for a migraine now!" she groaned.

She got up and carried the book with her over to Aunt Kathy's seat, where her purse was stashed. Many bottles of sleeping pills. Far too many to need on a short trip. She carried a mug with a picture of the family on it: Kathy, Uncle Dez, and Desmond. Mallory remembered this picture. She found the upstairs curtain of her room, pulled aside just so she could see them take their family photo for their Christmas cards.

When Mom found out, she'd been furious to be left out, mainly for Mallory's sake. Aunt Kathy had calmly explained, "You are guests. Welcome guests who can stay as long as they like, but guests. My husband and son are my family."

And now they're gone and you're desperate to bring home whatever family is left, even if it's the ones at the bottom of the barrel.

A loud buzzing caught her attention, and she looked down. A silver Sundry worker was writhing on the carpet.

"Shit, did I step on you?" she asked, bending down and reaching her hand out. But the Sundry stopped writhing abruptly and took wing. She watched it, puzzled. It had looked like the bee she'd stepped on when she was young.

She did a cursory look at the luggage. Nothing stuck out at her except the hard musical instrument case. Lovely had said she didn't know if she could play again. She'd probably want this.

Mallory shouldered Sam's backpack and Lovely's case and climbed down the ladder. She reached the airlock door just in time to see Stephanie walk out to the center of the ossuary, hold the fabric sack in her hands, and start vibrating.

30

PACTS AND ALLIANCES

ROM THE DOORWAY, Stephanie stood while the ossuary addressed her. Even the older, evolved Gneiss in the corner of the ossuary had begun to come alive. They were spending
their years it would take to naturally ascend, dozing a bit and waking to talk with others like them, and then dozing more. Now they
were all awake.

One of them began a low rumble, engines starting.

These various body parts and a ship that got up too early
couldn't stop her. They were only capable of brief bursts of energy
before they had to go dormant again to work on healing. There
was only one way they could rush their reformation, but they
wouldn't.

That was unethical. They wouldn't commit her crime in order
to stop her from committing the same crime.

Would they?

Oh, yes, they would, Grandfather said in her head. *They are
righteous. You are an abomination.*

"Just like you," Stephanie said out loud. She looked back at the
humans. "Do not come in here until it's over."

I can be your second. Just let me know, Ferdinand said, just so
she could hear.

Please. I do need you, Stephanie answered, loath to show vulnerability to the humans.

Xan gestured at the smaller human, the one who had a long coat over her. "I need to get her to *Infinity*. We can reach the other medbay from another shuttle bay."

"What's wrong with her?" Tina asked, lumbering over.

"I don't know. She doesn't look that badly injured, but she's really out of it," Xan said, his forehead creasing. That meant worry, right. He cared for this human.

"She will have a worse fate if they find out there's an injured human out here," Stephanie said. "Remember what I told you. I release you from our pact. It doesn't matter at this point."

"Why would they attack? What kind of threat could we possibly be to them?" Lovely asked.

Stephanie and Ferdinand left the hallway to enter the ossuary. Behind them, just within earshot, Xan said, "Stephanie told me earlier today. We're not a threat to them in there. We're fuel."

WHEN STEPHANIE HAD gone to see Ren that morning, she had not planned on revealing an ancient shame of her people to Xan, but also she didn't expect to walk in on what very likely was a murder taking place.

She'd had it with her grandfather. She was going to talk to Ren about Eternity's agreement not to allow her off the station unless she was with her grandfather or an Eternity-approved shuttle. The old rock thought she was capable of regicide just because she tended to move faster than the average Gneiss.

He had also promised to be the family's shuttle, but once they got to Eternity, he decided he liked it and wouldn't budge. She kept up with his care, hoping he would change his mind, but nothing happened except she was wasting her time.

She would have been happy to buy a new shuttle, she had the

savings, but then she would have two shuttles to maintain, two berths in the shuttle bay to pay for. She could park grandfather in the ossuary with the other old dusty ships, but he liked the busy shuttle bay better, and he wasn't dormant right now.

Too bad one wasn't allowed to sell one's grandfather.

She'd been stomping through the hall to meet with Ren—again—because his job was to help the residents of the station and he had done nothing but get in her way.

She hated him. She'd warmed to some other sentients since moving to the station, especially the humans, but she hadn't met a Gurudev she'd liked. The most powerful one among them certainly wasn't giving people a good impression of their species.

She pounded on the door of the Station Heart, yelling, "Ren, I know you know I'm here. I need to talk to you and Eternity now!"

Nobody answered, but then a high-pitched keening cut through the hallway. It seemed to be coming from everywhere, like the siren alarms, but this was definitely a cry of pain.

She raised her fist to pound again, but the door slid open suddenly and her fist came down and almost caved in the skull of the human Xan. He jumped aside quickly, his eyes wide.

"What are you doing here?" she demanded. "I need to talk to Ren."

"That's going to be difficult," he said in a shaky voice, pointing to the body lying on the floor in a puddle of blood. The other human, the ambassador, was struggling weakly, tangled within the vine-like tendrils of the station's Heart.

"What did you do?" she asked in awe.

"Nothing!" Xan said. "I wanted to talk to Ren to make sure Eternity was going to keep her word and keep me here if Earth sends someone to bring me home. But when I got here . . . that." He gestured to the mess. Adrian let loose a muffled cry as another vine encircled him. "I don't know what she's doing to him."

Stephanie pointed to the mess on the floor. "Is Ren dead?"

"I don't know everything about their bodies, but he looks pretty damn dead to me," Xan said.

A plan began to form in Stephanie's mind, something occurring to her that never had before. It hadn't occurred to her because she'd never had the opportunity.

"Did you kill him?" she asked Xan.

"What? No! I found them like this. I don't know what happened," Xan protested. His hands were covered in blue blood, but otherwise he was untouched. "But fuck, everyone's going to think I did. Again." He frowned and pointed to Adrian. "Do you know anything we can do for him?"

"To separate two joined sentients? That's very dangerous. As that one is learning, I suppose. She could link to him, or devour him, or kill him. Whatever she does, I don't think she even registers we're here."

The idea poked at her again. The body on the floor was no more use to Eternity. But it could be of use to her. "I'll make a deal with you. I'll tell no one you were here if you let me have that body without question."

Xan shook his head. "No, I'll consider it, but I get to ask questions."

They were losing time. Eternity creaked around them as she struggled with her new host. Sirens blared from far off.

"All right, but come with me," Stephanie said. She picked Ren up by the robe he wore and they hurried out.

Eternity had begun sealing off the hallway with her films of bio-matter, but Stephanie just burst through the first film. Xan followed before another one could grow to replace it.

"So, spill, what's this about?" he asked, pointing to Ren.

She wondered how to make the explanation short and understandable without making her people look horrific. She remembered what she had learned about human history, and how they murdered a man and then worshipped him, and decided to go with the whole truth.

"You constantly need to eat to sustain yourself, right? Bio-matter? Plants and animals?"

"Yeah," Xan said hesitantly.

"We need sustenance too, but usually lava or rocks or something. You've seen us eat, after all. But in order for my people to grow—like to heal from a break, or ascend to another form—we need bio-matter. Plants will do. We love planets with high plant content. But to ascend to something highly complicated, another form entirely, like a shuttle, we need either thousands of years of sleeping among plant matter, or we can do it much quicker with the bio-matter from a sentient being to help us along the way."

Xan looked horrified. "You eat people?"

"We did, once," she admitted. "It's seen as unethical now that we know other sentients in the galaxy, but that means no one ascends in a timely fashion without committing a crime, or unless we're in a war, or unless we find a very generous dying person."

"Or come across a dead body," Xan said.

"Exactly!" She was glad he got it. "There are fewer and fewer Gneiss, so many of our older population are in the process of ascending. My grandfather doesn't trust me. He is worried my attitude indicates violence in my future, and he's decided that means I will kill our heir. So he stuck me here."

"How close do you get to your heir, usually?" Xan asked as they reached the main hallway.

"Pretty close. It's Tina."

"Tina. Tina is your heir. I mean, I like her, but I wouldn't trust her to put a stamp on a letter."

"My opinion as well, hence my grandfather thinking I am violent toward her."

"But you hang out with Tina all the time! What's to stop you from killing her?"

"As long as Ferdinand is with us, my grandfather thinks that's enough to stop me. But he doesn't consider the fact that I may be mean, but Tina is much bigger than me. She can, and has, beaten me in a fight. Anyway, I'm stuck here until Grandpa trusts me. And part of the time I just think he likes it here and doesn't want to move."

"I could take you somewhere in *Infinity*," he offered.

"No," she said bluntly. "We tried that, remember? *Infinity* won't go against her mother's wishes, and my grandfather got Ren and Eternity to agree to not help me escape. This is easier."

Xan looked at the body. "So you want that so you can . . . become a ship?"

"It's more complicated than that, but yes, essentially," she said.

"And you won't tell them you found me in the Heart with Adrian and Ren?"

"I won't," she agreed.

"Then take it. I'll keep your secret if you keep mine."

The plant waste of the station was dumped through a chute in the wall of the corridor close to the Heart, landing in the ossuary so the sleeping Gneiss could have bio-matter if they wanted it. She roughly shoved Ren into the chute so he would fall. With any luck, he'd end up in a bio-matter pile and go unnoticed.

IT WAS HARD to keep a secret among the Gneiss. Most adults could communicate by vibration, even on a space station, so as she hefted the dead body, her grandfather immediately knew what she was doing.

You can't.

"Look who's awake," she said. "And I very well can. Remind me of the person who helped you ascend? A Silence member who was lost in our canyon that you said no one would miss? At least I'm not a murderer."

"What are you doing?" Xan asked, following her.

"Arguing. My grandfather is disapproving of me, like always," she said.

"Will he tell security?"

Stephanie laughed. "Give up his own family? No, Gneiss don't betray each other. Or if they do, they don't stay around their own kind. He'll be mad as hell, but he won't tell on me."

Xan jogged to stay beside her. "Listen, we need a story. Mallory can't know I was in the Heart when this happened."

The keening stopped and the alarms started. Stephanie thought for a moment as the station lurched. "The station is very unhappy. I think our biggest problem has gone beyond what Mallory thinks."

The station heaved mightily, throwing Xan to the floor. The hallway lights went out.

Stephanie stayed standing, immovable. "I think we should hurry and maybe find Mallory," she suggested, lifting him easily to his feet. "We might need to evacuate. That would get Grandpa moving."

"THAT'S SICK," LOVELY said, staring into the open door after Stephanie had left them. "She's going to *eat* the guy who was in charge of the station and turn into a shuttle?"

"Yes," he said. "But remember, we eat animals and wear them. They see it as similar. Especially since she didn't kill him."

"But who did?" said Phineas. "You wanted to hide this so much, hide that you were in there, hide that you knew this about those rock people. What else are you hiding?"

"Shut up, everyone, you're making my head hurt," Calliope said. Xan sat next to her.

"We need to get you to the medbay, but Lovely says the station has cut this part off and the only way out is via shuttle. And there's a whole bunch of angry rock folk in there."

"Can you get me there, too, so I can keep looking for Gran?" Lovely said. "I can see if we can make a path. I'm not injured."

"No one should go in there," the white woman, Kathy, said. "It's dangerous. Mallory's in there." She clutched at her bracelet and fingered the charms.

"I think she'll be okay," Xan said.

"No, it's dangerous *because* she's in there," Kathy snapped. "She's death wherever she goes."

"That's harsh. If she's so bad, why do you want to drag her back to Earth?" Xan asked.

Kathy's eyes filled with tears. "Because she's family."

This woman was trouble, and Xan found it ironic as hell that he turned back to talk to the relatively stable Calliope.

"Can you remember what happened? What hit you?" he asked, touching her head and neck carefully.

She grunted in a negative way. "I was grabbed, and then I was fighting for my life. Something was strong . . . something punched my upper arm. I started fighting back, and I don't remember much after that."

"Yeah, I figured that." He smiled. "We'll get you some help. Some more of that bacteria stuff."

"I don't think that's going to work," Tina said. "She's leaking a lot."

Xan wanted to demand what Tina knew about it, but then he realized he was kneeling in blood. Calliope was sitting in a puddle. How had he not noticed it?

"Cal, where are you bleeding?" he asked, panic coursing through him. He tried to pull her trench coat aside, but she was sitting on it and seemed resistant to moving. He reached in between her and the coat and felt around. His hand slid against a blade, and he jerked back, hissing. Two fingers were cut. He reached back in more carefully and felt around until he touched the knife's handle. It had stuck in her back and dislodged when she sat, he guessed, which was when she started to seriously bleed.

"Oh, fuck, Cal!" he said, his voice hoarse.

Infinity, what can we do? Can you get us to a place with a medbay?

I can. But can you get to me now?

I don't know.

"We have to get her to the shuttle bay across the ossuary," he said. "Anyone have any ideas?"

"I can distract them," Lovely said.

"I'll go with," Phineas said. "They're moving pretty slow. I can hold my own."

"Phin, you two can't fight rocks!" Xan said. "I wouldn't do it, and I'm actually trained."

"Sure, wave your thin ass in my face, soldier-boy," Phineas said mockingly. "I can at least match them for size."

"It's not a body size thing, it's a density thing! Flesh meets stone; flesh loses!" Xan said, trying to find the wound on Calliope's back. "Fuck! Who did this to her?" he asked Kathy, who was sitting against the wall, her knees to her chest. Her bloody face was dripping on her khaki pants.

"I didn't see," she said. "It was all a blur. She grabbed me. I'm the victim here!"

"He's right," Lovely said to Phineas, ignoring Kathy. "We're gonna break into messy little pieces if we go in there." She edged a bit closer to the open door. "Although I think there's a way we might be able to help distract from both Stephanie and Xan."

Tina peered into the ossuary and then returned to them. "Her granddad is pissed. He may come here."

"I thought no one could get out of the shuttle bay," Xan said.

"Not anymore. The station is stable. Can't you feel her?"

"I've been busy, so no," Xan said.

Calliope grumbled something, and Xan leaned in to her. "Just stay quiet, H2," he said.

"C'mere," she said. Her eyes were alarmingly bloodshot with pupils of different sizes. "Listen. I have to confess some shit."

"I'm not a priest," Xan said, trying some levity. "And you're going to be okay."

"You're a shitty liar. You're not a priest and I'm not Catholic, so we cancel each other out. Just listen. They gave me a lot of instructions. Someone told me to bring you back, or kill you. Someone else told me to help you and give you some information." Her arm flapped in her lap toward her jacket pocket. "You'll want to look in there. One of the pockets has a hole, though. Hope it's still there.

"Listen. I'm sorry, man. For Falcon Dam." She looked away, and he had never before seen her hesitate to meet someone's eyes.

"It was both of us," he said.

"No. I was the one who stole from Buck in the first place. Made him attack you. Made you too hurt to pay attention to the equipment. Purposefully gave them a shitty radio."

"Shit, Cal," he said. He sat for a moment, then shook his head. "You are an agent of fucking chaos. I guess you also gave ordnance the norovirus?"

She smiled. "Probably. Also, I'm sorry for all the shit I stole."

He knew about this. Kleptomania wasn't endearing or cute, but Calliope always stole shit so stupid that no one ever cared, or even missed it. Until Buck, that was. "I thought you were going to get help for the klepto stuff?"

"I tried. They said, 'Try not stealing,' and I said, 'Okay, stop being an asshole,' and they charged the army five hundred dollars. But stop distracting me. I'm mostly sorry for agreeing to bring you home. The offer of a space trip and backdated pension was too good. They were half expecting me to die anyway." She smiled. "It was good to see you, though."

Xan wished he could wipe the sweat and blood off her face or give her some sort of comfort. "You always were a mercenary at heart."

"Just like Uncle Drop. I guess the only thing he didn't teach me was how to avoid getting pulled into a crowd and shanked." She leaned away from him and dry-heaved. "God, it hurts. If you ever make it home, will you make sure my uncle Drop gets my apartment key?"

"You're going to make it out of this," Xan said, dimly aware of Lovely shouting something from the ossuary.

"Don't bullshit me, Vulture," she said. "You know what death looks like as much as I do. Don't worry about sending my body or my shit home. Uncle Drop's in prison and there's no family left to do the burial ritual. Even if Drop was paroled, he hasn't touched hemp since Grandfather died, so I'm sure he won't want my body. Just give him my apartment key; that's all he'll need."

"Hemp?" he asked, frowning.

"It's a Korean thing, or so I hear. Stop interrupting. Xan. You were my best friend. Did I ever tell you that? We were awesome Vultures. I want you to keep my coat even though it has a fucking huge hole in the back. The pockets are really useful."

"I'm so sorry, H2." Tears clawed at the back of his throat.

"Me too, man. Glad you're here with me, though. Remember you promised to give me a Viking funeral? Too bad you can't do that now." She looked at the doorway to the ossuary and got a gleam in her eyes, sharp and all too familiar. "Hey, you know what would be fucking *metal*?"

"Oh, no . . ." he said.

Xan listened to her. He held her hand when she breathed her last, and found he could still be amazed at how weird and innovative she was, even up to the end.

* * * *

XAN HADN'T EVEN thought about Calliope in months until she showed up at the station. But he'd never felt like this when a buddy died. He felt displaced, adrift, numb. He was dimly aware of chaos around him, aware of his brother yelling something else in the ossuary. He was barely aware of Mallory's aunt Kathy leaning over Calliope, touching her neck.

"Hey!" Tina said, snapping Xan out of his stupor.

Kathy jumped back as if stung. "I—I think she's dead."

"No, she's just resting in a pool of blood," Xan snapped. He closed her eyes and carefully removed her coat. It was heavier than he expected; she had several secret pockets within. He mentally logged all of the items, as he was used to doing on the battlefield. He pulled out seven sets of earbuds, a portable hard drive, a block of violin rosin, a hair comb, a small notebook, a highlighter, a gold chain, a paperback novel, a gun (*Christ, Calliope . . .* he thought as he disarmed it), a knife, a thumb drive, a rock, and a sandwich bag full of dust and pills. He quickly pocketed the thumb drive and the baggie, then looked at the rest of the loot. "My God, Cal, did you steal from everyone?" he muttered.

He picked up the rock, which vibrated slightly. He dropped it, repulsed, and it rolled toward the ossuary.

Tina bent down. "So wet. Is she done dying?"

"Yeah. She's gone," Xan said. He took a deep breath and stood, facing Tina. "She had a message for you. Or Ferdinand."

"Ferdinand is in there to keep Stephanie from getting pulverized, so I guess it's for me," Tina said.

Xan winced, trying to find the words. "She's offering herself to you."

"Offer?" Tina asked, blankly. "Am I getting the right translation of that?"

He waved at the floor. "Her corpse. Her biomass. She thinks—

thought that it would be awesome to be turned into part of an alien shuttle or something."

"Or something?" Tina repeated.

"Stephanie told me that shuttles were common, but not the only way your people ascend. I don't know what else there is. But if you want to, there it is. With her consent. Her very enthusiastic request, since she can't be set on fire and go over a waterfall."

"Is that really an option when your kind dies?" Tina asked, fascinated.

"Not anymore."

Inside the ossuary, things had slowed, and the Gneiss seemed to orient toward the hallway. They probably heard everything Tina heard.

This was forbidden stuff, but also this was their *princess*, Xan remembered. Or a princess, anyway.

"But the only people who want biomass are in there," Tina said, pointing to the ossuary. "And Stephanie has what she needs."

"I don't know the different options; I am just passing along the information. She wants the most exciting funeral in all of human history. Can you give that to her?"

Tina looked thoughtful. "My father said that long ago, carbon-based people would offer themselves to royalty. But I thought humans saw death rituals as sacred for families."

"Yeah, but her family is almost all dead. Her only relative is in jail, so even if she wanted a traditional death ritual, no one can give it to her." He shrugged uncomfortably. "I won't be going home anytime soon, so I can't take her back, and I'm her only friend here. Maybe anywhere. I can't tell you what to do, but you should know that before she died, she said that helping you or Ferdinand ascend would be 'fucking metal.' That's a saying. It means really impressive and exciting. Rare, too."

Tina looked over her shoulder thoughtfully. "I will need to talk to my people."

He glanced at Cal's body and the pool of blood around her. "She's not going anywhere."

Mallory is going to be so pissed that she couldn't look at the body, Xan realized. But he didn't know where she was.

"Made it," Mallory said, coming out of the ossuary out of breath.

Xan walked over to her and wrapped her in a hug, holding her tight. He pressed his face into her neck, letting the tears come.

She was stiff in his arms, surprised and awkward, then held him back.

Just for a minute, treat me like the only human here that you can trust. Please.

He was pretty sure he hadn't said it aloud, but her arms came up and held him.

"What's going on?" she asked into his ear.

"Cal's dead."

She gasped, and her hug got tighter. "I'm so sorry."

"She was here to kill me, and save me." He paused, then decided it wasn't the time for the rest of the information. He pulled away, wiping his cheeks. "There's a lot to say in not much time, so just go with it, okay?"

She nodded.

He filled her in on the Gneiss evolutionary shortcuts, Stephanie's plans for Ren's body, and Calliope's deathbed request, complete with the descriptor.

He smiled despite his grief. "Tina is talking to her people, I guess, but I knew you'd want to see the body before they did anything, so you have to examine her now."

Mallory took a moment to let all that sink in, then she nodded and put down the instrument case she had slung across a shoulder. "That's a lot. But okay. Help me lay her out flat."

With practiced ease he wished he didn't have, Xan got Calliope straightened out on the floor and then rolled her over to expose her blood-soaked shirt. Kathy watched them, frowning.

Mallory took very little time examining the ugly stab wound in Cal's back and the knife, and gave a quick look at Cal's other injuries. Xan picked up the contents of Calliope's pockets while she examined the body and sorted them on the ground.

"All right," she said softly. She had politely ignored Xan when he made a strangled sound at the sight of Cal's forearm tattoo of a vulture, and waited for him to compose himself. "I have all I need. Is Tina taking the body?"

"She hasn't decided yet," Xan said. "What's going on in there? Is my brother okay?"

"He and Lovely were trying to distract the Gneiss, but I'm not sure it worked. Now they're trying to get back here, but it's a mess. They may need help."

"What can we do?" he asked, glancing at Tina for her input, but she didn't respond.

Mallory picked the case up and handed it to him. "Lovely might want this. I found it on the shuttle."

"Why would she want an instrument in the middle of a battle?" he asked, baffled.

"Call it a hunch," she said.

Xan snapped his bloody fingers as he remembered one last thing. He pointed to the floor beside Cal, where he had laid out nearly all the things found in her pockets. "Something you should know—Cal was a kleptomaniac. Looks like she took something from almost everyone."

"Really . . ." Mallory said thoughtfully, looking at the items. "I don't see anything of mine."

He pointed to the novel. "Isn't the book yours?"

Mallory grimaced and picked up the dog-eared, coverless paperback. "I didn't realize it. This is the omnibus of the last three murders I dealt with back home. I wrote it, but it's not mine. Didn't everyone say that guy who died in coach was reading my stuff? I bet it's his." She flipped through it thoughtfully.

"Great, all right, make sure they do right by Cal's body. I'm going to get my brother back," he said. He wrapped Calliope's coat around him and dashed through the door into the frigid ossuary.

Mallory stared at him in disbelief, but he didn't stay to argue.

The ossuary was erupting in more and more slow chaos, like a tornado in slow motion. He tried to dodge the grasping hands and twitching legs while trying to spot where Phineas and Lovely had gone.

The room's energy had split into two, with some of the Gneiss focusing on Stephanie, but others flat-out attacking the two humans farther out from the door. Their side of the battle looked like they were fighting a rockslide. On one side, Ferdinand was guarding a motionless Stephanie, punching any Gneiss that came near, and on the other, Lovely and Phineas were . . . throwing rocks.

Xan ran up to them. "Why are you throwing rocks at other rocks?"

Phineas didn't stop picking up anything from pebbles to fist-size rocks and hurling them in any direction. "Where have you been? This distraction's for your hurt friend, isn't it?"

"She's gone," Xan said bluntly. "But you're distracting them from Stephanie, so keep doing—what the hell are you doing, anyway?"

"The rock dude, the good one, told us that to actually attack, these broken folks need to put themselves back together," he said. "We wanted to make that hard for them. See?"

Lovely demonstrated and threw a rock toward a moon-colored marble arm that was groping along the floor, inching toward a leg made from identical stuff.

Phineas pried a stone hand off his calf with a grunt and heaved it away. "I'm sorry about your friend."

"Yeah," Xan said, looking at the writhing floor. "So you are just violating countless graves?"

"Tina said they weren't dead," Lovely said. "Besides, they want to kill that one. And she was definitely alive." She gestured toward Stephanie.

The vibrations of the angry waking Gneiss began to sound more like words, the translation bug picking out words like *heretic* and *anathema* and *violation* and *hungry*.

"They're getting angrier," Xan said. "We need to get out of here."

"She might still need us," Lovely said, pointing at Stephanie.

"We can't protect her!" Xan said.

"Hold up," Phineas said, his large hand coming down on Xan's shoulder. He pointed. Across the huge ossuary, two shuttles still sat dormant like giant stone dice, but a third was hovering now. The green bushes around them were a black, shriveled mess, while the gently drooping leafy plants and the mushrooms on the walls withered.

"They're sucking the life from the room; they're going to go after us eventually," Xan said, wading into the pebble sea that had surrounded them.

"So they're mad at her for using carbon to change, and they use carbon to stop her. They're completely hypocrites," Lovely said in wonder. The grass under her feet went black, and she jumped to a stone area mostly free of pebbles, stumbling a bit as those few pebbles made their way under her feet. Then she righted herself and got a good look at Xan. She tilted her head. "Is that my violin?"

"Mallory found it on the shuttle, and somehow thinks that you should have it right the fuck now," he said, handing it to her with a shrug. Behind them, Phineas heaved another arm as far as he could. "But we need to get out of here," Xan added.

"You want us to leave?" Lovely asked. She pointed to the Gneiss. "What about them?"

Stephanie stood still, almost resembling a statue herself. Ferdinand kept the others off her. The light went out in her eyes, and Xan's heart lurched.

I can't lose someone else today.

Ferdinand didn't look alarmed, so the humans held back to watch, occasionally kicking away the grasping hands.

Between Stephanie's feet was the decomposing body of the unfortunate Gurudev. She wasn't letting it out of her possession anymore. Sheets of rock sloughed off her like mica, falling on the dead body. When enough had come off her to cover him in an overlapping, scaled pattern, she stopped, and the rock scales flexed, forming a full cocoon around Ren's body.

The room raged around her, still moving slowly by human standards, but getting in front of a wounded or incomplete Gneiss still seemed about as smart as being in front of a car that's "only" going five miles per hour.

Stephanie's cocoon pulsed hypnotically, and Xan didn't hear the whoosh of the arm until it was almost too late. He jumped to the side and the arm smashed into his shoulder blade, knocking him over. The pebbles surged and rolled over him.

Phineas?

They sought his ears, his mouth, his nose. He thrashed, trying to get up, but they pulled him down like quicksand. His nose was shortly plugged with pebbles, leaving him with no option but to eventually open his mouth, which no doubt would kill him.

His arms were held down with more and more pebbles.

This is how Calliope died. Being pulled into a riptide of panicked aliens in a truly unique situation that no one could train for.

But this is what four fighting was made for. And it was even more challenging, since he was stripped of sight, sound, smell, and even taste simply because he couldn't open his mouth.

I wish Cal were here.

But she wasn't, and they'd had no way to test how to fight with just one sense. Calliope was dead, and he would be next.

At least Phin will inherit and stop blaming me. Did he throw that? Where is he? Just watching the Gneiss pebbles do what he didn't have the guts for?

He tried to focus on all the sensations around him, most of which were the scratchy weight of sentient gravel, and for a moment could feel every inch of his body. But the only thing he was increasingly aware of was asphyxiating. He struggled once more, and just barely opened his lips, hoping to steal some air, but sentient aliens no larger than grit saw their chance and began to worm their way inside.

A large hand grabbed his collar and the thick trench coat, lifting him out of the morass. He got his feet under him and shed the gravel that still tried to cling, but surrendered at last to gravity. He spat and scraped at his face and ears to dislodge any of the persistent hangers-on, and looked back at Phineas, panting.

"Why did you do that?" he asked, his dry mouth delivering more of a croak.

Phineas blinked at him. "You're my fucking brother."

"I thought you'd welcome the chance to get rid of me. Then that inheritance would be yours."

Phineas shook his head slowly. "Dude, don't you get it? I got nothing left! The earthquake took our parents. The aliens took my brother. Grandma took my family by telling me I'm a bastard. She took my inheritance. Then the stairs took her. The only things I have from this family are cigarette burns and a brother whose death would have required the weirdest fucking epitaph in the history of Earth."

Xan winced and coughed. He would be damned if he swallowed any of those goddamn Gneiss. No matter how small. He looked up at his brother. "Phin. Take the house. Take the land. I have nothing but shitty memories of that place anyway. And you haven't lost me. I don't know if I can come home again, but I'm always going to be your brother."

He hugged Phineas briefly, but looked down at their feet. The pebbles had been working together to make a whirlpool. It wouldn't bring them down, necessarily, but it could hamper their movement. And Xan did not want to fall again.

A piercing noise cut through the ossuary, startling the brothers. It was a high note from Lovely's violin, one sustained note that sounded like a siren.

Xan clapped his hands over his ears. "What is she doing?" he yelled.

"She told me when we got here that the pebbles were vibrating at a low G. She wished she had her instrument. She's got it now, so she started playing notes to either match or counter the noises they were making. They just got stronger with a low G, but when she hit the high one . . ." Phineas half grinned, half winced as he gestured around the ossuary, where the Gneiss were mostly dormant now. The pebbles had stopped their surging, and the shuttle, while still hovering, had stopped rotating.

"Did she save me or did you?" Xan asked, coughing.

"Both," Phineas said.

Even though the pebbles had stopped their surging, Ferdinand also stood dormant, Stephanie cocooned at his feet.

"Shit," Xan said, and ran up to Lovely. "You need to stop playing; it's affecting Stephanie and Ferdinand!"

Lovely grimaced. Sweat beaded on her lip, and she winced in pain as her left hand stretched to sustain the high G. "What do we do, then? They'll just wake back up."

You can call for help, you know. I'm right here. Infinity's voice was still light in his head as if he were not facing down moving rocks and a violin was their best weapon.

"What can you do to help me in here?" he asked her out loud.

You'll be fine. Keep the woman playing. Make your way over here. Bring the Gneiss, too. I like her.

"What is your plan?"

One day you'll trust me.

"Can you tell Ferdinand?"

He knows. But he needs the music to go away.

"Keep playing, and follow me," he shouted to Lovely and Phineas, and angled toward *Infinity*, seen beyond the open door to the airlock.

Movement caught his eye on the far side of the room where it opened to the hall, and Tina's large, pink frame appeared. Xan froze in shock, spying Mallory on Tina's back, peeking over her shoulder.

I present to you the future queen of the Gneiss planet Bezoar. Her ascension is complete, Infinity announced in his head.

Xan shook his head. *That planet is so fucked.*

31

. . .

TWO HUMAN SYMBIONTS

MALLORY KEPT HER eyes flicking from the doorway through which Xan and the others had disappeared, to what was happening by Calliope's body, to her grim-looking aunt.

Tina had accepted Calliope's offer and was doing whatever Gneiss do when they absorb another sentient being.

"I don't know exactly how to do this," Tina had said cheerfully as she peeled thin layers of herself off. "So we'll see what happens."

Mallory had something on the edge of her awareness, a clue or even the solution. She just needed to think. Calliope's stab wound had had a shiny substance on the edge of it, but she couldn't place it.

A blue Sundry scout crawled around the doorway to the ossuary. It moved sluggishly, probably due to the chill. Above it, two silver Sundry crawled on the ceiling, vibrating so hard they were mostly blurs. Keeping warm?

Kathy looked in Mallory's direction, away from Tina. She caught sight of the Sundry. "Oh, disgusting! There are bugs here too?"

"They're another sentient race, and you need to treat them

with respect," Mallory said. But her words didn't have a lot of strength.

She rubbed her face. Aunt Kathy came up and sat down beside her, taking her hand. Hers was cool, while Mallory's was sweaty. Kathy's charms bumped against Mallory's wrist.

"Honey, you don't belong in all this chaos. It's not natural, and all these *aliens*," she said.

I thought you said I was chaos. "Where'd you find your bracelet? And did you get a new charm?" Mallory asked, looking at Kathy's wrist.

"I found it in my pocket!" Kathy said, delighted. "The doctors must have put it there. And I love my cute little alligator," Kathy said, releasing Mallory's hand and touching the charms. She started with her first, the feather, and then ended on the alligator. The little jaws were hinged so they could open and close.

"A large reptile doesn't seem your style," Mallory said. She shifted so she could watch what was happening in the ossuary.

"You have to know this is no place for a human, especially someone like *you*. You tried to get away from the murders and they followed you. So there's nothing to do now but come home with me. With Dez gone"—her voice hitched briefly—"and my beautiful boy in jail, I don't have much left. I've missed you so much."

Mallory made a noncommittal noise, trying to gently separate from her aunt, who had clasped her hand again. This was going into a place of poor-me and unappreciated mother and so many tears.

"I was there when your mother died. Then your teacher died, and I was there. Your guidance counselor? Remember that? I was there to hug you tight and remind you I am here for you. It's been a traumatic life, honey. Come home with me."

"You said I was chaos and curses and murder. Not sometime in the past—I mean, like an hour ago," Mallory said, shifting over again. The iron grip didn't let up. "You didn't want me there when I was growing up. Why now?"

Kathy looked like she was trying to decide between outrage and grief. She let grief win. Tears welled up in her eyes. "Desmond didn't make parole. I was thinking if you came home you could help me get him free. You know those clues so well."

"I was less than useless during that investigation. You told me that. What do you think I'm going to do to help now?"

"I thought some distance would have helped, and maybe we could work together to think of something," Kathy said. She sniffled and patted Mallory's hand. "And I like you just fine, honey."

"Is Stephanie doing all right?" Mallory asked Tina, ignoring Kathy.

"She seems fine, even though your friends are not," Tina said. Her voice sounded far away. "Ferdinand has her."

"What about you? You don't have a helper like Ferd," Mallory said. "Do you need one?"

"Oh, sure, the second is so that no one tries to pulverize you when you're vulnerable," Tina said. "But I'll be fine. If anyone harms me, the rest will turn on them."

"Tina, you have the most unearned confidence I have ever seen. I'm glad you don't need me to protect you from murder rocks," Mallory said.

Tina chuckled as she disappeared into her own cocoon, wrapping Calliope's mica-enshrouded body in her arms.

"I hope she'll be okay alone," Mallory said.

"Why do you care so much about these aliens? Why not put your focus on the humans, where it belongs?" Kathy snapped. She took a calming breath, then smiled again. "Come home, honey. I could use the company, and you're clearly not safe out here. Just tell me you'll think about it."

"I will," Mallory said. Her voice felt very far away. Aunt Kathy had said something about the people in her childhood who had died. Her mother, her teacher, her counselor. She had said it almost like a counting game.

Kathy started talking about Mallory's childhood, highlighting some of the birthdays and holidays that she somehow remembered differently. She glanced back outside and saw Xan go down into knee-deep gravel, which flowed over him.

She scrambled to her feet, finally breaking Kathy's grip on her hand. She glanced over at the giant cocoon of Tina, which seemed to be coming along a lot faster than whatever Stephanie was doing. "Tina! How much longer do you think you'll be?"

Of course, there was no answer. Phineas and Lovely tried to reach Xan, but a swirling maelstrom of pebbles had formed, and they couldn't get close. Then Lovely took out her violin.

She couldn't leave Tina but also couldn't watch Xan get mauled by Gneiss. Kathy watched her, outrage coloring her cheeks.

Lovely hit a very high note, stretching her left hand as far as she could to hit a clear, piercing note on the violin. At the same time, Tina's cocoon cracked, then split, spraying rock shrapnel everywhere. Mallory shielded her face, feeling the shards cut her hands and cheek. When she peeked again, Tina lay on the floor like a fetus. She was large and humanoid, and seemingly the same as before. Bulkier, for sure.

Mallory ran to the door to see if her friends were safe. In the ossuary, the tide of rocks had calmed, apparently because of Lovely's music. Phineas was helping Xan up, and they were running toward the airlock, Lovely keeping the Gneiss at bay with that one piercing note.

"FUCKING METAL," came the roar up the hall. Mallory snapped out of her shock.

Tina was awake and standing. Now she looked considerably different.

"Shit," Mallory said, taking a step backward. She glanced at the ossuary, where Stephanie was still in her cocoon and Ferdinand protected her. "How did you do that so fast—"

"FOUR REASONS: ONE—BECAUSE I'M FUCKING METAL!" Tina bellowed. "TWO—because it's harder to become a shuttle. Whole lot of internal changes. I don't even know where to begin. Three—I didn't want to become a shuttle. I wanted THIS. Fourth—I am a goddamn princess, and I think there's something in my metabolism that wants to be a walking war machine. Or something. Who knows? Come on!"

She approached, taking large steps, nearly running. Kathy cowered; Mallory winced in anticipation.

Tina had gained half of her height and stood over twelve feet tall. She was still humanoid, with two arms and legs and something resembling a head, but that's where the similarities with other Gneiss ended. Now she looked like a sentient war mech. She was still pinkish red, but smoother, like polished pink metal instead of rough stone. She turned and looked over her shoulder at Mallory. Panels in her shoulders dropped, showing the barrels of a weapon. Below the barrels were straps like for a backpack or basket.

Tina with a weapon . . .

Aunt Kathy shrank against the wall in fear. Tina thundered past her without acknowledging her. She reached Mallory in three steps and extended her huge hand toward her.

"This is going to hur—" she said, and then the breath was knocked from her. Tina picked her up as if she were a doll and placed Mallory on her back. A human-size seat was built into a backpack, and if Tina didn't look like a war machine, she might have resembled a new mother on a hike, with baby Mallory in her carrier. But no, instead, Mallory held on tight, trying not to think of the new weapons barrels uncomfortably close to her on Tina's shoulders.

Mallory ducked when they neared the door, but Tina just missed clipping the top of the doorjamb with her own head. Then they were in the ossuary.

This was probably what Xan had complained about—Mallory running into situations without plans—but she didn't have a lot of control this time. She was along for the ride.

Not that she would have chosen to be anywhere else in the galaxy right then.

"Your princess is here," Mallory announced, "and she's fucking metal!"

"SHIT, YEAH, I AM. WHERE DO I SHOOT?"

"Why do you think I know? This is your people's fight."

"Why do you think I brought you along?" Tina asked. "I need a navigator. I can't do this on my own!"

"That would have been good to know from the beginning!" Mallory took a quick look around the ossuary, and the tension in her chest relaxed as she spotted the humans in the airlock by *Infinity*. Xan had stopped to stare at them, but Phineas and Lovely pulled him aboard. "The humans are okay. Let's check on Stephanie and Ferdinand." Mallory tried not to wonder whether Tina would need a driver for everyday things. Mallory wasn't sure she had that kind of time.

"My people tried to form a hivemind with the pebbles, but your friend's music stopped them," Tina said. "That's what Ferdinand says, anyway. They aren't looking for their own bodies anymore; they just are working together as one."

"That works for the Sundry, right?" Mallory asked.

"It's not our way," Tina protested. "Our brains don't work well like that. The Sundry are a bunch of little minds; only the queen sees everything, and even she doesn't see it all at the same time. I don't know if we can separate each person when this is over."

The Gneiss seemed to be confused, some moving to intercept Tina and Mallory, but they were sluggish and distractable. Others rolled or crawled off to corners; some just lay dormant where they were.

Most seemed confused. Not all. Tina pointed and said, "Oh, and look, Ferdinand's father is going to fire on Stephanie."

"That ship is his father?" Mallory yelled, looking at the hovering shuttle. It was sleeker than Stephanie's grandfather, and she could see gun ports slowly swinging around. "Where's his mom?"

"Cargo ship, I think. She's docked at another station," Tina said. Her voice lowered to a whisper. "Divorce."

"Can you talk sense into the ship? Flex that princess title and all?"

"Oh, no, definitely not. My family has money and titles and not much else. Stephanie's family loves the class system and worships anyone with a title. But the ruling family gave us a shithole planet to control. We're mostly a joke." Tina planted her feet and focused on Ferdinand's dad.

"You're refreshingly chipper about this," Mallory said, plugging her ears and wincing in anticipation of the attack.

"Well, I like jokes." Tina's body lurched, and small rockets exploded from her shoulders into the shuttle.

Mallory wondered if pairing the foul-mouthed volatile assassin with a Gneiss lacking impulse control was the best idea, but none of them, including the Gneiss, knew exactly what would happen when the two beings merged. *I hope Stephanie doesn't turn into more of an asshole because of Ren.*

The rockets did minimal damage to Ferdinand's dad, who didn't pay much attention to them. Still, Tina's mighty feet crushed any rock she stepped on as she started off again to help Stephanie.

"Aren't you hurting those rocks?" Mallory asked.

"Well, they want to hurt Stephanie, and once they figure out what I've done by ascending with a human, they'll want to hurt me whether I step on them or not. So screw them," Tina replied.

Unfortunately, they weren't able to be in two places at once. Stephanie was now a standing sarcophagus, the micalike scales multiplying to cover her and the dead Gurudev she held. Discarded Gneiss arms and legs battered her feet, and Ferd Senior didn't seem concerned with the princess firing rockets at him as he swung to aim at Stephanie.

"We should get in front of her to block the attacks," Tina suggested.

"Should we?" Mallory asked. "I'm squishier than you, remember?"

"Let's go!" Tina said.

Stephanie lay prone at Ferdinand's feet, but at least he looked more alert now. The pebble tide, the ones that could still move, that was, now fell on her, covering her entirely. Ferdinand kicked them off as best he could as Tina approached.

"I have a better idea!" Tina said. She kicked aside Gneiss trying to get at her, stomped on a few others, and shrugged off the random pebble attacks. She seemed tougher than most Gneiss, which Mallory hadn't thought was possible.

Mallory scrambled to hang on in Tina's backpack as the new mech reached out two arms like a forklift and squatted down to Stephanie.

Ferdinand helped lay the cocoon in Tina's arms. It was growing at a visible pace now.

"Tina, can you handle this? She's growing," Mallory asked.

"Totally. She just needs the airlock," Tina said, and they headed toward the airlock.

"What are the pieces of Gneiss trying to do to her, anyway?" Mallory yelled.

"They want to break her," Ferdinand said, following them. "They aren't good at thinking things through in this state; they're just super-mad. They can be irritating. But my dad, he's the real threat."

"Would he fire on us?"

"Do you want to find out?" Ferdinand said.

Mallory risked a look back. The ship's gunports tracked them. "Hurry, please," she said to Tina.

Tina started kicking arms and legs out of her path as she picked up the pace. Her greater size and new functions? Abilities? Role as a war machine? Whatever it was, it made Tina faster and more nimble than other Gneiss. Tina outpaced Ferdinand toward the airlock. Until recently, the airlock had been built into a wall covered in lush vines. Now black and withered strings hung limply.

"We're going to space her?" Mallory yelled.

"She'll be safer out there than in here," Tina said. "She's becoming a ship anyway."

Stephanie was already twice as long as before.

When Tina bent down to let Stephanie roll out of her arms, Mallory took advantage of her proximity to the ground and jumped down.

A moment later, a loud boom sounded, shattering the backpack that had protected Tina's passenger.

Ears ringing, shocked, Mallory fell into the airlock, sprawling over Stephanie's body, which resembled a giant luge. She rolled off and landed on the floor on the other side, where she lay, trying to get her senses back.

She blinked, hearing more stomping. Tina had turned away from the airlock, her back a shattered mess. Mallory didn't know where Ferdinand had ended up. Tina seemed to be yelling at Ferdinand's dad or something, who continued to fire in their direction. The airlock door closed. More running feet. She struggled to sit up.

Xan was in front of her, pulling her to her feet. He was shouting something and pointing at *Infinity*, and then Stephanie.

Stephanie grew, stress fissures appearing in her rocky chrysalis.

Another boom, and the blast hit above the airlock, causing part of the cave-like wall to crumble onto Mallory's shoulders. Stephanie was now half the size of her grandfather and still growing.

Mallory remembered she'd had a thought right as she had been plucked up by Tina to go on an adventure. What was it?

She wiped dust and blood from her eyes and squinted at Xan, who was shouting and pulling at her arms. Why was he in a hurry? They were away from all the murderous Gneiss. They had rescued Stephanie and given a princess a bunch of guns.

Why not?

The muffled white noise started to clear, but her ears were ringing louder. Xan's voice started breaking through. "—open the airlock!" Xan cried in her ear, and she finally looked up. From the sound of the booms, Ferdinand's father was still firing on the airlock door to get at them. If he broke the airlock mechanism—

Xan's hands closed on her upper arms and yanked, pulling her out of the way when the airlock opened and two humans and three shuttles were sucked violently into space.

FEATHERS.

Mallory gasped and opened her eyes. She felt battered beyond belief, with multiple bruises and cuts all over her body. Her head and neck and hands tingled as if she had just come in from a very cold night.

Which she had. She was inside now, she was pretty sure. It looked like a dimly lit dry cave. They lay on a purple rock floor, with gentle light coming from the ceiling.

"Xan? Stephanie?" she asked, her voice coming out in a croak.

"That's me," a voice said softly. The lights dimmed, then brightened. "Hard to talk, still."

"Well, you're flying, providing oxygen, and somehow gravity. I guess you saved us?"

The light grew brighter. Then it began to blink. "Help Xan," Stephanie whispered.

Xan needed help? She'd thought he was passed out. Mallory crawled over to him and carefully straightened out his limbs. Nothing seemed broken, but a light frost had formed on his face and hands and arms. He wasn't breathing.

"Oh, no, no, dammit, Xan," she said, straightening his head. "I don't remember anything from CPR except what I've seen on TV!"

She willed him to breathe, but his chest stayed still. Cursing under her breath, she angled his head back a little bit to open his airway, apologized in advance, held his nose closed, and put her mouth over his and blew. The effort she needed to force air into lungs constricted by cold, clenched muscles was harder than she expected, and she sat back, head swimming. Pump the chest, right. She laced her hands together, one palm over the back of the other hand, and pumped his sternum, hoping she got the right spot. Three pumps, or five? She did three, breathed for him again, and then did five.

"Stephanie, is there anything you can do to help me?" she said desperately. "He needs to get back inside to get medical attention!"

The lights flared twice, slowly, as if she regretted having to say it.

So Mallory started pumping again.

Two minutes later, her already abused muscles screaming and black spots floating before her eyes, Xan took in a great wheeze of air on his own and then rolled over, coughing violently. Mallory sobbed in relief and rolled off him.

She lay down on her back, gasping, Xan coughing next to her. "You're okay," she said to no one in particular, her hand flopping on his shoulder in a sad attempt to comfort him.

"Mallory? Where are we?" he asked weakly, rolling over to face her.

"Inside Stephanie, as far as I can tell. She saved us after we got spaced."

"Is *Infinity* okay?"

Stephanie's light flared. "Yes," Mallory translated.

"Good," he said.

"Did Phineas and Lovely make it out?" Mallory asked.

"I got them into *Infinity* and then tried to get you. You were pretty shell-shocked."

She squinted at the ceiling. "You didn't get to safety on *Infinity* when you could have?"

"Not with you still outside," he said, coughing.

They lay there gasping, spent, as Stephanie did Gneiss things around them. The room shifted and grew in different areas, first in length, and then the ceiling got higher.

"No one would believe me if I wrote this in a book," Mallory said offhand.

Xan chuckled weakly. "I don't believe it now. What a fucking mess."

"I know, I know," she said. "It's no fun being around me."

He sat up, rubbing his chest where she had been compressing. "You? I was talking about me. I'm pretty sure most of this is my fault."

"In what way?"

He paused, thinking. "What the hell. At Fort Bowser, I came across some classified info. It concerned a drug that the army was developing that would be a weapon against the aliens."

"Which aliens?" Mallory asked.

"All of them, or as many as they could test it on," he said grimly. "At high doses, the drug severs their symbiotic relationship. As I understand, for some that's an inconvenience, but some feel enough of a shock that it kills one or both of the pair. I got word to someone close to the president and started working for her because the army had been lying about how dangerous this was. I guess someone found out my part in this, and there was a plan to kill me at Billy's party. You know what happened after that. Now, Calliope is—was—an old army buddy, and Phineas is my brother. I'm pretty sure they were here to take me back. If none of that had happened, then we wouldn't be in this situation."

Mallory laughed, too tired to follow up. "Xan, you're *here* because of me. If I hadn't gone to that party, the murder wouldn't have happened, you wouldn't have had to run, you wouldn't have ended up here with one shirt to wear for months. Mrs. Brown committed the first murder I ever solved. She and Lovely are here for me. Aunt Kathy is definitely here for me. That dead kid, Sam? Here for me."

"You think the murder attempt at the party was your fault? Did you not hear anything I just said? You think the army wasn't mad at me for the information I had until you showed up?"

"It's not that simple, but I think, yeah, maybe they wouldn't have gone for you that night. I don't know!" She rubbed her head. "It's confusing."

"You've been blaming yourself this whole time?" Xan asked. He was genuinely baffled.

"Well, yeah, you heard my aunt. Chaos and shit follow me everywhere I go. I show up at a party, someone dies and someone else gets abducted by a passing alien ship? That doesn't happen everywhere."

"If they hadn't gone for me at the party, they would have looked for another opportunity. And *Infinity* coming by was pretty wild, but no, it wasn't because of you."

She scooted away from him so she could sit and lean against the cool wall. *Are we really flying through space in a rock that used to be our friend?*

"I'm half convinced I'm dying and having the weirdest near-death experience," she said. "But you know I have to ask: What was Calliope talking about? Killing someone in your past? I'm guessing that wasn't normal army killing?"

He sighed. "We worked together in a mortuary division. We had an . . . incident." He swallowed and then forced himself to continue. He told the story of the lost patrol at Falcon Dam.

"That was last year. We got sent to separate bases and hadn't spoken in months. Then she came here, and she flat-out told me that she was a mercenary for the army, not enlisted. They hired her to—well, I'm not actually sure. She told me some conflicting information. But she also thought the army was sending her on a suicide mission. She said I'd find some information in her pockets about her missions. Plural."

"Where were you supposed to find a device to read a thumb drive in an alien space station?"

"I can get Infinity to read it. Stephanie might be able to, now."

The light flared, and Mallory smiled.

Xan continued, looking like he was confessing something big. "There's something else I haven't told you: my connection with Infinity is one of the reasons why Eternity decided to let humans aboard. They thought humans couldn't form symbiotic relationships with other species. But then two of us did."

"Who was the other one?" Mallory asked.

He stared at her like she was a moron. "You really don't know? Mal, the other one was you."

"But I'm not—" she said, feeling like the wind had gotten knocked out of her again. "I'd know if I was connected to another species, wouldn't I?"

He shrugged. "I don't know. I know because Infinity talks to me. If you don't have that, then I don't know how you tell. But she did say that you'd been connected for longer than she's known me and that the bond is strong."

"But—hang on, that's impossible. You got here before I did!"

"I'm telling you all I know, Mal. Our connections to aliens made Eternity reassess the human race."

"So, we made human tourism possible and we're the ones who get screwed?"

"Catch-22 of sorts, yeah."

"But how do I find out who I'm connected to?"

"Why don't we get to safety and see if we can ask someone then?" Xan asked. "Stephanie, are we going to the docking bay?"

The light flared. "Safe now," Stephanie said.

"That's good. Phineas and Lovely will meet us there," he said.

"Phineas and Lovely," she said, getting that faraway feeling again. "Calliope's dead. Tina and Ferdinand are in the ossuary. Mrs. Brown is still missing. Aunt Kathy." She looked at Xan in alarm. "We left Aunt Kathy."

"We'll check on her when we get back. *Infinity* says the station is stabilizing again." He made a face and rubbed the back of his head. "You have to check on family no matter how bad they are. My grandma fucked up some serious stuff for me and Phin, but she raised us."

"What happened to your parents?" she asked.

"Car crash when Phin and I were kids," he said.

"That's awful. I'm so sorry," she said. "My mom died when I was a kid . . ." She stopped talking. There it was, the flare in her brain, the feeling of a puzzle piece clicking into place that usually came when she figured out who the murderer was. But her mother hadn't been murdered. *Had she?*

She had died on Mallory's eighth birthday. Mallory had been outside playing, and her mom was sick in bed inside the house. Mallory had stepped on a bee and screamed. She hobbled to her mother's bedroom window to see if she could get comfort and saw—her memory refused to give it to her, there was a blank space there—and then she was waking up in the hospital after the allergic reaction to the bee sting. Her uncle had been very upset, and it was not just because of her, but because her mom had died the same day.

She hadn't died. She'd been killed.

"Oh, shit," she said. Goose bumps broke out over her body, making her skin shiver. The bee on the ground hadn't been a bumblebee. "It was a Sundry scout that stung me when I was a kid," she said, and now the memory was clear. The fat yellow-and-black body was replaced in her memory by a huge blue hornet.

She closed her eyes and tried to block out everything, trying to remember that day. She'd seen what looked like a blue butterfly and had run to look at it. That was also a Sundry, her memory informed her. She had stepped on another scout in the grass. Screaming, she ran to her mother's window.

"I blacked out after I got stung," she whispered. "I thought I had gone into shock from the sting, but now I remember—I was drowned in sensory overload. After I got stung, I was looking through my own eyes, but also I could see myself, and I could see my uncle pulling into the driveway, and I could see my aunt in the room with my mother. And then I passed out. That was the first death I ever saw. After that, they started to happen regularly. But I remember almost all of them."

"Almost?"

"My uncle's death. People at the party say I witnessed it, but I didn't remember anything. I was talking about how I could see where everyone was and what they were doing when I was hiding, so the cops didn't consider anything I said as usable."

"What are you saying?" Xan asked.

"Kathy. She's the key to all of this. And—oh god, the charm bracelet!"

Xan sputtered a confused comment, and she waved her hand, talking over him. "My mother was a maid who used a feather duster. Aunt Kathy has this terrible, tacky charm bracelet. She always wears it. She's got a feather on it. She's got other trinkets too, like an alligator."

"Which means what?" Xan asked, shaking his head as if he was already prepared not to believe her.

"Aunt Kathy wants a happy suburban life with a picket fence and the perfect family. She hated my mother. No proper suburban home has a sister and her kid living with them. After Mom died, Kathy said I would be her daughter." She shuddered at the thought. She had never accepted Kathy's pleas to call her Mom.

"But an alligator?" he pressed.

"She loved the goddamn suburbs, don't you see? My uncle wanted to move away from the burbs into the freaking eastern North Carolina swamps. So she killed him and stayed in her perfect house. It backfired when her own son was blamed. Maybe she thought she could pin it on someone else at the party. Like me. But she killed her husband and used an alligator as her trophy."

Mallory had found Kathy a few hours before the party, crying over photos she'd put on social media, pictures of their house and family. Holidays and vacations, always with wide smiles. Mother, father, and son. Perfection. (The foster daughter was behind the camera, always.) During the party Kathy had maintained the smiling hostess mask, welcomed everyone, kept the drinks filled, kept the dip cold, and then, when people had gone home, she removed the thing that would harm her suburban life.

"But your aunt has a lot of charms on that bracelet," Xan said, his eyes widening.

"Yeah. So she must have killed more. Christ, there's an apple as one of the trinkets, and a teacher at my high school died. She buys her trophies at Pandora."

"You can't get more suburban white serial killer than that," Xan said, shaking his head. Then he got very still. "She was there when Calliope got shanked."

"And she was sitting by that kid in the shuttle, the one that died," Mallory said. "Half the people said he'd been a big fan of mine and even annotated my books. They said he had a message for me. They all assumed he was a fanboy who might or might not be dangerous."

"Right," Xan said. He fished around in the coat Calliope had been carrying. "Look in there."

Mallory took the book—the omnibus Sam had been reading—and opened it. Words here and there had been highlighted: her aunt's name (Sonya, what she had called her aunt in the book), any reference to past murders, either solved or not solved by Mallory, and any mention of imagery or charms.

"He saw the pattern that I couldn't see 'cause I was too close," Mallory said. Then she added, "The book about my uncle's murder came out recently. Sam couldn't have solved it, could he? It was the murder I admit in the first chapter I couldn't solve."

"That would explain why he was acting so upset," Xan said. "He was sitting next to a serial killer."

"She must have killed him." Mallory felt inexplicably saddest about this one. "The poor kid would have blown her cover. I don't know how she did it yet, but I'm sure it was her. I'll figure it out."

"But there's still the question of what set Eternity off to attack the shuttle."

"I'm betting it was partly Kathy hitting the kid, and Adrian pulling Ren free from his connection and possibly attacking him. And the drug severed the connection?"

Xan rubbed the back of his head, shaking it. "Goddammit. I didn't want to think this, but I think Cal must have gotten the drug into the kid. She had it on her when she was here. But she didn't mention that when she died."

Mallory raised an eyebrow. "Was she likely to?"

"She apologized for damn near everything else," he said. "She was the reason I got attacked the night before the Falcon Dam incident, which put the whole damn disaster in motion. She admitted to stealing from all of you. She was dying. What did she have to lose?"

Mallory grabbed at her hair as if to pull ideas out of her head. "Christ, there's a serial killer on the station."

32

· · ·

THE KIDS ARE ALL RIGHT

MRS. ELIZABETH BROWN had nothing but memories. They bubbled up like pudding on the stove, back when pudding wasn't instant. Back when it was good, even with that skin on top.

There had been the shuttle, sitting on Lovely's right so they could hold hands. She was determined to get some help for her. When they got to that station, she would walk up to the first alien she found and demand some care for her granddaughter.

She'd gripped Lovely's hand tightly. Despite her love of winning contests, Mrs. Brown hated traveling. She hated driving, and she definitely didn't want to fly on a plane. She thought international vacations simply invited jet lag, stomach upset, and misunderstandings with people who didn't speak English.

She hadn't even been to Canada because she wasn't sure if she would understand the local vernacular, or French. The idea of customs and border crossings made her sweat, since the only thing she hated more than travel was law enforcement of any type. Cops, border patrol, security guards. They all became very interested when a woman with a murder record wanted to enter their country.

She hadn't traveled in several years because of her time in prison, but age and confinement hadn't warmed her to the idea.

And now, here you are, in fucking space.

Mama always told her that the internal voice was where you put the unladylike language. And Mrs. Brown always had, until she married a comedian who swore like a sailor with a flask of whiskey in one pocket and a filthy thesaurus in the other.

Takeoff. She closed her eyes, felt Lovely clutch her clammy hand.

You're in fucking space, *woman, enjoy yourself!*

She smiled, wondering how her Michael would see her now. What would he think of the woman she'd become, buttoned up on the outside and scared of leaving the house on the inside?

But fear died when it came to keeping family safe. *I gotta keep our granddaughter safe. I wish you had gotten to know her. She's a lot like me.*

"Did you say something, Gran?" Lovely asked, looking up from her e-reader. They'd reached space, and now there was not much to do until they made the jump.

"Nothing. Just nervous," she said, smiling.

"You doing okay?" Lovely asked, a frown creasing her perfect brow. Her skin was darker like her father's, who had favored Michael's complexion instead of Mrs. Brown's lighter mixed heritage. Lovely's hair was in one large braid that looped around her head like a snake. She wore a light leather jacket and jeans, her heavily bandaged left hand held gingerly against her chest. "Your ear isn't hurting, is it?"

"Right as rain. Say something in French," she said, leaning her right ear toward Lovely.

Lovely laughed. "Gran, I studied German."

It took Mrs. Brown a moment to realize that Lovely had said the comment in German, not English, and that the translation bug was working.

"I'll be damned," she whispered.

They sat in the first of six rows in what was clearly the economy section of the shuttle. In the front part of the shuttle, sitting right behind the captain, were the diplomats and bodyguards and a few VIPs who Mrs. Brown suspected were those billionaires who weren't famous but got treated like royalty because of money.

Her cabin seemed to be full of people who looked like they would be more at home on a cheap Greyhound than on the first interstellar shuttle. She wondered if they'd gotten lucky like her, or if they were better than her husband had been at hiding his wealth.

After he'd gotten his first big check and made his first outrageous clothing purchase—needed it for the stage, he'd said!—she had put a stop to that right fast. "You don't need to wear your money on your sleeve. And someday you're going to want to retire, and those ridiculous pants won't fit anymore, and you'll wonder how we're going to pay for your kidney dialysis when the hospital won't take thousand-dollar sunglasses as collateral!"

He had laughed when she said that. He always did. He made the world laugh, but she made him laugh, and that was enough.

That big man looked like he had money but didn't want to look like he did. She knew the type. She wouldn't recognize his name if he did tell her. An actor? She hadn't seen movies in years. He clearly didn't want to be recognized. Maybe it was a publicity stunt, sitting among the little people.

When she'd gotten up to use the lavatory—a horrifying experience, since clearly alien parts were different than human parts—she'd gotten a good look at the people in economy class. Two people caught her eye, sitting in the very back of the shuttle. Both white, one middle-aged, one college age.

The woman ignored everyone and everything, staring into space and playing idly with her charm bracelet. These were real charms, heavy metal, with chips of diamonds to indicate the alligator's eyes and the center of the star.

The kid was reading a thick, battered book and occasionally

marking things with a pink highlighter. After she'd gotten back to her seat, he started pacing the aisle, looking around with wide, frightened eyes as if he'd seen a ghost and was looking for someone who might believe him. After his third time passing by, Mrs. Brown was about to say something, but the Asian woman got up and took him to the back of the shuttle, where she spoke to him in low tones.

"Hey, are you cool?" she asked.

"Yeah, yeah," he said, sweat beading on his brow. "Just nervous, I guess. I—I mean, just nervous."

"I've got some Valium. I can give you one."

Wait. How did I remember this? Their backs were to me, and they were behind me.

While he paced, the white woman in the row next to his had pilfered the kid's book and was flipping through it. Mrs. Brown couldn't see her face, but a subtle flush moved up her neck.

No. I didn't see that.

The Asian woman returned to her seat, stopping to turn around to wave once at the boy. She reached into her bag for a gaming device. The boy came back to his seat, wiping water off his mouth with his hand. He put a water bottle in a cupholder in the seat in front of him. The book was back in place.

"Was that a Charlotte Queen book you were reading?" the white woman asked him.

"Oh, uh, yeah, I'm a huge fan," he said nervously. "I hope to meet the author."

"Maybe I can introduce you," the woman said. "I'm her aunt."

"I know," the boy said, his face pale. He was terrified of her.

The intercom popped on, the captain's alien voice coming in but sounding like English to her ears. "You are in for a treat, although an intense one, passengers! As this will be your first trip to Eternity, the station will reach out and touch your mind. It may be disorienting at first, but rest assured you are completely safe."

"Touch our minds?" the woman behind Mrs. Brown said, her voice tight.

"How is it disorienting?" Lovely asked her, but before she could answer, Mrs. Brown was overwhelmed by a sense of splashes of color, the scent of baked goods, the feel of fur over her skin, the laughter of children, and the taste of chipped beef on toast.

"Shit on a shingle?" he'd asked.

Nearly at her limit with his bullshit, she'd taken the plate back. "I happen to like it. Cook your own meals if you're going to talk about my cooking like that."

And he'd laughed at her irritation. He was nothing like Michael, who had laughed to make her laugh. What had she been thinking when she married this man? "That's what my granddaddy called it. I'll eat it, baby. Tomorrow you'll make me something better." Then he'd squeezed her wrist, hard.

He'd been telegraphing this more and more, trying to assert himself as the boss and threatening violence, but never with his words. He hadn't hit her yet, but the tight grasps, the meaningful looks, they all hinted at something yet to come.

The poor bastard couldn't have known. She'd changed her name after her first prison sentence. And she was usually so prim and proper, he couldn't have guessed the beast within her that took no threat lightly.

Shortly thereafter, the plate shattered against the wall, then a punch, a scream, a thump, and a splash of blood on her hands. And she would do it again if she had to.

Her senses overloaded, she fell back in her chair.

Hello, Mrs. Elizabeth Brown. I think we will be great friends.

You can call me 'Lizabeth.

Shortly thereafter, a scream, a thump, a splash of blood on her hands. But not Mrs. Brown's hands. Not her blood.

Then nothing but overwhelming pain and rage.

HOW THE FUCK do I know all this?

She floated in darkness but was able to breathe. *Am I dead?*

The breach had opened; she had been sucked through. She was vaguely aware of pain, of limbs breaking. But the pain hadn't followed her.

How did she remember so many details of the shuttle? She hadn't been positioned to see what she had about her fellow passengers.

The darkness faded, and she was standing in a corridor lit with red light. "Mama was right, I guess. 'That girl is heading to hell.'"

She opened the first door she came to, and the red light intensified. A tree that looked choked with red, thorny vines stood at the center of the room, the branches growing into the ceiling and the roots growing through the floor.

"You poor thing," she said automatically, and walked forward to start pulling the dangerous weed off the tree.

Help me.

She wondered if she should be messing with alien plant life, but you didn't need to grow up in the South to know that a tree suffering under invasive growth needed help. She patiently pulled the vines off the tree, gently prying where thorns had pierced the bark and were leaching the health from the tree.

Her hands were raw and bleeding by the time she got the final vine down, but why should she have thought to bring her gardening gloves to space? And even if she had, Lord knows where her purse ended up.

Another vine, this one looking more like ivy (or poison ivy; she could never tell) reached from the tree's branches toward her, tentatively touching her bloody hands.

Help. This wasn't a plea. It was an offering.

She felt she stood on a cliff's edge. She wasn't sure what was at the bottom, but she did know that if she went back it would likely mean going back to jail for violating parole and then dying of cancer. Everyone had to die sometime, though, right?

She took the vine and closed her eyes.

"JESUS, WHAT A mess," she said, looking around. She was still in the room with the tree, but around her were splintered shards of mirrors. Each one reflected something from a different point of view.

They shattered me. This is what I've put together from your minds when you slept, but none of them fit together.

Mrs. Brown walked around and looked at each mirror. Each one showed the moment in the shuttle when Eternity had touched their minds.

"They said you had found another host. Where is he? Why did he let this happen?" Mrs. Brown asked.

No. Not him. I never agreed. It was a bad pairing. He's gone. It hurt.

"Okay, okay, calm down. What do we have to do first?"

We have to fix breaches. Inform my daughter that I'm all right. Stop—stop the fight in the ossuary.

The breaches were like her grandchildren's skinned knees. If she thought for a moment, she could see them, even feel them. She mentally sealed one with a thought and some TLC.

"This is going to take some time. I haven't done anything like this before. And I don't know your daughter—you'll have to do that."

A sense of a shuttle, a sense of relief, a sense of urgency.

"And what's wrong in the ossuary? A cold graveyard, and a bunch of rock people. There's a big brawl; they're fighting among themselves and some humans got involved?" There: Lovely and that tall man. "Oh, that won't do. What has that girl gotten herself into?"

She's protecting others.

"Well. That's all right, then. Let's get back to the breaches."

She peeked into the ossuary from time to time, checking on her granddaughter, her pride and joy, playing her violin (a terrible tune, though, she'd have to talk to her about that) and making the rock people confused with the vibration. Now, she was safe inside a shuttle.

The rock people continued fighting, a plucky young mech facing down a craggy old shuttle. She had fired rockets precisely at the old ship's weapons, disarming him with little damage. He fired once more, missing the mech and hitting the airlock controls. The airlock opened and the three shuttles and two humans were ejected into space.

"We have to do something," Mrs. Brown said, trying to figure out what the station could do. But there was too much to understand, and no time.

I can't focus on too much at once while there's still damage inside. They're fine. The young shuttle has picked them up.

"And my granddaughter?"

Safe aboard my daughter.

"I'm having the strangest day I've had in a long time," she muttered. "But those young folks will be all right. Pity about the young army woman, though."

She will be remembered. Very, very well remembered.

Two humans aboard one shuttle, two aboard another, one tragedy, a whole mess of humans in one of the medbays, and one mess of a human on his way to medbay: the old host. Not nearly as good as the new host.

One missing. Mrs. Brown frowned and searched for the middle-aged white woman, finding her outside the ossuary, weeping and trying to wipe dried blood from her hands. Then she spied something beside the door to the ossuary. She picked it up.

All accounted for. More breaches, then. She focused.

33

· · ·

DIDN'T KNOW SHE HAD IT IN HER

MALLORY PACED, LIMPING on her left leg and ignoring it. Her head almost brushed the ceiling; Stephanie was still enlarging the room.

Xan's chest ached where she had given him CPR, and everything ached because of the spacing. And fuck, he'd had a long day.

"My mom. She killed Mom. And then it was my teacher. And then it was my guidance counselor! I left for college then, so who the hell knows who else she killed. There were more; there had to be. That goddamn bracelet. But she killed my uncle. Just because he wanted to move."

Xan had propped himself against the wall, wincing. "Sounds like she had one love in life, and he was about to take that away from her. Why are you in a hurry? You've got her, once we get back to the station. That was the other thing I was going to tell you before—" He waved an exhausted hand at the door to indicate their spacing.

"She killed Sam because he had figured her out," Mallory said, shaking the book like an angry street preacher.

"Why Calliope, though?" Xan asked.

Mallory thought for a moment. "When Kathy came to, she

was freaking out and had to be sedated. She didn't have her bracelet on. Would Cal have stolen it?"

Xan nodded. "Most definitely. But how did Kathy find out, or get it back?"

"Maybe Cal had a change of heart, gave it back," Mallory suggested.

"And your aunt would have left that part out? Unlikely. But Cal did say something about a hole in her pocket." Xan put his hands deep into the hidden pocket and, there. One of the pockets had been empty when he had gotten it from Calliope, probably because of the large hole. He held the coat open to show Mallory the hole in the interior pocket.

He patted his pockets while Mallory continued to think aloud. There was one very large and obvious thing missing, and he was afraid he had lost something through the pocket with the hole.

"Cal dropped it and Kathy found it. Kathy would also have wanted to know where the kid's book ended up. If she knew Cal had that too, then she would have worried Cal would figure it out."

Xan rubbed his forehead. "God, and I bet Cal hadn't read a book since high school. Cal was killed for being in the way. And by the way—"

"Same as Sam," Mallory said, nodding and pacing. "And everyone else on that shuttle. And who knows, at this point she might be going for the others just for the psychotic hell of it."

"Mal. Can I please tell you something?" Xan said, feeling so tired of trying to get her to listen to him. "First off, Eternity's fine. It was real bad there for a bit, but she's better now."

"Did she get a new host?"

"Yeah, but *Infinity* can't really tell me who yet." He frowned and tried to ask *Infinity* again, and then shook his head. "She keeps sending me images of an old lady wiping something off a child's face."

"Mrs. Brown? Holy shit," Mallory said.

"Secondly: apparently the Sundry had been scouting planets for First Contact possibilities way before any of the other races. They could blend in because of our other insects. That scout you stepped on when you were younger, that was when you got connected to the Sundry."

"But what does it mean that I'm symbiotically connected to the Sundry? It's not like they benefit me or anything."

He shrugged. "They're a hivemind. Like a big computer. Were you good in school?"

"Not especially. I was okay, but . . ." She lost her train of thought for a moment. "The day I got stung, my aunt killed my mom. Does that mean the Sundry are what makes me trigger murder? That's not a benefit!"

She had a point. "Look, all I know is that the hivemind told *Infinity* that you are connected to them. The blue hive, anyway. They're different from the silver. Some of the blue Sundry didn't want you to remember. It might change your way of living."

"What, I'm like a science project being observed?"

"Don't know," he said.

"But I've been seeing them around us all day! And they never offered to help me or tell me what they know!"

"Mal, I'm the messenger here."

Mallory sat down hard on the rocky floor. Her eyes were glassy. "What does that mean now? Can I talk to them like you do *Infinity*?"

"I don't know, can you?"

A buzz sounded from the top corner of the room. It was a silver Sundry.

"I'll be damned. They do get everywhere," Xan said. "Why don't you ask her?"

Mallory stood and held her hand out to the insect, which fell into her palm, wings buzzing weakly. "I can't communicate. There's only one of her."

"You can send to the hivemind. They just can't communicate back," he said. "Scouts go out on their own all the time to send info back."

Infinity sent two messages to Xan. The first message Mallory was going to hate. The second made him go cold all over again.

"*Infinity* says that one thing you can do to communicate with the whole hivemind, both ways," he told her, "is to let that silver sting you."

INFINITY EXPLAINED THAT if the blue Sundry had stung Mallory on Earth, she was only connected to the data collection half of the hivemind. They didn't do much with their data; they just collected it. The silver Sundry were the action part of the mind. They used the information.

"It seems that most of the time they're in agreement, but there's been a schism," Xan said. "But if you let the silver sting you, then you'll have both halves."

"And this will do what for me? We have an omniscient space station connected to a shuttle connected to you. Can't Eternity just tell us what's going on? Or talk to her when we dock?"

He didn't answer, trying to think up a good lie. "Eternity is still sealing breaches and calming down the fight in the ossuary. She sees all when she's well. She's far from well right now." Then he sighed, resigned. She should know. "And there's one more thing. *Infinity* says no one can land in the shuttle bay yet. There's something going on."

"What now?" she asked, looking suspicious.

"I'll tell you when you wake up," Xan said. He took her hand. "I got your back. This won't beat you. You need to find your aunt. Before something else happens."

She went very pale. "I'm allergic. I've got an EpiPen back in my room, but if we can't dock . . ."

He stroked her hand and made her shiver. "Mal, what will she do with no one to stop her? You're the only one who can do this. Stephanie and I will protect you. Promise."

"All right. I'll let you know what I find out. If I survive."

"You've already survived being shot at by a pissed-off old shuttle and being spaced today. Also, you were carried around in a wild mech's backpack. A bee sting should be easy."

"Says the guy who doesn't need an EpiPen to stay alive in the summer," she muttered. She took a deep breath. The wasp waited patiently on her hand. "All right. Do it."

A thought hit Xan like a bucket of water. *She really thinks this is going to kill her. And she's doing it anyway. Jesus, she's not impetuous; she's trying to make up for what she thinks she's messed up.* Before he could think it through, he leaned in and hugged her. She stiffened in surprise, and just when she started to hug him back, she went slack.

The wasp sank its stinger into her right hand, and Xan winced as the scout crawled away from the puncture wound, which was oozing blood and a clear venom.

He leaned over and felt her breath on his cheek. Still breathing. Good.

"Hang on," Stephanie said.

"To what?" he demanded, looking around the bare stone room.

Something shook the ship, and Mallory bounced up in the air, her head coming down on the stone floor with a crack.

Xan scooted over to the corner and pulled Mallory into his arms so he could cushion her head on his chest if they lurched again.

The shuttle rocked again.

"Is the coast clear?" he asked aloud.

"No," Stephanie said.

I had to go back to the shuttle bay for a passenger, Infinity sent back.

A panel of rock about two feet square slid aside on the wall, revealing a strong pane of . . . quartz? Diamond? Didn't matter—Xan only knew that he could finally see outside. Eternity was in front of them, already looking much better since the last time he'd seen her from outside. Her colors were returning to swirling blue and red, and there were no apparent leaks or breaches. It looked like Stephanie was flying toward the shuttle bay, albeit slowly.

But closing in was the massive rose-pink cube that was Stephanie's grandfather. He raced toward Stephanie at an alarming rate.

"Is he trying to stop you? I didn't think he had weapons," Xan said.

"He has impressive density and ramming capability. My hull hasn't had time to get strong enough to withstand that," Stephanie said. She sounded much stronger now.

Gramps didn't have a lot of familial love: he came straight for Stephanie. Xan winced and prepared himself for the blow, holding Mallory tighter.

Stephanie dropped, leaving Xan and Mallory briefly airborne. Xan hit the ceiling painfully, and then crashed down. He swore, trying to keep himself and Mallory free of broken bones.

Leather straps came out of the wall. "Strap yourself down," Stephanie said. She banked right and Xan scrambled into the restraints and grabbed Mallory again before she could bounce away from him.

A copper-colored streak went by the window. She appeared again, going in a different direction. Xan realized *Infinity* was creating a sort of cage by flying around Stephanie faster and faster.

Gramps appeared again. Stephanie maintained her speed toward Eternity. The shuttle shook slightly again, but it didn't feel like a hit. Then the entire shuttle vibrated, and Xan could just barely sense the words intended.

"FUCKING METAL PRINCESS!"

"Tina?" Xan shouted. Then the floor shook again, and the

massive mech launched, suddenly visible from the window, spraying her rockets backward to help her with momentum. He winced as one came right for them, but *Infinity* intercepted it.

Tina headed like a missile toward Gramps. She didn't fire any weapons, just got closer and closer, and Xan realized he was watching a game of chicken between two people who didn't know the rules.

"What is she doing? He'll pulverize her!" Xan said, watching in horror.

"No," Stephanie said.

And as they neared each other, Gramps veered off at the last minute, shifting his trajectory wide so he wouldn't collide with Stephanie.

"She's royalty," Stephanie reminded him.

"Right, this whole mess was due to him trying to keep Tina safe from some imagined threat, wasn't it?" Xan asked.

"Exactly," Stephanie said. "And when we dock, one of you is going to tell me what the hell is going on with Tina."

Xan smiled in relief. "That's a long story," he said. He watched *Infinity* leave them to collect Tina, who had done nothing to slow her pace toward Eternity. She still flew headfirst like a missile. A vastly optimistic and stupid missile.

Now that things were quieter and his own breathing had slowed, the sound of Mallory's wheezing reached his ears. In his arms, Mallory struggled to breathe, her stung hand turning purple and starting to swell.

"Hurry, Stephanie," he yelled. "Mallory won't last much longer."

34

. . .

A LOT OF DAMN NERVE

MALLORY DRANK FROM the data firehose.

At first, the stinger was excruciating. She could dimly feel the muscles in her hand tightening into a fist and not letting go. She felt Xan's embrace, and then his warmth was gone.

The hivemind took her.

Too many eyes, too many ears, too many tastes she didn't understand, far, far too much information—she wanted to close off all methods of sensory input to stop the flood, but out of all the noise she felt one singular presence.

Just relax. We don't control the information. We simply accept it. Your job is to help witness, help process. You don't have to do all the work, silver scout 42 whispered to her. It didn't keep to the usual form of communication, and Mallory realized she wasn't using her translation bug to hear this.

Her subconscious slowly unfolded from its fetal position and opened itself to the information, and it swept over her.

Only two things now pulled at her awareness, inside and outside the station.

Inside, her aunt Kathy marched up the hallway, Calliope's gun—*Calliope's gun?*—in her pocket.

"Where did she get that?" she asked.

Your human companion dropped it.

Kathy demanded to know where the shuttle bay was from anyone she passed. Most ignored her, the stress of their day vastly eclipsing the needs of one loud human.

Outside the station, Mallory watched the battle as Xan did, but from the compound eyes of the scout aboard *Infinity*, not her own.

All of the other data were still washing through, but those two scenes stayed with her like seeds in her teeth.

Do you see now?

"No," she said. "See what?"

You don't cause the murders. You don't attract them. They attract you. You're not aware of it, but when the probability of a murder is high, you go there to witness.

"I'm like a murder-sniffing dog?"

I suppose, the scout said, sounding unsure.

"Then what happened with Eternity? Did I sense all of this and decide to come here months ago?"

Of course. The hivemind that you had access to was here. They were seeing the problems with Ren, and the dissatisfied Gneiss, and the chances of Infinity *to collect a passenger on Earth. There are many, many things at play. You will never understand every single one. But they worked together to bring you here.*

Mallory was so baffled at this information that she just sat and soaked in more data as Aunt Kathy continued her search for the shuttle bay.

A Sundry had stowed away aboard Grandfather, transmitting his point of view of the battle. Sundry were on every ship. They slipped in everywhere and observed.

"Why me?"

You were a test. We wanted to see what your brain would do with a taste of the hivemind's logic. Your love of details made you follow violent situations. We gave you our venom, which can enhance bonding in some sentients, as well as be the base for healing drugs.

"Heal? I went to the hospital and nearly died."

Our pure venom can kill if we intend. You have done well with our connection. You may stay if you like.

Mallory felt cold and, back in her body, could feel her hand swelling up. "Stay?"

We wanted another sentient to bring another point of view to the hivemind.

"But I'm human. I can't take all of this all the time."

Your body is dying. You need to be with us.

"Dammit, that's not fair, why are you killing me? Why sting me if you knew I was going to die?"

There was a chance you wouldn't react this strongly. There was a chance you would.

"Well, fuck. What is Kathy doing now?"

There is a 76% chance she will shoot one of the humans, 23% chance of shooting another sentient. There's a 0% chance she will successfully steal a shuttle and a pilot to get back home to Earth.

"Zero. Why?"

Eternity can't see the threat yet. She is too busy fixing the problems with the station and bonding with her new host. But if the human takes a shuttle against its pilot's will, there is zero chance of it reaching jump distance before Eternity attacks.

"What can I do to stop Kathy? Does this connection of yours help me? Silver Sundry do shit with all that collected data, right?"

A pause; even the deluge of information slowed as the hivemind deliberated.

No.

Mallory drifted along, confused. "No? You're not even going to go through the probabilities?"

No.

"I thought you were the ones who acted, who did things! Then what the fuck is all this for?"

To give us a human's point of view. The voice sounded puzzled. "I thought this relationship was mutually beneficial!"

We can keep your mind alive in the hive if your body dies.

"That's not a benefit when you're the ones who killed me! This is bullshit."

If she was going to die, she had better do something to help her friends. *Infinity* had docked, its Sundry spy watching Phineas and Lovely exit the ship.

She thought for a moment, wondering if her pounding heart was panic or the shock her body was experiencing. She focused, trying to find a specific pair of compound eyes that were gathering the right information.

Two Sundry watched Kathy brighten as she found the shuttle bay. Mallory saw through their eyes and felt the alien workings of their minds. They saw the murderous human and the two innocents. They calculated new odds as to chances of death.

She sent an order. *That's no good. Move.*

No. Stop. This isn't the way.

"You assholes broke the way of things when you took me without consent into your hivemind," she said, and told the Sundry, *Sting.*

It resisted. She pushed again. *Sting. Don't kill, but sting her face. Make it hurt.*

Resist.

The hivemind as one assaulted her. *No. This is not the way we do things.*

You've got a lot of damn nerve. Fuck it. I'll sting.

She concentrated, and the wasp's wings began to buzz. She took control of the Sundry but wasn't able to manage the complex muscles to command the wings to fly, and instead of flying, she fell onto Kathy's shoulder, tangling in her hair.

The Sundry fought her for control, and the hivemind screamed at her.

She couldn't have the perfect target, so she went for the first piece of skin she could, at the nape of Kathy's neck.

Kathy screamed, mostly in shock, and Mallory let the Sundry go. Kathy's reaction was to slap the stinging insect away, but instinct made her do it with her right hand, and that one held the gun.

Now. One more thing, Mallory thought sternly as Kathy crumpled, leaving a spray of blood and cartilage on the wall.

MALLORY'S HEAD SPUN, and she wondered how long it would be until she suffocated for good. She had an odd sense of seeing Stephanie dock from both outside and inside. Her hatch opened and Xan ran out.

YOU BROKE OUR rules. The hivemind, both sides, were pissed.

"You never told me the rules. And what about my rules? You stung me without consent. You didn't give me a beneficial symbiotic relationship," Mallory said. "I've heard about your intergalactic whatever regarding symbionts. You have *laws* about this shit, and you didn't follow any of them."

We must come to an agreement, the Sundry said at last. *We will contact you in a cycle or two.*

"And if your venom kills me in the meantime?"

She gasped, tightly as if through a straw, as another puncture invaded her thigh. This one was far away and not nearly as painful. A few more tight breaths, and her airways began to clear.

She opened her eyes. She was still aboard Stephanie, and Xan, Lovely, and Phineas stood over her. The perky mech face of Tina peeked in from the outside.

She looked at Lovely. "I found your grandmother."

* * *

MALLORY WAS SITTING up and enjoying breathing when Mrs. Brown entered the shuttle bay. The blue and silver Sundry had gathered and were sitting on the walls and ceiling. But when Mrs. Brown came in, they immediately left the area. Mallory felt a tinge of fear in the back of her head, where she still had an uncomfortable sense of buzzing.

Lovely nearly tackled her grandmother in a hug, both delighted and demanding to know where she had been and if she was okay.

Mrs. Brown immediately started directing the shuttle bay workers as if she were a youth group leader at a summer camp. She had several busy shuttle bay techs checking *Infinity* and Stephanie for damage and directed drones to recover the wreck of the Gneiss grandfather, who was still hurtling away from the station. Stephanie had said he wasn't out of control; he was pouting and wouldn't come back on his own.

She ordered all the humans to the medbay for treatment, telling Eternity to give them human-sized rooms. Tomorrow they could talk.

THAT NIGHT, HER hands still aching from being swollen but overall much better, Mallory had a visitor.

Xan stood there. He was wearing a new T-shirt and Calliope's cleaned and mended coat, and had bathed.

"Almost didn't recognize you in a new shirt," she said, stepping aside to let him in.

"Yeah. I don't feel great robbing the dead, but Mrs. Brown insisted I get some new clothes from the shuttle since the only other option was borrowing from Phineas, and we're not the same size."

"What's up?" she said.

"Both Calliope and Phineas brought me thumb drives. I wasn't able to open the private data on one without the other. How the person who sent these figured the likelihood that I would get both drives from them is beyond me." He took the offered chair, and Mallory sat on her bed to listen.

"A file on Phineas's drive said that the officer who set it up wanted to make sure my brother would know their plans and help protect me." He shook his head. "Looks like they didn't know as much about me and my family as they thought. But the encrypted data tells everything about the God's Breath project. Calliope was sent here to test the drug on aliens, but she wasn't the only one. Seven other people on the shuttle were given the pill, including your aunt."

"No shit," Mallory said, covering her mouth in shock. "So all that stuff about bringing me home and being a family . . ."

He shrugged. "May have been true. You said her thing is happy suburban life. She doesn't have family without you, so maybe the offer from the army made it worth it."

"You thought Cal dosed the kid, but she said she gave him a Valium, right? What if she was telling the truth and Kathy was the one who dosed the kid and clubbed him?"

"That is possible," he allowed. "At least we won't be remembering her as the one who caused those dominoes to fall. Although she did plenty of other domino knocking. Cal was the kind of person who just ran around taking nails out of horses' feet to see what kingdoms she could conquer."

"We could interrogate Kathy when she wakes up," Mallory suggested. "I know Mrs. Brown wants to do that before she goes home. But who were the other six who had the drug?"

"They were all first class," Xan said. "Dead."

"So Kathy dosed Sam," Mallory began, "and when Eternity touched his mind, the drug weakened her connection with Ren.

Then Kathy clubbed Sam. Then what, Adrian pulled Ren out of the physical connection with Eternity? Which ended up killing Ren?"

"Yeah. But here's something else I found out on Cal's thumb drive. She had three missions. She was to test the drug on the station, arrest or kill me, but also, she had to try to get you back to Earth. The government wants *you*, Mallory. Maybe even more than me."

"For what?" she asked, baffled.

"They want to weaponize you. They figure if people die near you, then you might be a good weapon. That was why they tried so hard to get you to Billy's party."

"You're kidding." She stared at him. "Even if that was how I worked, there's so much chaos that there is no way to actually target someone. And Calliope never said anything like that to me. She never hinted that she wanted to get me back to Earth."

"She could have been waiting for the right time," he said, twisting his mouth as if something tasted bad.

"So if I go back—"

"They most likely will arrest you on an imagined charge and make you work for them."

She smiled bitterly. "No one believed me for so long when I thought I caused the murders. They probably won't believe me when I say that instead I'm attracted to the murders, not really a murder catalyst."

"Looks like we're both stuck here for a while, then," he said. "At least the station host likes us now."

"Hah. You didn't throw her in jail."

"That's probably water under the bridge. You saved her life, remember."

"Then she saved mine, so that debt is paid." Mallory sighed. "Anyway, what ever did happen to Adrian? Is he healing?"

Xan smiled and tried to bite it back. "He got carried around the station all day by a very angry security officer. He's being treated, but he's pretty messed up. Mentally and physically. A bad connection with the station can be pretty harmful."

They sat in silence for a moment. Mallory finally broke it. "Thanks for, well, everything today."

He grinned at her. "You saved me more than once. Goes both ways. Do you know what you're going to do with the Sundry?"

"Shit. Right. Yeah, I know. I am not going to do anything. I don't like them very much, and they're pretty pissed at me for my move with Kathy, but they're too useful. Xan, they just collect data. So much data that they don't use. They knew about God's Breath, didn't tell anyone."

He stared at her. "They knew about it. They could have prevented this?"

"Yeah. I only understand a tiny bit, but they're more interested in seeing the outcomes of different actions. They almost never manipulate data; they just like to watch. We're a soap opera to them."

"How did you find out?"

She sighed and rubbed her forehead where a throb still sat, refusing to move. "If I can meditate, I can touch the hivemind again. If I fall asleep just a tad, I can kind of touch it. It's hard, and they don't like it when I do it since we're not really friends. But I don't think they can stop me."

"Is it safe for you to do that?"

Mallory laughed. "Has that stopped us doing anything we've done in the last two days?"

"I guess not." He stood. "I need to check on *Infinity*. Stephanie needs some sanding, and Tina, God, she will always need help."

"Okay," she said, standing and walking him to the door. She held up her still-swollen hand. "I can help when this thing heals."

She opened the door for him. He stepped outside and said, "See you at breakfast?"

"Yeah," she said. She swallowed the lump in her throat. "Thanks for keeping me going today. I'm glad you're here on the station."

"I had to pull out the tough love. But you handled it." He took a few steps down the hall and then turned back. "Listen, do you remember being on Stephanie when the Sundry stung you?"

"It's pretty fuzzy," she said, frowning. "I'm not sure. Did I say something stupid?"

He smiled slightly. "No, not at all. I'll see you tomorrow."

She watched him go, too emotionally worn out to feel much of anything. She needed a friend more than anything on the station, and if he wanted to pretend he hadn't hugged her, she'd respect that.

She hadn't remembered. But the hivemind had.

THE HUMANS (MINUS Kathy and Adrian, both in the medbay), Ferdinand, and Tina met the next morning for breakfast. Mallory and Xan were so stiff from their adventures that they could barely move; they'd learned that the magic healing bug goo, as Phineas called it, wasn't given for "minor injuries." Ferdinand served them and sat down with them. Tina sat on the floor, with several tables moved aside to make room for her. They all had stories to tell and were desperate to knit them together to make sense of the previous day.

But first, everyone wanted to hear about Mrs. Brown.

"You're part of the station now?" Lovely said. "What the hell does that mean? When do we go home?"

"Honey, I'm not going home. There's very little for me back home except for dealing with parole violations and cancer treatments that won't work," the old woman said firmly but kindly.

"What about your family?" Lovely demanded.

"You can come visit whenever you like," Mrs. Brown said. "For free. Hell, move here if you want. But understand that I'm much better off here." She glanced at Phineas. "You both visit. There's not a lot left of our merry little band that survived. That terrible woman doesn't count."

Kathy had survived the gunshot, disintegrating most of her ear and bursting her eardrum when the gun went off. She was heavily sedated and confined while she healed.

They frankly weren't sure what was going on with Tina. Calliope was technically dead, and her body was gone, but talking to Tina was a completely new experience now.

"I need to get Kathy to confess; that's about all that will get my cousin out of jail. I don't know if I can tie the older murders to her," Mallory said. She glanced at Xan. "I also need to know if she dosed Sam."

"Oh, I can tell you that, dear," Mrs. Brown said, frowning at her literal boiling beverage. "We need to get some coffee aboard. But on topic, from Eternity's memories I was able to see Calliope give Sam a white pill. The weaponized pill was blue, if I understand correctly. I haven't seen who got it to him, but I know it wasn't your friend.

"The station is at her full capacity now and can piece together the situation that led to the shuttle attack," Mrs. Brown continued. "There will be a number of questions from Earth. I'll be inviting a delegation here to retrieve the bodies and the criminal and to hear how this will play out. I will make locking up that woman one of the requirements of humans coming here. As well as the safety of our permanent residents. And no military. Eternity will know."

She looked pointedly at Xan. "Speaking of military and what they tried to do, I understand a few of our human visitors brought some of that God's Breath drug aboard. What has become of that?"

"I went out with *Infinity* and spaced it," he said. "I got the idea when we were sucked out of the airlock, but Stephanie caught us too fast for me to dump it then."

"There is none left on the station," Mrs. Brown said, rather than asked.

"None that I know of," Xan said.

"Good. Like I said, I will set up stipulations to protect you, and—"

"You don't have to protect—" Mallory started to say, but Lovely shook her head.

"Don't even think about telling Gran what to do. Best you don't fight her."

"And what the hell were you thinking, Tina?" Mallory asked, focusing on the massive seated Gneiss. "Just launching yourself at Stephanie's grandfather like that?"

"Stephanie's grandpa didn't want her to hurt me and thought he was protecting me. So I thought if I was going to get hurt somewhere else, he would have to follow."

"That logic is incredibly dangerous," Ferdinand said.

"It worked, and it was fucking metal."

Mallory leaned over to Xan and Ferdinand. "Is Calliope really dead? 'Cause Tina sounds different."

Ferdinand hummed briefly. "What she did was an ancient practice that our people haven't done in centuries. Stephanie's grandfather was one of the last, and he said he would never tell how he did it. I think Stephanie and Tina let instinct take over. But it's hard to study the effects of an illegal act since no one wants to admit if their ascension was natural or not, so I don't know much of the details about it. I'm actually afraid of the long-term ramifications of this. What Tina's family will say. What happens when my father wakes all the way up. The ossuary is locked for the near future until everyone there calms down."

"Eternity is monitoring the situation," Mrs. Brown said.

"What about you?" Lovely asked Xan. "What's your plan now that you have a spaceship to keep you safe?"

"It's dangerous, but I'm taking Phineas home and we're going to bury Grandma. I need to get some legal documents going to transfer the land to him," he said. "But I'll be back."

"I'm sure *Infinity* can keep you safe for the duration of a funeral, and a quiet meeting," Mrs. Brown said firmly.

"Or alert every nation's military that I've come home," he said. "We'll see."

"Nah, you're not risking all that for me," Phineas said. "Grandma won't be allowed in sacred ground. She was too mean. A funeral will probably be me pouring her ashes under the porch and saying, 'Don't fucking haunt me, Grandma,' or something."

"Or you could bring them to space and release them into a star or something," Mallory suggested.

Phineas snorted. "Like she deserves that."

"And Lovely, are you going back to your job?" Mrs. Brown said.

"It'll take some PT, but I think I can get back to playing. Playing without your pinky finger isn't easy, but it's not impossible. And after everything we did yesterday, playing for an orchestra without a pinky and without aliens attacking me doesn't seem scary at all." She took a hesitant sip of the beverage in front of her, winced, and put it down.

"Are we good, Mrs. Brown?" Mallory ventured. "I understand if you don't like me, but a lot has been going on, and—"

Mrs. Brown firmly interrupted, "There are a lot of times in our lives when we have to do what's right. That night, two of those rights collided. I killed an abuser, and you reported me doing it. You've since saved my life and my granddaughter's, so I'd say we're even. But moving forward, more humans will be coming to the station. Can you handle that?"

"I think so. I still would prefer to understand this ability I have, and the Sundry and I aren't on the best terms," she said.

"No one is on good terms with them, if they let others get harmed with no action," Mrs. Brown said. "Unfortunately, cutting off ties means no more access to the translation bugs since the Sundry maintain the species language databases."

"You're not going to ask Stephanie to take you somewhere else?" Xan asked Mallory. "You've pretty much got your own shuttle now."

"And leave all my friends?" Mallory shook her head. "Nah. I'm done running. I'd like to give living a chance."

TWO EPILOGUES

. . . .

1

WHEN PEOPLE APPROVED of your interest, it was called a passion.

When they disapproved, they called it an obsession.

They didn't say Einstein was obsessive. They said he was brilliant. Curie, Mozart, Dickinson, Hemingway. They were all passionate about their work.

But according to his family, his professors, and his therapist, Sam Washington was *obsessive*. He needed to get a life, focus on school, stop stalking people on the Internet. His fanaticism bordered on dangerous, they said.

He didn't think he was dangerous because he was completely open about his passions. He didn't hide his scrapbook in the basement away from prying eyes. He ran a detailed fan website. He'd never threatened anyone. He'd never before even tried to approach the person he was passionate about.

And it wasn't even a sexual thing. Even with his roommate's posters of scantily clad women, people still reacted more strongly to the printouts on his side of the room, complete with annotations.

His roommate, Jackson, had moved out months ago.

"Why do you think you're so interested in Mallory Viridian?" his therapist, Dr. Bridge, would ask. She was a heavy woman in her late twenties who wore handmade dresses and red lipstick and radiated sexy self-confidence that totally distracted him. He had been dismayed when he had learned she would take his case, not because she was so attractive, but because she didn't read books and he knew she wouldn't understand.

"I've always been into mysteries," he said. "My parents and I used to watch the old classics, *Miss Fisher's Murder Mysteries; Father Brown; Murder, She Wrote; Midsomer Murders;* Poirot; Marple; all those old shows. We used to have bets on who the murderer was, and whoever lost had to do the dishes."

"Are you close to your parents?"

"Sure, I guess," he said. "We watched TV together. Dad gave me twenty dollars when I got a good report card."

She nodded and made a note. Sam worried they would be calling his parents, and he really didn't want them to. To his relief, she returned to the subject at hand. "But the Mallory Viridian books are allegedly based on true crime," she said. "That is quite different than scripted mysteries."

"I believe she technically calls them novels," he said, "but I've cross-referenced every single thing I could in her books with whatever news and public record police reports I could find."

"Police reports aren't public record in North Carolina," Dr. Bridge protested. "How did you find out those details?"

He sighed. She was too smart. "Fine. I bribed someone at the county records office. And took the reporters who covered Mallory Viridian out to lunch."

"Also a bribe," she said. "So you have cross-referenced everything involving Mallory's cases. Again, I ask, why?"

"Because they're amazing," he said. "The situations she found herself in, the ways she solved cases! The dusty pepper shaker in the senator's house! The torn seam in the yoga instructor's pants! It's amazing! And it's a damn shame," he added, feeling the familiar irritation rising, "that she wasn't allowed to go for her PI license. Is it legal for the authorities to block that? That doesn't seem legal. She worked a night shift in an animal hospital and writes books when she would be the most amazing PI in existence. And now she's left the damn planet forever!"

His face was warm, and he was panting now, and he was just getting heated up, but Dr. Bridge appeared unfazed. "Are you angry that she's gone, or are you angry that she's not solving any more crimes for you to read? Are you angry that you never got a chance to meet her and tell her of your admiration?"

He blinked at her, shaking his head. He had gathered one small nugget of hope that this one might understand, but she was like the rest.

"You don't get it. I wasn't stalking her. I don't want to hurt her or anyone around her. I don't want to fuck her or anything." Saying the unfamiliar profanity felt like spitting out a tack. "I want to tell her that she got one of her cases wrong!"

HE HAD METICULOUSLY recreated each of Mallory's murder scenes. He did it in LEGO bricks because after the first one he did with Barbie dolls, people got weirded out. Little blocky murder scenes were much more palatable to his roommate. Before he left, anyway.

He even followed German video game laws and made the bloody scenes green instead of red. He made every effort to not creep people out.

The murder where Mallory had been a pizza delivery woman who had arrived at a house just after a murder had occurred was a sloppy one, but no one could blame her. She had no idea about her future. But, through the novel, the news items he could find, and an unedited manuscript he had bribed one of her first readers to give him, he worked out exactly how she figured out the crime, which clues were important, and which ones were red herrings. He was proud of that one, and had featured it on his site.

He had put toy Mallory in a green jumpsuit work uniform from Space Case Pizza, carrying a flat white square reminiscent of a pizza box, and had managed to carefully paint a black eye on the middle-aged woman answering the door, trying to hide the grisly murder scene behind her. It would have been an obvious case of self-defense, but the woman had killed others earlier in her life—also, apparently, in self-defense—and her efforts to hide the murder, blame a nonexistent home invader, and the . . . efficient way she had killed her husband all came out after Mallory had spotted two key pieces of evidence the cops had overlooked: the ring that had cut her face when the victim had punched the murderer somehow ended up on a chain around *her* neck (she'd nearly hidden that in plain sight) and the small hairpin in her bun that was the murder weapon that had stabbed so precisely into her husband's jugular.

All right, admittedly, in that diorama he had used fake blood to stain the scene. It had just been too grand.

DR. BRIDGE LEANED forward, her pad tilting in her hand. He could almost see something written there. She caught his eyes with her icy blue stare. "I'm trying to believe you, Sam, but despite your claims, this fixation you have does sound like stalking behavior. It feels unhealthy. You know where she's worked, and what shift? How do you know she left the planet for good? If you thought she was wrong, why didn't you write her an email instead of stalking her in person? Surely someone who's good at digging up facts can find that email address," Dr. Bridge had pointed out, a frown deepening the dimples in her cheeks.

He shook his head, the denial hot in his throat. "If I'm going to communicate with her, I am going to do it in person. I just wanted to get a sense of who she was, if she would be open to talking. But she tries hard to keep herself from people."

"That's not surprising," Dr. Bridge said mildly. "What do you ultimately want out of this passion you speak of? Mallory is gone, there will be no more books, so far as we know, and you're a young man in college. How can we move past this?"

"We," Dr. Bridge had said. As if she were ready to help him when she thought he was as crazy as everyone else did. He just stared at his hands and didn't look up.

"I just want her to know that she got one of her cases wrong. And maybe I could have emailed her before, but I can't now."

"What did she get wrong?"

He shook his head. She would laugh at him. "Never mind. You wouldn't believe that I solved a case that she had trouble with."

"Are you interested in private investigative work yourself? Or investigative journalism?"

Sam shrugged. His goal had been to meticulously go through Mallory's books from the last three years. He was in college because his dad told him he had to go. He hadn't really thought about the future much.

"Okay. I think we've had some good progress here, Sam," she said. "Thanks for coming in and sharing all of this. I'd like to see you twice a week to start with."

"Twice a week?" he asked, his head snapping up. "Am I that crazy?"

"'Crazy' is ableist and rude, Sam," she said, frowning. "I think we need to talk frequently so that you can learn to refocus your attention on things like college and your future. As you yourself said, this fixation has played out as far as it can go. You can't read any new Mallory books, you can't follow any more murders she's investigating, and you definitely can't stalk her anymore because you're on Earth and she's not."

He remembered the doctor's deep dimples as she smiled at him, trying to be comforting and supporting. He had seen her three times after that, trying to tell her what she wanted to hear and barely processing her part of the conversation.

The bill for the next semester was due, and his bank account was full. It was his parents' money, but Dad liked Sam to get the sense of what a dollar was worth, so even though they provided the money, Sam was in charge of paying the bills. So this time around he took that money and bought into the lottery for a seat on the first shuttle to the alien space station. He was going to go find Mallory and talk to her. He was going to tell her where she was wrong. He was going to help.

Now, sitting on the shuttle to pursue his grandest dream, he thought about his therapist, and her dimples, and her advice to move on. He thought about her advice to email Mallory.

He thought about Peter, the friend on his floor that he had a crush on. They'd had a joke that so many things in TV shows could be fixed if someone just picked up a phone and called someone else. But no, so many things had to be conveyed face-to-face. "I can't tell you now, not over the link!" insisted Michael Garibaldi from *Babylon 5*. Then he severed the connection and was shot in the back.

Maybe Sam just wanted to meet her in person. Maybe he wanted to go to space. Maybe he had tried to email her, but it didn't reach the space station. Maybe—he couldn't remember any more maybes. He couldn't remember much of anything except for being on the shuttle and putting together that more than one person had a connection to Mallory. He remembered thinking maybe he shouldn't just up and talk to someone if he thought they might be a killer. But the Asian woman had given him a pill, and he had stopped caring.

He drifted now. It had been forever since he'd taken the pill and knocked it back with his water, which had tasted a little funky, now that you mention it. It had been a minute since he'd taken it. The woman across the aisle scared him a lot, but he couldn't remember why. She sat near him, fingering the charms on her bracelet. That famous bracelet, famous to no one but him. *Infamous, then.* Mallory mentioned it every time she had referenced her aunt, and it featured heavily in the final book.

He thought about Peter, and how he wished he had told him how he felt.

Then the grandest moment of his life happened: the sentient space station Eternity entered his mind to learn about him and welcome him, and then her grasp on his mind slipped right off like it was greased, and she fell into the void.

Then he fell after her.

2

THE HUMANS PHINEAS and Lovely made it back to Earth thanks to *Infinity*. They carried considerable information describing the disasters that had hit them. They interviewed extensively. They had to explain that everyone else from the shuttle was dead or staying aboard Eternity. Earth officials were welcome to clean up the mess, but no military. They carried a message from Eternity that Mrs. Elizabeth Brown would be staying aboard permanently, and no parole officers were welcome either. Human visitors were welcome after the investigative team finished its work. Also, that Earth would need a new ambassador, since Adrian Casserly-Berry had been gravely injured and was still recovering, and their second ambassador had died without ever reaching the station.

Under the cover of night, Xan Morgan also returned to Earth, where he and his brother poured their grandmother's ashes and all her cigarette ashes under the porch and then drank beer all night while they searched her records for their family's documents. The next day, a lawyer and a notary arrived, and Xan made Phineas his executor and transferred his inheritance to him.

Phineas surprised him with the arrival of a personal shopper, bringing Xan a new wardrobe to take to his new home so he could trash that shitty ARMY shirt. But Xan kept Cal's coat, which was strangely free of bloodstains after the trip on Stephanie. They got it patched, and Xan reminded himself not to ask Stephanie where the blood had gone.

Adrian Casserly-Berry did survive his adventure with the Phantasmagore, the Silence member, and the broken drone. He remembers almost none of it. That was a mercy.

Their tedious day had Devanshi and Member 2331 unable to find any good information on the location of Mrs. Brown. When they tried to appeal to the Sundry, they found the insects sequestered angrily inside their nests.

Devanshi then learned that there had been a riot in the ossuary, a space battle between three shuttles and a mech, two Gneiss performing forbidden rituals that enraged their whole population, a new human host for the station, and a new drug threat to her people, all while she had been just looking for information while lugging around a wet bag of injured human.

Devanshi retired. That was it. She'd had it.

She made close friends with Silence Member 2331 and learned how to program drones. Mrs. Brown and Eternity were thrilled with her innovations. They also worked on studying the human body and began developing bionic prosthetics for anatomy, starting with an eye for Adrian.

Adrian had become, if not a friend, at least a pleasant, quiet companion. It was surprising what tasting the power of one of the strongest minds in the galaxy and finding oneself lacking will do to an ego. Devanshi actually found herself becoming fond of the wet bag. He mostly read books and watched media from all the sentients. He stayed away from murder mysteries.

Devanshi enhanced her drone and named it Fenris.

When her engineering skills advanced past broken drones and broken humans, she delivered herself to the security team again, not as another grunt, but as an electronics expert specializing in drones to better communicate with Eternity. They, and Mrs. Brown, welcomed her. Mrs. Brown arranged for a group of Earth prosthetics dealers to come aboard and sample her wares.

One day, Mallory Viridian came to her, asking for a drone to help her. She'd had a new case land on her doorstep involving another human shuttle and a missing boy, and the Sundry and Eternity refused to get involved.

"That is our specialty," Devanshi said, and got to work on Fenris 2.

ACKNOWLEDGMENTS

While we would love to claim that a book bursts forth fully grown from our heads like Zeus birthing Athena, it's a gross oversight to pretend that no one else had a hand in it. I'm very grateful to the crew at Ace, mainly my infinitely patient editor, Anne Sowards.

My fantastic agent Seth Fishman picked me up when I was a bit adrift and helped keep me sane and focused through the final drafts of this book. Thanks also to Mary Robinette Kowal, steel goddess of kindhearted patience, for everything she has ever done for me and for SFF at large.

I want to thank the guys from clipping., Jonathan Snipes, William Hutson, and Daveed Diggs, for the use of their songs to reference in this book, but also for creating the album *Splendor & Misery*. Any fan of that album should be able to see its influence on this book.

I want to emphasize that the pandemic fell in the middle of writing this book, and it was a challenge to keep going sometimes. We clung to whatever rafts of escapism and entertainment that we could during that time, and two of the rafts that got me through that year were the game Blaseball (from the Game Band studio) and the band the garages, who make music inspired by the game. Thanks specifically to band members rain and Mother Love Blone

(Max Cohen) for letting me use one of my favorite songs in this book. R.I.V.

During the writing of this book, I took space advice from Dr. Pamela Gay; hand injury advice from Misty, Rory, Colton, and Sara from North Carolina Center for Physical Therapy; bacteria advice from Dr. John Cmar; gold smelting advice from artisan Kim Crist; army advice from Kim Rieck and Chris Lindsey; and violin and Ben Franklin weirdo quartet history and advice from Kyle VanArsdelan. I was unable to fit Tartini and his deal with the devil into this book, but I'll try again in the future.

The community built from my podcast and streaming audiences have all been supportive and amazing, some lending their names to dead bodies via our Discord channel and on the livestream. Thank you, Fabulists!

Authors can't survive in a vacuum. Thanks to Richard Dansky, Alasdair Stuart, Kellan Szpara, Cory Doctorow, and Jim Kelly, and thanks forever to the secret cabal of space drunks. I couldn't do it without you.

Thanks to my parental units, Donna Smith and Will Lafferty, for supporting my interest in writing for so many years. And thanks to my family, Jim and Fiona, for being my rock, my anchor, my peace.

Lastly, the book would not exist without Jennifer Udden and Rebecca Brewer. Thank you both so much for everything you taught me and the chances you took on me.

Photo by Karen Osborne

MUR LAFFERTY is an author, podcaster, and editor. She has been nominated for many awards and has even won a few. She lives in Durham, North Carolina, with her family.

CONNECT ONLINE

MurVerse.com
🐦 MightyMur
🟣 Twitch.tv/MightyMur

Ready to find
your next great read?

Let us help.

Visit prh.com/nextread

Penguin
Random
House